Born in Dublin in 1969, Emma Donoghue is an Irish emigrant twice over: she spent eight years in Cambridge doing a Ph.D. in eighteenth-century literature before moving to Canada, where she lives with her French partner and their two children. She also migrated between genres, writing for screen and stage as well as contemporary and historical fiction. Her international bestseller *Room* was a *New York Times* Best Book of 2010 and a finalist for the Man Booker, Commonwealth, and Orange Prizes; the screenplay won her Oscar, Golden Globe, and Bafta nominations.

You can discover more about the author at www.emmadonoghue.com

AKIN

Noah is only days away from his first trip back to Nice since he was a child when a social worker calls looking for a temporary home for Michael, his eleven-year-old great-nephew. Though he has never met the boy, he gets talked into taking him along to France. This odd couple, suffering from jet lag and culture shock, argue about everything from *steak haché* to screen time, and the trip is looking like a disaster. But as Michael's ease with tech and sharp eye help Noah unearth troubling details about their family's past, both of them come to grasp the risks that people in all eras have taken for their loved ones, and find they are more akin than they know as they unpick their painful story and begin a new one together.

Books by Emma Donoghue
Published by Ulverscroft:

ROOM
THE WONDER

EMMA DONOGHUE

AKIN

Complete and Unabridged

CHARNWOOD
Leicester

First published in Great Britain in 2019 by
Picador
an imprint of Pan Macmillan
London

First Charnwood Edition
published 2020
by arrangement with
Pan Macmillan
London

Photographic illustrations by Margaret Lonergan
Photograph on p. xii: Myrabella, Wikimedia
Commons, CC BY-SA 3.0 & GFDL; photograph
on p. 418: Yad Vashem – The World Holocaust
Remembrance Center.

A catalogue record for this book is available
from the British Library.

ISBN 978–1–4448–4553–2

Published by
Ulverscroft Limited
Anstey, Leicestershire
Set by Words & Graphics Ltd.
Anstey, Leicestershire
Printed and bound in Great Britain by
T. J. International Ltd., Padstow, Cornwall

This book is printed on acid-free paper

For my beloved kinsmen
Denis and Finn

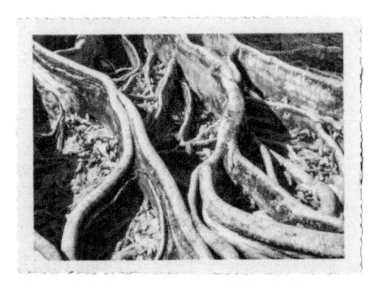

Akin, *adjective*
1. related by blood
2. similar in character

Contents

1. The Call 1
2. Twenty Questions 56
3. Takeoff Speed................................112
4. The Promenade 159
5. Neither Here nor There..................212
6. The Law of Closure........................261
7. *Nom de Guerre* 302
8. Schooled 342
9. Decisive Moments..........................379

Acknowledgments 419

1

The Call

An old man packing his bags.

Hard not to read the situation metaphorically, Joan commented in his head.

Noah corrected her: not old. He was only seventy-nine, till next Monday. When he'd been young, your seventies had counted as old, but not these days. Say, youngish up to sixty; then middle-aged, or young-old, through the sixties and seventies. Ancient Romans used to distinguish between senectus (still lively) and decrepitus (done for). Sharp as ever, hale, hearty — surely Noah could still count himself in the senectus camp?

And these were only literal bags he was packing — well, one slim carry-on and his leather satchel. Also, his destination was neither heaven nor hell. Though the mention of Nice, or the French Riviera, or the South of France generally, did make people roll their eyes in envy, especially in a New York February.

Noah was going to Nice for his eightieth. He hadn't been since he was four. There'd been nothing pulling him back to his hometown; after all, he didn't know anyone in that part of the world, not since his grandfather had died in 1944. That had freed his mother (Margot) to join his father (Marc) and little Noah in the

1

States. (He'd still been Noé, then.)

Noah folded another shirt. He wasn't flying out for another three days, but he liked to get his packing done early, to leave time for last-minute chores. Meticulous, he found each balled pair of socks its nook.

He'd never been a keen traveler — because of his rather yanked-about childhood, he supposed. Going to American Chemical Society meetings, all he'd cared about was whether he'd find himself stuck with the graveyard shift (8 a.m. on Sunday) for his paper on, say, polyvinyl-chloride fibers. He'd accompanied Joan on most of her work trips, though as the decades went by she'd started turning down all the invitations she could, everything but the most prestigious keynotes; she recoiled from the prospect of extra nights in hotels. She and Noah had never vacationed much, either. When Joan wasn't in the lab or on the road, she liked to be at home, buried in a novel, Miles Davis on the record player. Or dropping into sleep in their bed (double; queen was too wide). Back to back, her leathery soles touching Noah's.

I miss that too, Joan said.

Which was nonsense, of course, because there was no Joan to miss anything anymore: no soles, no souls. These remarks of hers were generated by Noah's brain, using their not-quite-forty years of marriage as an algorithm. A neurological tic.

Was that five pairs of socks or six? He counted them again.

For the past nine years, on his own, Noah had kept himself too busy for vacations. There'd been

2

hints that he should retire, of course; barbed remarks from colleagues, cost-cutting ones from the dean, benevolent ones from women friends, to the effect that Noah should learn to kick back, live a little, join a choir or take up tai chi in Central Park. His little sister, Fernande, was the only one who'd never suggested it, even though she'd retired from her receptionist job with relief at sixty-five. She must have guessed that her widowed brother needed to stay tethered to the surface of the earth. Having classes to teach — the hard slog of preparation and performance and marking — had reassured him of that much.

Noah supposed what had finally nudged him over the line was his imminent birthday. *Professor in his late seventies* sounded rather admirable, but *professor in his eighties?* He'd had no intention of carrying on long enough to end up a laughingstock. Students were harder to impress since the turn of the millennium; they sat there with their external brains, their little screens, ready to fact-check you if you fumbled a formula.

No, it was better to call a halt before the first time Noah's wits deserted him at a podium. *Retired*, though; the moribund ring of the word. But then, it had been only a month. Of course he'd have plenty to do. Who could be bored in New York City? It was just a matter of picking how to spend his days. He'd declined the title of *professor emeritus;* pottering around campus doing a little independent research struck him as pathetic. If Noah was going to study, it would be some quite new subject. Or a hobby; he was sure he'd come across something of interest. He just had to find his feet. His first venture was this trip.

Once he'd zipped up his case, he went to fetch the recycling tub from the kitchen and carried it into the spare room. This had been his and Joan's home office, but after her death the sight of it had weighed on him, and really he'd preferred to work on campus, so he'd turned it into a guest room. Though now Noah couldn't remember who his last guest had been. The double bed was always made up, as if ready for a visitor; tidier that way. Several times Joan's friend Vivienne had suggested he invite a refugee to move in, but Noah couldn't face housing some stranger.

He knelt to tug Fernande's boxes from under the bed. Only three left to deal with; just personal papers. (He found objects more troubling.) The Swedes had a word for when you spared your family by tidying up your own stuff in advance — Noah couldn't call up the syllables, but it meant 'death cleaning.' It had been Margot who'd sorted Marc's effects. (Did you have to be dead for your belongings to be called that, he wondered?) Fernande had done it in turn for Margot, and then for her own husband, Dan, and she'd helped her brother after he'd lost Joan, too, though Joan had been so ruthless about clutter (tossing Christmas cards on the first of January) that there hadn't been much to do. So Fernande's death last year was the first time Noah had been given this task to do alone. He was nearly done, he promised

4

himself as he sat on the edge of the bed.

Hospital invoices, her powers of attorney, Living Will and DNR — irrelevant now. Recipes, postcards, photos, appeals from charities, offers from The Great Courses — recycle them all. It was odd to be disposing of the remnants of a younger sister's life, when logically Noah should have gone before her. Deciding what to keep for sentimental reasons was tricky because there was no one left but Noah. The knack, he'd found over the past year, was to keep sentimentality at bay; to ask, about each item, *Does anyone need or want this?* until at rare intervals a real feeling flooded over the levee.

This afternoon he found himself saying yes to just three items: the wedding menu from 1982 (Prawn Cocktail, Chicken Vol-au-Vents, Profiteroles); a photo of Fernande in 1990, wild-eyed with bliss after her home birth, a newborn Victor on her chest (those eyelashes!); and a curling sheaf of comic haiku she'd made up for everyone at the Thanksgiving table in 2002. A postwar baby with chipmunk cheeks, Fernande had always had a warmth and lightsomeness foreign to Noah, eight years her senior.

Clippings from magazines, straight into the recycling. Letters in handwriting Noah couldn't make out, Get Well Soon cards . . . let it all go. What did a life add up to — Fernande's, anyone's? The papers were almost overflowing the tub. Like leaves, he told himself grimly; grow, shed, rot, repeat.

The minute Noah was done, he was going to treat himself to a cognac as well as a cigarette.

5

(The third of his never-more-than-seven a day.)

Just as he tossed a copy of *Marie Claire* from August 1992, his fingers sensed an odd stiffness. He leaned over to pick it out of the tub. Tucked in the middle, a rigid mailer with nothing written on it — cardboard on one side, brown paper (softened by years) on the other. August 1992: that was the month after Margot's death. The envelope felt empty till Noah slid his fingers in. He recognized the sharp edges. Photographs.

He tugged them out, pulse thumping just in case they were Père Sonne's. Half a dozen or so, black and white, clearly old from the format (two and a half inches by three and a half, he'd guess). From the clothes, hair, and general aesthetic they looked 1930s, '40s maybe. Mostly taken in the street; the setting plausibly though not definitively Nice. Noah polished his fingerprints off the top one (a dandyish man with a cane, caught in profile). But as he leafed through the photos — nine in total — disappointment came fast. None of these bore Père Sonne's stamp. Besides, they were no good.

Slipshod, unilluminating. A Belle Époque building, for instance, cropped at the fourth floor. An awkward close-up of a box, rectangular, inscribed with a circle, a dash on each side. This stock scene of a middle-aged couple on a bench, seen from behind. A woman with coiled hair, again from the rear — was that angle in vogue at the time, he wondered, the equivalent of pursed-lip selfies today? A shot of children's feet trotting by was cute in a generic way. Tree roots, not even particularly well framed. None of the subjects was looking at the camera apart from one smiling boy with neatly combed dark hair who had to be small Noé, though Noah didn't quite recognize himself.

He had to assume it was his mother who'd taken all these. But she must have known better, after decades working with — for — under — her mighty father. Surely she would have borrowed Père Sonne's superb Contax, or even one of his little portable Leicas. This shot of an empty street, for instance — had she meant to press the shutter just then?

No commercial studio's stamp on the backs, only jotted letters in two cases: *MZ* for the woman seen from behind, *RJ* for little Noah. (Unless it was *R.J.*, a pair of initials? In which case the boy wasn't Noah at all.) That meant Margot must have printed them herself, in the reeking darkroom in their apartment near the Cours Saleya.

He couldn't think of anyone else's brain to pick about this but Vivienne's. Besides, he'd owed her a call for months.

'Excited for your big trip?'

'I suppose.' Noah often caught a faint whiff of the patronizing in Vivienne's tone; a hint of the kindergarten teacher. She wouldn't have been his choice, as a friend — nor vice versa, he supposed. They'd inherited each other from Joan, who'd been Vivienne's best friend ever since they'd seized on each other as the two Jews in first grade in their tony New York girls' school in 1942. 'How are your people?'

'The kids and so forth?' she asked.

Noah knew that Vivienne's great-granddaughter in Texas was starting ballet, her grandchildren there and in Oregon were doing postgraduate degrees, and her grown kids in New Jersey and Tel Aviv were going through the minor health indignities of their fifties. 'No, actually I was thinking of the Sudanese in your spare room.'

'Oh, the Abdullahs are Yemenis. They're fine, more than fine — they're pregnant.'

Noah rolled his eyes. If the couple raised a child in Vivienne's apartment, would that give them squatters' rights? Well, let the bank worry about that; she'd reverse-mortgaged the place and was spending the proceeds on her pet causes. (She'd always been a do-gooder — the polar opposite of Joan, whose research was of such clear importance that she'd felt entitled to be selfish in her time off.) Noah occasionally warned Vivienne to keep enough for paying strangers to wipe her butt in the end, but she insisted, on the basis of extensive genealogical research, that no one in her gene pool made it past eighty-five.

He remembered what he was calling about. 'The thing is, I've found these old photos in the last box of Fernande's stuff — '

Even if Vivienne had been right here in the hall with Noah, he'd have had to describe them, as she was legally blind. (She'd announced it last year, in an email so perky as to sound proud.) Losing her sight in her early eighties had barely slowed the woman down. She used software that read aloud whatever was on her screen; she'd had the tech guy set it to

'Male Australian' to remind her of Frank.

Noah did his best to summarize the images, leafing through them awkwardly with one hand.

'Doesn't everyone have some crappy photos — lots of them?'

'But why would my mother have bothered taking these — early '40s, I'm guessing, when she was still in Nice, without me and my father — and printing them, and holding on to them till the end of her days? Then she gave them to my sister, or more likely just left them in a drawer. And why didn't Fernande mention them to me?'

'No names at all?' Vivienne asked.

'Just what look like initials on the backs of two.'

'Well, you might spot some of the locations when you're in Nice. As for the human subjects, maybe try the public library. They'll have some kind of local history collection. If you find any names, give me a shout.'

Vivienne was in touch with distant cousins all over the world, having subscribed to various data-bases and sent off a saliva swab to a lab. Noah supposed a sense of tribe was crucial if you'd lost your parents. (Her father in the Holocaust, her mother in its long aftermath.) Just when Vivienne's sight had started really failing, she'd gone off to stay with a family in Spain who'd turned out not to be related to her at all, but she had no regrets; said it was very jolly.

Some kind of beeper went off at her end now. 'I must hang up, my group's phone-bombing Congress about the Muslim ban.'

9

'OK,' Noah said, 'enjoy.'

He knew Vivienne would rise to that. 'It's not about enjoyment, it's *tikkun olam.*'

Repairing the world, the Jewish obligation. 'I know. I'm only ribbing you.'

★   ★   ★

Noah was eating his usual poached egg on an English muffin in the kitchen when the phone rang. Vivienne again, with further tips?

Jangle jangle. *She can leave a message,* Joan advised, though she'd always answered, herself. (Before personalized ringtones, the two friends had used a signal to identify themselves: call once, hang up, then call back.)

Not many people but fundraisers and telemarketers bothered Noah at home these days. If it wasn't Vivienne, this call would probably turn out to be a recording or a robot. Fernande had been in the habit of calling her brother for chats at random intervals — to cheer him up, he suspected. But now, why was he still paying monthly fees on the thing? (A *landline*, that was the modern word — like a skinny root anchoring a tree to the earth.) That was how the corporations made their money: our mindless, lifelong habits.

Jangle jangle. He hurried down the narrow hall to stop the clamor.

'Noah Selvaggio?' The woman pronounced it uncertainly but more or less accurately.

'That's me. But if you're selling something — '

'You're the uncle of Victor Pierre Young?'

10

That familiar dread. What was it this time, old debts? Crimes, unpunishable now? 'My nephew died more than a year ago.' It hurt Noah's throat to say it.

'I'm aware of that, sir. This is Rosa Figueroa from the Administration for Children's Services. I'm contacting you in connection with Michael Young.'

'Oh.'

'Excuse me?'

'I just said *Oh*,' Noah told her foolishly. What must the child be now — nine, ten? He reckoned the years: eleven, actually. How word of the pregnancy had appalled Fernande and Dan: Victor making such a blunder, when he was still an angel-faced teenage boy. The woman was still talking, but none of it was making sense to Noah. 'I'm sorry, Ms. — ' Her name would come back to Noah in a moment, once he stopped grasping for it.

'Figueroa. Rosa Figueroa,' she repeated in the too-clear enunciation middle-aged people used with those who were past middle age.

'Could you back up for a moment?'

'I'm exploring Michael's kinship resources,' she told him.

Had Noah misunderstood — was this some kind of genealogy project, then?

'He's been living with Ella Davis, his grandmother, but she's just passed.'

For a moment he thought she meant something like an exam, and then he got it. 'I'm very sorry to hear that.' To fill the silence: 'What was it that . . . '

11

'Complications of diabetes. She was only sixty-three.'

That made seventy-nine sound like the height of luck to Noah.

'And her husband died back in the '90s,' Rosa Figueroa added. 'So now we're looking for somewhere for Michael.'

Noah was at a loss as to how he came into this. 'Why is he not with, ah,' — Angela? Amanda? — 'Amber?'

'She's currently incarcerated.'

He groaned inwardly. 'For what?'

'I wonder, could we focus on the child's immediate needs, Mr. Selvaggio?'

Noah cleared his throat. 'I'm just racking my brains as to how I can be of any assistance to you. I've never met any of these people, myself. My sister died soon after Victor, and her husband, ah, a long time before that.' Dan had lasted long enough to have a pretty good idea of what kind of son he'd raised — *incorrigible*, that was the word people used to throw around. But too early to know that Victor would soon follow him, which was a small mercy, and one not granted to Fernande.

'Yes, sir, that's exactly why I'm getting in touch. You appear to be the last of Michael's kin here in New York City.'

That old-fashioned word again. Kith and kin, kinsfolk, kindred; like something out of J. R. R. Tolkien. Did she mean legally or genetically? In what sense could you really be kin to someone you'd never met?

'Mr. Selvaggio?'

This social worker couldn't be thinking of bringing the child here, to Noah's apartment.

No. It struck him that, like so many other seniors, he was the target of a phone scam. The woman had gotten hold of the names of relatives of his, for some equivalent of the Spanish Prisoner trick — the Nigerian fortune constantly being offered in illiterate emails.

Put down the phone, Joan told him.

'Sorry not to be of more use, Ms. Figueroa' — no trouble remembering the name the crook had given, now, if he took a split second to get the vowels in the correct sequence — 'but I've got to go now.'

'Please.'

It wasn't the word but Rosa Figueroa's tone that made Noah pause, receiver halfway to the cradle. She did sound like a real person, and so weary. 'It's just that I don't see how I can be of any practical help,' he told her. 'Certainly not in the immediate . . . I'm off to France next week, as it happens. Maybe after I get back we could speak again.'

'This can't wait. I met Michael for the first time myself this morning. There's nobody at all to look after him.'

It wasn't subtle, how she was playing on Noah's sympathies. He wanted a cigarette.

'Could you come and meet his mother with me, tomorrow morning?'

'But — '

'Let's all just sit down and put our heads

13

together, all right, to see what can be done for this child?'

Noah sighed.

★   ★   ★

Noah smoked as he leaned out the kitchen window — a waste of heat, yes, but these apartment buildings stayed so baking from October to April you couldn't survive without opening a window once in a while.

Incarcerated. Was Amber Davis just as much of a fuckup as his nephew had been? Possibly more so. Hadn't she been a grown woman (though not quite old enough for it to have counted as statutory rape) when she'd gotten the lanky, lovely fifteen-year-old into her bed and conceived this unfortunate Michael?

Noah was trying to get the sequence straight. Victor's adolescence had had such a disastrous domino effect it was hard to remember the order and duration of each awful event. He was pretty sure that word of the baby had come after Victor's truncated stay in that so-called therapeutic school upstate (which had almost bankrupted Fernande and Dan before getting shut down) and after he'd run away from their house in Brooklyn for the second time, with Fernande's jewelry and a checkbook. She'd gotten her gold back, but it had been melted into a lump. The judge had placed Victor in a group home, then, but he'd run away from that too. Always minor-league stuff, but it added up: possession of marijuana, Ritalin, loitering,

14

trespass, disorderly conduct . . .

What Noah couldn't remember was, had Michael been born before or after the Limited Secure Placement? Fernande and Dan had been encouraged to call that his *group home* too, though the fence was of razor wire this time. (Orwellian, the dialect of the justice system.) Noah had visited twice, on his own; Joan had always been busy. The place was just two subway stops from the elegant brownstone where Victor had grown up, but a world away.

Then when he'd been let out after ten months, the boy had 'crashed with friends.' Noah had never gotten the impression his nephew was actually living with the young woman and their son. Fernande — more than Dan — had badgered Victor to let them meet their grandchild, but he'd been elusive. When she'd asked if they could send baby clothes, he'd asked for money instead. And then at seventeen, for something petty — violating parole by skipping school? — Victor had been sent off to juvie, a hellhole of a residential center up near Albany. That fence had been sixteen feet high, Noah remembered from his single visit. Victor had come back with kidney damage from a beating.

From that point on, all Noah had heard about his nephew's doings had come via Fernande. She and Dan had managed to meet the mother and child a couple of times; she'd reported that Victor was 'quite involved,' though Noah didn't know what that meant: changing diapers? Paying support? Noah had seen a few photos and nodded dutifully. He couldn't remember what

15

the little boy had looked like, now, except that he hadn't inherited Victor's looks.

He stood up, stubbed out his cigarette, and tugged the old window shut. He could have made more of an effort with his nephew, he supposed. But it had all felt like such a goddamn waste of breath.

The moment that stuck in Noah's memory like a sliver was when he'd made himself go into his and Joan's home office, a few months after her death. (He'd have avoided their bedroom, too, if it had been practical, as well as the bathroom and kitchen and living room; even the rubber mat by the door where she left her winter boots, and the key hook on which she balanced the little roll of dog-shit bags.) Those four rectangular spaces on the office wall, like ripped-out teeth: Noah's last Père Sonne prints. He knew at once that it must have been Victor, who'd slunk off during Joan's funeral while everyone else was eating and taken them off the wall, then smuggled them out of the apartment.

When Noah had called Fernande about it, she'd burst into tears, but it wasn't shock. Victor had sold hers long ago, she admitted. The only photos by their *pépère* that had stayed in the family were gone now; locked away from the world in some collector's vault. 'What's the difference?' Victor had responded. 'You guys would've donated them to some museum sooner or later.' He was nineteen, so it would be adult prison this time. As a favor to her, Fernande begged, would Noah please, please not call the police?

He hadn't. But he hadn't forgiven his nephew either.

Noah had stopped asking Fernande for news at that point, though when Victor's name came up she always spoke with a determined positivity. He'd chosen to assume the best, or the least worst: that his nephew had finally calmed down in his twenties, as so many wild boys did, and become more or less law-abiding. (Amber and little Michael were still in the picture, though having a child to support could be as much hindrance as help, Noah imagined, to someone like Victor.) But maybe Fernande had hidden the worst from her brother, or maybe she hadn't known the half of it herself.

How could anyone bear to be a parent? Like contracting to love a werewolf.

His sister's retirement, which should have been a well-earned respite, must have been one long fretting and losing. First Dan — after a stroke, pointless rehab, another stroke — and then, three years later, Victor. Fernande had had to identify her son laid out on a refrigerated tray in the morgue in Queens: still exquisite in all his features, not yet twenty-seven. Farther east on Long Island, the day before, a motel chamber-maid had found Victor on the carpet, veins full of heroin and fentanyl.

Which had never made sense to Noah, because he hadn't thought of his nephew as that kind of user. (A dope-smoker since twelve, but not what they used to call a *junkie*.) Drugs had their own irrational logic, he supposed, and these days everything seemed to be laced with something worse. If you weren't quite sure what you were taking, could you be held accountable for doing it, and for leaving your son fatherless?

If it came to that, Noah wondered now, which of our decisions were ever entirely our own?

Never to reach twenty-seven. He'd felt hurt that Fernande hadn't asked him to go with her to identify her son. What else was a brother for? But he supposed that on such a day, company was no consolation. And she must have known that he'd given up on Victor long before.

Joan, in his head: *Come on, surely you have things you should be doing?*

Noah stood on the pedal of the garbage can and threw away his cigarette butt.

★ ★ ★

Next morning, he writhed in his seat at the women's correctional facility. (The latest euphemism for *prison*.) Whenever he tried to straighten up, the molded plastic prodded him in the wrong part of his back. Rosa Figueroa was across the table, and the speechless notary public, Lucas Weinburg (brought along for what she called *witnessing*), on his left.

Noah was still rattled from the journey. An hour and a half up the Hudson, through snow flurries, in Rosa Figueroa's cluttered and underheated sedan, with Lucas Weinburg in the back, apparently asleep. The social worker looked about fifty; worn but not burned out, with only a little gray in her black curls, and a birthmark on

18

her cheekbone, which Noah liked her for. Also one of those discreet hearing aids. She turned out to have a caseload of twenty-four children. When Noah had asked how she remembered who was who, she'd laughed darkly and said the system was in such crisis that she and her colleagues were just doing triage.

After that, the two of them had made desultory conversation about bad news in the headlines till they'd reached a pretty hamlet ('full of Hollywood types,' she'd told him). Then a sharp turn through a gate in a double barbed-wire fence, into the parking lot of the prison.

Behind Noah, a baby wailed on and on. Children, all ages; he hadn't expected quite so many of them. It hit him now that when a mother was sent to jail, her kids were receiving just as long a sentence. He thought of the boy, Michael.

'All right, Mr. Selvaggio?'

'Perfectly.' He didn't mention his back. It wasn't advisable to admit to aches and pains after seventy, or younger people wrote you off.

'There can be delays.'

Noah disliked statements of the blindingly obvious, but the woman was just being civil.

'Just as well it's a Sunday. They don't allow contact visitation during the week.'

He cocked an eyebrow.

'Seeing her in person,' she explained, 'not just by video link. Ms. Davis is actually only entitled to visitors on Saturdays, since her name's in the first half of the alphabet, but the sergeant agreed to make an exception for a hardship visit because of the urgency.'

Video link would have been fine by Noah. He'd have preferred to stay at arm's length from this whole mess.

'Also we're lucky New York State doesn't insist on the full visitor-application process,' Rosa Figueroa told him. 'You just need the permission of the inmate.'

Noah's head was aching. Nothing about this felt lucky. He'd agreed to this appointment with the *inmate* out of a sort of guilt by association with Victor, her onetime . . . partner? Also as a posthumous favor to Fernande. She'd managed to meet her grandson on only a couple of occasions, but she'd spoken of him with a wistful fondness. If he was in desperate need of a roof over his head for a week or two, Noah supposed he could manage that much, after Nice.

Not that he believed any old guff about the dead looking down, like spy drones hovering. His baby sister was long past being herself. Like Joan, like all Noah's dead — like he himself would be, at some point — Fernande was humus, dust. And a memory trace, he supposed, not to get too mumbo jumbo about it; a fingerprint of feeling left on her loved ones. So as a nod toward their shared past, Noah was here right now, on this hard, slippery chair.

The baby's sobs rose again.

Beside Noah, Lucas Weinburg (clearly used to such places) was reading his way through the *Wall Street Journal*.

The guards — some men, some women, in

navy blue — occasionally escorted an inmate to a chair opposite her visitors. Noah couldn't work out the rationale for the order they arrived in; it seemed to him that his little group had been waiting the longest. In their dark green overalls, the prisoners looked like park rangers. The decor was bucolic, too. Amateurish murals on the walls: the wooded shore of a lake with a bald eagle overhead, and a deserted sandy beach with a single palm tree.

Noah's sports coat hung too lightly, and his right hand kept moving to pat it. No wallets were allowed; Rosa Figueroa had made him leave his in her glove compartment, together with his phone, his cigarettes: all contraband. They seemed to Noah more likely to get stolen from her car. He had been allowed to bring in his passport, as ID, for lack of a driver's license. At the metal detector he'd been sniffed up and down by a German shepherd, then patted down by a male guard in an intrusive way, and asked twice if he had a pacemaker (presumably because he might have forgotten). He'd had to sign a statement agreeing that he'd been shown the rules of visiting — mostly prohibitions on spandex, slit skirts, bandanas, and flip-flops.

'So, Amber. What did she do, to wind up in here?' He'd heard it was a faux pas to ask that question in prison, but did the same go for the visiting room?

Rosa Figueroa's mouth twisted. 'Well, the charge was criminal possession of a controlled substance in the second degree.'

Why was she putting it that way, with an

emphasis on *charge* — surely she didn't believe Amber was innocent? 'Which substance?'

'The police found crack cocaine, meth, and oxycodone in her car.'

Noah judged the young woman, of course he did; like hackles rising along his spine. 'She's a dealer, you're telling me?' What used to be called a *pusher*, the kind of parasite who was to blame for stupid deaths like Victor's. Amber had chosen this life, inevitably gotten caught, dumped her child on her own mother in one of the last pockets of Brooklyn resistant to gentrification. *Dying* mother, as it had turned out.

Rosa Figueroa shook her head. 'I don't think so. Ms. Davis had no priors, no involvement with law enforcement at all. She helped her mom find a Section 8 apartment in a town house, away from the projects. My sense is, she was doing her best for Michael, for all of them. I believe his dad — Victor — had done time?'

Shame heated Noah's face. 'Only as a juvenile.'

'Excuse me?'

'He was a child.' Too loud. 'Legally.'

'Right. But given the history, I'd say ninety-nine to one the stash was your nephew's.'

Noah bristled. 'Then why wouldn't they have arrested Victor?'

The social worker shrugged. 'Maybe Amber took the fall. She'd have known he'd get a longer sentence, with his previous convictions.'

This struck Noah as unconvincing and lurid. 'Surely if what you're claiming were true, it would have come out in court, at her trial?'

She inhaled as if summoning all her reserves of politeness. 'Oh, Mr. Selvaggio. Nobody gets a trial these days.'

Noah felt rebuked for his naïveté.

'Amber would have been looking at three to ten years. Possession in the second degree is a Class A-II felony — up there with crimes like predatory sexual assault against a child.'

That startled him.

'Her public defender — well, they're run so ragged, sometimes it's months before they have a chance to meet their clients. It was probably on his or her advice that Amber accepted a plea of five.'

He swallowed. Five years.

Over near the left wall, an inmate put her head down on her crossed arms and a little boy stroked her braids.

What was keeping Amber? Not that her time was her own, Noah reminded himself. He supposed prison was like the military, that way: hurry up and wait. 'And how long has she been here?'

'Almost eighteen months.'

It struck him that she couldn't have supplied the heroin and fentanyl that had done in his nephew, if she'd been locked up months before he died.

Rosa Figueroa went on: 'As a nonviolent first-time offender, very compliant, Amber actually has minimum-security status. But New York's closed down almost all its minimum-security facilities for women, so she's held in this medium-security one.' Her eyes slid from table to table. Women chattering, or sullen, or rocking toddlers in their laps. She murmured, 'You'd be surprised how many of them are banged up because of their men, one way or another.'

Noah could tell she was trying to visit the sins of the nephew on the uncle. 'If you've no actual proof the drugs belonged to Victor,' he barked, 'it seems tasteless to keep speculating that this is all his fault.'

Rosa Figueroa's lips parted as if she was about to say something else. Then closed. 'I beg your pardon, sir.'

An inmate gave an officer with a camera a plastic token, then pressed up against her tattooed man in front of a daubed approximation of a yacht. Belatedly Noah realized the murals were backdrops, where the prisoners could pose with their visitors; aspirational scenes of freedom.

A guard moved to separate the two. 'Brother-sister pose!'

Reluctantly the couple pulled their bodies apart and stood facing forward, his arm slung over her shoulders.

No indication that it would be Amber's visitors' turn anytime soon. That baby began shrieking again. Noah tried to tune out the sound, as New Yorkers learned to do for car alarms, honks, and sirens. 'If Amber's all that compliant,' trying out the jargon, 'wouldn't she soon be eligible for parole?'

'Sorry, could you repeat that?'

He kept forgetting about the social worker's bad ear. 'Parole.'

Rosa Figueroa shook her head. 'There's no parole on determinate sentences for felonies.'

'Oh.'

'And the maximum good-time credit is one-seventh, so the earliest she could hope for, in terms of conditional release, that would be two years and nine months from now.'

The wails of the baby went up a notch. Noah wanted a cigarette so much his fingers were curling.

Too bad, Joan said. She'd always despised the habit. It particularly galled her (or at least the neurological replay of her who'd taken up residence in Noah's head) that he'd smoked his first cigarette on the day of her funeral. Perverse, to have resisted the social pressure to light up — so strong in the '50s and '60s, beginning to taper off only in the '70s — for most of his life, then succumbed in 2009, of all years. He hadn't meant to spite Joan; he'd just needed something else to do with his hands when they reached for her and closed on nothing.

'Davis,' a guard called, and gestured to their table. 'Inmate Davis!'

A girl in green walked over and lowered herself into a seat beside Rosa Figueroa. Young woman, Noah thought, correcting himself. Shirt tucked into her pants, work boots. White painted nails, hair pulled back in a smooth blond ponytail, eyes sunken behind thick glasses. A hard case, he could tell that much at a glance. But unnervingly young.

Rosa Figueroa introduced herself as Michael's caseworker. 'I'm very sorry for your loss, Amber

25

— may I call you that?'

A nod, stone-faced. 'They wouldn't let me go to Mom's funeral.'

'Really?'

'Said the documents hadn't come through in time.'

'That's a real shame.'

'Where's Michael?' Amber scanned the room.

'I'm afraid I couldn't arrange in time for him to join us today.'

The young woman's glance flicked over the two men sitting opposite her.

Rosa Figueroa introduced Lucas Weinburg and Noah. 'Can I get you something, Amber, a drink?'

'Coke. Cheetos.'

Noah couldn't help despising her a little for wanting junk food at a time like this.

'Mr. Weinburg,' Rosa Figueroa asked, 'could you possibly . . . '

The notary public stirred. She handed him a fistful of coins and he headed off to the vending machines.

'Well.' She made an attempt at a smile. 'Your son's been staying in the apartment next door to your mother's, at a Bernice Johnson's.'

A rapid nod. 'Berni's a good woman. Mom knows her from church.'

'But she's got four of her own living with her, so . . . '

Hands clenched, the white nails digging into the palms. 'Are you going to apprehend Michael?'

A weirdly formal verb, Noah thought.

'I hope we won't have to consider removal,' Rosa Figueroa told her.

Another strange word, *removal*, he thought: like transporting a corpse.

'Our agency focuses on family preservation. It's all about kin, these days. If he could be placed with a relative . . . '

'Has Grace been in touch with you yet?'

Rosa Figueroa checked her notes. 'This would be your sister, Grace Davis?'

'Yeah. Grace Drew, that's her married name — she still goes by that since they split up. She's got two little girls, they know Michael. Grace will definitely' — Amber broke off — 'I'm ninety-nine percent positive she'll take Michael for me, now there's no one else.'

'I've had some difficulty tracking her down. The number I was given, it seems it's no longer in service.'

Ah. Of course he wouldn't have been anyone's first call, Noah realized. How long was the list of names the social worker had tried before reaching his?

'She moved, but I think I remember her cell,' Amber told her. 'And you could try Instagram.'

'Sure, write it all down for me, any details at all would be a help.' Rosa Figueroa slid a notebook and ballpoint across the table.

The guard frowned.

Could pens be sharpened into shanks, had Noah read that somewhere?

'I'll keep working on finding your sister,' Rosa Figueroa said as Amber started writing. 'But in the meantime, can you think of anyone else?'

27

Noah felt quite invisible. A certain relief came with it. This young woman didn't know him, and neither did her son; how could he possibly be considered *kin*?

The pen halted as Amber looked into the middle distance. 'We have some cousins on Dad's side.'

'Mm, they were in your mother's address book, but the last whereabouts I could find for them were way out of state — Utah and Nevada. It would be less disruptive to find Michael a temporary placement right here in the city.' Rosa Figueroa turned her body toward Noah. 'This is where Victor's uncle could come in. Mr. Selvaggio's a widower, no children of his own, and he's offering your son a very comfortable home.'

Hold on, she was twisting his words. Noah's voice came out hoarse: 'Open to the possibility, I said.'

Both women stared at him.

'Just in the short term, as a bridge.'

Say 'One week,' Joan proposed.

'For a couple of weeks, maybe. Until this sister of yours turns up,' he said in Amber's direction.

Rosa Figueroa was nodding. 'That's so helpful.'

'Hold on.' Amber's lip curled. 'I don't know this guy from Adam.'

'Well, likewise.' Noah hadn't been expecting tears of gratitude, but what about basic manners?

'If you don't mind my asking, how old are you?'

28

He was finding this whole conversation embarrassing.

Rosa Figueroa jumped in. 'Seventy-nine, but he's in excellent health.'

The age his father had died, it struck Noah now.

'He's a retired university professor, owns his own apartment in Manhattan, with an empty bedroom.' She'd drawn all that out of Noah on the drive.

'A stranger,' Amber said.

Noah spoke up: 'Technically correct.' What, this was a job interview now? Had he asked for any of this? He never should have answered the phone. 'I'd be doing you a favor for the sake of — '

'I'm not looking for any fucking favors, mister.'

As her voice swooped up, the guard glanced their way.

'What do you want with some boy you've never laid eyes on? You could be a chomo for all I know.'

Noah's ears were ringing as he rose to his feet. Was *chomo* some variant of *homo*?

'Amber, I know you've been through a lot.' Rosa Figueroa had her hand over the other woman's. 'Mr. Selvaggio . . . '

Noah couldn't tell whether she meant to defend him or appeal to his kinder instincts, but he sat back down anyway, mostly because other visitors were staring.

Amber wrenched off her glasses and stuffed them in the pocket of her overalls.

29

The notary came back and deposited the soda and cheese puffs on the table.

'Of course I checked state and federal crime records, as well as the sex-offender registry,' Rosa Figueroa was murmuring. 'He's never been arrested — never had a parking ticket, even.'

Not that Noah had anything to hide, but it was a little unnerving to be investigated. 'I don't drive.'

Amber pulled back her head, turtlelike, as if that oddity counted against Noah; proved him incompetent rather than a lifelong New Yorker. She sat there slugging her Coke, a convicted felon, judging him.

'The key thing to remember is, he's fourth degree of consanguinity to Michael, which would be enough for my agency to consider it informal kinship care.'

Amber was drumming on the table now, a flamenco riff of anxiety.

'See, this would be voluntary — you'd be choosing to leave your son temporarily with his father's uncle — and I'd be involved just in an advisory capacity.'

'All right, all right.'

Noah thought Amber meant she agreed, but no, it turned out she was just working up another head of steam.

'What I don't get is why you're *advising* me to trust my eleven-year-old to this creepy old guy.'

Rosa Figueroa spoke very low. 'Because a family member is the only alternative I can see to taking custody of Michael today and placing him in a group home.'

Those perfect brown eyes stared.

Noah tried to steel his heart. A small, homey residence with qualified foster parents — it couldn't be anything like Victor's Limited Secure Placement behind rolls of barbed wire, could it?

Let's not kid ourselves, Joan said.

Noah squeezed his eyes shut. They'd failed Victor; not just Fernande and Dan, but Noah and Joan. Something had gone awry as that dazzling boy had entered his teens, and none of them had figured it out in time to save him.

'In which case, Amber, your parental rights . . . '

The young woman erupted. 'I haven't done anything to lose them!'

'I know.' Rosa Figueroa was gravel-voiced. 'I'm so sorry. But any time your son spends in the system would go on your record. My superiors could make a decision that it's in Michael's best interest to terminate your rights before you're released.'

Amber's eyes glittered.

It was only then that Noah grasped why the social worker was behaving in such a rushed, unorthodox way. She wasn't naïve enough to assume that Noah would do a great job of this. She was just trying to keep one kid from being sucked into the pipeline. Because of the holy word *kinship*, her harried superiors, glancing at the paperwork, weren't likely to object.

None of this seemed fair. Dealer or not, this young woman had already lost years of freedom, her boyfriend, her mother, and now she was about to lose her only child. To prevent that,

31

Rosa Figueroa was scraping the barrel, and Noah was all she'd managed to scrape up.

'Hopefully it would be just for a little while,' Rosa Figueroa told Amber in the kind of voice you might use to calm a horse. 'If Michael stays in the city, remember, he'll be close enough to visit.'

Still not a word from Amber, but her eyes brimmed.

'Why don't we see how it goes, give them a chance to get to know each other, just on a trial basis? Meanwhile I'll track down your sister.'

A tiny nod.

'All right then.' Rosa Figueroa flashed a grin at Noah. 'Let's start on the paperwork.'

A poke from Joan. *If ever you're to extricate yourself, now's the moment.*

But it felt as if Noah had passed that turnoff in the road some time back. 'All right. In principle.'

'What's that supposed to mean?' Amber asked.

'I'm certainly willing to, open to having the boy stay for a few weeks, if when we meet we, ah, we get along all right.'

Amber crossed her arms, creamy nails like a shield. 'Oh, you expect to get along right off the bat? So, like, if Michael's not feeling chatty you'll take a pass?'

What was she hiding about her son? Or was Noah being paranoid? Maybe it was just that Amber had reason to fear this arrangement would fall apart as others had. He pointed out, 'Michael may have something to say about the matter.'

She pursed her lips.

'Of course the boy's views will be taken into account. But if we're going to try this,' Rosa Figueroa warned, 'you both need to sign off on it today.'

Silence from Amber.

Noah managed a nod.

Rosa Figueroa popped open her briefcase. 'Here we go. 'Designation of Person in Parental Relationship.''

What an odd phrase, Noah thought. 'Of course nothing can actually happen, in terms of his moving in, till after I get back from France next Monday.'

Amber's eyebrows soared as if he'd said he was jetting to the moon.

'I'm leaving this Tuesday,' he reminded Rosa Figueroa. 'The day after tomorrow.'

Her face wore its exhausted look again. 'I didn't realize it was coming up quite so soon.'

Noah was almost positive he'd told her. Maybe she'd missed that detail because of her hearing problem. Or was she counting on a seventy-nine-year-old not being entirely sure of what he'd said?

'The thing is, Bernice Johnson's been more than patient, but she can't keep Michael past tonight,' she went on. 'Couldn't your vaca-tion . . . '

'It's not a vacation. It's a very long-awaited, overdue visit to the place I grew up.' *A bequest from my sister*, Noah wanted to add, but that sounded pampered.

'Can't it be postponed?'

'No, it can't! I'm going for Carnival — that's

like the Christmas of Nice. The flights, the hotel . . . ' In peak winter season, the prices were already exorbitant. 'I don't know what it would cost to start changing everything.'

Amber's mouth tightened.

On Noah's university pension, it struck him, he was probably more comfortably off than anyone else in this awful room. Still, he didn't mean to be manipulated into demolishing his plans. 'This trip has taken a lot of organizing, and I'm not going to put it off.'

'Then you could maybe take Michael along?' Rosa Figueroa suggested.

He blanched at the prospect.

'That's crazy,' Amber said.

'Listen' — Noah got to his feet, looking at neither woman but the space between them — 'I'm willing to look after Michael from next Monday, for a few weeks. Take it or leave it.'

'Anyway, you can't drag my boy off to Europe, he's in *school*.'

Amber's disdain provoked Noah. 'Well, if it came to that, what could be more educationally stimulating than a visit to a famous city that's two-and-a-half thousand years old?'

'I could speak to Michael's principal.' Rosa Figueroa's face was alight. 'It would be the trip of a lifetime.'

'But — ' *I want to go on my own*, Noah wailed in the privacy of his head. *Not shackled to some random boy.*

It was a half-remembered glimpse of Victor that stopped him from walking away. Dressed as a zombie for Halloween: plastic chains clattering

34

behind him, an ax through his beautiful head.

Noah let himself down heavily onto the seat.

'Passport?' Lucas Weinburg broke his silence.

Rosa Figueroa looked sucker-punched. She turned back to the young woman. 'I don't suppose Michael has a passport?'

A blank look. 'No, and he doesn't need one.'

Relief, then, like a shot of glucose in Noah's veins. He wouldn't have to do this after all.

Rosa Figueroa seized one of Amber's hands. 'He's going into a group home in East Flatbush, or he's going to France. You choose.'

Tears plummeted off Amber's jaw onto the scored surface of the table.

Noah couldn't stand this. He whipped the clean cloth handkerchief out of his pocket and put it to her knuckles.

Amber pressed his handkerchief over her eyes, hard, like Justice's blindfold.

Rosa Figueroa breathed out. 'What time are you leaving on Tuesday, Mr. Selvaggio?'

What if Noah said, 'First thing' — would that get him off, even at this eleventh hour? 'Late,' he found himself admitting. 'A night flight.'

'If we pay the rush fee . . . fingers crossed we'll get it by Tuesday afternoon.'

A murmur from Lucas Weinburg: 'Wouldn't count my chickens.'

'No, we can make this happen.' Rosa Figueroa squinted as if consulting her mental files. 'There's a form that lets us apply for a passport on Michael's behalf, and another for you to consent to a relative taking him overseas,' she told Amber. She scowled down at her watch. 'I'll

35

run out to my car and find them online. The problem is, how to get hard copies, because visiting hours end at, what . . . '

'Two thirty.' Amber sniffled.

Noah wondered if the young woman wanted this mad scheme to fall through, without its being her fault. Would she rather the devil she knew (at least by reputation) — the *apprehending*, the *removal*? She looked down at his handkerchief, the cotton wet and translucent in places.

'I have a portable printer I can hook up to my phone in the car,' Lucas Weinburg mentioned.

'Bless you!' Rosa Figueroa thrust her keys into his hand.

Noah sat useless while the notary sloped off and Rosa Figueroa started filling in the Designation of Person in Parental Relationship form with Amber.

Ballpoint in midair, the young woman studied it. 'It doesn't say anything about kin.'

Rosa Figueroa checked the wording. 'That's true, you can designate any adult. But it's as a kinship carer that I'm proposing Mr. Selvaggio.'

Proposing? Strong-arming a prisoner into consigning her eleven-year-old to a geriatric stranger on the brink of leaving the States; Noah couldn't decide whether Rosa Figueroa was a powerhouse or a loose cannon.

The social worker asked, 'Have you anyone else in mind who's willing, able, and can get here in the next ten minutes?'

Amber shook her head. Took a shaky breath. And signed.

36

Noah's turn. He skimmed the form. (He remembered Joan making him go through a publishing contract clause by clause, even though it was only with a university press and would make him a lifetime total of some four hundred dollars in royalties.) 'NOAH SELVAG-GIO, a person over the age of eighteen . . . the care of the following child/children/incapacitated person(s) MICHAEL JEROME YOUNG D.O.B. 06/17/2006 . . . Any authority granted to the person in parental relationship pursuant to this form shall be valid (check appropriate box and initial) . . . '

He looked up. 'Thirty days? A couple of weeks, I said.'

'That's just in case,' Rosa Figueroa said, placating.

The 'person in parental relationship' was authorized by the parent to get the child immunized, consent to mental health treatment, permit absences from school . . . Noah finally found the line for him to sign.

After all the hurry, they had time on their hands, waiting for Lucas Weinburg to get back through security. Noah watched the clock.

Rosa Figueroa wrote down Michael's school details, doctor, and dentist for Noah. Also Noah's address and number for Amber's reference, and Amber's inmate number and the correctional facility's details, 'so you can stay in touch.'

Noah tried to think of pertinent questions to ask. But what came out of his mouth was, 'You and Victor . . . '

Amber's eyes flared. 'Vic.'

Was that her name for him? *Tell me how it all happened*, was what Noah wanted to say.

But really, he could imagine. He'd seen puberty lure away the little nephew who'd once wet his pants laughing at a Monty Python video with Noah, and metamorphose him into a handsome devil: height, sideburns, a reek of plausibility, a libidinal swagger. Amber might have had no idea Victor had been only fifteen when they'd met; of course he'd have bullshitted about his age as well as everything else. The couple would have been careless, many times or once, and one time was often all it took for the young.

Joan and Noah had never had to have the conversation; never had a pregnancy scare. They'd always been careful, because it had mattered so much not to have their lives interrupted — their work lives, yes, and their life together. Noah didn't care if that sounded ruthless, or pathetic.

'This Valentine's would have been our twelve years.' Amber folded up his handkerchief.

Noah found her tone unreadable: loving, raging, lamenting? Fernande hadn't known how to get in touch with the young woman when Victor died; not realizing that Amber was in prison, she'd had to assume they'd broken up. But Amber spoke as if she and Victor were lovers, even now. 'It must have been a shock,' he said.

Don't pussyfoot, Joan advised.

He spelled it out: 'The overdose.'

'That shit was never his poison.' Amber almost growled it.

Confused, Noah tried to meet Rosa Figueroa's eyes. But she was jumping up, because here came the notary, a sheaf of forms in his hand.

★ ★ ★

Manhattan was noisy with cold wind.

Back in his apartment, Noah called Vivienne. Twice in one weekend, after months of silence; the woman would think he was wooing her, or getting dementia. He wound up his summary: 'So I seem to have sabotaged my big trip.'

'No, no, this will do you good, you old fart-in-the-mud.'

'You still sound like an immigrant. It's an *old fart* or a *stick-in-the-mud*.'

'You sit down in the mud and fart in it,' Vivienne insisted.

'What have I done to bring this on myself?'

'Well, now it's happened, it'll pull you out of the mud,' she told him.

Try new things, if you wanted to reduce the cognitive deficits of aging, the *New York Times* was always advising: do crossword puzzles and brush your teeth with your nondominant hand. Of course there were losses; Noah wasn't senile enough not to have noticed. He knew he got distracted when reading, these days. (Mind you, wasn't everyone like that, since the internet?) He had to look up facts he'd known all his life, and resort to paper and pen for arithmetic. Joan had sworn by a simple maxim: keep working

39

like a dog. But then, she'd only had to make it to seventy-four, herself; her mind (twice at sharp as Noah's to start with) crystalline to the end.

'When men retire they need projects, or they tend to keel over the first year.'

That was what had happened to Frank, so Noah couldn't argue. 'Michael's not a project. He's a bereaved child who deserves a home.'

'Yes, yes, but you'll do for a couple of weeks,' Vivienne said. 'Besides, such a tale! This child your sister tried to reach out to, all those years ago, this boychik who was lost . . . '

Noah thought of the Prodigal Son. 'Hardly *lost*. He's been with the Davises all along. He just didn't know us Youngs and Selvaggios.'

'Well, high time he did.'

Us, what *us* was there now? Eleven years ago, there'd still been just enough of them to constitute some kind of clan. Of course Noah and Joan would have been willing to meet Victor's girlfriend and son if he'd ever proposed a get-together. (If he'd ever reached out to his aunt and uncle for any purpose other than ripping them off.) But now Noah was the only one left of his own generation or the next; too late for any *family preservation*.

'Don't underestimate the blood tie,' Vivienne added. 'Like calls to like.'

Noah loathed this kind of mysticism. 'Strands of DNA do not sniff each other out.'

But she was already going on about a woman in Philadelphia whose daughter had been abducted at birth. The grieving mother had run

40

into a girl at a party six years on and somehow *known*, and made an excuse to steal a sample of her hair . . .

Joan had been even more of a cold-blooded scientist than Noah; how had she put up with this ditz? 'I have to go now. You wouldn't believe the paperwork involved.'

'All right, well, mazel tov.'

He let out a scornful grunt.

'Bon voyage, anyway.'

Noah sat down with his tablet and bought the kid's flights first, because you couldn't even apply for a passport without proof of immediate travel, paid in full. The app kept glitching. He missed travel agents. (Joan had left everything up to theirs, preferring to save her brain for what it was best at.) No seats left on his New York to Nice flight, so Noah had to change to a later one — ugh, more tiring — and add *Master Michael Young*. (Why did airlines insist on addressing male children as if this were the eighteenth century?) The whole eleventh-hour farrago was costing more than two thousand dollars, on top of what he'd already spent on a trip that he now considered a write-off. A trip an eleven-year-old who'd never left the States before might very well hate.

Complete purchase?

Noah clicked on the green button.

★ ★ ★

Monday at 8:55 a.m., on a freezing corner down in SoHo. When Noah spotted the social worker running up, he dropped his butt on the sidewalk

— almost letting his latte fall too — and ground it out.

Rosa Figueroa nodded at him as she talked on the phone. 'Mm, but only because his grandma was dying . . . Yes, I can assure you, it'll be very enriching.' After another minute she clicked off. 'I've gotten the truancy probation officer off your back for now, but when you're back from France, Michael can't miss another day of sixth grade.'

Splendid, Noah was already in trouble.

'Oh, and the principal wants him to keep a diary.'

A log of any mistreatment? Times that Noah might send him to bed hungry, or wallop him, or lock him out of the hotel room?

'For literacy, cultural studies.' Rosa Figueroa covered a yawn.

Oh, a travel diary.

'How heavy a smoker are you, Mr. Selvaggio?'

'Very light.' A faint hope: might that disqualify him as a foster parent?

'You know not to expose Michael to secondhand smoke, keep all cigarettes and lighters locked away?'

'Sure, fine.'

'What about alcohol?'

Noah managed not to roll his eyes. 'I was born in France. We're known for our moderate and civilized use of wine.'

'Anything else at all by way of recreational — '

He cut her off with a shake of the head. It was pure hypocrisy, interrogating him at this point, as if she hadn't already put all her eggs in his frayed basket.

42

The two of them had to pass through a metal detector, into the passport office, and — NO WEAPONS, FOOD, OR DRINKS — the guard gestured for Noah to drop his latte and half-eaten muffin in the garbage.

He and Rosa Figueroa took the elevator to the tenth floor, collected a ticket (D452) from a machine, and sat on more plastic chairs to wait for one of the so-called passport specialists. Rosa Figueroa's name would always conjure up pressure on the buttocks for Noah. That was how it was, approaching eighty: everything got close to the bone.

'Proof of travel?' she asked him, like a fretful mother.

Noah handed over the printout. (A *hard copy*, they called it now, as if it were steel rather than flimsy paper.)

'Expedited fee for will-call service?'

Noah patted the pocket that held his wallet.

As the minutes ticked by, he tried to relativize this line. The worst days of Soviet Russia, breadlines of a thousand people. Or that Beijing traffic jam, a few years ago, that had lasted twelve days.

'Should be here by now.' Rosa Figueroa checked her phone again.

'Who?'

She looked at him oddly. 'Michael has to be present for the application.'

Evidence that the child was real, Noah supposed, rather than part of some passport-selling scheme. He found himself sick with nerves. A bald, skull-faced senior citizen, that's

43

what he looked like.

No child's idea of a good time, Joan joked.

Noah stared down at the names Rosa Figueroa had filled in. 'Statement of Exigent/Special Family Circumstances for Issuance of a U.S. Passport to a Minor Under Age 16.' A whole category of words survived only on governmental forms meant to intimidate citizens, words even a professor could get through his life without saying aloud: *exigent, issuance*. He struggled to make sense of the fine print. The circumstances counted as *exigent* if Michael's health or welfare would be jeopardized by not getting a passport immediately. *(Quick, I must see the Mediterranean or I'll fall into a decline!)* This request might qualify as a 'special family circumstance IF the minor's situation makes it exceptionally difficult or impossible for one or both of the minor's custodial parents/legal guardians to apply in person or provide the notarized, written consent.' A situation such as Amber being locked up and Victor being dead?

Noah watched numbers change on the screen over the booths. D445. C926. A188. Quite random, perhaps — meant to break applicants of any expectation that it would be their turn soon. 'So what does Amber do all day?' He wondered if they had a writer-in-residence in her *correctional facility*. You heard of lifers getting PhDs, sometimes.

'Various programs.' Rosa Figueroa flicked through her papers. 'Parenting,' she read, 'Life Skills slash Budgeting, Alternatives to Aggression, Introduction to Building Maintenance.'

44

Oh dear.

'Also she's working in a Signs and Metal Shop for twenty an hour.'

He blinked. 'That has to be more than twice minimum wage.'

'Twenty *cents*.'

'Sorry — of course.' Hot-faced. The only word that came to mind was *slavery*. 'She can't even get her GED in there?'

Rosa Figueroa's head tilted. 'Amber graduated high school when she was eighteen.'

Ah. He shouldn't have assumed she was a dropout. 'I just thought, with the drugs . . . '

'She has no record of any substance-abuse problem. Never failed a urine test, even.'

'My mistake.' But could you really work in that world without being sucked in?

'She studied business at a community college for almost a year,' Rosa Figueroa added, leafing through the file, 'before she moved back in with her mom for the birth. While Michael was little, she worked at a local discount store.'

Nineteen when motherhood hit her like a truck: so she couldn't be more than thirty now. Victor must have been gone so much, walled up in his various *placements*. Had he been any use to Amber at all?

D448, said the screen.

Then, immediately, D449.

Noah checked the little scalloped ticket; they were D452. If the boy didn't turn up in time, they'd miss their appointment, the whole improvised plan would fall through, and what then?

45

'By the way,' Rosa Figueroa murmured, 'I got a friend in the NYPD to take a quick look at Victor's record. He was arrested that same night as Amber.'

Noah stared. A little more than three months before he'd died.

'Also, he'd previously served a year in a men's prison for dealing. This was in 2014 to '15.'

His mouth was dry. 'We . . . I never heard that.' It occurred to Noah that Fernande — ashamed of her son — must have decided to keep that adult sentence to herself. Late 2014, that was when Dan's strokes had begun. Was prison, rather than callousness, why Victor hadn't been at his father's scattering? Fernande hadn't said. Then again, Noah hadn't asked. Or had she not even known? Instead of calling his worn-out parents and asking for another expensive lawyer, had Victor gone it alone? 'Only a year. How come Amber got five?'

'More weight.'

Noah thought she meant morally. Then he realized it was a technical term: grams of drugs.

'For August 2016 — the night he and Amber were picked up in her car — the record's pretty minimal. They seem to have let Victor go the next day, and no charges were filed, whereas they threw the book at Amber.'

'Well, then. The police must have known the stash was hers.' But this rang hollow even as Noah said it. Since when were American police so reliably discerning?

She gave a tiny shrug. 'Legally, there are always a number of factors at play, arrangements . . .'

46

It was Victor who was selling those drugs. Joan, like a hammer tapping in his head.

We don't know —

Come off it! In all kinds of trouble since he was thirteen, a convicted dealer . . .

Oh Christ, Amber's doing his time for him. Five years.

Facedown on a carpet, three months after they'd let him go. What was it Amber had said about the overdose? 'That shit was never his poison.' Pushers made a point of abstaining from their product. So why had Victor succumbed and pressed the plunger, in the end? Maybe it had been too much for him, life without his girlfriend. Life outside, the freedom that should have been hers.

Idiot. Stupid, useless wastrel. You weren't meant to speak ill of the dead, but some-times . . .

'Anyway,' Rosa Figueroa said. 'Between the two of them, Amber and her mother seem to have done a great job with Michael. Even stayed on top of the paperwork. Birth cert, Medicaid card, immunizations, school reports . . . '

'A smart cookie, is he?'

She didn't respond.

Noah felt awkward. 'I mean, I remember his father as distinctly clever.' He'd taught Victor to play chess, around eleven or so, and soon the boy had mopped the floor with him.

Rosa Figueroa closed the folder and smoothed it with her hand. 'Michael's a good kid, he's on track. But he hasn't been performing up to his capacities in a classroom setting.'

47

'You mean he's flunking?'

She shook her head. 'There's a Behavioral Plan in here that indicates he can be oppositional, makes bids for negative attention . . .'

Oppositional Defiant Disorder, that was one of the many labels the specialists had tried hanging on Victor, before he started refusing to talk to them. When Noah had looked it up, the so-called symptoms had seemed to boil down to being adolescent. How did it help to medicalize rebellion? 'Any concrete examples?'

'Well, Michael was recently suspended for three days for being found in possession of a knife.'

Pocketknives had been normal in Noah's childhood, but bringing one to school nowadays, he supposed that showed poor judgment. A psychologist had once told him at a cocktail party that if you didn't teach impulse control in the first four years . . .

'But I know that school, and it can be an intimidating environment.' Rosa Figueroa gave a little grimace. 'Though the new principal seems to be trying to turn things around. Anyway, the knife incident is not typical. You just need to know it's likely Michael's going to act out and test your boundaries, especially while you two are getting acquainted.'

D450, said the screen.

A woman hurried in and stared around.

Rosa Figueroa leaped up. 'Ms. Johnson?' And then, as the woman hurried up to her, 'Did you get the passport photos?'

'Ain't had time. I applied at the Burial Claims

48

Unit like you said, but they only going to pay me back nine hundred, and the cremation come to fourteen hundred ninety-five.' Bernice Johnson was stern with stress.

Not till then, while Rosa Figueroa was assuring her she'd speak to the burial claims people, did Noah notice the boy trailing in the woman's wake. Her hand grasping not his, but the sleeve of his puffy coat.

The small face pale, blank; no obvious resemblance to Victor. A ball cap with a flat brim pushed off to one side and an angular Y with an N over it, in exotic lettering; Noah couldn't remember if that meant Mets or Yankees.

'Well, let's get to it.' Rosa Figueroa hurried them all over to Photograph Service. 'Oh, Michael, sorry,' she threw over her shoulder, flustered, 'this is your father's uncle who's going to be taking care of you for a little while, Mr. Noah Selvaggio.'

The boy let out a small, explosive sound.

A sob? No, Noah decided, a snigger. 'Hello there,' was all he could think to say.

No response from Michael.

'I'm going to be late for work. You be good now,' Bernice Johnson told the boy. 'Keep your head straight. Don't be no stranger.' She mashed a kiss on his ear before she left.

At the photo booth, Rosa Figueroa was already filling in yet another form in a rapid scribble.

Waiting beside the child, Noah decided to risk it. 'Is it the surname? Is that what made you laugh?'

Eyes on his phone, Michael appeared not to

hear him. Noah noticed it had cracks radiating from a hole.

'When I first came to America, I used to get teased a lot for that.' *You sell vag or something?* 'This was back in 1942.' How unreal that sounded now, an ominous date from the history books.

'You're how old?' Michael still wasn't looking at Noah. His voice was a child's, but getting husky, unless that was put on for machismo.

'I'll turn eighty in a week.'

'You don't sound like an immigrant.'

'Well, I arrived at the age of four, and kids are adaptable.' Noah winced. This kid had just lost his grandmother, on top of everything else; how fast was he supposed to adapt to that? 'But I am French.' Though as a US citizen Noah always felt rather a fraud, saying that. *I'm from France,* was that any better? 'So are you, partially.'

'No I'm not,' Michael snapped.

' 'No sunglasses,'' Rosa Figueroa read from the instructions, ''no earphones, no headgear' — so cap off, please, Michael.'

The boy took it off and sat on the stool. His brown hair (nearer to Amber's shade than Victor's) was buzzed short in a way that reminded Noah of convicts in old movies.

'Better not smile,' he said in the boy's direction as he was paying the photographer.

'Why not?'

'It's whatchacallit, biometrics. The distance between the edges of your mouth and your eyes, that kind of thing, the proportions get distorted by a smile. You'll look less like yourself — I mean your usual self.'

50

'What if I usually smile?'

In Noah's two-minute experience of this child, he didn't.

Michael was glued to his phone again.

'Eyes up, please,' the seen-it-all photographer called.

'Do a neutral face,' Noah suggested.

'What do you mean, neutral?' the boy asked.

'Not smiling, not frowning, just as if you're calm.'

'Like dead?' Now he played possum, jaw hanging, eyes staring, torso lolling off the stool.

Rosa Figueroa spoke up. 'Michael, can we please get this done before we miss our turn at the passport desk?'

'"An unaffected smile is permitted,"' he called out, pointing to a sign on the wall. He stumbled over *unaffected*, but there was nothing wrong with his reading.

Noah hid his irritation. 'I guess they must have changed the rule. But *unaffected*, that means nothing goofy or over the top.'

Michael pulled a sinister grin with his fingers hooked in the corners of his mouth.

Noah might end up losing two thousand dollars to the airline because this kid wouldn't stop monkeying around.

'Sit up straight, please.' The photographer suppressed a yawn.

'Phone away,' Rosa Figueroa told Michael.

He only tightened his grip on it.

'That's OK, it's just a head shot,' the photographer said.

Once released from the stool, Michael put his

cap back on and pulled it all the way down.

They had the envelope of warm prints in about a minute. (The electronic sign over the glass booths still said D450, so they hadn't missed their slot.) In the pictures Michael looked older, Noah thought; harder. But really, eleven — that was barely formed.

He sat down on the plastic seat beside the boy. He noticed a tiny hole in Michael's coat, a bit of fluff sticking out.

Go on, Joan said, *make more sparkling conversation.*

'I'm sorry about your grandma.'

Rosa Figueroa caught that. 'Sounds like she was a wonderful lady, she'll be missed. I bet she's looking down, watching you right now.'

The boy's small face showed nothing at all.

The sign jumped from D450 to C927, then straight to D452, and Rosa Figueroa leaped up as if she'd been electrocuted: 'That's us.'

★　★　★

Out in the bone-rattling wind, afterward, Noah tingled in anticipation of the large coffee he was going to enjoy, by himself this time, in a not-too-trendy café, before he went home to gather his forces. 'How should we get Michael back to school?' he asked Rosa Figueroa in the most responsible voice he could put on.

She frowned at her watch. 'Hardly worth it. I have to be in Downtown Brooklyn for a hearing by twelve thirty, and before that I need to make a couple of calls . . . but maybe we could fit in the home visit now?'

She wasn't really asking, Noah gathered, and the home in question was his apartment. 'Ah. OK. I haven't had a chance to tidy up, but . . . ' That was the whole idea, he realized; it wouldn't be an accurate spotcheck otherwise.

Michael was playing with some ball-shaped electronic game, oblivious to the cold.

Rosa Figueroa fretted over her laminated bus map.

'Let's treat ourselves to a cab.' Noah said it lightly, like a line from a Noël Coward play. Would she guess that he was so worn out he thought he might drop down in the street?

She made only a token protest.

To fill the silence in the taxi, Noah said, 'I used to work in Brooklyn, as it happens. I taught for more than forty years at a university.' Though the engineering and applied-sciences campus had been five miles from Ella Davis's notorious neighborhood.

He won't be interested in your career, Joan pointed out.

Snagged in traffic. Noah watched the ticker mount. Would the boy think Noah was a billionaire? It was all relative, he supposed. Rich enough to take a yellow cab, but not a limo with a peaked-cap driver; what did you call that?

'What's up with that hat?' Michael didn't look up from his beeping globe.

Rosa Figueroa wasn't wearing one, so the boy must mean Noah's. His hand flew up to adjust the sit of his old fedora. 'What's up with it?'

'Why are you wearing it?'

'Why do you wear yours?'

Michael shrugged.

Noah tried again. 'What's that game you're playing?'

Several seconds passed.

'Can you answer the question, Michael?' the social worker murmured. 'Mr. Selvaggio just wants the two of you to get to know each other.'

Enough of a further pause to be insolent before Michael said, '*Mind Reader.*'

'Is that right?' Noah asked. 'It reads your mind?'

A scornful sound in the boy's throat.

'So . . . you think of something? And then?'

'It does a question about the thing, you say yes or no — '

'Oh, that's an ancient game,' he said with relief. 'A TV show, and it was on the radio before that. People have been playing Twenty Questions for centuries.'

'Nobody's even had electricity for centuries,' the boy muttered.

Rosa Figueroa roused herself. 'So, you know where your uncle's going to take you tomorrow, Michael? France! If your passport comes through.' Faltering.

'He's not my uncle. Cody's my uncle.'

Hang on, who was Cody? 'Is he your aunt's husband?' Noah asked.

'Mom's brother. He lives with us.'

Noah looked at Rosa Figueroa.

'Cody Davis has been staying at their mother's on and off this past year,' she admitted.

'Then why can't — ' Noah stopped himself.

54

'Didn't you say on the phone that I was Michael's only relative in New York?'

'After we ruled out Mr. Davis. He's on disability — in chronic pain. You're the only one in a position to be able to offer care.'

And how could Rosa Figueroa possibly have known whether Noah would have it in him to *offer care*? 'What's wrong with him?'

'He uses a wheelchair, I believe from an injury he suffered, years ago. That right, Michael?'

The boy nodded over his electronic ball.

'You must be missing him, too, as well as your grandma.'

'Is this Cody still at the apartment?' Perhaps with some kind of hired support . . . If Noah could throw money at this situation, he'd do it in a minute.

'Landlord kicked us out already.' Michael's voice was bitter.

'I think your uncle's with friends in Queens for now,' Rosa Figueroa told him, 'but I'm sure you'll see him soon.'

So this Cody was motherless and homeless too. It was all such a disaster.

'And Mr. Selvaggio is your great-uncle, which is another kind of uncle.'

'What's so great about him?' Michael wanted to know.

Whether that was ignorance or wit, it did make Noah smile.

2

Twenty Questions

Noah surveyed his neighborhood out the cab window with new, uneasy eyes. The Upper West Side really wasn't that tony — less so than the Upper East Side. He and Joan had bought this apartment before prices had skyrocketed in the '80s. Still, as the cab pulled up to his building he found himself self-conscious about the scalloped canopy over the entrance, the uniformed doorman. It must all look pretty snooty to Michael.

The elevator clanked on the way up to the ninth floor. *See,* Noah wanted to say, absurdly, *the place could do with some refurbishing, I'm no Daddy Warbucks.*

At his door, he found himself struggling to turn the key. Rosa Figueroa was right behind him, no doubt assessing everything from his fine motor skills to the prints in his narrow hall. (Was the Egon Schiele drawing borderline pornographic?) As the invaders filed past him, Noah tried to see his apartment through their eyes — fine-boned chairs, thin Persian rugs on the walls, unbroken shelves of *Proceedings of the National Academy of Sciences* and *Organic Letters.* He just hoped the child wouldn't break anything.

'Michael, want to take your coat off?'

The boy ignored Rosa Figueroa.

What was she scanning for: sketchy room-mates? Whips? Mysterious white powders? Or dangers that Noah wasn't even aware of? No, more like absences of crucial things that kids needed.

Noah didn't even have to be the best of a bad bunch, he told himself, because there was no bunch from which he'd been selected. If the social worker judged him not up to the mark, so be it: she could tear up that Designation of Person in Parental Relationship and take Michael away with her to the group home. The sad fact was, for her to do that, there'd probably have to be a serial-killer collage on Noah's bedroom wall.

'Where's your dog?' Michael wanted to know.

'Ah, dead, sorry,' Noah said. He never registered the heated sleeping pad in the corner anymore, or the mangled chew toy. Unhygienic; he should get rid of them.

Michael didn't even glance at the rippled surfaces of books, the CDs, the vinyl (mostly jazz). Still wearing his backpack, he parked himself on the curved end of the black leather chaise longue. *That's a genuine 1969 LC4, designed by Le Corbusier, Charlotte Perriand, and Pierre Jeanneret in 1928*, Noah wanted to tell him. *A marriage of geometric purity and ergonomic perfection.*

'Could I see Michael's room?' the social worker asked.

The spare room looked perfectly all right — patchwork quilt draped over the footboard,

57

reading lamp, empty dresser and closet. Just nothing like an eleven-year-old's room.

When they returned, Michael didn't appear to have moved from the chaise longue. Head down, studying his beeping ball.

'Anyone hungry?' Just for something to say. But what on earth could he offer them? He always had stuffed olives in his cupboard. Marcona almonds dusted with rosemary. Maybe a can of Campbell's Thick Creamy Mushroom.

'Nothing for me, thanks.' Rosa Figueroa spoke in the self-denying tone of someone who would really rather say yes. 'Michael?'

'What's your wife?'

That your wife, was that what the child meant? Or, what was she, career-wise? Noah crossed to the large photograph in the cluster over the chaise longue. 'Joan was a scientist. There she is receiving an Outstanding Lifetime Achievement Award.'

Michael turned around to glance at the picture.

Noah had let it be known that the AACC shouldn't shilly-shally, because of the tumor. And there was Joan again, that same year, at a Women in Chemistry fundraiser, nodding and smiling and speechifying till she trembled. In those final months, she'd squeezed herself out like a lemon. 'See who's shaking hands with her?'

Rosa Figueroa let out a respectful gasp. 'That's Hillary Clinton, who was nearly president,' she told the boy.

'So what's your Wi-Fi?' Michael asked.

Not *wife*; Noah heard correctly this time.

58

Discomfited, he said, 'The password? I'll have to look it up.'

Michael got up, still strapped into his backpack, turtle-humped. He roamed the room, picking up books and papers like some burglar, putting them down in the wrong places. Noah's hands itched to stop him.

'Smoke detectors?' Rosa Figueroa seemed to be running down a mental list.

'One in the kitchen,' Noah said with a gesture, 'another in the bedroom.'

Michael located the black plastic modem, flipped it over, and started copying the long code into his phone.

'Oh, and your principal wants you to keep a journal, Michael. Maybe Mr. Selvaggio will help you do a family tree? Or just describe whatever from your trip. When I was your age my folks took me to Niagara Falls, and I've never forgotten it.'

Michael looked to Noah like he'd rather forget all of this.

Eyes on Noah, Rosa Figueroa jerked her head toward the kitchen.

He led the way. 'You might as well call me Noah,' he said over his shoulder.

'OK, sure, if you'll say Rosa.' Her tone went from soft to crisp. 'I notice your medicine cabinet isn't locked.'

'Sorry, there is a key, I just . . . ' *Need to find it.* 'I'll lock it.'

'Great.'

Didn't she realize Noah had no competencies in the parenting field at all? The last — the only

— minor who'd ever stayed the night here was Victor. (Who would almost definitely have raided their meds, Noah realized now.)

'His school information is at the top of the file. Listen, these placements don't always work out, and it's nobody's fault.'

So she'd decided he was going to fail at this. Noah felt (could it be?) oddly stung.

'If you're not coping — or if Michael's freaking out — get in touch earlier rather than later, all right?'

He nodded, unable to speak.

Rosa checked her watch. 'At this age kids say, 'Leave me alone,' but they need you not to. Just keep trying, listening. The goal is to make him feel safe.'

Noah nodded.

'You might have better luck once I'm out of your hair.'

'He doesn't have any.' Michael, in the kitchen doorway.

Noah let out a nervous chuckle and rubbed his crown. He wondered if baldness seemed creepy to a child; like a mutation.

Rosa was zipping up her thin down coat.

He registered that she was leaving the boy with him *now*.

'Is everything clear, Noah?' She sounded as if she thought he might be losing it.

'More or less. Except — won't we need to collect the rest of his things at some point?'

'Got them.' Michael's shrug made his backpack jerk.

Could that really be the sum total of the

child's possessions? Like a gypsy, or a refugee.

'What if the passport . . . ' Noah's voice came out faint. 'If I haven't heard from them by the end of tomorrow.' *Will you come and take him back?* Better not to ask, especially in front of Michael; it would be hurtful, as well as showing weakness. Noah had signed the form, after all. He was saddled with this child, for an unspecified number of weeks. 'Well. I'm sure it'll turn up in time.'

Rosa nodded, her smile tight, and put a card into the boy's hand. 'Keep this somewhere you won't lose it, Michael, and message me if anything's bothering you at all, OK?'

''Kay.'

Anything fixable, she must mean; anything small. Not grief. Or fury at his fate.

'Or ask your uncle for his phone. Any hour of the day or night.'

'*Great*-uncle.' The sound was deep in the boy's throat.

★　★　★

When Noah came back from seeing Rosa to the elevator, the boy was in the kitchen (still in his coat and cap), staring up at the saucepan rack. No, to the left of it.

'Can I see the bird?'

Noah hadn't noticed the clockwork toy in years. He lifted it down and blew off the dust. The tiny automaton was upright, with beady metal eyes and a worn velvet body in orange, gold, and black. 'This was my grandpa's. He was

61

a famous photographer. My mom and I lived with him in France, during the war, and that's why I'm going there tomorrow, really.' He corrected himself: 'Why we're going.'

'Which?'

'Which what?'

'Which war?'

'The Second. World War Two,' Noah added for clarity. The bird's beak hung a little loose and askew, he saw now. 'My grandpa got this Pick-Pick Bird from a commercial photographer who was retiring. Used it when he was shooting kids.' They'd been a craze in the '20s — millions of them sold, pneumatic versions, even water-powered ones. Where were they all now?

The kid didn't look as if he were following.

'It's what photographers said, to get you to look into the lens: '*Le petit oiseau va sortir.*'' He fumbled for the American equivalent. ' 'Watch the birdie.' Anyway, this one, you wound it up and it walked around in circles, pecking at the ground.'

'Wound it up like how?'

Noah puzzled over the bird. There was a bald spot over the left hip, with a tiny hole; he put his finger to it. 'I suppose the key was detachable, and it's been lost.' By Margot, or Père Sonne, or the man he got it from, even; sometime in the last century, somewhere between Nice and New York.

'Design flaw.' For a moment Michael sounded much older.

'Indeed.' Noah supposed he could possibly track down a replacement key online, if he took

62

the trouble. But then what if it didn't work? On the whole, he'd rather not know that the mechanism was rusted up; would rather think of this Pick-Pick Bird as potentially full of movement and music. It reminded him of the old story about the emperor who chose a bejeweled wind-up nightingale over the dull brown one who used to sing to him so sweetly.

'This is him,' Noah went on, crossing to the photos on the wall, 'your famous . . . great-great-grandfather.' Was that right?

'Why does it go 'father,' '*grand*father,' 'great-grandfather,' but Cody's my 'uncle' and you're my 'great-uncle'?' Michael wanted to know. 'Shouldn't it be 'grand' before it jumps to 'great'?'

Noah furrowed his brow. 'No idea, sorry. That's me there in my mother's lap — Margot, she was called, your great-grandmother — with Père Sonne. That was his *nom d'artiste*. Like a *nom de plume* for a writer — a pseudonym? Or alias?' It was exhausting having to translate almost every word into vocabulary he imagined an eleven-year-old would know. 'His real name was Pierre Personnet. You must know singers with ludicrous stage names? Like, ah, 50 Cents.'

'50 *Cent*,' Michael said, pained. 'And it's Luda*cris*.'

Now Noah was out of his depth. 'John Wayne's real name was Marion, but he thought it sounded too sissy.'

'Who's John Wayne?'

'Never mind. My point is — '

Michael broke in. 'So my ancestor was famous

63

like Beyoncé famous?'

Noah had heard of her. 'He still is. But it's hard to quantify. They'd have different fans.'

'Bet Beyoncé has way more.' Michael was kneeling up on the LC4, staring at a photo from inches away. He put his finger to the glass. 'That me there?'

'None of these are of you, I'm afraid.' It occurred to Noah that he hadn't come across any pictures of Michael and Amber in Fernande's boxes. She must have taken some. Could she have thrown them away after Victor's death, when she thought his partner and child had slipped out of her life for good? 'That was Victor, between his parents — my sister Fernande and her husband Dan.' The image of the lovely boy hurt his chest like the thump of a bat. 'You're pretty like your dad.' A lie; Noah was trying to make Michael feel part of the family. But he must have put too much stress on the wrong word, because —

'I'm not *pretty*.' Michael spat it.

'No, sorry' — a yelp of mirth — 'I meant *pretty like* as in *quite like, rather like*. Handsome guys, both of you.' Noah was making this worse. The more often he said it, the less true it was. 'That picture was taken at a little party we had to celebrate the millennium.' He remembered a tedious argument with Fernande about whether (as he insisted) the true millennium wouldn't begin until a year later, on January 1, 2001. She'd been flippant, but Noah was a pedant, he knew; he'd like to have that quarter of an hour with his sister back now. 'Victor must have been,

64

what, nine?' Still undersized like Michael, before the tsunami of hormones.

'He had a motorbike,' the boy said.

'No, he — oh, you mean when he was grown up?'

'Took me for rides, sometimes.'

That sounded risky, typical of Victor. Had they worn helmets, at least? Noah pulled the cuff of his shirt over the heel of his hand and rubbed at the glass so his nephew's ghostly smile shone through again. Watching a child grow up, you convinced yourself that the soft-faced toddler and the laughing boy were being folded into the young man; told yourself that nothing would be lost. But that wasn't true. Time, the child catcher. 'To be honest, we didn't see much of Victor once he was in his teens. Christmases and so on. Joan was Jewish, but we celebrated all the holidays, in our secular way.'

'Sounds weird when you call Vic that.'

'Well, that was what he was, with us.' Noah's gaze went back to the smooth cheek. 'Originally, Victor' — a roll of the final consonant — 'because our family's French.'

Michael shook his head, mutinous.

'Send off your spit to the lab and it'll prove that a quarter of your ancestors came from France.'

'Your name, Noah, that's not French.'

'Ah, I'm really Noé.'

The boy frowned. 'Like, no way?'

Noah nodded. 'When I started kindergarten here, the other kids gave me a hard time for it.' He'd had no English when he'd reached New

York, and the first year had been one long blur of confusion. 'They used to point at me and shout, 'No way, no way!' So I kept nagging my dad till he let me switch to Noah.'

'This one time in fifth grade, someone told my girlfriend I liked someone else even though I didn't, so she ended it.'

Noah sucked in his cheeks so he wouldn't smile. 'Kids.'

'Always talking smack, cracking dumb jokes.'

Of the *yo momma* variety, Noah wondered? A father in prison might possibly bring tough-guy kudos, but a mother?

'Where are yours?' Michael was scanning the wall.

'My what?'

'Kids.'

'Oh, Joan and I didn't have any.'

'Why not?'

Clearly eleven-year-olds had no concept of which questions were rude; it was refreshing. 'Never wanted any.'

Without warning, Michael lounged full-length on the LC4. It slid with him, tipping toward the horizontal; he jerked it forward, then gave up and lay back.

'This is a famous piece of furniture,' Noah told him. 'You feel weightless, don't you? Floating.'

A grunt.

'It doesn't wobble at any angle, because of friction on the rubber tubes that cover the crossbar.' Joan's parents had asked her and Noah to pick their own wedding present. For almost

66

four decades she and Noah had used this lounger — separately, at different times of the day.

Michael pulled out his electronic ball again, as if Noah's voice was just background radio. *Beep, trill, beep.*

'Show me how it works?'

The boy shook the ball. ' 'Is it an animal?' Yes.' Pressing the button. ' 'Is it bigger than a bread box?' What the fuck is a *bread box?*'

Noah was startled. Then he realized the last question was Michael's, not the game's. Mildly: 'Mind your language.'

'Yes.' But it was the game Michael was saying *yes* to, not Noah. ' 'Does it live in water?' Sometimes. 'Do you love it?' Hell no.'

'What's the thing you're thinking of?'

'You have to guess. 'Could it bite you?'' Michael read aloud. 'Rarely.'

'Why *rarely*?' Surely a thing could either bite or not.

'I'd kick it in the teeth, that's why.'

'Alligator?' Noah suggested.

Michael shot him such a tetchy look that Noah knew he'd guessed right.

'Mind reader,' Noah said in a spooky voice, tapping his own head.

The boy switched off the game and was on his feet all at once. 'Is there anything to eat?'

Noah checked his watch: 1:27. 'Ah . . . what would you say to a slice of pizza?'

''Kay.'

They went down together, speechless in the elevator. 'Spooky,' Michael whispered.

67

'What is, the clanking? That's just the old cable.'

The boy shook his head. 'So quiet. Like everybody's dead.'

Noah assured him they weren't. *Just middle-class*, he thought. Considerate, sedate, well soundproofed. 'One of my upstairs neighbors practices her opera singing in the mornings. Is — was your grandma's place noisy?'

A small shrug. 'Parties, sometimes. One Saturday morning the bitch downstairs said she'd gut me for playing my music too loud.'

The boy was testing Noah with the foul language. 'Could you just call her a woman?'

'Yeah, but no, because she's a bitch.'

Before he could think of an answer they were in the lobby, and the doorman held the door of the building open for them. 'Julio, this is . . . a young relative of mine, Michael.'

The two of them exchanged nods.

On the street, Noah lit a cigarette. Surely outdoors didn't count as exposing Michael to secondhand smoke? Only to a bad example.

'You know that stuff's going to kill you?'

From the mouths of babes, Joan murmured.

'I'm hitting eighty,' Noah told both his interrogators. 'I've never had more than seven a day, and my doctor says my cardiovascular capacity is 'far better than it should be.' Besides, my wife and my sister did everything right and didn't get past their early seventies, so it's all a roll of the dice.'

Michael didn't dispute that. 'Cody used to smoke till I got him Juuling.'

'What-ing?'

'Vapes, you know? E-cigs?'

Noah nodded. 'Old dog, no new tricks.' He sucked hard on his cigarette, to get it finished, as he wasn't much enjoying it.

In the pizzeria, he found he had no appetite.

Michael held up two fingers, for two slices.

The man had his hair slicked back in what looked like a shower cap, and a net over his beard held on by a string. He served up the pizza on a cardboard triangle.

'Coke,' Michael added.

Noah said, 'Ah, I don't think so. It's a junky enough lunch without washing it down with sugar.'

'I want a Coke, motherfucker.'

Enough! 'Watch your mouth, Michael.' Noah turned to the man and said, 'A cup of water, please.'

'Dasani?' The man jerked his thumb at the refrigerator.

'All right, a bottle of Dasani water. Please.' Even if this was a rip-off, because surely you were entitled to water from pipes you'd paid for with your own taxes.

'Fine, *I'll* get the soda.' Michael pulled out two dollar bills.

Noah had no idea of the extent of his authority. And was this the first battle he was going to pick, really? Did he mean to shove the boy's money away and stage a showdown here and now? Instead he put on his best poker face.

The man sold Michael a big waxed cup of

Coke, after charging Noah for the pizza and the despised water.

As the two rode back up to the ninth floor, the bottle was painfully cold in Noah's hand. He thought he'd drink some, but his fingers couldn't manage the seal. 'You've got some sauce on you,' he said, pointing to his own chin. 'Would you like a napkin?'

'Got one.' Deadpan, Michael held up the flimsy white rectangle, then stuffed it back in his pocket.

Noah told himself not to rise to the bait.

In the apartment, Michael stayed in the bathroom for a long time.

Medicine cabinet, Noah thought, rushing to put his ear to the door. But he couldn't hear anything that sounded like pills rattling or hands wrestling with childproof packaging.

Maybe Michael just needed a few minutes alone? Noah knew how that felt. He leaned his ear on the door. *Il faut qu'une porte soit ouverte ou fermée.* 'A door must be open or shut.' That was one of Margot's favorite proverbs. Noah supposed the American equivalent was 'You can't have it both ways.'

In the kitchen, he had a glass of water and a few almonds and tried to start the *New York Times*.

A flush. The sound of water running in the sink, the bathroom door juddering open, footsteps going toward the spare room. That door shutting tight.

Noah hurried to the bathroom and spent ten pointless minutes rooting around for the tiny key

70

to the unlocked medicine cabinet. Giving up, all he could do was remove any obvious hazards — sleeping pills, cough syrup, painkillers. Unlike many of his contemporaries, he wasn't on a raft of prescription drugs. He frowned over a mini-bottle of hand sanitizer. Had he heard something about people stealing the stuff from emergency rooms for its alcohol content? This was getting ridiculous. He threw it all into a grocery bag and went into the kitchen to add a few dusty bottles of hard liquor (cognac, grappa, scotch).

His eye fell on a leaflet that Rosa must have left him. *Being a Relative Foster Parent.* At the top: 'Are you fit and willing to ensure your child relative's safety and meet his/her needs? Do you have the ability, motivation, and readiness?'

Too late now; Noah had signed on the dotted line. How did *readiness* differ from *ability*? Was it possible to be able but not quite ready, not today, not this week, though perhaps sometime in the indefinite future? 'The readiness is all.' Was that Hamlet? Margot and Marc used to take Noah and Fernande to Shakespeare in Central Park on summer evenings, though Noah's eyes had often slid away from the actors to the darkening sky, the first bats.

The next paragraph told him that he was now 'entirely responsible for the temporary care of a minor who has been placed outside his/her own place of residence.' But Michael no longer had a place of residence. His grandmother was ash, and his uncle was sleeping on somebody's couch in Queens. 'During a time of disruption, you are

71

giving a child relative a new home,' the leaflet went on, slightly more soothingly. Then exhortatory again: Noah was 'obligated' — was that the same as *obliged*, or more stringent? — to provide 'a stable, nurturing environment.' Also 'guidance, discipline, and a good example.' Like something out of a Victorian novel. 'Good-quality food.' Pizza and Coke. 'Proper toilet articles. Keep the child's clothes in good condition.' What did that mean — ironing? darning? 'Regular attendance at school and support with homework. Recreational activities and undertakings,' whatever they were. Generally, Noah was to create 'as many positive experiences as possible.'

He let out a long, ragged breath. What was he offering Michael but a further *time of disruption*?

'Mr. — Noah?'

Mister Noah: it had the ring of some apocalyptic street preacher. Well, better than Great-Uncle Noah. 'In here. In the kitchen.' He almost tripped over the clinking bag of hazardous goods as he got up; he stashed it in the skinny cupboard with the broom.

The face in the doorway was wiped clean of pizza sauce, at least.

'You should call me Noah.'

Michael stepped in. So small without his coat. Noah had been a shrimp himself, while other boys shot up past him.

'We should go out for some air,' Noah said with false cheer. 'Coat on.'

'There's air in here.'

'Exercise, then.'

72

Michael didn't have gloves but insisted it wasn't even cold.

Within a few blocks Noah found his steps turning toward Central Park. 'You must have been there on a school trip or something?'

'I don't remember.'

Noah paid an arm and a leg for a bunch of forced daffodils from a convenience store on the way. Michael didn't ask why, and Noah found himself too shy to explain.

He noticed how many trees there were behind absurd six-inch fences; signs saying KINDLY CURB YOUR DOG; advertisements for chamber-music concerts and chess clubs; brown-skinned workmen in safety masks, hauling away construction waste as paper-white little old ladies in fur collars stepped around them.

Michael walked along like a gunslinger, eyes taking everything in. What did this neighborhood *not* have, that he'd be used to, Noah wondered? People snacking and smoking outside convenience stores, maybe. Boarded-up doors, broken glass, payday loans, CA$H 4 GOLD, the odd addict shuffling.

When they passed Holy Trinity, Noah pointed it out. 'My mom used to bring us to Mass there, and weekly Confession. Your grandma, she was a churchgoer, wasn't she?'

'United Methodist,' Michael said. 'Never let us skip a Sunday, not even the day I broke my collarbone. I sang in the choir.'

Noah struggled to picture this boy in flowing

robes, harmonies raying from his mouth. 'Our father, Marc, he wasn't a believer. My sister Fernande stayed Catholic all her life, but I lost it early.'

'How come?'

'Ah . . . Once you place your trust in science, you generally find you don't need the other stuff so much.'

Great; Michael might report him to Rosa for indoctrination.

Entering the park, Noah remembered Fernande's skinny figure at the Bethesda Fountain, clutching her handbag as if she feared someone might steal its precious weight. How Noah's spirits had sunk, the day he and she had scattered Victor, and stayed sunken for months. A life erased, and so squalidly. *Not with a bang but a whimper.*

He wondered how Amber — in prison for months already, he knew now — had taken the news. How long before she'd been told, even? And in how much detail?

Maybe the night Victor had shot up, he'd been gnawed by guilt about all she'd done for him. But hadn't he realized that if he died, her doing his time would be for nothing?

Michael's gaze narrowed at the sight of a passing car. 'Lambo.'

'What's that?'

'Lamborghini.'

'Was it?' Noah turned his head but it was gone. 'So you like cars?'

Another small shrug. 'Good ones.'

'Such as?'

'Ferrari, Maserati, Alfa Romeo.'

'Ah, the Italians. Any American favorites?'

'Tesla's all right.'

'What about hybrids? Dan and Fernande had a Prius.'

Michael shook his head. '*So gay.*'

Noah blinked. 'You're saying their car . . . '

'Prius sucks big-time. Everyone who's into cars hates them.'

'I take your word for it, but don't say *gay* for *bad*, OK?'

Michael rolled his eyes. 'It doesn't mean *actual* gay. Kid in my class is gay, I don't hate her.'

Noah felt he'd lost his grip on the argument.

He trudged into the park, Michael beside him. Noah's steps were longer, but the kid's came faster. Noah stopped at the stand of gnarly black cherry trees and gestured with the daffodils. 'This is where my mother's ashes are, and Joan's, and Fernande and Dan's. You're a Young because of Dan — you got his surname, through Victor, see? Dan taught American history at a university. They did meet you when you were tiny, and your mom.' Maybe Amber had been prickly, impossible to befriend; maybe it was Victor who'd insisted on keeping his old and new lives apart. Too many hurt feelings and absences to sort out, at this point. 'They would have liked to see more of you.' He went on just to fill the silence. 'A rabbi at a party, once, he told Joan that Jews shouldn't be cremated, it was an act of disrespect and violence to the body, and you know what she told him? 'So is rotting. And at least cremation's faster.''

A tiny snigger. Then, soberly, 'Cody's got Grandma in an urn.'

'Oh, your uncle? Right. What's he planning to . . .'

'Dunno.'

'When we get back from France you can talk to him about it. I'd like to meet Cody, myself,' Noah added with forced enthusiasm. 'You must miss him.'

The boy nodded. 'And his PlayStation.'

'His what?'

'For gaming. We play *Minecraft* and stuff together, but he doesn't like my first-person shooters.'

Cody sounded like a proper uncle. To get the next bit over with, Noah said, 'This is where your dad's ashes are too.' Dark clouds were massing, and the wind was making his eyes water. 'It's technically illegal, disposing of human remains here, so Fernande and I didn't, you know — ' He made a grand gesture of tossing something high into the air. 'We just bent down discreetly and sprinkled them around the base of a tree.'

'Which?'

'I can't remember, I'm afraid. One of these black cherries.' Noah patted a ravaged gray trunk. 'They'll be blooming in a couple of months.' He looked down at the daffodils in his other hand. 'Want to leave these here for your dad?'

''Kay.' Michael took the pinched bunch in their wet paper. He set them on a tree root and walked away.

Noah couldn't bear to leave it at that, as he followed the boy toward the path. 'Victor . . . He was such a charmer.' That sounded like a euphemism for con artist. 'What I'm saying is, he had a lot of potential.' Even worse, in a way; a retrospective indictment.

'Doesn't everybody?'

Noah's mouth twisted. 'I suppose.'

'They're always drilling it into us at school. Posters on the walls, 'Unlock Every Child's Potential,'' Michael quoted in a satirical falsetto. ''You Will Never Have This Day Again, So Make It Count.' 'Believe in U! B U, Cuz Nobody Else Can B.' I mean, who the fuck else do they think we think we're going to be?'

Did he expect Noah to agree that no-hoper kids of the urban underclass were being peddled a pack of lies? Or did he want to be contradicted and urged to believe? Sidestepping the question, Noah said, 'I bet you never used that kind of language in front of your grandmother.'

'Of course not.'

'Well, then.'

'If I'd ever cussed Grandma out, she'd have . . . I don't know what,' Michael said fervently. 'Chores every day, home from school by four thirty, no hanging around on the corner or she'd tell Mom on me. Grades slipped, I had to go to Homework Club. If I talked back she'd turn off the Wi-Fi. One time I talked smack about Grandma's casserole, she took my phone for a week.'

Noah raised his eyebrows. Not some sweet lady looking down on her grandson, then; an

77

angel with a flaming sword. 'So what would she say if she heard you using obscenities?'

'Listen, Mister, she's dead, and what the fuck do you care how I talk? I'm only your problem for a couple weeks.'

Michael had a point, Noah realized. This hiatus, this peculiar holiday with his great-uncle, it was hardly going to have any lasting influence on his diction.

Feed and water him, Joan suggested, *and let yourself off the hook.*

The cold was creeping through Noah's thin leather gloves. 'Want to go get a hot chocolate, to warm up?'

'Can I have a Coke?'

'I don't think so.'

'How come, don't they both have sugar?' Michael asked.

Noah struggled to formulate a case, in his head, for the more nutritional qualities of hot chocolate. Besides, it was the calories in hot drinks that warmed you up, not the joules. Noah had probably just offered hot chocolate because it was a taste of his own childhood: *chocolat chaud* after ice-skating in Central Park. 'I guess so.'

'Coke, then?'

The kid's logic was too much for Noah. 'OK.'

In the convenience store, Michael glugged his pop. 'What did your dog die of?'

'Mendeleev? A tumor. Bichon frises are horribly prone to them.'

'Meddle what?'

'Mendeleev, after the Russian chemist who

78

devised the periodic table. You've heard of that?' Noah pulled out his phone case as illustration.

'Duh.'

Noah took that as a yes.

'Why've you got it on your case?'

The last Christmas present Fernande had ever given Noah; he was resisting upgrading his phone, because then he'd need a different-size case. 'I like it.' *I love it* would have sounded sappy; *I put my faith in it*, cultish. 'It's a sort of family tree,' he added, remembering Rosa's request. 'The universe is three-quarters hydrogen,' putting a fingertip to the first element, 'one-quarter helium. All the rest is just a rounding error.'

'Huh?'

'A mere sprinkle.'

'But we're carbon-based life forms, aren't we?'

'Humans? We're mostly oxygen by mass, actually — or hydrogen, if you're counting atoms.'

You're going to bore the pants off this child, Joan warned him.

'But carbon's what firms us up, yes, because it's' — 'a slut,' the guys used to say in Freshman Chem, though Noah wasn't going to tell Michael that — 'friendly. Carbon wants to bond with everything else.'

Michael frowned at the phone case. 'I don't see how that's a family tree.'

'Well, a set of characters, if you like. Superheroes and villains,' Noah suggested. 'For instance, mercury's a standoffish element, keeps to itself.'

'Batman.'

'Right. So if you eat mercury — don't, by the way — it passes right through you, unchanged. Historians have tracked Lewis and Clark's route through the Wild West by the mercury laxatives left behind in latrine pits.'

That made the boy smirk.

'Each element is rather like the rest of its . . . ' Noah wouldn't say *period* because this was an eleven-year-old boy. 'Its row mates, but it's much more closely akin to its group, that's its column' — his finger skimming vertically, now — 'because they've each got the same number of electrons in their outer shell.'

'Can we go?'

As soon as you thought you were having a breakthrough moment with this kid, he left you flattened.

Michael threw his can in the trash as they walked down the block.

A man whizzed past them, flipped up his board to hold it vertically at the curb, then sped off across the intersection.

Noah thought to ask, 'Do you skateboard?'

'Skate.'

'Oh, you prefer skating? Ice or roller?'

'It's called skating, dude.'

'No, but I'm just asking whether you do it on ice or dry land.'

Michael punched an exasperated finger in the direction the man had gone. 'Nobody says 'skate*boarding*' anymore.'

'Ah, I see. And do you yourself like skating?'

A scowl. 'Mom got me a board, but last year

80

some eighth-graders jacked it.'

That startled Noah. 'You knew who'd taken it?'

'They skated right past, dissing me. Grandma said' — Michael quoted — '"This is a test from the Lord, are you going to hold on to your wrath? Are you going to pass the test?"'

'What did passing the test involve?'

'Not getting into a fight.'

'And did you pass?' Noah asked.

Michael nodded grimly.

That sounded Stoic as much as Christian. 'Your grandma must have been an impressive lady.'

The boy's eyes slid sideways. 'Are you making fun of her?'

'Are you kidding? Why would you think I was — '

A shrug. 'She wasn't some fancy-pants scientist.'

'I bet she was worth two of me.'

'Three.'

Silence stretched again as they walked. But that was all right, Noah told himself; he was still new to this. Besides, surely people didn't have to talk every minute of the day. Joan and he had spent harmonious hours at a time in the apartment without exchanging a word. The skateboard story nagged at him, though. 'Couldn't you have reported them, at least, the kids who robbed you?'

'Called the cops?' Michael was openmouthed.

'Or told the school,' Noah suggested.

The boy's head swung from side to side.

'Snitches get stitches.'

'What?' Even the word was old-fashioned, ridiculous. Like *rat, fink, canary, stool pigeon:* shades of film noir.

'You just don't do it,' Michael told him. 'Like on stop signs, after the STOP, taggers put SNITCHING. One time a seventh-grader came in with a T-shirt that said SNITCHES END UP IN DITCHES, the principal made him take it off.'

'But Michael. Really. Why would you protect them when they stole your skateboard?'

'It's not about protecting *them.*'

'What's it about, then?'

Michael spoke very low. 'Not being a punk-ass little bitch.'

Noah gave up for now.

A fire escape loomed above them in the gathering dusk. Every childhood had its own unspoken rules, he reminded himself, and at the time they seemed unbreakable, perpetual. 'When I was a kid we played in the streets till it got dark. Ring-alevio — that was a kind of hide-and-seek in teams, all around buildings, up onto the roofs sometimes.'

'Cool.' Michael suddenly sounded younger. 'Was it dangerous?'

'Nobody seemed to think so, then.' Kids might have fallen, but nobody would have been likely to shoot them, at least. 'Capture the Flag, Steal the Bacon, I Declare War . . . ' They were all variants on war, it struck Noah now. He supposed children acted out the headlines of their day.

'What's that?'

82

'I Declare War? Kind of like dodgeball.'

'That's banned at my school.'

'Oh, for god's sake!'

Michael objected: 'Aren't you a atheist?'

Noah corrected him: '*An* atheist.'

'That's what I said.'

'It's *an*, rather than *a*, when it's followed by a vowel: *an* atheist.'

'Like, you're *an* asshole.'

He supposed he deserved that one.

No one would have reason to expect you'd be a natural at this stuff, Joan pointed out.

Nor had his own father been, after all. Well-intentioned but stiff: no wonder Marc had asked an agency for a nanny the minute he'd heard from Margot that she was sending little Noé to New York in the summer of 1942. Father and son must have been practically strangers, after two years apart. Strange, Noah's childhood; he'd been like a beanbag tossed between his parents. Blame the times.

★   ★   ★

Back at the apartment Noah told Michael he could watch TV, if he liked. The truth was, he was desperate for half an hour off.

'Nah, I'm good.' The boy curled up on the couch with his cracked phone. He scrolled, flicked; delicate finger movements, as if he were stroking a kitten.

Noah hovered. He wondered what Michael was looking at; which particular contaminated rivulet of the internet was pouring into this growing brain. 'I'm surprised you haven't sliced your fingers open on that screen. Why haven't you' — *replaced it*, Noah was going to say, before he considered the price of such repairs — 'taped over it, at least?'

'We only had Christmas tape. And crime-scene for Halloween.'

Noah tried not to judge. He went into the kitchen and emerged with a roll of clear packing tape and a pair of scissors. 'May I?'

Michael pursed his lips.

'Come on, it's driving me mad.'

The boy turned his phone off and handed it over.

Noah made a neat job of it: three overlapping rectangles, holding all the-little shards in place. The lock screen read UNLOCK IF U WISH 2 DIE, with a close-up of a shark's teeth. He checked that the screen was still responsive to the heat of his finger, through the tape. 'You don't seem to have any service. Who's your provider?'

'Huh?'

'How do you make calls?'

'I don't.'

'What, calling's too old-fashioned? It's all messaging these days?'

'Apps and shit.' Michael snatched back his phone.

Noah finally got it: *He doesn't have a phone plan*. That would be too expensive. This was somebody's discarded phone the kid was using for messages and games, catching Wi-Fi where he found it.

'Your wife — what did she get that prize for?'

84

Noah's eyes followed Michael's to the photo of Joan on the wall. 'Ah, she helped create a new drug.' The word sounded wrong. 'Medicine, for people with cancer.' Decades of tireless slog, as well as flashes of brilliance.

'Did you do that too, save lives?'

'Afraid not.' From as far back as Joan's postdoc at Memorial Sloan-Kettering, it had been clear that their paths were forking — hers, up toward the limelight. Of course Noah had sometimes felt jealous, or more like crushed into insignificance. The two of them had joked about it; it was that or quarrel. Strangely, it had helped when the gap between their statures began to yawn so wide that Noah hadn't had to rate himself on the same scale anymore. 'I've spent most of my career working on polymers. Large molecules made of chains of chemicals.'

'Plastics? Like that floating shitpile twice the size of Texas?'

So even middle graders had heard about that. 'Yes, artificial polymers are found in the Pacific garbage patch, and in your earbuds.' He glanced down at the boy's red-and-white sneakers. 'Your soles, too. And wood, and cotton, they're polymers as well' — gesturing at Michael's hoodie — 'and so are your hair and nails. Your DNA, even. You know how that molecule's shaped? A double spiral.' Noah drew it on the air. 'Like a twisted rope ladder.'

But the roving beam of the boy's attention had swung around, and clicked off.

Strangers, still. It didn't help that they were technically related, Noah decided. When the human genome was mapped, pages of gobbledygook were found after each legible gene.

★　★　★

In the kitchen, he considered his cupboards. Penne; who didn't like pasta? He put on a big pot of water to boil.

When he was checking the weather forecast on his phone he saw he had a text message from Rosa from hours ago. *How's it going?* He must have failed to hear the alert while they were outside. Weary, he thought of replying with a message of his own, *Fine.* But that would sound as if he were hiding something.

So he called back instead. 'Ms. Figueroa? Rosa? Sorry not to get back to you till after work . . . '

'Oh, I'll be at the office a while yet,' she told him, rueful.

He imagined her trying to check up on all twenty-four of her charges. One for every hour of the day and night. 'We were out for a walk.'

'Great. Any questions so far? Concerns?'

'Not really.' Or scores of them. Where to start?

'Could I talk to Michael for a minute?'

'Sure! Yes. I'll give him my phone and I'll, ah, be in the other room.' *So he won't be afraid to speak up.*

After Noah had handed the phone to Michael and shut the door, he stood in the kitchen with NPR on to make it clear that he wasn't eavesdropping. He listened to the tail end of an interview with a composer who sounded as if

Noah should have heard of him. He stirred the penne. The minutes crawled by. He ran down a list of all the complaints Michael might be making.

Michael was suddenly behind him. Noah nearly scalded himself.

He took his phone back and said 'Hello,' but she'd gone.

'Dinnertime,' he told the boy.

'I'm not hungry.'

Was the pasta an unfamiliar shape or something? Noah's eye veered to the fruit bowl. 'Kiwi? Pear? Satsuma?' He wished he had some plain apples to offer, or bananas.

'Nah. I'm tired. I'm going to bed.'

★   ★   ★

Noah tossed clams and olives with his pasta. And a glass of red wine for his heart. On impulse he wrapped the Pick-Pick Bird in a bit of bubble wrap and brought it to his room to add to his suitcase, tucking it into a shoe for protection.

He found the boy standing there with Marc's hand, holding the leather cup and straps.

Noah thought of saying, 'Stay out of people's bedrooms.'

Michael slid his right palm into the cold grasp of the prosthesis. He shook hands with it, and Noah saw him flinch a little as the fingers moved in his.

'Careful.'

The boy spun around.

'That's a hundred years old.' The sense of time made Noah dizzy.

'Some kind of robot thing?'

'It's my father's second hand. Well, his third, actually, if you count the one he lost, but the second metal one.'

'Diabetes?'

Noah stared.

'Grandma had three toes amputated,' Michael told him.

'I'm sorry to hear that,' he said absurdly. 'No, my dad's hand was blown off in the first month of the war — World War One, this was.' Along with half a million other young men injured or killed beside the River Marne. 'He'd have bled to death except one of his pals got a tourniquet on him fast.'

Michael's eyes were big. 'Who won?'

'That day? The French and the British. But then the Germans dug trenches to hide in, and it was four years of stalemate.' Groveling in the mud, waiting to die. 'Marc was lucky, he got invalided out, sent back to his aunt in Monaco, and missed the rest of the war.' A talented painter, before; afterward he'd gone to university and found a late-blooming second gift for interpreting art. He'd never complained of pain, that Noah could remember, but he must have had some, phantom or otherwise. Noah thought of Amber's brother in his wheelchair.

'Why his aunt?' Michael wanted to know.

The boy had to be hoping his own Aunt Grace would turn up soon, with the two little cousins.

'His parents had both died of an infection called TB.' Strange, how the majority of wartime deaths came by illness rather than bullets.

The boy nodded. 'I know kids with that, they have to take pills for nine *months*.'

Noah had read about the comeback of tuberculosis in New York, but only now did the statistic become real. He took Marc's prosthesis from the boy. Its darkened creamy coloring was like no skin he'd ever seen; no wonder Marc had worn gloves for nine months of the year. 'So the army gave him a fairly primitive wooden hand at first, then this high-tech one. If they could claim they'd sent you home fit for civilian life, they only had to pay you a tiny pension.'

'High-tech?' Michael sneered.

It was a marvelous thing, for its time, displaying all its smooth seams, and a square panel on the back of the hand that held its gears and levers. 'This was cutting-edge tech bionics, for intellectuals — desk workers,' Noah translated. The middle-class hand. 'My dad couldn't do any heavy lifting with it, but he could count banknotes, turn pages, use a pen, tie a necktie . . . '

'Did it freak you out?'

Noah shook his head. 'I never knew him without it.' One of those things a child took in his stride; adults were mysterious anyway. 'Now, Selvaggio, Marc's surname, that's Italian. It sounds like *salvage*, but it's actually from *savage*.' He improvised: 'One of our ancestors on his side might have been nicknamed Michael the Wild.'

A puzzled scowl. 'You said you were from France.'

'Well, Nice is a border town. Tossed back and forth between France and Italy for centuries.'

The kid's eyes slid away, toward the bedroom door.

Noah yawned hugely. 'You have everything you need?'

A nod.

'Goodnight, then.'

★ ★ ★

Awake at 2 a.m.

Hydrogen, helium. Lithium, beryllium, boron, carbon, nitrogen, oxygen. Fluorine, neon, Noah chanted silently. Back in Freshman Chem in the '50s, they'd made everything into jingles, learning by heart the essential tools of their trade. *Sodium, magnesium, aluminum, silicon, phosphorus, sulfur, chlorine, argon.* When Noah couldn't sleep, in his mind's eye he traced the top three rows of the beautiful battlemented castle. He could sing the names straight down, too: *Hydrogen, lithium, sodium, potassium, rubidium, caesium, francium.*

No good; this litany wasn't soothing him the way it usually did.

Maybe because of the ticking time bomb across the hall, Joan whispered.

While Noah had still been teaching, he'd occasionally taken an Ambien to get back to sleep, but he'd always hated the next day's grogginess. He preferred to soldier on, with *À la*

90

recherche du temps perdu on his e-reader. (He chose Proust because of how little story there was to hook his attention, and how fuzzily he grasped what the more obscure French words meant.)

Instead Noah heaved himself out of bed. He crept into the spare room to check on Michael.

Faint snores. In the light that spilled up from the street nine floors below, the kid was visible only above the jaw: round-cheeked, looking half his age. Noah thought of patting his shoulder, through the bedding, but held back in case of startling him awake.

★   ★   ★

At 6:23 he woke again with a jerk. His shoulder ached as if he'd pulled a muscle in his sleep. These days everything hurt faintly, or sagged; the nerve endings in his soles prickled with little electric shocks when he got onto his feet. Crannies in Noah's mouth where certain teeth used to be; bad breath; a permanently dripping nose; only the most theoretical, residual libido. There was nothing serious wrong with him but an iffy hip, though. His doctor was pushing the operation, but Noah didn't think he'd bother, at this point.

Top priority this morning was to make himself coffee.

After that he went to the spare room and tapped on the door.

The room was empty, the bed stripped. Noah stared. Like a hospital bed after someone had died. Had Michael run away in the night? *Shit shit shit shit shit.*

Noah thundered down the hall. Ducked into the kitchen, the living room, even (briefly confused) into his own room. He trembled in the passage. He needed to call Rosa — and the police, he supposed? — but first he had to pee.

He sat down on the toilet seat because he was shaking so much. The shower curtain was pulled across. Something was hung over the rail, dripping on the slatted wooden bathmat. Sheets? He washed his hands, then called, 'Michael?'

Nothing.

Then, from the living room, 'Uh-huh?'

The boy was in the corner behind the door, in a sort of nest of the duvet and pillow. His Twenty Questions ball beeping in his hands.

Noah dithered between *Good morning* and *Hi* for too long; ended up saying neither. 'Have you been up for long?'

A nod. Dark circles under the eyes.

'Half the night?'

Michael shrugged.

How to measure time when you were awake and alone in some old guy's spooky old apartment?

'It can be hard to sleep in a new place.' Noah didn't ask about the washed sheets. Too young for wet dreams, surely? Well, you never knew. He went off to the bathroom to squeeze them out before he forgot, and bundle them into the dryer.

Shower and dress. It took Noah half an hour, these days; there were few things he couldn't do at all, but he did nothing fast anymore. It wasn't

92

as if he was in any hurry.

This Brooklyn school, P.S. whatever it was. Roughly ten miles away, but more like nineteen by Google's recommended driving route, and an hour and seven minutes by subway. There and back to drop Michael off and pick him up again this afternoon, that meant the best part of five hours of Noah's Tuesday. A travel day, too; he'd be worn out before he even got on that plane. *If the passport turned up.*

When he went in to ask what Michael would like for breakfast, he found the boy slumped sideways onto the carpet, face on a curl of duvet.

Sleep that knits up the raveled sleeve of care, balm of hurt minds. Lord knew this child could do with a bit of that.

★ ★ ★

When the boy finally stumbled into the kitchen, he still had the duvet wrapped around him.

'English muffins? Cheese? Muesli?'

Michael shook his head, raccoon-eyed.

'Good-quality food' and all that. 'You have to have something,' Noah said. 'You didn't have any dinner.'

'There's stuff at school.'

Noah peered into the refrigerator. The end of a packet of sliced bread. 'Toast?'

A yawn seized Michael. ''Kay.'

'Oh, and eggs — what about some eggs?' The packing date on the carton read *JA 25*, but Noah knew they were perfectly safe for four weeks after that.

93

The kid shook his head and climbed onto the second stool.

Joan's stool. Not that Noah said so. He put the bread in the toaster and laid out the butter, a plate, and a knife. Poured a glass of milk. Did kids need dairy for their growing bones, or was that a myth promulgated by the agricultural lobby?

'It's brown,' Michael said when he saw the toast.

It seemed self-evident, but Noah responded gamely. 'Mm, that's a Maillard reaction. Above 285 degrees, the sugars in the bread caramelize and pyrolyze — they break down into little chunks like charcoal.'

'No, but it's *brown*, dude.'

'Oh, you mean whole-wheat bread — yes, it is.' Clearly it wasn't just rich kids who were picky. Noah drained his lukewarm coffee.

Michael was hacking at the butter. 'And what's up with your butter?'

'It's just cold.' All year round in this building the choice was refrigerator-hard or a rancid puddle. Noah could spread the butter on the despised brown toast himself . . . but that would be babying the boy. 'Did yours come in a tub? At your grandma's? If so, it wasn't butter, it was a spread — butter diluted with water and vegetable oils.'

'Better than this shit.' Michael ground a wedge into the toast.

He was just being loyal to his grandmother, Noah reminded himself. To his whole stolen life.

The boy pulled out his phone and was soon

94

immersed in a silent game.

Terrible manners, but if Noah said 'Put that away,' he — as well as Michael — would be forced to make conversation.

When the toast was gone, Noah asked, 'Do you need a bag lunch?'

'There's a canteen.'

'Money for the canteen, then?'

A tiny pause, before Michael said, 'Nah, I eat free.'

Noah was impressed that the kid hadn't just accepted the cash. 'You have your books?'

The shake of the head could mean either that the school required none or that Michael didn't have his.

Noah found he didn't care enough to ask — not today, at least. 'What do you use for a bag?'

'My backpack.'

'OK. Then everything you don't need today, leave here.'

The boy looked suspicious.

'It'll be perfectly safe.' *Nobody comes in but the cleaner once every two weeks*, Noah almost added, but that sounded aristocratic. 'Go brush your teeth.'

No answer. Which could mean either *I don't need telling* or *Fuck you*. Michael went off down the hall.

Noah called after him, 'I presume school starts at nine?'

'Eight-oh-five.'

'No!' He checked his watch, gnawed his lip. How had the time run away with him? 'That seems horribly early.'

'It's a renewal school.'

'What does that mean?'

'Gotta go an extra hour a day because we're dumb.' The bathroom door closed.

Noah should have countered that, but he was already online, checking whether they could get there any faster in a cab. No. Damn it! Late, the very first time.

A surge of ruthlessness. Noah went and knocked on the bathroom door. 'Michael, would you mind missing one more day of school?'

A hollow laugh.

Great, Noah was sliding into absenteeism already. Set that against one measly point for getting whole-wheat toast into the kid.

If the school called, he'd say Michael was suffering from exhaustion due to bereavement.

Noah decided to enjoy the fact that at least he wasn't on the L train right now. He leaned out his front door to collect today's *New York Times* from the sisal mat, and read it at the kitchen counter. A long article about this year's commemorations of the end of World War One. (Noah found it incongruous when people said 'celebration.') The last surviving combatant, from the Women's Royal Air Force, had lasted right up until 2012. Noah also learned that Britain had formally pardoned the more than three hundred WWI deserters it had shot at dawn. He supposed people were more forgiving of qualms and panics nowadays, more fascinated by the traumatized victim than the hardy hero. He thought of Marc's hand; he hadn't been the

Six Million Dollar Man, but he had gotten by.

Insurance policies specified a lump sum for each limb, didn't they? Which reminded Noah: he'd better call his company to get Michael added to his travel and medical coverage as a temporary dependent.

But after being kept on hold for twenty minutes, as he worked away at one corner of the crossword, he abandoned the attempt for now.

He found himself looking up stats on Michael's school. Percentage of free-lunch recipients, suspensions, new speakers of English, bullying, state math and reading scores, rates of attendance (that gave him a twinge of guilt). What shocked him most was the percentage of students living in shelters. How could you do your homework if you didn't even have a home to work in?

Then he tried 'travel France kids.' Much unhelpful advice along the lines of 'Strap your baby to your chest and tackle the Louvre super-early.' For teens, it kept recommending 'Bribe them with delicious ice cream.'

French parenting seemed to be all the rage, at least among American book-buying women enthralled by the fact that Gallic kids could sit up straight at the dinner table through four courses. Noah tried to remember: had he retained this skill after he'd come to New York at four?

He read up on the concept of the pause — how French mothers waited a few minutes before picking up crying babies, to give them a chance to settle themselves. (Or perhaps to teach them not to expect instant gratification?) He couldn't recall his little sister crying much at all. He wondered if Margot had slid into indulgent, Anglo-Saxon ways for her second go at motherhood, after the war. Had she felt bad at all about the two-and-a-half-year *pause* when she'd stayed away from her son?

That was cruel. But those small photos he'd come across in Fernande's box — only three days ago, was it? — they'd unsettled him.

Noah went into his room and got them out for another look. That one of a poseur with a cane. (No, that wasn't fair; it had been as common for a stylish man to sport a cane in the 1940s as it was to wear sunglasses today.)

Though Margot had often mentioned Nice — her childhood, and youth, and early days of marriage — she'd never said much about the time she'd spent with her father, without husband and child, during the war. Shouldn't those years have been the most interesting? Refugees flooding in, then the Italian army, then the Germans . . . Noah had always assumed she preferred to forget. But if the images in the envelope were from that period, then for all their obscure subjects and shoddy aesthetic, they hinted at preoccupations of his mother's unknown to Noah. A time in her life to which it seemed he'd been only a footnote.

It struck him now that the cane might have been a matter of need for that man, just as for Margot herself, after the war. (She'd hurt her knee in a fall.) So many things could have stunted the gait back then: different-length legs,

98

a club foot. Noah considered the silhouetted face; a certain tightness and fatigue, suggesting chronic pain? On the other hand he was chic, as if he might break into the tap routine from *Singin' in the Rain* at any moment. Who was this dandy? And why had Noah's mother treasured a picture of him all through her married life?

He paused next at the cropped shot of the frilly building that looked like a hotel. A closed, arched door, with elegant moldings and wrought-iron balconies; four rows of windows. *Il faut qu'une porte soit ouverte ou fermée.*

Which reminded him to put down the old photos and email the Hotel Belle Vue ('a gracious souvenir of the Jazz Age Riviera,' according to its website, 'mere minutes from the legendary Promenade des Anglais') to add a bed for Michael. Noah's first impulse was to ask for a second room, no matter the expense, but then he remembered the boy might drink miniatures from the minibar, electrocute himself by dropping the hair dryer in the bath, abscond. So Noah added *Enfant 1* to his room reservation and asked for two *lits jumeaux* (twin beds) instead of the double he'd specially requested before. '*Je serai accompagné par mon petit-neveu.*' Was that right for 'I'll have my great-nephew with me'? Perhaps the English word should be *grandnephew* instead of *great-nephew*. Both sounded implausible to Noah, somehow; foreign.

His French was badly rusty now; he'd barely used it in the quarter-century since his mother's death, and even before then it had been a matter of one-sided conversations in which Margot had addressed him in French and he'd disappointed her by lapsing into English.

If by any chance the Belle Vue didn't have a room with twin beds, he typed, could the child please be provided with a . . . cot, or camp bed, or rollaway. How did you say that? '*Lit d'enfant*,' he wrote, as an umbrella term for child's bed.

Michael, in the doorway. His T-shirt said SERVER STATUS: OFFLINE.

How long had he been standing there? Noah wasn't used to having to close his own door for privacy. 'I like your shirt. Does it mean *asleep* or just *zoned out*?'

A shrug for an answer. Michael eyed the walls, the Tiffany bedside lamp, the window blinds, the bare hardwood floor. (Noah was determined not to be one of those seniors who began their decline by tripping on a rug.) 'Are they by the famous guy?'

Noah looked where he was pointing, at the photos on the bed. 'Père Sonne? No, no. It's a bit of a puzzle, actually. I think my mother took them, in the '40s, but I don't know why.'

Michael held up his phone. 'Me and my friends take random pics all the time.'

'But film was expensive back then, so people usually thought before they clicked.' He held up the one of a woman with her hair up, snapped from behind, and the one of the empty street. 'Also she printed them, and brought them with her to America' — when there was so much she must have had to leave behind — 'and held on to them for half a century.' Boring old dead people:

100

he could tell he was losing Michael. 'This building, for instance,' Noah added, 'I just wish I knew what it was.'

'Have you googled it?'

'What would I look up?' he asked, sarcastic. ' "Building, probably in Nice"?'

'Googled the actual pic.' Michael poked it with a finger.

Noah used the edge of his chenille bedcover to rub the print off the surface. 'Sorry, I don't know what you're talking about.'

'Just scan it in and hit Search, old man.'

Noah stared. Why hadn't one of his students mentioned that such a thing was possible? (He was reminded of the first time he'd put together a bibliography on a PC — around 1988, this would have been — and how he'd painstakingly cut and pasted all the titles into alphabetical order by author before Joan told him that the computer could do that with one command.) 'Really? I must find a scanner right away.'

Michael grunted with annoyance. He held the photo against the white wallpaper and snapped it with his phone. Tapped in a few words, then held his screen out: 'Best guess: Hotel Excelsior Nice.'

Flabbergasted, Noah grinned. 'You're a genius.'

'Nah, you're a dumb-ass.'

He couldn't disagree.

After the boy wandered off, Noah looked up the Hotel Excelsior. It hadn't been knocked down yet, this elegant, cream, 1890s terraced palace.

This four-star boutique hotel's restful atmosphere belies its location in the beating heart of Nice's Musicians' Quarter just 3,117 feet from the famous Promenade des Anglais and 493 from the Train Station. The quirky decor of its different 42 rooms with travel inspired wall murals recall the Excelsior's roots as a coaching inn purveying recuperation for nobles and their horses.

He was amused by the specificity of the distances and the creakiness of the English.

On the hotel's own website, a last-minute Carnival deal: just one Comfort Suite still available. He canceled the Belle Vue and booked this one.

★   ★   ★

For lunch he took the boy out to buy supplies in a deli around the corner. Michael seemed overwhelmed by the variety, so Noah offered him the plainest of options: ham, white bread. 'What fruit would you like?'

Michael shook his head.

'Come on, what about grapes? Lovely and sweet.'

''Kay.'

'What do you think of the Upper West Side?' Noah ventured to ask as they were walking back with their paper bags.

'Huh?'

'This neighborhood.'

He thought Michael might mention the trees,

102

or the handsome buildings. But the boy said, 'Lots of old white people.'

Yes, it wasn't half as diverse as what the boy was used to. When Noah was a kid, he wouldn't even have seen whiteness, let alone named it.

As they passed a stoop, Michael asked, 'Did somebody get offed here?'

'What? Where?' Noah jerked around.

Michael pointed at a cluster of balloons tied to the handrail.

The boy thought it was some kind of memorial, Noah realized. 'That means a kid's birthday party.'

A nonchalant nod.

Walking on, Noah recalled a recent headline about a study of reading tests across New York neighborhoods. Each recent local murder had a stupefying effect, pulling children's scores down by two or three grades. It made sense to Noah, in terms of brain chemistry; the fight-or-flight response superseded all abstract thought.

Michael turned his head to gape at a pair of silken Afghan hounds going by, pointed black faces held high above the cluster of Lhasa apsos and shih tzus. 'That dude has like *eight* dogs.'

'Oh they're not his, he's just the walker.'

The kid's forehead creased.

'He's paid to take them out, while their owners are at work.'

Noah couldn't tell if Michael thought this was the coolest job or the most ridiculous thing he'd ever heard.

Back in the apartment, as he and Michael ate their sandwiches on the kitchen stools, he glanced through the boy's agenda. On each weekly double-page spread there was a perky message in Comic Sans: *What skills do you need to go from your house to the store?* or *Planning ahead helps you avoid stress.* But what skills would help a sixth-grader prepare for contingencies such as his mother's imprisonment, his grandmother's death? *Every day eat a variety of fruit and vegetables to keep healthy.*

'Have some grapes,' Noah said.

'I did already.'

'Where are the stems? Have they become invisible?'

Coldly, Michael took a grape.

★   ★   ★

Downtown, the photography center had a more complicated floor plan than Noah remembered.

Michael was dragging. 'Why haul my ass all this way to see some picture?'

At last: Noah came to a standstill in front of the large crisp print. So gorgeous; his fingers itched to hold it one more time.

Père Sonne [Pierre Personnet] (French, Marne-la-Coquette, 1860–1944 Nice)

Tuyeau de Cuisine [Kitchen Pipe]
ca. 1942 [?], [printed mid-1960s].
Black-and-white gelatin silver print.

Gift of Dr. Noah Selvaggio and
Dr. Joan Chubatovsky, 1992.

It had raised a few eyebrows back in 1969, he remembered, Joan keeping her own name. But if her Russian grandparents, who'd fled the shtetl back in 1903, had gotten through Ellis Island with *Chubatovsky* intact, she wasn't going to trade it in.

'Hey, that's you, vag-seller.' Michael put his finger to the information panel, where it said *Selvaggio*.

A guard barked behind him: 'No touching.'

The boy's hand recoiled.

'We donated a whole set of still lifes after my mother died,' Noah said. 'When Père Sonne was too old to get around much, he started doing close-ups, portraits of objects, and he called the whole set 'Objection.' It could be a pun, see — the *objects* are registering their *objection*.'

Way over his head, Joan commented.

Noah tried again. 'This drainpipe may be saying, 'Hey, look at me . . . ' '

' 'I'm a dumb-ass drainpipe,' ' Michael suggested, ' 'big whoop.' '

Noah countered, ' 'I'm a drainpipe, and I don't have to symbolize anything because I'm useful and beautiful all on my own.' '

The boy let out a snort.

'This print has been valued at somewhere in the low five figures.'

Michael worked out what that meant. 'You're shitting me.'

'Shh!'

'Suckers.' He cocked one finger at the photograph. 'I could snap better than that on my phone, easy.'

'*Easily*,' Noah told him.

'Huh?'

'*Easy* is the adjective. To say how you'd snap it, you need the adverb, which is eas*i*ly.'

The boy let his eyes roll back in his head.

Noah knew he was being petty. 'And sorry, you couldn't have taken that picture. It's all in the composition, how it's shaped.'

'It's shaped like a fucking drainpipe.'

'Now you're being disrespectful.'

'Because my great-great hasn't earned my respect with this piece of crap.'

Noah tried again. 'See how the pipe curves just above the floor, as if it's a tired person who's longing to sit down? The paint flaking off at the join, and the rust eating into it? That drip forming at the seal, it seems to slow the moment right down. And Père Sonne took the shot from just the right angle so the pipe's shadow would look like a liquid leaking out — like blood, even.' His long, spatulate finger hovered over the spot.

'Sir! Move away from the exhibit or I'll have to call Security.'

'I wouldn't dream of touching it,' Noah snapped at the guard, as he stepped back. 'For your information, I'm the donor of this particular work.'

The guard's face was unconvinced.

'There's more of his work upstairs,' Noah told Michael.

The boy rubbed his eyes. 'Can we go?'

'Just a quick look?'

'I'm tired.' He did look wrecked.

106

'All right,' Noah said. 'I just need five minutes in the shop.'

Michael wouldn't take an interest in anything there, even though Noah would have been glad to buy him a book or a craft set. The boy leaned against the wall, arms wrapped around himself as if he didn't trust them not to knock something over.

Noah glanced at the *O* to *S* bookcase, between *PENN, Irving,* and *PLATT LYNES, George.* This was where he'd picked up a few studies over the years; specialist monographs on how Père Sonne fit into late nineteenth- and early twentieth-century portrait photography, *plein air* versus studio work, the art of the Mediterranean, social realism, the cult of celebrity in the 1920s . . . But now an unfamiliar title hooked his gaze: *Père Sonne: A Life's Work* by one Max Harstad. He snatched down the heavy paper-back and checked the copyright page: new this year.

Thrilled, Noah couldn't resist skipping right to himself in the index: 'Selvaggio, Noé Pierre, son of Margot Isabelle Selvaggio née Personnet, grandson of P.S., 329, 342, 389–94, 427.' Though when he flicked back to those passages, they turned out to be mere mentions of occasions when he'd been with his grandfather in Nice.

Noah's memories of his first years were few and slight. Making caverns of stones on the beach; low radio music at night; the warm savor of tobacco from a pipe. His *pépère's* pipe, surely, since Marc had been broken of the habit back in 1914 by having his hand blown off.

★ ★ ★

As they walked to the bus stop, Noah's eyes watered in the buffeting wind. He thought to check his phone: no messages from Rosa or the passport people. If it didn't come through by the end of the working day — what was he going to do?

Cancel his trip, he supposed, as he wasn't a complete monster. But he'd always resent it.

'So your dad didn't live with you guys.'

'What's that?' Noah looked down at Michael.

'Back in France. You and your mom lived at your grandpa's?'

'We were all together at first,' Noah told him. 'Marc had been a fervent fan of Père Sonne's, published essays about his work.' He must have stood out from the crowd of acolytes, for Margot; older, maimed, interestingly melancholy. 'But after I was born . . . I think it just got too small in that apartment.'

He meant metaphorically small, but Michael nodded, leaning against the bus shelter: 'Cody got the bed.'

'Sorry, I'm not following.'

'When his girlfriend kicked him out, he had to crash at our place, and Grandma said Cody needed the bed more than her so she went on the couch instead of me, and I got a mattress.' Michael must have seen Noah wince, because he added, 'I liked it. Didn't hurt my back like the couch.'

'How's the bed at my place, by the way?'

A surly shrug.

Noah wasn't trying to make the boy say anything disloyal about the life that had been ripped from him less than a week ago. 'Anyway, if you share a home with a renowned genius . . . I think it gets a bit exhausting.'

'Not for Jay-Z.'

Noah must have looked blank.

'With Beyoncé!'

'Oh, right.'

'Probably different if you're *both*, like, world-famous,' Michael added.

Noah thought of those decades of fielding calls for Joan. 'Anyway, my father moved out for a while, when I was small. I never got the full story.'

'Was he running around on her?'

This child was the strangest combination of ignorant and worldly. Noah and Fernande had discussed that possibility, but . . . 'I don't think so. Then Germany invaded, or at least took over the north of France, and Marc went ahead to New York with all my grandfather's prints and negatives — to get them away before the bombs started dropping, see?' Had Margot hurried her husband onto that ship, Noah wondered now, or begged him not to go? Could Marc be said to have abandoned his wife and toddler? Or had everyone behaved in a very civilized fashion, focused on keeping the art and the artist safe?

Père Sonne had wangled his son-in-law a position at a Greenwich Village gallery, Noah knew that much, and Marc had carried on burnishing the old man's reputation and arranging some crucial sales. 'Then when I was four, things got scarier' — Noah was glossing over the Italian occupation of Nice, and the far worse German one — 'so my mom sent me over to my dad in New York, without her.'

Michael yawned.

'Oh, what the heck, we'll get a cab home.' Noah stepped to the curb and put his arm up. If they were by any chance flying to France tonight, it was going to be a long one.

★ ★ ★

In the lobby of his building, on the mahogany bench, sat Rosa.

Flustered apologies all around. She'd been kept on hold so long by some branch of city bureaucracy that her phone had run out of juice. 'How're you doing, Michael?' she asked as they went up in the elevator.

''Kay.' The boy looked run ragged, as if Noah had set him to work in a sweatshop the moment she'd left.

'He's just tired.' What, was Noah some expert now? 'Had a bad night. Sleep-wise,' he added, in case Rosa thought he meant a psychotic break. 'He didn't seem up to going to school — '

Michael's eyes slid sideways at Noah, letting him know that he'd detected the bullshit.

' — so we, ah, took a cultural day and went to a gallery.'

'Did you call it in?'

'What's that?'

A sigh Rosa couldn't quite restrain. 'On the first page of his file, with all the numbers, there's one to register an absence on the school's automatic attendance system.'

'Oh, sorry. I'll know for next time.' Great — that sounded as if Noah was planning a lot of absenteeism.

Upstairs, Michael went straight down the passage.

'Well, he seems to be making himself at home,' Rosa said, and slid a navy-blue rectangle out of her purse.

The passport. Noah didn't know if he was relieved or disappointed. He felt slightly sick. Time to marshal his strength.

He found Michael slumped on the Le Corbusier lounger.

''Is it a specific color?' No. 'Is it brown?' Rarely. 'Does it come in different types?' Yes.'

'Good news,' Noah told him. It sounded bleak, somehow. He made sure to smile as he held up the passport.

Michael nodded, eyes returning to his game.

Noah found himself remembering a *New Yorker* cartoon: *About your cat, Mr. Schröd-inger — I have good news and bad news.*

'What are you grinning at?'

'It's hard to explain.' Or rather Noah could have explained Schrödinger's refinement of Heisenberg's uncertainty principle, but there'd be nothing funny about it by the time he was done.

3

Takeoff Speed

LaGuardia was a hell of detours and obstacles these days. Noah sucked on a last cigarette outside the door.

Michael hung back, taking a picture of . . . what, Noah wondered? The stumpy air traffic-control tower?

Something occurred to him. 'Have you been on an airplane before?' he asked the boy.

A shake of the head.

'But you must have been to an airport?'

Why must he have? Joan wondered.

Noah stubbbed out his butt and put it in the garbage, then beckoned Michael through the automatic doors.

'To Paris, then Nice? Very *nice*.' The check-in agent smirked.

Noah had a feeling she used that pun every time.

'Any bags?'

'Just carry-on.' He'd avoided checking in baggage ever since a trip to Santiago when Joan's suitcase had gone astray, and she'd had to give a very important paper in the slightly less crumpled of Noah's two linen jackets.

In the security line now, he and Michael were halfway along the third segment of the zigzag. 'What are we waiting for this time?' the boy wanted to know.

'They have to check everybody thoroughly,' Noah told him.

'For what?'

'Anything dangerous.'

'Like what kind of dangerous?'

Noah leaned down to murmur in his ear. 'I'm not going to say, because passengers have been arrested at security just for talking or joking about this kind of thing.'

'About bombs and shit?'

'Shh!'

A couple were being wheeled through the metal detector one after the other. Noah tried to decide whether they were older than him. It struck him that being able-bodied was a temporary condition, what with the weaknesses of infancy and age, and all that could go haywire in between.

Almost eight o'clock, when Noah next checked his watch. 'Do you know we spend three years of our lives waiting in line?'

Eyes on his phone, Michael appeared not to hear.

The prospect of an overnight transatlantic flight with this boy was making his stomach tight.

What were you thinking, taking this on? Joan marveled.

Oh shush, you.

Was it some atavistic clan loyalty? Helping your sister's descendants pass on some of your genes was strategic, he supposed.

Noah jumped at the sound of that fake-shutter

113

snap. Michael was photographing the full-body scanner. 'Put that away, it's illegal to take pictures.'

'Seems like everything's illegal here.'

Their turn at last. Noah read the sign: 'You and I don't have to take off our shoes and jackets. Over seventy-five, under twelve, they assume we're harmless.'

'That's bullshit! I could easily be a — '

'Shh!' Was the kid baiting him now or did he just not get it? 'One joke and they'll pull us out of line.' *And I'll go to France without you*, Noah would have liked to say, but that would be childish, and petty. As well as unconvincing. A terrible thought: 'You don't have anything . . . sharp on you? Like what you brought to school that time?'

The kid's cheek twitched furiously. Didn't he know Noah would have been told about the knife? 'That was for protection.'

Too late, anyway. The guard was asking if Noah had a pacemaker.

He made sure Michael's toiletries were out of his backpack, and took his own tablet out of his satchel. The man on the other side of the metal detector was beckoning the boy through.

Noah watched him go. Nothing beeped.

Buckling up his satchel again, beside Michael at the conveyor belt, he said, 'None of me is metal, yet, but my eyes do have acrylic glass lenses implanted. That's another handy polymer.'

Michael leaned in close to peer into Noah's face.

Noah flared his eyes. 'Can't see them, can you? I'm one of the only members of my retired academics' speaker club who can read a menu. How's your sight?'

Michael shrugged.

He supposed — hoped — they tested these things at school. 'Personnets have good vision. Well, my mother had a problem later in life, she could see almost nothing in her left, but that was because of an infection she got in the war.'

'I've got Grandma's glasses.'

For a moment Noah thought the kid meant he used them himself. 'Oh, as a . . . ' Not *souvenir*. 'A keepsake.'

'Huh?'

'You're keeping them for her sake — to remember her by.'

Gruff: 'I remember her fine.'

Noah yawned, needing more air. 'So, a trip to France. That'll be something to brag about.'

Michael shook his head, pained.

'No?'

'My teacher'll tell the whole class and they'll be like, 'Oh, that dude thinks he's all that.''

'Ah.' The perpetual, cruel dynamics of childhood; every tall poppy slashed down. 'Do I get the sense you don't like your school?'

Michael let out a huff of breath. 'I'm a gamer. I just put in the time till I can get online.'

On their way to the gate, they passed a framed poster of the Stars and Stripes made out of the names of the 9/11 dead.

'I heard that was Jews.'

115

Noah pulled up short and stared at Michael.

'Nine-Eleven, they all stayed home from work that day.'

Joan, give me strength. 'That's an anti-Semitic conspiracy theory.' The kid was looking blank, so Noah translated: 'A Jew-hating lie. Where did you hear it?'

A shrug. 'Snapchat.'

Was that slang for gossip?

'No offense.' Michael's eyes had slid off into the distance. 'I didn't mean your wife.'

Noah headed for the bookstore.

He picked up *Time* and *Scientific American.* He was confused by the jacket of a book called *Nice Is Just a Place in France* — it seemed a petulant accusation — until he realized that it meant *nice* as in *pleasant-mannered;* from the jacket he gathered that this was a satirical guide to being a *betch*, which he assumed was a variant on *bitch*.

Michael was glancing at tech magazines — *PC World* and *Wired.* Noah urged him to choose something from the Young Readers shelf. 'You must read books sometimes.'

'Not anymore.'

His world-weary tone made Noah laugh. 'Since, what, since you turned eleven?'

For an answer, the boy held up his phone.

'Oh, come on! When I was a kid I spent my whole allowance on books.'

'Because no internet.'

'There won't be Wi-Fi on the plane,' Noah warned him.

'How come?'

116

He pointed upward. 'Thirty thousand feet in the air.'

He insisted on buying the kid an expensive, shiny compendium of facts called *Incrrrrrrrrrrrrrrredible!* At the last minute, at the checkout, he added a hardback notebook with a pirate cover for the journal Michael was supposed to be keeping.

Noah bought a box of sushi and sashimi for himself, and chicken nuggets and fries for Michael. 'No soda,' he added, too late.

'It comes with,' the young woman said.

Michael was filling up a huge waxed cup at the Coke tap.

At their gate, he sat with bass-heavy music leaking from his headphones.

'Would that be rap?' Noah asked him.

'Huh?'

He gestured for the boy to take out the earbuds.

Instead Michael pressed pause.

'The genre, the style. Is *rap* the right word for it? Or *hip-hop?*'

'Don't even try.' Michael turned his music back on.

The young bearded man on Noah's other side was immersed in the Bible. *Good News*, debossed in gold on black leatherette. Noah found himself thinking of Schrödinger's cat again.

He tapped Michael on the shoulder.

The boy flinched and took out one earbud only. Rapid-fire, furiously articulated words spilled from it.

117

'Do you like jokes?'

'I guess.'

'So a doctor tells a patient, 'I have good news and bad news.''

'Uh-huh?'

'The patient wants to know the good news. The doctor says, 'They're naming a disease after you!''

A pause. 'That's not funny.'

'No?'

'Maybe when you're seventy-nine,' Michael conceded.

'Gallows humor, you mean — oldies laughing about death because we're on the brink of it?'

The boy shrugged. 'What got her — your wife?'

Noah could suddenly smell it, the antiseptic tang of the oncologist's office. 'Cancer.'

'Ironic.'

'Yes, she found that funny.' Her old enemy, yanking her down to punish her for the battles she'd won.

'Why does it say *doctor*?'

'Where?'

'On your ticket,' Michael said, pointing.

He examined his boarding pass: *Dr. Noah Selvaggio*. 'Oh, it's a courtesy title, because I have a PhD, what's called a doctoral degree. Meaning, I studied for years and years.'

'Doing explosions and shit, in your lab?'

Noah was starting to take the vulgarity in stride. 'Regrettably few.' In recent decades explosions had been frowned on by the health-and-safety folks.

'She had you whipped, right?'

'Joan?' He chuckled. 'At organic chemistry, at least, correct.' It was a pity she'd never met this kid; she'd have got a kick out of him.

'You're the bad guys?'

Noah frowned. 'Joan and I?' He guessed again. 'University professors?'

'Chemistry-ists.'

'You mean chemists. What makes you say that?'

'Dunno. Mad scientists? Poisoners and meth cooks and people who make . . . ' The boy's eyes shifted to the gate agent behind the desk. He mouthed *bombs*, and mimed one going off.

'Well, hang on now. I admit we've had a few sketchy guys on our team.' Alfred Nobel sprang to mind — founder of prizes to erase the nickname (Merchant of Death) he'd won by inventing dynamite. Or what about Haber, whose ammonia fertilizers had saved multitudes from starvation, but who'd overseen the very chemical weapons that would be used to murder millions of Jews, including his own relatives? Haber's Rule — Noah still knew it by heart: *For any given poisonous gas, $C \times t = k$, where C is the concentration, t is the time of breathing, and k is a constant. Doubling the concentration allows the time to be halved for the same effect.* He shuddered. Once you started poking into the details, it was hard to work out a karmic equation for any individual's effect on the world, not just the geniuses. 'The thing is, Michael, virtually any compound can be used to harm or help. Chemistry just means finding out what the universe is made of, every speck of air or drop of your blood.'

Noah realized that he'd lost the kid's attention several sentences back, and that their flight to Paris was boarding.

So they lined up and inched forward again. A man ahead of them offered his chunky smartwatch to be scanned instead of a boarding pass; Michael watched with what Noah assumed to be envious awe. *O brave new world.* But it wasn't Noah's world.

On the other hand, once you started thinking that way, you might as well turn up your toes.

Go on, give him the window, Joan prompted as they shuffled down the long tube onto the plane.

'You should have the view, as it's your first time.' Noah waved Michael ahead into the window seat. This left him with the middle, which he particularly disliked. Of course, it was dark now: no view but the runway lights. Michael was trying to take a picture of them out the porthole window.

Over the intercom, a flight attendant said, 'It is easier to pack coats around bags than bags around coats.' Then she repeated it in French, which made it sound even more like a zen koan.

'Shall I pop your hat up in the overhead compartment for you, sir?' her male colleague asked Noah.

'No thanks.'

'You don't want it getting crushed on the floor.'

Was there now some rule against wearing hats

120

in an airplane? 'I won't be putting it on the floor.' Noah set his fedora on his lap.

'You sure?'

Repressively: 'It's an heirloom.'

'What's an *air loom?*' Michael's eyes were already glued to a car-chase game on his seat-back screen.

'Something inherited. A precious antique.'

'That old hat?'

On Noah's right, in the aisle seat, was a woman in her fifties or sixties who seemed to have dropped off to sleep already. He should have remembered to use the bathroom at the gate; he didn't want to disturb her. *Destination weather: 4°*, said his screen. Which sounded on the cool side, but that was Paris; the South of France should be a lot milder. *Visibility: unlimited.*

'They do have Wi-Fi.' Michael tapped the icon.

'Really?' Noah leaned over to peer at the details. 'Nineteen dollars — they've got to be kidding!'

'Oh, I thought it was free.'

Noah felt a little bad, but not bad enough to pay $19. 'The movies are free. Watch one after takeoff.'

'Why only after takeoff?'

'Spread out your pleasures, young man. It's a seven-and-a-half-hour flight.'

Hat gently propped against his chest, Noah opened *Père Sonne: A Life's Work.*

The study seemed soundly researched, but irritating to Noah in the way academic analyses of one's relatives naturally would be. Max Harstad (professor of visual communication at a university in Texas) had dried and pressed Noah's genial, eccentric *pépère* into a historical figure, someone impelled only by his art. The family members came up only as specks of ordinariness blown in the face of high ambition. Margot — Noah had jumped ahead to the turn of the century, when she was born — was the special case: the artist's beloved only child, model, equipment porter (she dragged his tripod, light meter, and cameras through the cobbled streets of Nice on a little cart), studio and business manager, secretary, and archivist. His irreplaceable helpmeet, especially from the age of twenty-nine, after her mother, Isabelle, had died. When her father's eyes were tired, in the evenings, Margot had played piano: Chopin, Debussy, Satie. (Those sweetly melancholy ripples, the soundtrack to Noah's childhood.)

He was hoping for hard information about Margot's war years; details about some of the locations and individuals in her mysterious envelope of slapdash photos. But he soon realized that Harstad was leaving out anything that didn't inform the great man's great work; there was no mention of the fall that had damaged Margot's knee, for instance. She always seemed to be busy nursing her father and cooking, as well as answering his mountains of correspondence and helping him conceive, plan, take, develop, and print his photographs. The only other claims on her time that Harstad mentioned were doing the flowers at church

— funny how these pious rituals were kept up, even in times of war — and somehow scrounging each day's food, as famine closed in on Nice that final summer.

On Père Sonne's art, Harstad was more interesting. For instance, Harstad pointed out that many sneered at the 'Objection' series for what they saw as a myopic turning inward, a cowardly choice of the aesthetic over the political, but the fact was, taking photographs in the street was outlawed during the war; the old man could have been arrested and had his equipment smashed if he hadn't turned to working indoors instead. Also, there were strong precedents for a preoccupation with the close-up still life: Ansel Adams with his pebbles and water droplets, Albert Renger-Patzsch's girders and eyeglasses. Wasn't it fair enough to say, even while tanks were rolling in, 'I care about this drainpipe'? Père Sonne's last series, by enshrining the lowly and the particular, could be understood to enact a symbolic, furious objection to Nazism.

Hm, that's stretching a point, Noah thought. Hadn't his *pépère* resolutely stayed out of politics through both the First and Second World Wars? Head pulled in, a turtle in his shell; while all hell broke loose in the streets outside, he'd held his grip on what had always mattered most to him: his work. Apart from writing the occasional mildly phrased letter in support of an arrested artist, Père Sonne had never risked drawing down on himself the attention of successive military regimes.

123

To explain this, Professor Harstad quoted Matisse (a contemporary and acquaintance of Père Sonne's in Nice) to the effect that an artist should close his doors to everyone, especially toward the end, and not waste a single hour. And Père Sonne was not unusual, in fact was typical of the French, in hanging back. Harstad cited a recent study showing that although so many had claimed afterward to have been involved in the Resistance, only around two percent — mostly students and immigrants — had actually committed themselves. Perhaps another eight percent had taken timid steps, such as reading underground newspapers. It seemed as if most French had been *attentistes* (wait-and-see-ers), even as their puppet government at Vichy was rounding up undesirables to send to Hitler's death camps.

Well, Noah couldn't throw stones; his times had been less testing. He'd been a little too old to be drafted for Vietnam, so his life had been spent cocooned in labs and classrooms. And after all, didn't his kind manage to ignore today's awful wrongs? Read the paper, shook their heads regretfully, sipped their lattes.

Noah noticed out of the corner of his eye that Michael was taking a picture of his own shadow, in profile, on his tray table, one hand held up in what Noah feared might be a gang sign. (But perhaps the kids all posed like that nowadays?)

'Shadow selfies,' he said, nodding. 'Photographers have been doing those for more than a hundred years.'

'No way!'

Noah riffled through *A Life's Work* till he found the images he was looking for, the charming 'Perspective' series. 'Look at this one of my mother in 1907.' A girl dancing on what looked like a cliff — unless the angles were exaggerating the height of the overhang? 'See the shadow of my grandpa's tripod?' He put his fingertip to the spot. Its placement on the stones hinted that Père Sonne was waiting below Margot. Watching, cold-blooded — very much the artist, at that moment, rather than the father? But also, Noah hoped, near enough to catch the little girl if she slipped off the cliff.

Michael squinted at it. 'Maybe he just messed up, letting the shadow show.'

Noah shook his head. 'Every shot was so hard to take, back then — especially outside, because you had to get the sun behind you and use the smallest possible fixed-focus lens. Besides, he was trained as a painter, lots of them were, and painters have always found jokey ways to include themselves in the picture.'

The next shot showed a slightly older Margot squeezed into a cleft in rough rock. It could have been a harsh desert landscape, or another planet even, rather than the French Riviera, and the girl a prisoner. But her slight smile suggested this was a game. 'You have to realize how ahead of his time the man was. Most portraits were taken in studios, all stiff and fuddy-duddy against backdrops, with props.' Noah thought of the awful murals at Amber's prison. 'But Père Sonne realized it was brighter outside so he could use a shorter exposure time, and that let his subjects,

125

the people he was photographing, behave more naturally.'

Noah turned the page. The girl Margot squatting this time, a tree looming over her like some hungry giant . . . but the window-sill hinted that this was just a garden shrub. Probably the Personnets' house in the hills above Nice? (Noah had searched for it online; it had been demolished and replaced with a center for *thalassothérapie*, which seemed to involve being rubbed with products expensively derived from the sea.)

'Can you find my mother in this one?' he asked. Taken from way above the stony beach of the Baie des Anges, when the shadows of the palm trees were long: dawn, or possibly dusk.

An impatient click of the tongue; Michael poked the page.

'That's right.' A black blob that turned out to be a hat with its shadow; a small child, foreshortened, dragging a bucket and spade as if girding herself for the long day's work of play ahead . . . or maybe tired from the day that was done.

In the next picture she seemed to be hanging in pure light, a blur of girl in a striped bathing suit, released from gravity, swallowed up by the sparkle of the glittering waves. Had Père Sonne tucked himself under another overhang from which he'd coaxed his daughter to leap past his lens into the sea?

'She looks kind of fun.'

'My mom? Oh, she was,' Noah assured him. He tried to marshal evidence. 'She did tricks

126

— licked her own nose.'

Michael nodded. 'I have a friend that does that.'

Who, Noah almost corrected him. 'About one in ten people can,' he said instead. 'Doctors call it Gorlin sign.'

'Did you get it?'

'Inherit it from Margot?' He shook his head and demonstrated: his tongue tip was a good inch below his nose. 'Yeah, she was a force — always lively, even though she had health problems.' Energetic, a taker of showers rather than long baths. (She'd had their tub in New York ripped out. Noah, raised without one, could never see the appeal of sitting around in your own floating scum.) 'She taught piano till she was in her eighties, refused to go easy on herself. Like your grandma, it sounds like?'

Michael ignored that. 'How come she's always a kid in these pics?'

'Well, Père Sonne ended the series when she was twelve.' Was it puberty that had drawn the line — had he wanted to show a girl's freedom, untrammeled by womanhood? (It occurred to Noah that his grandfather had almost never photographed Isabelle during their long, fond marriage.) Or could it have been Margot who'd rebelled against being his subject? But no, it didn't sound to Noah as if she'd ever said no to her papa.

Here she was in a snowstorm — sandstorm? — barely visible in the terrible shower and whirl of it; eyes screwed up, laughing or crying or both. Nice had no sand and rarely any snow, so

127

what was this stuff?

The notes explained that it was flour, flung into the air at a Corso Illuminé. 'This was her at a nighttime procession. It'll be Carnival time when we're in Nice.'

A flicker of interest from Michael. 'A fun fair, like Coney Island?'

'Well, festive, yes, but it's more about dressing up and parades of crazy floats, not roller coasters. They've been partying in Nice every February since 1294.'

But the boy's attention had switched away from the photos already, back to his screen.

As they thundered down the runway, Noah tried to recall his own maiden flight, New York to L.A., in . . . what year was it? Fernande had been a toddler in their mother's lap, so no later than about 1948. If he didn't remember the journey, that was probably because it had gone by in a flash, unlike his solitary transatlantic crossing on the ship. In California they'd eaten oranges straight off the tree, bursting radiant in the mouth, though Marc had insisted they couldn't hold a candle to the clementines of the South of France.

The screens were taken up with a safety video now. Ignoring it, Michael opened *Incrrrrrrrrrrrrredible!*, which featured colorful photographs and jagged captions, mostly about mysterious accidents, it seemed to Noah. The Bermuda Triangle, Malaysia Airlines Flight 370, a seven-year-old kid who survived going over Niagara Falls . . . Perhaps not the best choice of reading material for a first time on a plane?

The plane gathered speed. 'Don't be nervous,' Noah said. 'I remember I used to think how unlikely it was for a great metal capsule to stay up in the air.'

Michael gave him a scornful look.

How little Noah knew of what made this generation — this particular kid — nervous. 'Did you know, it's safer and easier to take off if the wind is blowing *against* us?'

'That makes no sense.'

'With a headwind there's more airflow over the wings, which helps lift the plane at a lower takeoff speed.' Noah mimed it with his fingers.

'Bullshit.' Michael kept shaking his head.

'Science,' Noah countered.

The plane tilted back and floated now. Sudden and blissful, that sensation of being pressed into your seat by an invisible hand . . .

After they leveled off, the boy was silent.

Drinking in all this new experience, Noah wondered, or maybe panicking? Or just bored?

'Something's up with my ears.'

'The air pressure in the cabin's less than when we're on the ground.' He should have warned the boy. 'Just yawn,' demonstrating. Now Noah really did need to pee, but he hated to disturb the woman to his right.

Old men are prone to bladder infections, Joan reminded him.

He pulled the pirate notebook out of his satchel. 'This is for your travel journal.' Though maybe pirates weren't as timelessly cool as he'd assumed. Would a plain notebook have been better? 'Well?'

'Thanks.'

That wasn't what Noah had been trying to make Michael say. 'It's to write or draw or stick things in, anytime you like.' From the bottom of his satchel he dug out a ballpoint inscribed *Pan-Am Chem Con 2003*, which still seemed to be working.

'Sweet.' Leaden.

'Why don't you start it now?'

'I'm good.'

Funny how that had come to mean *no*.

'The idea is to record things as you're going along, before you forget them.' Noah waited. 'A little bit, every day of our trip, maybe.'

Michael scored the cellophane with his nail and yanked it off. He held the notebook between his fingers.

Noah couldn't help himself. 'Did you want to start with a family tree, like Rosa suggested?'

Michael gave him a stony look. 'For all my new dead relations?' With the ballpoint, he scribble-sketched the classic wide-crowned shape of a tree.

'Hang on. Are you planning to put yourself on the trunk and your parents and grandparents in the crown? That's always seemed illogical to me. Surely the roots come first, then the trunk, then the branches, so wouldn't your grandparents be the roots?'

The boy heaved a sigh and drew a huge X through the silhouette.

'Michael! I didn't mean . . . ' The journal looked awful now; wrecked before it had been begun.

'You do it.' He shoved it toward Noah and dropped the pen on top.

'I was only raising the interesting question of how to represent a family visually.'

'Not interesting to me,' the boy muttered.

Noah thought of Rutherford-Bohr diagrams of atoms, with their dots and rings, or Lewis structures with their dots and dashes. (What on earth was that photo of Margot's about, the one that showed a circle between two short lines on some kind of box?) For an accurate diagram of ancestry, you'd need something more complicated than DNA's double helix, even. It was as if many tangles of seaweed had brushed together in the ocean, and two strands — the Young-Selvaggios and the Davis-whoevers — had knotted at a single point: Michael. But how to draw that?

Noah returned to *A Life's Work*, jumping to 1944. He'd never thought to wonder what his grandfather had died of, but from the vantage point of nearly eighty, he didn't find 'natural causes' (at eighty-three) quite sufficient as an explanation. The photographer had had ongoing bronchial problems, it turned out, and a previous abscess on the lung, and the fuel shortage that brutal winter hadn't helped. Margot and he used to fox-trot to the gramophone to keep warm. (Noah enjoyed that detail.) Père Sonne was taking a tar cough syrup containing chloroform, and belladonna cigarettes for asthma, which sounded alarming to Noah.

Here was an oddity: when their apartment building was being converted into offices in

131

1968, Harstad mentioned in a footnote, a reporter had tracked down Madame Dupont, Père Sonne's former twice-weekly *femme de ménage*. (Noah thought he remembered a cleaner in a housecoat and head scarf. Hadn't she brought a little girl with her sometimes?) She'd told the reporter that Madame Selvaggio hadn't come home for two nights in a row in the middle of August 1944, and her father had worried himself sick. Madame Dupont had had trouble persuading a doctor to call more than once or twice, in all the chaos of Liberation, and Père Sonne had slipped into unconsciousness on the fifth of September.

Noah reread the whole paragraph. Two nights? What the hell had Margot been up to? For such a devoted daughter to stay away from her frail father that long without a word . . .

But this could be a scurrilous invention, the old housekeeper trying to cash in on her memories by beefing them up.

What was it her little girl had been called? Something out of a song. Michelle? No, the detail slid further away as Noah tried to hook it.

The woman to his right was awake now, so Noah got up stiffly and beckoned the boy to follow him.

'I don't need to.'

'Right now, Michael, so we won't have to disturb our neighbor too often.'

When they'd come back and clambered into their seats again, Noah saw that two pages of the boy's notebook were filled with a crudely drawn airplane shooting up into the sky. From one oval window, a stick figure in a ball cap pantomimed excitement. In a speech bubble: *Me (Michael Malcolm Young) in the sky and not dead yet, unbefuuckinleevable.* 'I like the drawing. But remember you'll be handing this in to your teacher?'

A small groan. 'Negative consequences,' Michael said in a parodic singsong. He went to work with his ballpoint, covering *fuuckin* with a black shape.

'What's that you're adding?'

'Some bird flying by, about to get his ass blenderized in the engine.'

'Which engine? This is an Airbus 380, the world's largest passenger airliner. It's got four — there, there, there, and there.' Noah indicated with his finger.

Michael added flames spurting out of each spot.

'So now the plane's on fire?'

Noah spoke more loudly than he meant to, and the woman to his right gave him a horrified glance.

'Nah, just turbocharged.'

The flight attendants handed out those little steaming cylinders.

'Is this a snack?' the boy asked.

'No, a hot towel, to clean our hands.'

Michael liked that, Noah could tell. And the free Coke from the cart. (He ordered it before Noah could think to say *water*.)

Noah had a cognac, himself. He took a baby aspirin to reduce his chances of a flight-related heart attack or stroke. Though it increased the risk of intestinal bleeding, so . . . six of one, half-dozen of the other.

At dinner he put his fedora back on to keep it out of harm's way. Michael peeled back the foil from his special child meal, which didn't look any more appetizing than Noah's salmon in goo. 'We ate already. You don't have to have any,' he told the boy. 'By the way, if you feel sick, there's a paper bag in the seat pocket — '

'I'm good.' Michael crimped the foil back down.

Noah would have loved a cigarette about now. Instead he watched an exhausting film about a nineteenth-century fur trapper surviving a bear mauling.

Michael's choice featured a horribly scarred superhero, strippers, and torture. Noah poked his own Pause button, then — taking three tries at it — Michael's.

'Hey, I was watching that!'

'It seems extraordinarily violent.'

'Nah, it's just messing around. Fourth wall breaks all the time.'

Noah had no idea what that meant.

With his phone, Michael snapped a close-up of the frozen screen: the superhero's face in a rictus of agony. 'I'm strictly D.C., but Marvel's funny.'

'You must be too young for this one. What's the rating?'

'So's yours violent.' Michael gestured at the trapper's bleeding face in the snow.

'Well, that's history.'

'What's the difference? It's all blood.'

Noah puzzled over that one. 'It's educational to learn what our ancestors lived through.'

'*Deadpool*'s educational too, about the future. Mutant-cell regeneration and shit.'

'Would your grandma have let you watch it?'

Michael's face contracted.

'I wasn't criticizing her,' Noah rushed to say.

'She didn't care about *movies*. She just wanted me home, off the corner,' Michael growled. 'Safe.'

'OK.'

Each went back to his own screen. But Noah had lost the thread of his wilderness epic. Brooding over everything Ella Davis must have toiled to shield her grandson from, for as long as she'd been able.

★ ★ ★

Noah woke with a start in the dimmed cabin, and his screen said *Time to destination: 2 hours 37 minutes.* He shouldn't have slept at all; groggy, haggard. His hip throbbed.

Hunch and drop those shoulders, Joan ordered. *Circle those feet, if you don't want some deep-vein thrombosis.*

Noah made a few half-hearted movements, which hurt.

To his left, Michael was slumped in the kind of wormlike position that looked as if it would cause damage, except that he was so young.

Noah tried *Père Sonne: A Life's Work* again. For lack of shampoo, and because hair salons closed down, he read, Frenchwomen often wore

135

turbans during the war. Their shoes had soles of wood or cork, laces of string, newspaper for insulation. Had Noé had a pair of clogs at three or four, or was he making up that memory? He thought of the clomping sound of wood on cobbles, and the hush of cork.

Only when the breakfast cart was clinking past did Michael uncoil, rubbing his eyes.

Noah leaned past him to shove up the shade. A fluffy white expanse. 'Look, snow!'

But the boy was hard to fool. 'You must be high, dude.'

He grinned. 'Why don't you take a picture?'

'I've seen clouds before.' Michael looked instead at the double spread of photos in Noah's book. 'Hey, same kind of dumb-ass hat as yours.'

'You've got a sharp eye. That's my grandfather wearing this hat, on a visit to his dealer in Paris in 1934.' Standing beside Robert Capa, though Michael was unlikely to have heard of Capa either.

'Hell no! The same actual hat?'

'Hell yeah.'

That made Michael grin.

Noah turned the fedora upside down and traced the darkened sweatband. 'See that pebbly pattern pressed in? They stopped doing that in the late '20s.' Margot must have brought the hat with her to New York, in 1944. It had sat on Noah's dresser as a reminder of his *pépère*, until one day at the university when it had occurred to him to put it on, for a joke. Since then he hadn't worn it every day, but whenever he did wear a hat it was this one.

136

Michael wrinkled his nose. 'The leather's all greasy. Didn't you or your grandpa ever clean the thing?'

Noah examined the torn cloth of the lining; a mysterious stain on the brim. 'I'd be afraid it would fall apart.' It came into his head that ineradicable wrinkles in vintage clothes were known to conservators as *memory*. Why was he able to hold on to such arcane details, when he occasionally fumbled for the code for picking up his voicemail? Over a lifetime you packed your brain tight with data, like an overstuffed suitcase, only for it all to fall out in the end. He stroked the fine brim. 'The hat itself is felt. Rabbit and chinchilla.'

'It's made from a fucking bunny rabbit?'

The woman to Noah's right quivered.

The kid's language is not my problem, he told himself; *I'm only a temporary carer. A fill-in.* 'And a chinchilla, a sort of South American squirrel.' Endangered nowadays, no surprise. His fingers gripped the concavities at the front. 'These are called the *pinches*.'

'Shouldn't it be in a museum or something?'

'Oh, they have his photographs. I'm keeping the hat.' Noah set it back on his head.

'So where'd he get his handle?'

'What?'

'His street name.' Michael tapped *Père Sonne*, the serious black letters across the book's jacket.

'Well, artists often had nicknames based on their real names, like . . . ' Nadar, Christo, Izis; the boy wouldn't know them. 'Have you heard of, let's see, Man Ray?' he asked without much

137

hope. 'Even more famous than my grandpa. He began as Emmanuel Radnitzky.' Maybe he'd been trying to sound less identifiably Jewish. 'Look, here's a picture of Man Ray that Père Sonne took in 1922.' Noah leafed through the pages to find the ambitious night shot of the man dancing cheek to cheek with his own camera — or rather pretending to dance but standing still for a sharp focus, while the crowd on the Promenade blurred around him. 'But to answer your question, my grandpa's surname was Personnet, which in French sounds almost the same as personne — meaning no one.'

Michael frowned. 'Person means no person?'

'Confusing, isn't it? So Père Sonne sounds like no one, but also like father — that's père, in French — and just to complicate matters, sonne is French for ring.'

'Like bling? A gold ring?'

'No, that's hague. Sonne means ringing, like the sound of a phone. So the whole name means father rings, but also no one.'

'Daddy Ring.' Michael tried it out. 'Daddy Nobody Ding-a-Ling. Kind of creepy. Or Nodaddy Ding.'

What Père Sonne had signed on the back of his prints was actually PS, it struck Noah — postscriptum, what you put at the end of a letter in either French or English when you had one more thing to say. And the man did always have one more thing to say, artistically; he'd been inexhaustible.

A grinding sound rose from the airliner's belly, and Michael twitched.

'That's only the wheels being lowered,' Noah told him. 'Look down, you might get a shot of the Eiffel Tower.'

But the cloud cover was thick, so Paris was invisible.

Michael hunched, pressing his ears.

Why did it hurt so much more when you were a child? 'You need to yawn,' Noah urged him, 'to equalize the air pressure in your Eustachian tubes.'

In unfamiliar pain, the kid was unreachable.

'See what the air pressure's doing to this?' Noah asked it loudly as he showed his weirdly crumpled water bottle.

Michael straightened up, intrigued, and snapped it with his phone.

'Now let the air in . . . ' Noah unscrewed the cap, and the bottle gasped and swelled.

★   ★   ★

His right ear was slightly blocked up from the flight; he tugged at it and stretched his jaw, achieving nothing. Waiting for the elevator in the terminal, he pointed to a sign that said *Aéroport de Paris-Charles de Gaulle*. 'De Gaulle was the leader of the French Resistance, during the war.'

'Your one, not your dad's one?' Michael mimed his right hand being severed.

'That's right, World War Two.'

The boy whistled a sad four-note tune. Then, seeing Noah's blank face, he did it again more slowly, spacing out the notes.

'What's that, the theme from *Close Encounters*?'

Michael looked equally puzzled. 'The Resistance in the *Hunger Games*, dude. The mockingjay call.'

'Well, unlike in your fantasy movie, this was real. *Resisting* the Nazis. You know, like fascists today? White supremacists?'

A casual nod: 'The alt-right.'

'Don't call them that. They're not an *alternative*, they're the same old racists. Anyway' — Noah tried to remember his point — 'when the Germans invaded, the French had to decide whether to let the enemy boss them around, or fight back.'

'I'd have fought back like the Gaulle guy.'

'Well,' Noah said bleakly, 'probably most people thought that, till it came to the crunch.'

He set his watch six hours forward. 'Let's see your phone?' But Michael's device had reset automatically, to 10:35. Noah was confused, until he saw that the boy had already managed to log into the airport's free Wi-Fi. These kids, it was like breathing. 'Your body clock will still tell you it's four thirty-five,' he warned Michael. 'Have you done time zones at school?'

A long yawn.

Noah wondered if that meant *no*. 'It's still night over Brooklyn, see, but here in Paris the sun's been shining for hours.'

'No it's not.' Michael jerked his head at the expanse of glass, the dull gray.

'Well, it's up, at least.'

They would have had a two-hour layover if

140

they hadn't landed late. *Layover* struck Noah as misleading, with its suggestion of lolling on benches at a Roman feast rather than scuttling between terminals, with further delays because some administrator behind glass was mwah-mwahing and chatting with colleagues instead of dealing with the line of drooping tourists. Damn it, the two of them would be lucky to make their next flight. Noah didn't run, these days, as a matter of policy.

'*Douanes* — that means *Customs*,' pointing, just to take his mind off the length of time he'd been chafing in this line already. But why would *Customs* mean anything to a child who'd never crossed a border? 'Where they check you haven't brought in too much of anything,' he explained. What else? '*Entrée interdite*, 'Entry is forbidden.''

'You're like a human Google Translate,' Michael muttered.

'Oh, so you'd rather guess all the words on your own?'

'We'll be back in America in six days, right?'

Such a short trip, and would any of it be what Noah had hoped for? 'But you might study French at school sometime.'

Michael puffed out air to suggest the unlikelihood of that.

Some of the signs came with their own stern translations: *Passport Control, Submit Now.* Michael did take a picture of that one, with his left hand holding up its middle finger in the foreground.

Noah secretly sympathized, even as he

141

murmured, 'Stop it before the guards see you.'

When it was finally their turn he handed over their passports, and the Letter of Consent for Travel of a Minor Child. His ear was still woolly; he could make out the agent's questions through the Perspex barrier, but only just. '*Son grand-oncle*,' he said: he was the boy's great-uncle.

The agent turned his gaze on Michael and switched to accented English. 'Who is this man?'

Looking for confirmation this wasn't an abduction, Noah realized.

Michael stared dully.

Noah tried pushing the Designation of Person in Parental Relationship form into the hatch, but it crumpled up. He pointed to it and said, '*Voilà, je suis ... une personne avec une relation quasi-parentale à ce garçon.*' *Parentale*, legally, not *quasi-parentale*; when Noah got flustered he erred on the side of pomposity.

'He is what to you?' the agent demanded of Michael.

'*Great*-uncle,' the boy said.

'He is great?'

A snort.

'*Son grand-oncle, monsieur. L'oncle de son père*, his father's uncle,' Noah added so clearly and loudly it sounded as if he was calling the man an idiot.

Their passports finally got stamped.

Michael didn't comment on the encounter. Worn out, Noah wondered? The boy would be used to hearing foreign languages in New York, but not to finding himself trapped inside one.

142

After all the hurry, they had a little time to kill before their flight to Nice. Noah glanced at the newspapers as they passed a bookstore. His eye was caught by something about *La haine la plus ancienne*, the oldest hatred: a sharp rise in anti-Semitic hate crimes already this year.

At the gate, Noah settled down with his biography.

'Mother of butt!' Michael muttered at his small screen.

Noah's mouth twitched with amusement at the phrase. 'What's the problem?'

'Out of ammo.' Almost tenderly to the menacing figures, 'Too good, boyo. You ready to square up?'

'The red feathery marks, what are they?' Noah asked.

'Where I've shot someone.'

Stylized blood, then, but Noah couldn't tell if it represented the bullet's path toward the victim or its exit trajectory. 'How do you know who's the enemy and who's not?'

An impatient shrug. 'Just have to guess. It's pretty much run and gun at this point.'

The game struck Noah as relentless. Even watching over the boy's shoulder was exhausting. But clearly it enthralled Michael.

'*Oh* yeah,' the boy crooned to a fallen avatar, 'you just got schooled.'

Noah supposed a new form of fun such as video games always triggered a moral panic about its capacity to rot the brain and pervert the character. Like comic books, when he'd been a kid. *À chaque âge ses plaisirs;* 'Every age has

143

its pleasures.' That old proverb floated up unprompted — was it one of his mother's? *Chacun voit midi à sa porte*, that was another Margot liked: 'Everyone sees noon at their own door.'

A ferocious face loomed on Michael's taped screen, then a clash of limbs. The scene exploded.

'What's the rating on this one?' Noah asked.

'Why d'you want to know?' Michael muttered.

'Just curious.'

'M.'

Middle, Noah wondered? 'M for what?'

'Mature.'

That made him laugh. 'Is that what you are?'

'But like, if a cigarette gets stubbed out in someone's eye you don't see it close up,' Michael added.

'Delightful.'

'The graphics resolution on this is for shit, though.'

'On this game?'

'On the phone. The game's made for a console.'

Noah thought of the boy's uncle Cody and his PlayStation, out of reach in Queens. 'Why bother playing it on this, then?'

'Duh.'

Meaning *better than nothing*, he supposed.

★ ★ ★

As they filed onto the smaller plane, Noah took the window, this time; he refused to miss out on

144

his first glimpse of Nice since 1942. In fact, it struck him that he'd never seen his hometown from the air.

When they reached the Mediterranean they flew out over it as if heading south to Algeria, oddly, then turned back to approach the coastline from the water. Noah kept thinking he'd spotted Nice, but it would turn out to be Antibes, or Cannes; the whole stretch was so built up, sprinkled with the whites and oranges of apartment blocks, that he couldn't tell one resort from another. Surely this was Nice, now, the long curve like a ballerina's arm, the Baie des Anges? Tiny boats leaving their streaks. Feeling bad for hogging the window, Noah nudged Michael and flattened himself back against the seat, chin tilted up, so the kid could see past him. 'The whole area's called the Côte d'Azur, the Blue Coast, and this particular stretch is the Bay of Angels.'

A cursory glance. 'How's it like angels?'

'Well, doesn't it look heavenly?' Mountains slanting down across a pale blue sky to a more vividly azure sea edged with rippling foam.

'How come you've never been back till now?'

Thrown by the question, Noah said, 'I don't know. I've been busy.'

So low, now, as if the plane's wheels might touch the water. No sign of land yet.

Michael was looking distinctly nervous.

The runway appeared underneath them at the last minute, and they were touching down.

★   ★   ★

145

In the baggage area, soldiers in camo toted machine guns. Michael lifted his phone to —

Noah pushed it down.

'What the fuck?'

'Just keeping you out of trouble.'

'This is my mom's phone I'm looking after.' The boy's eyes were ablaze. 'You smack this phone, I'll smack you.'

'Michael, I didn't *smack* it.' Noah thought of the day Amber must have put her phone into her, what, nine-year-old's hands and said she wasn't going to be needing it for a while, could he keep it safe for her? 'I'm sorry, but the soldiers, they might think we're — ' He didn't say the word *terrorists*. 'Photos put them on edge, they feel spied on.' A certain irony there. France was so surveilled and militarized, since this wave of attacks had begun in 2015, that half its total forces were patrolling its own streets. '*Tapis Bagages*,' Noah read aloud, to change the subject. '*Tapis* means *carpet*, like tapestry — it's a carpet of baggage.'

Joan asked, *You do realize you're talking to yourself?*

The carousel was dotted with gliding suitcases. Noah saw signs in Cyrillic lettering, which suggested that Nice was still popular with the Russians. He felt wobbly; how could Michael move so energetically after the night they'd had?

Noah got euros out of the machine. 'I need a coffee and a croissant before going any further.'

All Michael would accept, at the café, was some kind of gourmet re-creation of an American iced doughnut.

146

Noah's *café crème* came as a tiny puddle of espresso in a big cup.

'That's a rip-off right there,' Michael muttered.

'No, I get to pour in all this hot milk, see?' Noah loved being able to do it himself, making it milky enough but not too milky.

The boy scanned the other customers. 'Are French guys all gay, or what?' he asked in a low voice. '*Actual* gay, I mean.'

Noah counted four men having coffee, two of them with their legs crossed at the knee, one with a lemon cardigan draped around his shoulders. 'Not necessarily. They just aren't afraid of things that American men call *sissy*.'

'Huh.' Michael inserted his entire doughnut into his mouth. He took a selfie of himself with eyes bulging as if he were suffocating.

Noah averted his gaze.

He missed his sister, suddenly. He should have come here before now, with Fernande.

A few summers after Marc's death — this would have been the mid-1970s — she'd pressured Noah into signing up for what she'd called a 'nostalgia trip' (though she'd been born in New York herself), to surprise their widowed mother by 'whisking her home.' Privately Noah had thought it a terrible idea, because of the surprise and the season; the heat and crowds on the French Riviera in August were as bad as in Manhattan. He'd been relieved when Margot, getting wind of the plan — Fernande hadn't been able to resist dropping hints — had turned it down civilly. She'd offered no explanation but the proverbial one: *On ne se baigne jamais deux fois dans le même fleuve.* ('You can't step in the same river twice.')

But why hadn't he and Fernande gotten around to going some winter, just the two of them? Noah couldn't remember, now, if she'd ever raised it; if he'd failed to hear the suggestion.

As her executor, last spring, reading her will (a free downloaded form she'd filled in by hand, but valid), Noah had been both touched and irritated to find that although the proceeds of the Brooklyn brownstone were to go to a children-at-risk project, Fernande had set aside a lump sum that Noah was obliged to spend within a year on *SOMETHING FUN!!!* (That was his sister all over: hadn't she been their small family's bonus prize, free giveaway, *something fun?*) So here he was. Not that he expected this to be pure FUN!!! even before Michael Young had been added to the itinerary, but he knew it would please Fernande to think of him finally making the crossing.

Would have pleased. Such convoluted grammar death required: what tense to describe the hypothetical emotions of a woman who didn't exist anymore? Someone on NPR the other day had been talking about how he'd 'have hated to die without having heard' a certain revelation. Which made no sense — you could hardly be tormented by not knowing a secret if you never learned there was a secret to know — but Noah got what the fellow meant.

★ ★ ★

Outside the terminal, the sun stabbed him in the pupils and the air smelled almost floral, despite the tang of fuel. Noah lit up with desperate gratitude.

The boom made his cigarette fall from his hand. Like a volcano blowing its top, or an avalanche; most of all, like a bomb.

'Jesus Christ,' Michael cried, in a half-crouch.

'I remember this!' Pulse still banging, Noah checked his watch. 'It's a cannon on the hill over there, in the middle of town. They fire it every day at noon.'

'What for?'

Noah shrugged, Gallicly, and picked up his cigarette.

The taxi ride was long, sluggish, and so expensive that he told himself to pretend euros were worth the same as dollars. At least, en route, there was art. Guarding a traffic circle, a giant made of boulders shackled together with barbed wire. A huge bronze woman, peeking from a cleft in the gray facade of a hotel. A massive metal swoosh like a lopsided smile, with tourists perched on its shorter end.

Noah tried out his French on the driver, who insisted on answering in fluent English, telling him Nice was still pretty quiet but would be 'super crazy' by the weekend.

'They're expecting half a million tourists for Carnival,' Noah passed on to the boy, 'on top of the third of a million people who live here.'

'Fun in the sun, yes? Three hundred days,' the driver remarked, trying to catch Michael's eye in the rearview mirror.

'Three hundred sunny days a year,' Noah explained, 'or so they claim.'

The concrete ribbons of roadway were thick with vehicles. Two-seater Smart cars looked like toys to Noah. Michael was whispering the names of his favorites, incantatory, as he spotted them: 'Maserati. Ferrari. Another Maserati!'

'Nice was where car racing really got going,' Noah told him. 'The first hill climb, drag race . . . ' He riffled through *A Life's Work*. 'Wait till you see this. A factory owner called Leon Serpollet broke the seventy-five-miles-per-hour land-speed record, and my grandpa was right there.' The photo had remarkable depth of field, from the car's wheel looming in the foreground all the way back to the mountains in the distance.

'Seventy-five, that's not *fast*.'

'This was 1902! The thing was powered by steam. They nicknamed it the Easter Egg.'

Michael grinned at the ovoid contraption. 'That driver looks like a baby chick breaking out of the shell.'

Now their taxi was snagged in traffic. Noah pointed out a huge mural on the windowless side of a high-rise. It showed cypresses, palm trees, and the sea beyond; a picture of what it had replaced. Cynical or poignant? Better than no view at all, he supposed. 'You could take a picture of that.'

'Why?'

'Well, you're quite the shutterbug.'

'What did you call me?' Michael demanded.

'It means someone who takes a lot of pictures.'

Noah made the old-fashioned clicking-at-eye-level gesture. 'I'm just saying you could get a good shot of that mural, since we're stalled here anyway. It's very Nice, very typical.'

'*Trompe l'oeil*,' the driver supplied.

Noah hadn't heard that phrase in so long. '*Trompe l'oeil*, that means the style that tricks the eye,' he told Michael. 'Back in Renaissance times — '

'It doesn't trick *my* eye,' Michael scoffed. 'Why don't you take your own pics?'

'Oh, I haven't traveled with a camera in donkey's years.'

'Duh, use your phone.'

'I mean, I don't . . . I want to see things, but not have lots of photos to deal with afterward.' Oddly enough, Noah had never felt very comfortable with a camera. Made awkward by his grandfather's fame, he supposed. Of course he used to take holiday snaps; Joan had liked looking through the albums in moments of leisure. But for the past nine years, there'd been nothing Noah felt the need to record. He was just freewheeling, at this point; the race was pretty much over.

Billboards for junk food, circuses, water parks slid by. So far, nothing rang much of a bell. Noah asked the driver if the film industry was still thriving.

'All gone.' The man explained that a plane landed every two and a half minutes, so it was impossible to record clean sound anymore.

'There wasn't even an airport when I was four,' Noah said to Michael. 'From Marseilles

— west of here — I went by ship to Barcelona. From there, another ship took me all around Spain to Portugal, then across the Atlantic.' He could picture little of his journey except the time he'd thrown up on deck and slipped in the puddle. He must have missed his mother badly, but it was hard to disentangle that feeling, now, from the general confusion of the voyage. Marc had been chafing on the docks in New York, waiting for a boy he must have known he wouldn't recognize. 'My father had been gone for two years already when I turned up.'

'How come?'

'Well, my mother . . . ' What was the right verb for it? 'She didn't feel able to leave Nice when Marc did. American universities kept offering Père Sonne jobs, to get him away from the war, but he wouldn't budge. And she wouldn't let me go without her, not till it looked like the Italians were really going to invade, in '42.' Then she'd sent little Noé off, and stayed on with her father because someone had to.

At least, that was the family's explanation. But those snapshots . . .

He pressed on. 'There was a matron on the ship in charge of us' — Noé must have been one of the only Gentile kids fleeing the Continent on that voyage, though he'd understood that only later — 'and then in New York, I had a nanny to teach me English. A pretty nasty one.' Miss Sprule must have seemed meticulous during her interview, and Marc had been working such long hours at the gallery, how could he detect the nanny's mean streak? But if Noah didn't hold a grudge against Marc for hiring her, or for having stayed an ocean away from his son for the previous two years, he had no right to resent Margot either. Mothers always got the lion's share of blame. 'Well, parents did what they had to, you know? The war was an awful time. The Italians surrendered, but the Nazis moved in right away. Then the Allies started dropping bombs, and Père Sonne died.'

Michael produced a convincing machine-gun mime, with sound effects.

'No, of pneumonia. So Margot joined me and my father in New York, and the next year Fernande — your grandmother — was born.'

Noah had always assumed that his sister's conception had been an accident, since his mother and father had been 45 and 53 respectively, and too Catholic (Margot by conviction, Marc by upbringing) to consider ending a pregnancy. But now he was struck by the possibility that she'd been a reconciliation, a celebration of having come through what the French called *les années noires*, 'the dark years.'

Michael was staring out the taxi window.

Kids bereft of parents and homes could be said to be living through one long wartime, Noah realized. Did Michael blame his mother for being out of reach?

'By the way,' he said, an awkward segue, 'as soon as we get back from France, I can take you up to see your mom.' He made a mental note to find out how to arrange a visit: by bus, maybe?

'It's all a mix-up.' The boy muttered it to the glass.

153

Noah waited for more. 'Amber being . . . '

An impatient glance. 'In the slammer. She didn't do it. She's always on my back, saying, 'You stay away from that shit!' '

Did the boy know or guess that the stash had really been Victor's? 'Yeah,' Noah said warily, 'I think there may have been a mistake.'

'Goddamn government.'

So this was how Amber had softened the truth: she'd blamed it all on Uncle Sam and done her best to steer Michael down quite a different path from his father's.

Minutes passed. Noah found his head lolling back against the seat. He didn't want to slip into a doze, or he'd be completely discombobulated when they pulled up at the hotel. He tugged a magazine out of the seat pocket: *Plaisirs d'Azur*. It was bland, gushy stuff about '*le lifestyle des expats*.' He puzzled over what distinguished an expat from an immigrant; it seemed the word was reserved for whites from the West who decamped to sunnier climes.

As the traffic loosened, Noah began to recognize glimpses of the hills that hugged the city on three sides. High on a wooden slope, that little white dome . . . He pointed it out. 'There's the observatory, for stargazing. I remember we went up there in a cart pulled by a mule.'

The kid looked incredulous. 'When was this, cowboy times?'

'Mules are better than cars on a dirt track. They never slip.'

'We nearly there?' Michael let out a huge yawn.

'Nearly.' Actually Noah had no idea. 'You know, we complain about how tiring travel is, but our ancestors would have called us pussies. Coming down here from Paris used to take two weeks by road, and when you got to the river Var — just past where the airport is now,' jerking his thumb over his shoulder, 'you had to hire local *passeurs*, ferrymen, to drag your carriage through the water. Or carry you on their shoulders, even.'

The kid was looking at his phone again.

'Ah, back to the screen.'

'You talk a lot, dude,' Michael murmured without looking up.

'Well, I was a teacher.'

But not anymore.

★ ★ ★

Five floors high, six windows wide. Since his mother had snapped this hotel, the dull black doors had acquired a *Hotel Excelsior* in gold on the columns to either side, and an *H.E.* in tasteful neon scrollwork overhead. Once past its gracious lobby, the *quirky decor* the website boasted of began to hurt Noah's eyes: old trunks had been whimsically converted into coffee tables and cabinets, the wallpaper and stair carpet covered in magnified scribbled words as if guests were trapped inside a can of old postcards. But Noah supposed everywhere else was probably booked out now for Carnival.

Their Comfort Suite was decorated in electric blues, with a gaudy painting of the Prom filling the wall behind the bed. Also a see-through Philippe Starck chair, which Michael found hilarious. But the only bed was the slim kind that passed for a double in Europe, and (how absurd) a mesh-sided crib stood wedged between it and the radiator. 'Damn it, I asked for a child's bed!' He must have used the wrong term after all.

'So where am I going to sleep?' The boy was already curled up in the crib.

'I'll sort it out. Get out of there before you dirty the sheets.'

But Michael panted through the mesh like a dog. He held his phone at arm's length and took grotesque selfies.

Noah unzipped his bag and hung up his shirts and pants.

'So how come your mom took a pic of this place?'

'Beats me, Michael.'

'That one with the hair all up, is that her?'

Noah slid from the envelope the headshot of a woman seen from behind. 'I don't think so.'

'She could have snapped herself from the back, except I guess they didn't have selfie sticks yet.'

'Oh, I'm sure there were ways: a string to pull the shutter release. But it says *MZ*, and Margot was *MP*, for Personnet, then *MS* after she married my dad.' Coiled hair, black, dark brown? Hard to tell in black and white. He remembered his mother with sleek silver hair; she'd stopped coloring it brown in what, her fifties? This woman could have been anything between twenty and eighty, or a dummy in a wig, even.

156

The shoulders of her jacket were boxy, with that slightly homemade look. Noah thought aloud: 'It's not glamorous enough to be a fashion shot. Maybe a how-to picture for an article on hairstyles?'

Michael smirked.

'Yeah, well, your sneakers will seem silly, too, in seventy years.'

'They're genuine Air Jordans,' the boy told him in an offended tone. 'Hey, maybe *MZ*'s a handle, like Nodaddy Ding's.'

'Oh, a pseudonym?' Noah didn't really think so, but . . . 'Possibly.'

Michael went into the bathroom. 'Two toilets!' he called.

'If one of them has a little faucet, it's a bidet, for washing your butt.'

A squawk of disbelief.

'Well, you asked.'

'Wish I hadn't.'

Noah heard the repeated shutter sound that meant Michael was photographing the bidet.

Hopefully no butts are involved, Joan murmured.

The boy wandered back into the room. 'Why aren't the pillows normal?'

It was the usual European bolster-and-square-pillow combo. 'The whole point of travel is to learn there's no such thing as normal.' Noah got out his toiletries bag. He straightened up and noticed Michael struggling to press his phone charger into the outlet. 'Stop!'

The boy goggled at him.

'You could fry yourself,' Noah said in a

157

shaking voice. 'The voltage in Europe is 220. Twice as strong as back home.'

''Kay,' Michael said in a small voice. He sat on the edge of the bed and hugged the bolster with his arms and legs like a wrestler.

'You can use my adaptor as soon as I've charged my own phone.' Noah let himself down now too, and fell back on the mattress. Just to be flat for five minutes; the sweetness of horizontality.

'What are we waiting for?' Michael wanted to know.

'I need a little down time.'

'I don't.'

'We've been up all night. Give me a minute.' Noah managed to toe off one shoe, then the other, before his eyelids fell.

4

The Promenade

From a dream of lost passports, Noah awoke with a start to the whir of a photo being taken. Behind the phone, Michael's unsmiling face was looming over him.

He reared up.

'Thought you died in your sleep, maybe.' In only a red T-shirt and sweatpants, without a hoodie to create the illusion of bulk, Michael looked even younger.

'So your first reaction was to take a picture?' Noah rubbed his face, feeling foul. He wondered if Michael had seen his grandma laid out. He supposed Rosa would expect him to get the boy expressing his feelings. Women generally —

Not me, Joan pointed out.

Well, no, Noah conceded. *You're the exception to all rules. Why do you think I picked you?*

It was me who did the picking, she reminded him.

They'd met over the university's first oscillating U-tube digital density meter. Joan had been the elder by three years, much better looking, and at least twice as clever, with that knack successful people had of knowing which chances to seize. All Noah could congratulate himself on was that he'd been wise enough never to let go of his luck, his Joan. He'd known he'd be playing second fiddle; maybe one spouse always did. (Hadn't Margot and Isabelle both done it for Père Sonne?)

'You were asleep forever,' Michael complained.

'It was only a nap. How did you pass the time?'

The boy held up his phone. 'Thirty-one kills.'

'Lovely.'

Noah's generation had gotten more fresh air, he decided, but also probably more fractures, playing such perennial favorites as Johnny-on-the-Pony (in which one team leaped on the backs of the other until the whole human pile crashed to the ground). He wondered now how a gamer like Michael had broken his collarbone.

Every bit of Noah was aching from last night's flight. He remembered the stretches: Chops, the Superman Pose, Dynamic Hugs, the Silverback Gorilla. While Vivienne could still see, she'd affixed a leaflet to his freezer with (an extra joke) a magnet of Matisse's *La Danse*. But Noah didn't want to attempt the moves in front of Michael, who might try to film the humiliating ritual.

He called down to the front desk and had a tense conversation that ended with the management promising to swap the crib for some kind of child's bed by tonight. Then he thought to log in to the Wi-Fi and scan in some of his mother's other photos.

'Found what they are?' Michael asked.

Noah shook his head and tilted his tablet to

160

show the boy. For the rectangle with the circle between two dashes, the only suggestion offered was 'Best guess: house door.'

'That's not a door,' Michael said disgustedly. 'More like a gravestone.'

'You think?' Very abstract for a tomb, though, and where was the name?

For the dandy with the cane, Noah was offered a set of 'visually similar images,' but they were just random white people, not similar to the man in the photo at all.

Michael pointed: 'Some of these aren't even guys.'

Noah was amused to recognize that face as Greta Garbo's.

'You think he was, what, a friend of your mom's?'

There was something in Michael's tone; it made Noah look at him hard, then at the dandy again. What could this fellow have been to Margot? 'He is what to you?' as the passport checker had asked this morning. A sexy devil, leaning on his cane. Noah shook his head to dislodge the cobwebs of suspicion.

'Hey, let's say your dad *did* ran around on her' —

'Did *run*.' Noah automatically amended the participle.

— 'so once she was on her own, she paid him back with this guy . . . '

This really wasn't a conversation to have with an eleven-year-old. Besides, the mathematics of marriage wasn't as neat as that. 'I very much doubt it,' Noah said repressively.

161

But his pulse was racing. A banal theory; all the more likely to be true. Two years unencumbered by husband or child; two years of assignations at the elegant Excelsior? Then, what, had things soured between Margot and her limping playboy, or had he been killed or torn away from her in the chaos of Liberation, and for want of any other future she'd sailed for New York to try being Madame Selvaggio again?

Schlocky, Joan complained. *I'm not buying it.*

Michael was channel surfing now past chat shows in French, soaps in Italian, English-language news.

'You should do your journal before we go out for lunch. A little every day,' Noah told him.

A wordless groan.

'Like killing rats.'

The image made Michael's eyes bulge.

'Whack each one as soon as you see it, so they can't form a pack.'

The boy dug into his backpack for the notebook, and Noah began the not-to-be-rushed business of getting his shoes on.

★   ★   ★

The February air was perfumed. A lemon tree was ripening, dangling over a wall. Noah felt his shoulders relax. He spun around until he spotted a burst of open blue sky: the seafront.

'Freaky.' Michael had stopped to examine a four-wheel motorbike, parked next to a one-person car with a zipped plastic window. 'And I've never seen so many turds in my life.' He

162

jumped over a particularly moist, orange-tinged pile.

Noah nodded. 'Make things beautiful, then let your little dogs crap all over them: I'm afraid it's the French way.'

'I've got to post this one.'

For a surreal moment he thought Michael wanted to send the dogshit by mail. But the kid was only taking a close-up of the coil. Michael edited the image with rapid tweaks of finger and thumb.

'If you're really fond of someone, here,' Noah told him, 'you call them '*ma petite crotte*' — 'my little turd.' '

'You're shitting me!'

When they rounded the corner, the crescent bay opened out like the curve of a dancer's arm. Gigantic palm trees shook their heads all along the sweep of the Prom. Behind the line of gracious buildings, the city sloped up toward the darker mountains with their swath of snow.

Six lanes of traffic to cross to get to the sea: an appalling development since Noah's day. 'Wait. Michael! Give me your hand.'

'Hell no.'

'Then just hang on till I say it's safe.'

'It's safe, dude,' Michael called from three lanes across.

Noah paused on the median strip under a lush shrub: oleander? Bird-of-paradise bushes, each flower preening with its crest of orange and blue and a long tapered beak outlined in flaming red. The massive palm trees had bark scored horizontally, and the same pattern appeared on

163

the lampposts as an homage.

A knot of tourists whizzed by on identical heavy blue bicycles.

'Watch out for the bikes!' Noah scuttled across the next three lanes to join Michael.

As the two of them turned west, past the ice-cream cake of the Hotel Negresco (snowy walls, pink dome), the wide expanse of path was thick with promenaders. Sun-leathered women arm in arm with wizened men; kids wobbling and veering on those scooters with two little wheels in front. A tangle of ancient joggers ran by. A teenage girl walked past with jeans half unbuttoned over a thong bikini, which appalled Noah. Boys on in-line skates zoomed through obstacle courses of little orange cones or upturned plastic cups that they'd laid out, it seemed, for the pleasure of mastery. So many North African faces and head scarves — from the former French colonies, of course. Panting slightly, Noah caught up with the boy. 'This is called the Promenade des Anglais, the place the English walked.' A big lungful of the salt-sweet air. 'It stretches for five miles.'

'Are those *people* in the water?'

Dark spots on the waves. 'Yep. It's so mild here, some Niçois — locals — swim all year round. My dad said it was easy enough if you never broke the habit.'

'Hard-core,' Michael murmured.

Though several of these swimmers were wearing wetsuits with neoprene hoods, Noah noticed. Maybe this generation was a bit tenderer than previous ones.

'How come your family didn't move back here after the war?' Michael asked suddenly.

Oddly enough, Noah had never considered this. 'Ah, things were pretty rough in Europe.' This very Prom, for instance; defaced with concrete barricades and rolls of barbed wire. 'Parts of the city were smashed up, rival gangs feuding, not enough to eat . . . ' As he spoke, this all sounded to Noah unnervingly like Michael's ungentrifiable corner of Brooklyn.

He leaned over the rail to look at the bright blue wooden deck chairs and parasols laid out for rent on the gray beach below.

'How come there's no sand?'

'I don't know,' Noah said. 'It's all pebbles around Nice.'

'Why did the French make the English walk here, was it a punishment?'

Noah grinned at the idea. 'Actually it was a luxury thing, having time to go for a walk. The English were the swanky visitors, before the Russians, and then the Americans. 'Winter swallows,' they were called, here for the sun.' He was summarizing what Max Harstad's book said about the grandmother Noah had never met, Isabelle Personnet of the bad lungs. (Though she'd lived another half-century, as it turned out, and what had finally killed her was a bowel complaint.) Noah wondered whether Pierre — who, on the evidence, had begun as an undistinguished painter — would have reinvented himself as a fearlessly original photographer sooner or later, somewhere else, if he hadn't had to bring his wife south to Nice.

Was genius a weed that sprang up anywhere, or did it need a particular habitat? 'Lots of them had TB and hoped the sea air and sunshine would cure them. Unfortunately, bacteria don't care about the weather.'

Michael had found a fallen palm leaf, dried into a sword, and was swiping and stabbing at the air with it.

Noah looked down at the broad path underfoot, dark pinkish tarmac. 'Actually, I seem to remember the Prom is named for the Anglos because they paid for it. During a famine — the orange harvests had failed — visitors got so tired of being bugged for spare change that they hired the beggars to build a walkway.'

'Why didn't they just give them the money?'

'Well, rich people used to think handouts made people lazy.'

Used to think? Joan repeated, sardonic.

Noah found himself brooding over Michael's grandma, dead at sixty-three. Was that what it came down to — was it money that had kept the branches of this boy's family tree apart? Not so much Victor's perversity as a standoffish squeamishness on the part of the haves (Youngs and Selvaggios) vis-à-vis the have-not Davises? How hard had Fernande really tried to connect with Amber and this child? Noah would never know, because he'd never asked her.

He pushed on with the story. 'So instead they forced the starving men and women to build this road for pennies.' Like Amber metalworking while Noah and her son basked in the sunshine.

166

'Children too, younger than you, lugging basins of dirt.'

'*That* shit shouldn't be allowed.'

'Too right.' Noah thought Michael meant child labor, until he followed the boy's gaze to a middle-aged man in a skimpy Speedo. 'Oh, that's just what European men swim in.' Though Noah noticed some of the younger lollers on the stones were in American-style board shorts.

'Tits, even!'

A young woman, stretching out on the stones just under them, was untying her bikini top. Noah shushed the boy sharply.

'If she lays it all out, she has to expect to get looked at.'

'Toplessness on beaches is no big deal here. Let's go find a restaurant,' Noah added, beckoning him away from the rail.

'There's churros.' Michael nodded toward a snack van.

'No, no, a proper meal.' Noah led them back across the Promenade.

They passed canopied tables with suave young waiters calling, 'Hello, *ciao, hola.*' The Belle Époque villas were curvaceous, garlanded. 'See all the decorations on these buildings? The fancy metalwork?' Noah pointed up at a scroll with curlicues.

Michael grimaced, shaking his head. 'All these faces spying on me.'

True, now that Noah looked for them; painted or carved eyes peeked down from nooks and crannies, like a crowd of fairy watchers.

'This frilly shit . . . ' The boy gestured at

167

columns in faux-marble; cement meticulously painted to resemble the more precious stone. 'Life's too short.'

Preoccupied by hunger now, Noah plunged down a side street. 'Well, all the more reason to spend your limited time making something that will last.'

'What'd you make? If you never discovered any meds for cancer.'

Nettled, Noah said over his shoulder, 'I'm not dead yet.' A pathetic answer, because what exactly did he plan on making, in however many years he had left?

He walked into the first restaurant he saw that didn't display its menu in English.

But *déjeuner* was long over, Monsieur.

Noah had forgotten how seriously they took the rhythms of their day here. He was embarrassed to be caught asking for lunch at three in the afternoon; he'd have blamed it on jet lag if he could have remembered the French word.

Finally he found an all-day brasserie with menus in French, English, Italian, and Russian. Several women were lingering over coffee with their little dogs.

Noah ordered himself cod with aioli. Michael picked a burger and fries.

'*Un sirop, Coca?*' asked the waiter.

Michael caught that syllable. 'Coke,' he answered before Noah could say no. He was tapping on his phone already, copying in the Wi-Fi code printed on the menu.

Hoping to distract him from his screen, Noah

flicked through the biography. 'Let me show you what men used to swim in, nearly a century ago.' There, a wasted D. H. Lawrence, skinny as a changeling behind his beard and in a shoulder-to-knee striped swimsuit, emerging from one of the dressing huts that once stood on this beach. The photo was slightly overexposed, eerily bright. Max Harstad suggested that Père Sonne had been hinting at the notion of death as a reclothing, the shedding of a skin. 'How would you like to have to wear one of those?'

'I would *end* anybody that tried to make me.' Then, 'Look, more soldiers.'

Noah watched them pass outside the windows, one a pony-tailed blonde, like some Botticelli with an assault rifle. 'Well, I suppose right here is where the attack happened.'

'The Nazis?'

Noah shook his head and lowered his voice. 'This was just a couple of years ago, a street party for Bastille Day — that's like the French Fourth of July. Right after the fireworks this man drove a truck into the crowds, zigzagged along for over a mile, hunting people down.'

'Holy fuck.'

For once, the kid's word choice seemed justified. 'They had to cover the bodies with tablecloths till the ambulances could get to them.'

Noah jerked slightly as their waiter slapped down a basket of baguette rounds, a slim bottle of mineral water, a glass of red wine.

'Where's the butter?' Michael wanted to know.

'This is how they serve it here.'

169

'Dry? Don't they have any butter?'

'They just don't spread it on their bread at lunchtime. Tell me, what kinds of things did your grandma cook for you?'

'Depends on the time of the month.'

That startled Noah.

Michael snorted. 'Not *that*! You're sick, dude.'

'Well, what was I supposed to think you meant?'

'First of the month, the welfare check comes in, and Grandma's — ' He stopped, fumbling for the right tense. 'She always cooked up a storm, ribs and stuff.'

Noah got it. 'Whereas four weeks later . . . '

'A week or two, max.'

'What would you do then?'

'Well, snap.'

Was this a catchphrase of some sort? 'What does that mean?'

'Duh — SNAP, the card for buying food? But that runs out fast too, because me and Cody are always hungry.'

This had to be some modern form of food stamps. 'So, ah, then?'

A shrug. 'It's all about what's left at the food pantry. Soup, pasta sauce, puddings. Some people go early in the month to get the better stuff, but Grandma never wanted to till she had to.'

Noah understood that. He looked into his wine so his face wouldn't show what he felt.

Then he went off to wash his hands, though the toilet was nasty enough that he regretted it. It was almost comforting to find France had refused to change in this respect.

When Noah got back to the table, Michael was huddled over his phone again. 'What game is that?'

The boy shook his head. 'That crazy-ass guy in the truck. Killed eighty-five! A third of his vies were Muslim like him.'

'Keep your voice down,' Noah whispered urgently. 'Lots of people here understand English.'

Michael put the screen up to Noah's face. 'Is that a leg?'

Blurred footage — taken with a phone right after the attack, it looked like, by someone stumbling along the Promenade. 'Turn it off.' Noah stabbed his finger at the screen but couldn't get it to pause. One long, low-res nightmare; grainy shapes all over the sidewalk, like broken mannequins.

'Game over,' Michael was saying with a kind of awe. 'People throwing babies over fences — '

'Shh!'

The boy finally turned off the screen.

'Our waiter might have been here that night,' Noah told him. 'It's not a goddamn movie.'

'Mom's going to get me a better phone when I give her this one back.'

The kid's pivots in topic and mood made Noah dizzy. He wondered if this device would be entirely obsolescent by the time Amber got out, in more than two more years.

'When's our food coming?'

'When it's ready,' Noah told him. 'Have you had some bread?'

'It's stale.'

'You've heard 'The customer's always right'?'

'Sure.'

'Well, that's in America. Not here.' Noah tried a slice of baguette, but it was indeed hard. (Their fault for lunching so late.)

Michael watched the tennis match showing on a silent TV.

Then the waiter was sliding rectangular plates in front of them. Noah's cod looked perfect, with an assortment of spring vegetables.

'What the crap is this?' Michael demanded.

Noah sighed. 'Is it that French burgers don't come with buns? For a starch, you have the fries.'

'No way is this a burger. It's all raggedy and bleeding.'

Noah had forgotten to warn the waiter that Americans liked their meat broiled into submission. 'They mince the meat up fresh, on the day, and cook it rare — for less time — so it's more tender. Try it.'

'Not in this fucking lifetime.'

Noah reminded himself how the kid must be feeling: off-balance, out of his depth, at sea. He beckoned the waiter over: could the young man's *steak haché* possibly be cooked a little more?

It seemed rude to start his cod until Michael's meal came back. 'Would you like some of these vegetables in the meantime?'

The boy curled his lip and stared at the tennis on the TV.

So Noah ate in silence.

The waiter returned Michael's plate a couple of minutes later with barely veiled disdain: the meat brown, the fries even harder-looking.

Michael pinned the burger with his fork and sank his knife into it. Then threw the cutlery down. 'Still bleeding.'

Noah said, 'That's just the juice of the meat.'

'It's blood, dude! Like the juice of *your* meat would be if I stuck this in you.' Michael snatched up the steak knife again.

Noah looked away from the jagged blade and carried on eating. 'It's only pink. That degree of doneness is called medium.'

'Well, I call it dog food.'

Bereaved, Noah reminded himself. Jet-lagged. Culture-shocked.

Michael tasted a fry. 'I need ketchup.' He darted off.

For a moment Noah thought he was running out of the restaurant.

The boy came back with a cage of bottles from an empty table: mayonnaise, mustard, even genuine Heinz ketchup.

Well, one point for problem-solving. 'Are the fries all right?'

Michael shrugged. 'This is like a kiddie portion. They're cheap, the French.' He ate all the fries except two that had touched the puddle of pink juice.

While Noah was paying the bill, Michael went off to the bathroom. He came back to announce, 'Some lazy-ass pissed on the seat.'

Outside the restaurant, turning back along the Prom, Noah told him, 'In my day it was mostly squat toilets.'

'Huh?'

'Two footpads over a hole, and you crouched down — ' Noah held onto a gold-painted fence and tried to mime it.

'Ew!'

'Well, at least there was no seat to get dirty. But drunks did tend to pee down their legs.'

'Where are we going now?' Michael asked.

'Just strolling.'

The boy let out his breath loudly in protest. Then, 'How come that blonde's got horns?'

Startled, Noah spun around, but it was only a poster for Marine Le Pen on a lamppost. 'Somebody's drawn them on to say that she may look nice, but her party's ideas are like Hitler all over again.'

The boy's head turned to follow a car. 'Another Maserati.'

That reminded Noah. 'Oh, a legendary accident happened on this street.'

'A big pile-up?'

'No, one car. An American ballet dancer, Isadora Duncan, she had on this long scarf and it got caught in one of her wheels.'

'That couldn't happen, dude.'

'Picture an old-timey convertible, with its big wheels sticking up above the side panels, and no mudguards. She got yanked out and dragged — ' Noah made a strangulated face. Then wondered what Rosa would think of his choice of topics. Well, let her try keeping up conversation with this kid all day without resorting to the vulgar and the macabre.

'Was she more famous than our Nodaddy Ding?'

'Far more famous. Isadora's fans used to break the windows of restaurants to get at her. She said we should dance barefoot, the way our bodies told us to. She sunbathed before anyone else . . . ' Noah was flicking through *A Life's Work*, trying to find the iconic close-up of the dancer doing a backbend on the strand, the sea sparking through gaps in her draperies.

'This ballet woman was white?'

'Ah . . . yes.' He showed the picture.

'Called it,' Michael said with a snort. 'Back in Africa people've been sunbathing and dancing barefoot like forever.'

'Fair enough.' Discomfited. 'I suppose all I mean is that she made it fashionable.'

Michael asked for his ice cream in a waffle cone but Noah said no, because the add-ons were always overpriced. So then Michael chose some strange product out of the freezer: tiny pellets of ice cream that he knocked back like peanuts.

Made in USA, Noah read on the discarded packet. So much for educational stimulus in a two-and-a-half-thousand-year-old city; really this week was about junk food in a different time zone.

Tourists passed in Carnival masks, all sequins and feathers, with strings of beads. Michael was goggling at a man on a recumbent bicycle. 'They're good for the back, apparently. They spread the weight,' Noah told him.

'Wouldn't get much respect, though,' the boy said, frozen dots almost escaping out the side of his mouth. 'But I'd go in one of *those*, all right.'

175

He nodded at a passing rickshaw.

'As the cyclist or the passenger?'

The boy grunted at Noah's stupidity. 'Passenger.'

Noah read the price on the pedicab. 'Eighteen euros for half an hour? What a rip-off. If you did the pedaling, how much do you think you'd make in, say, an eight-hour day?' He waited. 'Do the math.'

'You do the fucking math. I'm on vacation.'

It's going to be a long week, Joan said.

They passed a palatial casino with hordes filing through its grand Deco doors. Sloganed T-shirts and ball caps rather than black tie these days. France still got more visitors than any other country in the world, Noah had read. Tourists were never attractive, en masse, but he supposed they were an index of peace and all its mundane joys.

'Can we play?'

'What, baccarat?' Noah joked. 'Blackjack, roulette?'

'Just the slots.'

'Ah, I don't think they let minors in.'

As they walked on, Noah mulled the notion of gambling, of fortune good and bad. Victor with his excellent prospects and lousy luck. 'There's a story about a guy who wins the lottery.'

'Oh yeah?'

'His neighbors say, 'Lucky you!' The guy tells them, 'Wait and see.' He goes out to celebrate and gets in a crash, breaks his leg. Everybody says, 'Bad luck!' He says, 'Wait and see.' Then he — '

'Something good this round?' Michael asked.

Noah nodded. It seemed as reliable a measure of intelligence as any other, that the kid could spot a sequence by the third term. 'He falls for the doctor and she marries him, lucky man! He says, 'Wait and see.' At the wedding he chokes on a fishbone — '

'And he doesn't say anything after that.'

'You get it. Every silver lining has a cloud. As my mom used to say when we were fretting over the chances of something, '*Qui vivra verra*.' If you live, you'll see.' He fumbled for a better, less literal translation. 'Time will tell.'

'Yeah,' Michael said, 'but if you've had seventy-nine years of silver linings already' — he turned on Noah, finger cocked like a pistol — 'you've got no right to bitch even if you drop dead today.'

'Your logic is impeccable, young man.'

Noah was tired again, but they had to do something, anything, before going back to the hotel; all they'd achieved so far was eating.

He paused every time they passed a famous painting reproduced on ceramic at the very spot the artist had stood to work. Most of them had been badly cracked; he wasn't sure whether this meant that people resented art or that drunks would hit anything.

A headland, in front of them. Where the Prom curved around its base, a gigantic sundial was embedded in the sidewalk. 'Kind of cool, right?'

'Kind of lame,' Michael said. But he stood on the right spot and held his head stiff. 'Does my shadow say the right time?'

'More or less, allowing for Daylight Savings.' Noah walked to the concrete barrier; the seafront was high above the waves at this point. He was startled to see young people diving from the rocks. 'About fourteen miles to our left is a tiny country called Monaco — blink and you've missed it — and then Italy,' he told the boy. 'The ancient Greeks settled here first, back before the time of Christ, and they named Nice for Nike, goddess of victory.'

'Like my Jordans?' Michael tilted up one sneaker.

Noah studied it with confusion till he spotted the swoosh. 'Oh, Nike. Right, same goddess. We could go see where they fire the cannon from,' he said, craning up at the green bulge of the Colline du Château. 'It's called the hill of the château — the castle — because it used to have a castle on top.'

'And now it doesn't? Big whoop.' Michael's tone was deadpan. 'Got to check that out ASAP.'

'Well, it's a significant absence. This was the most impregnable fortress on the Mediterranean, till the King of France blew it up and said it was never to be rebuilt.'

'Wait up, isn't *this* France?'

'Ah, now it is, but until 1860, Nice was' — how to explain the complex dynamics among the dynasties of Savoy, Anjou, Piedmont-Sardinia? — 'ah, swapped around between different bosses. There's actually another theory about how the city was named. In Niçois — the local dialect — '*ne za*' means 'neither here,' so the name might mean that Nice is neither here nor there, an in-between place, not really in one country or the other, see?'

Michael only rubbed his eyes.

'My point is, without the fortress there was no military stronghold, so as a sort of booby prize Nice got to become a tourist mecca instead.' Which was why Pierre Personnet had brought his wheezing Isabelle here on the train, this formerly isolated town between mountains and sea, between countries and principalities, where he could metamorphose into Père Sonne. Ergo Margot, ergo Noah and Fernande, ergo Victor, ergo Michael. So many other dots on the map; other ways it could have gone. Maybe history really boiled down to how the hell did *we* happen to happen?

Michael let out a leonine yawn.

'It's a lovely climb to where the fort used to be, and a famous view.'

'Of what?'

'Well, this, but more, farther,' sweeping his arms through the air.

'Pass. Unless we can go in that little train.'

Noah turned to see. *Le Petit Train de Nice*, it said along the side of one of the crammed trailers strung like beads. 'That's not a train, just an open bus, pretending.'

'I know that.'

'And anyway, we don't need a ride, we've got legs.'

'Can we just go back to the hotel?'

Give the kid a break, Joan advised.

★ ★ ★

179

Noah didn't let himself nap again, but he did lie down to look at more pictures in *A Life's Work*. The early 'Valétudinaires' series of celebrity invalids struck him as being much more about death than convalescence. A wan Katherine Mansfield, fingering the crumbling stonework of the arch that enclosed her like a tomb; old Renoir painting in his wheelchair in a garden, brush clutched like a last weapon in a fist deformed by arthritis. Stunted little Toulouse-Lautrec, mugging in drag. Chekhov with drink and pipe outside a café on the Prom, eyes shut against the sunshine: an ancient statue, or a sleeper, or a corpse.

On the narrow camp bed that had replaced the crib while they were out, Michael lay sphinxlike, propped up on his belly. His eyes shifted from side to side, thumb tapping the screen in an uneven, staccato rhythm.

Noah read the caption under the night shot of a young woman called Marie Bashkirtzeff, wrapped up in furs; according to the caption, that weird glint in her eyes was the reflection of the first Casino Pier burning down. How typically perverse of Père Sonne to turn away from the big news of the fire to the watcher; he'd always been committed to the individuals, and to his view of them rather than their own. He never took a fee, preferring to keep a free hand, according to Max Harstad; he supplemented his family money by selling prints and books of his work instead of taking commissions.

'Here's one my grandpa took in 1883, on that hill you wouldn't go up.' Getting off the bed with

180

an effort, Noah showed the boy the picture of a man hunched over a walking stick, gazing down at the panorama. Again, the observer being observed. 'This fellow's a German philosopher called Nietzsche. He used to hobble up that hill every day.'

'Can't see his face,' Michael said. 'He could be anyone.'

Noah was reminded of the couple on the bench in his mother's photo, snapped from behind; also the woman with coiled hair; the dandy in profile, who might have been her lover. But on the other hand Noah might be making up the whole thing with the paranoia of a motherless child. 'Yeah, Père Sonne was fascinated by celebrities, but he made fun of them too. Maybe here he was suggesting we're all the same when we're facing death?' Noah was winging it now, trying to keep the kid interested. 'This guy was such a junkie, by the time he came to Nice, he was faking prescriptions for himself and signing them 'Dr. Nietzsche.''

Michael grinned at that.

But Noah was thinking of Victor. Should he have said *addict*, or *struggling with substance abuse*? Not that he was clear, even now, on what or how much his mercurial nephew had been taking. The thing that had destroyed Victor by twenty-six — could it be called his business, or his illness, or both?

Noah got out Margot's photos for another look.

The empty street might be the Prom, he supposed, because of its wide sidewalk; parts of

181

buildings, a bicycle propped against a wall, a parked car, a seagull picking at garbage. But if so, this snapshot had none of the picturesque aspects that centuries of artists had captured: the skirts, the parasols, the human flow. As if Margot had gone out of her way to pick a moment when nothing worth recording had been happening.

In the shot of himself, smiling little Noé, he looked about three or four. Had she kept it as a memento, after having to leave him on that ship in Marseilles? It was the only one of the set that seemed not to have been taken in a rush.

When Noah scanned it into the image search, the answer was almost comically guarded. 'Best guess: person,' with a link to a definition: 'A person is a being, such as a *human*, that has certain capacities or attributes constituting *personhood*.'

'Great,' he muttered. 'Google can tell it's a person! That one has to be me, though someone's put *RJ* on the back.'

'The kid? He's not you.' Michael reached over to pick up the photo.

'I know the resemblance isn't striking, but who else . . . ' Noah's voice died away as he looked at the picture.

'Nah.'

Michael was right. There was none of that indefinable likeness that made adults recognizable in their baby pictures. 'Of course she could have photographed one of my friends,' he said weakly. (Though he couldn't remember any, except perhaps Madame Dupont's little girl. Corine, was it? Caroline? Camille?) 'But to hold

182

on to it all her life . . . '

'You didn't have any brothers?'

He shook his head.

Michael spoke with a certain delicacy: 'You a hundred percent sure about that?'

Noah's unease was growing. Could Margot and Marc possibly have had a first child, earlier in the '30s, who had died? No, he couldn't believe they'd have kept such a secret. Anyway, the boy in the photo didn't look particularly like any of the family. (Though of course genetic resemblance wasn't always obvious.) This boy had dark hair, a pale face, had recently been ill, perhaps — or did all black-and-white images of children carry a shadow of mortality?

'One of my friends, he was playing handball with this kid that turned out to have the same dad.'

'No, no.' Noah's pulse was loud in his throat. If the dandy had been Margot's lover — If they'd had a secret son, with the initials *R.J.* —

This was absurd. Fathering a child might be kept hidden, but giving birth to one?

After she sent me away, maybe.

No: the reason she'd sent him away. Because pregnancy was something Margot might just possibly have hidden from her aged father, but not from the boy climbing into her lap, so she'd had to put Noah on that ship. If Père Sonne's sharp eye had let him guess, or if Margot had confessed — the photographer would have kept such a shameful secret in the family, wouldn't he?

Oh Christ. That unexplained absence of

Margot's that Madame Dupont had mentioned to the journalist; those two missing nights, three days. In a hospital, giving birth to this R.J.? Such rage, rushing through Noah's veins. The treacherous bitch! To bring this other baby into the world, and then —

Then what? The house cleaner would have said something if Madame Selvaggio had had an infant in tow when she finally came home. Could Margot's lover have taken responsibility for the child? Or had the guilty pair stashed him somewhere — an orphanage? Noah thought a vein might pop in his head. *Think.*

'No,' he said hoarsely. 'Definitely not a brother of mine. Even if they were, ah, involved, there wasn't enough time.' If Margot had given birth during those three missing days, this abandoned child would have been only a few months old when she'd moved to New York after burying her father. And even if he'd been born earlier, soon after she'd packed Noah off on the ship . . . 'The kid can't have been any older than two when Margot left France herself.' What kid? This boy in the photo was not Margot's. 'This fellow has to be three or four,' Noah said, punching his finger at the print, 'and she wasn't even here then.'

Michael squinted at it. 'How do you know it was her took it?'

But it went with the others, Noah thought: the same small format, the same lack of a studio stamp, preserved all these decades in the same envelope.

'Or any of these pics,' the boy added.

Could someone else have shot and developed

184

them, sent them on to Margot years after the war?

Come to think of it, what if they were random rejects, preserved by accident, that Fernande had mistaken for precious relics? Noah had spun this whole web out of his imagination. The story of R.J. the love child might be technically possible, but so were a million other parallel universes.

'I'm hungry.'

Noah was jolted out of his brooding state. It was on the tip of his tongue to ask, 'Again?' But that wasn't fair. Michael was a growing boy. 'OK, we'll go out soon. Though first — ' The demands of the present fell heavy on Noah; almost a relief. 'I should tell Rosa how you're doing.' But how *was* Michael doing? 'What should I say?' he asked over his shoulder, getting out his tablet.

The boy was back on his phone, what sounded like some kind of race-car game.

'Michael?'

'Like, a report?' Apprehensive. 'You going to rat on me about the knife?'

'What knife?'

'In the restaurant. I wasn't — '

'Don't be scared,' Noah told him.

'I'm not *scared*.'

'I just meant I'm not ratting on you about anything.' He sighed. 'Would you prefer to write it yourself, and I won't look?'

'Nah.'

Noah composed a one-liner to the social worker, telling her they'd arrived safely in France and everything was going all right so far. *Seems*

185

to be, he substituted for *was.* It still felt like a lie, but it was technically correct. 'What about your mom, now?'

'What about her?'

'How do you usually stay in touch?'

Michael shrugged glumly. 'She calls sometimes.'

Noah looked up the prison's Communications page. 'Outgoing calls FROM inmates only. No collect calls to cellphones permitted.' Damn. Could Noah send Amber a message to call them at the hotel? But then they'd have to time it just right, allowing for the six-hour time difference, and what if Amber tried and the guy at the front desk said he wouldn't accept a collect call, or didn't understand the American operator's English, and the whole arrangement fell through, with Amber left furious or panicking?

'We had a video visitation on my birthday,' Michael said.

'Really? That sounds nice.'

The small mouth twitched down at the corners. 'It's hard to remember all the stuff I want to tell her. If I say bye before the half hour's up, Grandma's like' — a fierce hiss — ' "That's a waste of money,' and Mom says, 'Let him go,' but I can tell she's crying.'

Noah gnawed his lip.

There was a 'convenient prepaid collect-call option' for cellphones, he found after further digging, but this had to be set up through a third-party vendor by calling an 800 number from within the territorial United States. Jesus, it might be simpler to use a carrier pigeon. 'What

186

about email? Can you email your mom?'

'I guess.'

'Sorry, but I don't know what that means. Yes or no?'

'*Special* emails. Grandma knew how.' Very low, muttered into his phone.

Noah's head was pounding with fatigue. He could always send a message via Rosa, but the woman was busy enough with her twenty-three other cases. (He thought, dizzily, of the multiple complications of all those children's lives.)

He went back to the web page. There turned out to be a rudimentary pay-per-message system: a hefty charge for every page, every picture, every video that would be free to send if you were in the outside world. Sickening, how these companies milked desperate families of millions of dollars. 'OK,' Noah said once he'd managed to set up an account with his credit-card details and downloaded the Correctional Communications app, 'we're through. Go ahead, write your mom a message.' He laid the tablet on the camp bed beside Michael. 'Tell her about the flight, what we've been up to so far.' Eating, walking, squabbling. 'I'll be back. Just don't hit Return till you're all done, OK?'

''Kay.'

In the bathroom, Noah ran the water till it was very cold, and splashed his face with it.

★　★　★

Outside a *fruiterie* about six feet wide, cherries and kumquats were piled lavishly on shelves.

187

'Choose a piece of fruit,' Noah said.

'Are they free?'

'No, no — you go inside to pay.'

The boy's eyes shifted from side to side. 'Don't people just grab them and run?'

'I suppose . . . ' Noah looked for a camera and found only a tilted circular mirror. He pointed it out. 'The staff keep an eye on the mirror. Anyway, pick something.'

'What's up with the grapes?'

'They're just bigger than you're used to, maybe. They've got seeds in them over here,' Noah explained. 'But it's easy to spit them out.'

The boy shook his head nervously.

'A banana, then? An apple?'

'They're scaly-looking.'

The apples were some lovely European variety, pinkish under a delicate filigree of brown. 'I'm having one of those,' Noah said, taking one. 'Come on, the bananas look identical to the ones in New York.'

Michael shrugged, so Noah grabbed a banana for him.

As they walked along he kept noticing store names in English, a sign of the creeping linguistic invasion: Star Hooks Shop, Azur Land, Bio City, Le Relooking, Modern' Copy (but why that apostrophe?). Even the huge vacuum the street cleaner was riding on was called Glutton.

As he munched his apple Noah tilted his head back, resting his eyes on stone ribbons, flowering tendrils of plaster. 'See that word?' A name high on a building. 'That was the architect signing his building. Like a graffiti tagger,' he suggested.

Michael rolled his eyes. 'Yeah, except I bet nobody arrested him.'

They boarded a silver bullet of a tram and leaned on poles opposite each other. 'Kind of like a bus on train tracks,' said the boy.

'Cool, isn't it?'

But Michael refused to go that far. He held his banana tightly as their tram curved around a corner.

The carriage filled up, and kept filling. A jolly woman kept murmuring 'C'est fou!' to her friend — how crazy this crush was, especially around Carnival. Noah belatedly remembered that you had to punch your ticket; he couldn't reach the machine, but another woman took the ten-ride card from his hand and fed it into the slot until it beeped twice, once for him and once for Michael. Her friend offered Noah her seat, which rather offended him. He shook his head, straightened up, and tried to look nearer seventy.

Each upcoming stop was announced with a different recorded voice, one of them a little girl's. 'Creepy,' Michael whispered.

'Eat your banana,' Noah told him.

Michael opened the stem end. One fastidious bite. Another.

'Tastes just like at home, am I right?'

In a robot voice: 'Yes master thank you master.'

'You said you were hungry,' Noah reminded him.

'Changed my mind.'

It was true that appetite could come and go unpredictably when you were having a week like this boy was. Noah remembered not eating a bite at Joan's funeral, then bingeing on leftovers a few nights later until he threw up.

They got down at Place Garibaldi, where bronze lions crouched in a fountain at the foot of a huge monument to the revolutionary. Michael ran along the guano-streaked stone edge, the half-peeled banana flapping like a bird.

Wasn't there a calypso song about a yellow bird? 'Don't go in the fountain, though,' Noah called.

'And wet these kicks?' Michael sounded shocked at the idea.

'These what?'

'My *Jordans*. Grandma got me these for my birthday, on layaway.'

The woman had gone back month after month, paying an inflated price for these sneakers, before she was finally able to take them home to the boy with growing feet? 'That was nice of her,' Noah said, dry-mouthed.

The boy jumped down, and the top half of his banana broke off.

'Michael!'

'Sorry.' The small face blank.

Noah couldn't tell when Michael was genuinely cowed and when Noah was being played.

Michael picked up the pale banana half, now with a cigarette butt stuck to it. He held it as if ready to choke it down.

'Throw it in that trash can over there,' Noah snapped. When Michael came back — 'Now eat the other half, at least.'

190

The boy took a few bites. 'The bottom's smushed.'

Because you've been holding it in a death grip for the last quarter of an hour. But Noah told himself to keep his powder dry; he had the whole week to get through. He took the limp banana out of Michael's hand and went to the trash with it.

An obedient convoy of tourists glided between them on Segways, following a guide with her hair in multicolored braids. 'Can we do that?'

'No.' But Noah seemed to be saying that every time the kid suggested something. 'Not right now. Maybe another day when I'm less groggy.'

Flocks spun over Place Garibaldi, swallows in their thousands, making billowing fabric of the sky. Or were they swifts?

Noah needed another coffee, so they went into a *salon de thé.* The glass case held *mille feuilles,* Opéras, crown-shaped Saint-Honorés, *financiers.* Amazing how the names were flooding back: had Noé's childhood vocabulary mostly been acquired in patisseries? Paris-Brests covered in flaked almonds, macarons in dazzling shades ... He remembered buying Joan an incredibly expensive tube of macarons somewhere in the West Village; every bright color had turned out to taste more or less the same. 'Look, these are *religieuses,* nuns — see their little heads and brown robes?'

Michael grinned at that. He was eyeing chocolate plaques shaped like elaborate masks.

Noah chose something decadent called a *palmier framboise,* two squares of buttery pastry sandwiching raspberry jam.

And for the young man?

'Hungry again, are we, now there's no fruit in sight?' Noah asked Michael. Then felt a little bad.

The boy picked out a pink pig with chocolate eyes.

Waiting for his coffee, Noah noticed daily papers hanging over dangling rods. He took down a local one and read about child migrants (mostly from sub-Saharan African countries) trying to get from Italy via Monaco into France, being kicked off the train at Nice by *gendarmes*. The police were said to steal the SIM cards out of the kids' phones and cut the soles off their shoes before sending them all the way back on foot without water. Many of those kids were now selling themselves to drivers in exchange for a ride across the border into France . . .

'*Votre crème, Monsieur.*'

Noah jumped, and rushed to fold the paper over its rail again.

The interior of the tearoom was full of lean elderly ladies and their shopping bags, and anyway he wanted a cigarette, so he carried their tray out to a small table under the colonnade. The metal legs of his chair grated on the flagstones. He sipped his coffee and bit into his *palmier*, getting powdered sugar all over his pants.

Two men of Noah's vintage went by, and he found he was searching their features for any resemblance to little R.J. in the photo. A war child, was that the phrase for it? (As if the war itself, rather than the suave dandy, might have seduced or forced Margot into letting it inside her, spawning a little version of itself.)

He tried to put his hypothetical half-brother out of his mind and followed Michael's gaze to the young skateboarders — no, *skaters* — zooming, sliding, and leaping around the fountain, skimming along its edge; the grind and crash of their small wheels. It occurred to Noah that he might get Michael a board as a goodbye present, when Amber's sister, Grace, turned up. Well, not goodbye, exactly — they wouldn't be strangers anymore. Maybe Michael could come into Manhattan for the odd Saturday outing?

The boy sank his teeth into the pig's head, then spat it out violently on his plate.

'What is it now?'

'That's not chocolate.'

'Did anyone tell you it was?' Noah scrutinized the decapitated pig. 'Looks like some kind of confectioner's cream, or a mousse, maybe. Try another bite.'

'Try my ass.'

Noah tipped his face up to the sun and asked for patience. After a moment, 'Would you like some of my *palmier*? It's just raspberry jam.'

Michael shook his head. He was tugging off the tablecloth clips and attaching them to different parts of his body.

'What are you doing?'

'Seeing what hurts.'

Boyish curiosity, or another sign of trauma?

Noah couldn't shake the image of Margot and her dandy man, and their hypothetical lost child, taking tea and cakes in Place Garibaldi.

Unless you've made up this whole rigmarole, Joan suggested.

Noah drew on his cigarette. Anchored only by the dishes and vase now, the paper tablecloth was flapping. 'It's going to blow away if you don't put those clips back.'

Michael leaned his elbows on the table, phone in his hands. 'No it's not.'

Tipping his head back to follow the wheeling swifts, Noah spotted a plaque on the column beside his chair: ICI TOMBA, 'Here fell.'

'A Resistance member called Paul Vallaghé was shot right here,' he remarked, 'in the last days of the war. My mother could have seen it. He was only twenty-four.'

'OK, I get it,' Michael said, eyes on his screen. 'Shit happens.'

Amber was in medium security because there was no room in minimum, Noah reminded himself. What was she witnessing, enduring, every day? And all because she'd let her family line get tangled with Victor's. Why was Noah expecting this boy to give a damn about the long-ago sufferings of others?

He tried to get at least halfway through his enormous *palmier*, as he had nothing to carry it in. But it was too much, the glorious butteriness of each flake.

Noah slid the envelope out of his satchel and let himself leaf through the prints. He wondered whether the hidden story they hinted at just happened to unfold during the war, or had it sprung from the war's dangers and allegiances?

Getting out his own phone, he typed in 'French war child' with one finger.

Then wished he hadn't. 'Estimated 200,000 war children sired on French mothers by German soldiers.' That statistic grabbed Noah by the stomach. But just because two hundred thousand women had had war children didn't mean Margot had: he clung to that. Besides, he had no reason to assume the dandy with the cane was a German soldier. He studied that photo again. In profile, the man had a very straight nose that could plausibly be interpreted as . . .

Joan tutted in his head. *Hitler didn't look Aryan, did he?*

True. And no way to know if Margot's lover had been a soldier, in any army. Yes, it would have been a plausible way for him to have injured his leg . . . but such an elegant suit. Then again, soldiers did wear civvies off duty. *Officer material,* Noah wondered? Nights at the Excelsior with his girlfriend, who'd conveniently sent her husband and son off to America? Had Margot, like so many other Frenchwomen, in fear or loathing or defiance, for fun or for food, taken up with one of the invaders?

Funny how the word *collaborator* meant something so benign in Noah's academic world: those who worked together on a paper or experiment. In wartime, the word lost all its overtones of collegiality. *Collabos,* that was the French slang version; after the war they'd strung up thousands from lampposts. Paramilitary *Milice française* fighters, informants, war profiteers, and what was that

195

special idiom for women thought to have slept with Germans? *Les tondues*, that was it, the shaven-heads — hounded through town after town in a brutal parade of vengeance.

Noah tried to remember if he'd ever seen any photos of Margot from the time she'd arrived in New York. Had her hair been long then, as in later years, twisted into a bun? Four-year-olds generally didn't care what their mothers looked like, or remember later. Her bad eye, which she'd always blamed on an untreated infection, but could it have been the result of a beating? Also her knee. And oh Christ, could her punishers have raped her too? But surely Madame Dupont would have told the journalist about it later, if Madame Selvaggio had turned up after three days with a shorn scalp and multiple injuries?

This was ludicrous. Just because his sister had been in possession of some old photos that included a man with a cane and a small boy . . . 'OK, shall we move on?'

'Where?' Michael asked.

'Ah . . . we could walk back to our hotel, but a different way.'

In his robot voice: 'Exciting.'

But first Noah remembered they should use the tearoom's tiny toilet, which was accessed — this cheered Michael — by sliding open a section of the partition wall.

They followed a long green park called the Paillon, new since Noah's day. 'I'm starving,' Michael said. 'Can I get a hot dog?'

'This is France. They eat proper sit-down meals. Where do you think we'll find — '

The boy did a ta-dah gesture at a van that bore a six-foot lurid image of a frankfurter labeled *Le Giant Hot Dog New-Yorkais*.

'Can I just say, if you'd had some of your burger at lunch, you wouldn't be so hungry.' Noah was getting out his wallet as he spoke.

'I'll get it my fucking self then.' The boy broke into a run.

'Michael!' Noah strode after him.

By the time he caught up, the boy was sitting at the picnic table beside the van, head on his arms. Crying?

'Listen,' Noah began.

Michael's dry face snapped up. 'Asshole wouldn't take my money.'

'Because you need euros here.' Noah held out a red ten-euro note.

'It says *New York Style* on the sign!'

Noah went up to the counter to order a hot dog and a bottle of water. The menu also included *Le Hollywoodais*, he noticed, and the pornographic-sounding *Le Very Big*.

'Coke,' Michael ordered from behind him.

'Water,' Noah said firmly.

With gas?

No. '*De l'eau plate, Monsieur, s'il vous plaît*.'

Michael devoured the hot dog, which — thankfully — came with a New York-style bun.

'*S'il vous plaît* means *please*,' Noah mentioned, 'and for *thanks* you say *merci*.'

Michael added more ketchup.

Noah nudged the water bottle toward him.

Michael ignored it.

197

Once the hot dog had been consumed, Noah said, 'Have some water.'

'Don't like water.'

'Is this some kind of thirst strike? Look, I'll make you a deal. I'll buy you soda with one meal every day we're here, so long as you drink water the rest of the time.'

A long, tactical pause. Then, ''Kay.'

On the next stretch of the park, Michael went up close to examine one of those gigantic, sword-armed plants, like a cross between a dinosaur and an octopus.

Noah tried to remember the name for it: agave? Bristling cacti sent up long columns with bursts of yellow and orange tubes at the top. Mouse-eared ones were topped with pink ovals, each with their own needles. Red succulent blooms.

Michael moved to stroke a little tuft.

'Don't — '

But he spoke too late; the boy was glaring at his fingertip. 'Fucking thing's left like a million spikes in me.'

Noah sighed. 'Don't rub, you'll only irritate the skin more. We'll have to tweeze them out.' One of his more adventurous freshman students had gotten a rash from a prickly pear that had lasted six months, he remembered.

'Then do it!'

'My tweezers are back at the hotel.'

As they walked, Michael kept examining his finger, and Noah kept reminding him to leave it alone.

The streets around the train station rumbled

with the low-level friction of suitcases on wheels. Noah could feel things getting busier as the first weekend of Carnival approached. Tourists lurched along under top-heavy backpacks (six times the size of Michael's). One tiny man had both a pack and a roller case.

There was their hotel at last. But Michael still lagged on the far side of the road, behind a parked car, looking down. 'Noah?' he called. 'What's this?'

He wondered if it was another champion dog turd.

'Something about . . . Auschwitz.' Michael tripped over the pronunciation.

Another commemorative plaque, then. Noah crossed back over and steeled himself to scan the white letters chiseled in black marble: *Les victimes avaient été internées dans l'Hôtel* . . . What the hell?

'It means our hotel, right? The Excelsior?'

Noah couldn't answer the boy; couldn't speak. Between September 1943 and August 1944, he was reading, the Nazis had requisitioned the Hotel Excelsior for its convenient proximity to Nice's central train station, and had held more than three thousand Jews here before sending them off to Drancy, the transit point for Auschwitz.

He goggled at the pretty balconies across the street. Usually a plaque was attached to the building or spot where something had happened, but in this case he could see why the owners would have wanted it on the other side of the road, preferring to emphasize the hotel's older heritage as a coaching inn. Noah was busy trying not to picture the charming lobby as it had been in 1944, crammed with huddled adults, big-eyed children waiting in every bedroom. 'We've, ah, somehow ended up staying in the Nazi HQ.'

'Wow.'

'Not wow. They locked up three thousand people here for being Jewish, then sent them off to be murdered in the camps.' Would Rosa approve of him telling the boy this? Noah didn't care; it had to be told.

Chastened, the boy scanned the hotel's gracious lines. 'How come your mom had a picture of this place?'

Something in Noah's belly torqued. 'I don't know.' It could be just a coincidence. Presumably people came to the bar here for cocktails long before the Nazis took over the building.

But why the photograph, then? Joan asked.

'Can we go to that?'

Michael was pointing at a garish advertisement for an old-style circus. (*Vrais tigres de Sibérie*, with a picture of a glowering tiger.) 'No.' He corrected himself: 'I mean not right now.'

'When, then?'

'Another day, when I'm over my jet lag.' Noah was repulsed at the thought of walking through the doors of the Excelsior, but that's where their baggage was, and they had nowhere else to stay. Besides — 'Your finger. Let's get those prickles out before they fester.'

Upstairs in the bathroom, Michael writhed away from the tweezers.

'Hold still, I have to pull them all out. It

shouldn't hurt.' If this didn't work, Noah would have to buy some glue. He toiled on, squinting at the boy's fingertip, securing the minute barbs one by one.

'Done?'

'I think so.' Noah released him.

'Goddamn plant.'

'Evolution protects those who protect themselves. You'll know better next time.'

'Not gonna be a next time.'

Did Michael mean he wouldn't be stroking that kind of vegetation again? Or that he was planning never to leave New York for the rest of his life?

★　★　★

Nine o'clock already.

Michael's journal entry was like some handmade parody of a children's book, illustrated with stick figures:

Today with my Super Great Uncle I did some real educashional stuff like seen a beach with no sand and giant dog turds and walked about a million miles.

The next page showed a Michael with hashtags for eyes and lightning coming out of his ears, attached to the wall by the cord of his phone. *Warning: Europeen Power Zaps Like Double!!!*

'Your teacher's going to think I let you get electrocuted, and I'm unfit to be looking after you.'

'Nobody's going to read this shit.'

201

Well, by the time someone did, it was likely not to be Noah's problem because Aunt Grace would be in charge. He handed back the notebook and got to his feet. 'Dinner.'

Turning down the first alley, they passed a beggar who looked like a bit part out of *Les Misérables:* draped in plaid blankets, with an old black coat and a flat-topped, vaguely military cap.

Michael kept glancing around.

'What's up?'

'Nothing.'

Under the next lamp, Noah told him, 'It seems perfectly safe here.'

'Like you'd know.'

Fair enough: Michael probably had more in the way of street smarts. And more reason to be wary of the kind of things that could happen the minute you stepped out your door. Noah turned into the next restaurant that still had its lights on.

Michael's *nuggets poulet avec frites* came fast, and he downed them even faster. The kid had figured out that the *menu enfant* always came with a choice of drink, so he was on his second Coke of the day. 'That's breaking our deal already,' Noah pointed out.

He shook his head. 'You said you'd only *buy* me one a day. This one is free.'

When Noah's *plateau de fruits de mer* arrived — with its giant prawns, sea snails, crayfish with long whiskers and bulging black eyes — Michael gaped.

The idea of the platter had appealed to Noah's

nostalgia, but his appetite quailed at the size. Mostly shell, he assured himself, sipping his glass of rosé. 'Want a picture?'

'Hell yeah.'

Noah had meant a view of the plate from above, but Michael seized the biggest crayfish with squeamish relish and held it close to his cheek, pulling a face as he snapped a selfie with the other hand.

'Shall I take one of you, for a better angle?'

'I'm good,' Michael told him.

'You can't have got much of the crayfish in the frame.'

'It's a selfie, dude.'

Every genre of photography had its own conventions, Noah supposed. 'I've never taken one, myself.'

'Seriously?'

'Whereas your photos — it's going to look like you went around France on your own.'

'Oh, I beg your pardon, Mr. Great-Uncle, sir. Should I be Instagramming your baldy head?'

Noah chuckled at the thought. He used an empty pair of shells as tongs to retrieve the mussels' little meats. 'Want to try?'

''Kay.' Michael picked up a shell and nipped at the tablecloth with it.

'I meant try a mussel.'

'Nah. They smell like pussy.'

Noah considered several possible answers: *That's incorrect*, or *That's misogynist*, or *You're the most consistently crass person I've ever had the misfortune to vacation with*. Instead what came out of his mouth was, 'Like you'd know.'

Michael snorted so hard, Coke ran out his nose.

Noah grinned. When this kid's hard shell inched open . . . 'You look like your dad,' he found himself saying.

Michael stared. 'No I don't.'

'Just a bit, when you're laughing.' Not Vic's beauty, but his impudence.

A long pause.

Noah wished he hadn't killed the moment.

'Vic was cool,' the boy said at last.

'Yeah?'

'He took us out to Mickey D's.'

Noah didn't know where that was. 'Did you see much of him, after your mother' — don't fudge it — 'went to prison?'

'Sometimes. The first time he came around,' Michael muttered, 'Grandma wouldn't let him in.'

Noah wasn't surprised to hear that. How enraged Ella Davis must have been by this young man who'd grown up with all the advantages and thrown them away; who'd bulldozed her daughter's life.

'He kept saying how much he loved Mom, how he'd trade places with her in a second if he could.'

Why hadn't Victor admitted the whole stash was his, then, the night they were arrested? 'He didn't suggest you move in with him?'

'He had to travel for his work.'

Noah privately rolled his eyes at that — his shambolic nephew, like some careworn business-man on the road . . .

'He said when Mom got out we'd live together, all three of us,' the boy said into his plate.

★　★　★

Taking the long way back to the hotel, Noah appreciated the lights strung through the trees. But they made him think of the war, as everything did at the moment. 'During the Occupation — when the German army took over from the Italians — you had to tape black over every window so American bombers wouldn't spot any lights. And there was a curfew, which meant everybody had to stay indoors after dark.'

'I know what a freaking curfew is.'

'Of course you do.' *Home by four thirty every day.*

They walked in silence for half a block.

'Mom and Grandma were all about the curfew,' Michael said.

'Yeah?'

'You come straight home from school now' — in a gravelly old-lady voice — 'and stay inside, live to be a man. Hanging around on the corner, you're going to end up getting yourself shot like Cody.'

Noah had never thought of rough neighborhoods quite that way before: like living under siege. 'Is that how your uncle ended up in a wheelchair?'

Michael nodded. 'He ran a corner store. Thugs came in for this guy they had a beef with, and one of the bullets hit Cody.'

'Oh my god.'

As they walked the last few blocks to the Excelsior, Noah tried to see the city through this boy's eyes. The ornateness, the prettiness, little oases of grass everywhere: did it strike Michael as enviable or just trivial? Windows full of shiny goods, families laughing on patios at ten o'clock at night. Nothing boarded up or burned out, rusted or crunching underfoot; no screeches of sirens.

But all Michael commented on was how close the cars were parked. 'They're like, touching,' he complained, squeezing between two fenders as he followed Noah across the street.

'Well, Europe's more densely populated than the States.'

Michael stopped to take a selfie with a wooden cutout of a wine bottle taller than himself.

★   ★   ★

The sight of the Excelsior made Noah sick. He should have already found them somewhere else to stay. Was it sheer laziness? No. Because of his mother's photo of this hotel, something in Noah felt compelled to mount these stairs to the blue room.

His eyes were sandy and his head was spinning. Only four in the afternoon, back in New York, but on the other hand he and Michael had barely slept on the plane. The ache in his hip was spreading right into his groin, down his thigh, even: too much walking. European pillows were all wrong: the small cylindrical bolster

206

pressed painfully on his neck, and the big square pillow Noah could use only by sliding his body so far down that his feet were crushed by the footboard. He tried folding the square in half, but that felt like a spring that would hurl his head sideways.

Michael was playing on his phone, his face grave with concentration.

Exhausted, but oddly enough not sleepy yet, Noah checked his email in case there were any messages from Rosa (or Amber, in response to whatever snitching of his own Michael might have done). Instead he found one from Vivienne with a link to a little museum about Nice during World War Two that she'd come across, 'to help work out whether your mother's photos do date from then. I've been in touch — ask for a Monsieur Benoit, he's there on Thursday and Friday afternoons.'

She was an interfering nagger, but it was all kindly meant.

Noah refolded the pillow. He couldn't keep at bay his worries about the Excelsior's black doors. Maybe Margot had just wanted a discreet, private reminder of the place she'd been happy with her lover. Her lover the Nazi, by any chance?

Now that's sexist, assuming she could only have come here for a man, Joan pointed out.

Noah tried again. His mind was so muddled.

Think like a scientist.

If the little R.J. in the picture was Margot's son, and born during the war, then his father might or might not have been a German.

If R.J. was not Margot's, then there was no reason to assume she'd taken a lover during the war. And if it wasn't to meet a lover, Margot must have had some other reason to come to the Excelsior, or at least to photograph its entrance.

If she'd taken that picture before September 1943, it was a weird coincidence that the hotel would go on to be commandeered by the Nazis.

If she'd taken the picture after September 1943, it had to have had something to do with the Nazis. And if not an affair . . .

He looked up 'France Nice collaborators war' on his phone. Mostly fans enthusing about games called *Gears of War* and *God of War*. Noah tried again, with different wording, and came across a headline that punched him in the chest: 'Up to a Million French May Have Spied for Germans.' Could that possibly be right?

The article quoted a new study claiming that far from there having been two smartly booted Gestapo agents on every corner, as in the movies, Nazi investigations almost always began with spontaneous tip-offs from civilian informants — the eyes and ears of fascism. These *indies* (short for *indicateurs*) were more familiarly known as *mouches*, flies, and their motivations seemed to have been personally malicious as often as mercenary or ideological: petty disputes between neighbors, colleagues, in-laws . . .

Noah forced his thoughts down that track.

Was it conceivable that his mother could have been one of those everyday monsters? A covertly self-righteous hag who tidied up her father's

208

studio and cooked his lunch before taking a streetcar to the Hotel Excelsior to denounce communists, queers, prostitutes, and above all, Jews?

But Margot was lovely, Noah protested, *inside and out. She taught kids to play piano.*

Close to a million French people did it, though; came to the invaders with information, to sell or just to offer as a gift. If the country couldn't shake off anti-Semitism today, think how rife it must have been in 1943. A well-bred, Catholic, intellectual woman, edging over to the *collabo* side of the line . . . was it really inconceivable?

Noah sat up, arms wrapped around himself. Impossible. He knew his own mother. Margot had always voted Democrat. (Hadn't she? Or had Noah just assumed?) She'd never expressed anything hateful. (Not in her children's hearing, anyway.) She and Joan hadn't got on particularly well, but Noah had chalked that up to Joan's abrasiveness; his wife had had little time for women without serious careers. But their conversations had always been perfectly civil. Surely if his mother had been secretly anti-Semitic, Joan would have sniffed it out?

Oh, now you've nothing to say? he complained. *Help me out here: could my mother have given aid and comfort to the Nazis?*

No answer from Joan.

Noah got into his pajamas and went into the bathroom. He used the various flosses and implements his patchwork of crowned teeth and bridges required. He was working himself into a

209

tizzy, he knew. Suspecting his mother of being a fascist informer just because she had a snapshot of a hotel!

None of Michael's things were in the bathroom, Noah noticed. He stuck his head into the bedroom. 'You can just leave your tooth-brush and so on beside the sink, you know. Nobody will take it.'

''Kay.'

Slipping under the sheets, Noah reached for the main switch. 'I'm turning off the light now.'

No response.

'You should get ready for bed too. OK, Michael?'

In the dark, the boy's face was creepily lit up by his small screen, the wavering glow of the game. His thumb flickered, sometimes tapped the screen. Focus, patience, swift decisiveness. Now and then Michael let out a frustrated gasp, but he never stopped.

Sounds of gunfire, at intervals. Small roars — of pain? Noah wondered whose pixel blood was getting spilled. 'That's all chemistry, too.'

'Huh?'

'Your game. Semiconductors such as silicon — they're elements with this amazing trick of letting electricity pass much more easily in one direction than the other.'

No response from the boy.

Phone off now, Noah should say. But he felt an already familiar weariness at the prospect of an argument. Looking after a child was like a bad dream about appearing in court without legal training. Added up, presumably the points

210

at issue mattered, but taken one by one they seemed irrelevant. And really, who was Noah to tell this boy when to go to sleep? Circadian rhythms kept teens up at night. Plus, Michael was jet-lagged. Plus, brokenhearted.

In the silence, Noah fell over the edge into a doze.

Waking a little later — an hour, maybe? — he sat up and found Michael still in his clothes, keeled over, off the side of the bolster, his darkened phone against his cheek. Noah slid the device out of his sweaty grasp and set it on the bedside table. He wondered whether Rosa would expect him to wake the boy to make him undress and brush his teeth. Well, too bad.

He watched Michael sleep, that reassuring regular rise and fall of the ribs. Not cute at all; powerful. A tiny sound, as if he was sucking his tongue. The extraordinary thing about children was that they changed all the time, Noah thought, but not by attrition, the way adults did. Kids were always growing, moving up, away from their only ever temporary carers.

5

Neither Here nor There

In the morning Michael was up and dressed and antsy. 'Can we get out of here?'

'Just give me a chance to dress. Are you that hungry?' Noah doubted the kid was getting enough sleep. Perhaps he should have taken the phone away from him last night, even if it had led to a fight.

'Did my mom answer?'

Noah rubbed his eyes and swiped his tablet, looking for the right app. 'Ah, not yet. Remember it's still nighttime for her. And she's probably . . . I doubt she's allowed at the computer whenever she likes.' Noah tried to imagine the compulsory beat of an incarcerated day.

Breakfast was served downstairs in a dining room with see-through chairs and pictures of palm trees. Old American pop played over the speakers. Noah's large *crème* was about a quarter the size of a New York latte, but he appreciated the hit. Michael turned up his lip at the cucumber water and rejected the croissants, but drank both their glasses of orange juice.

Would the boy's stomach be a vat of acid now? Oh well, vitamin C, at least.

'On Saturday, there's a Bataille des Fleurs — a mock battle — with people dressed up and

212

throwing flowers at the crowd,' Noah told Michael.

'Do we get to throw them?'

'Well, I think the idea is for us to catch them, as many as we can.'

'Lame,' Michael muttered.

'Then on Sunday night we're going to the Corso, the Carnival parade. But I haven't planned anything else. What kind of thing should we get up to today?'

A shrug.

'We could take a train to a town called Menton where they make pictures out of lemons. Huge sculptures — scenes, really.'

'Just lemons?' The boy was incredulous.

'Various citrus fruit. I guess they had a glut one February, too big a harvest, so they had to get creative,' Noah said. 'Want to check it out?'

Michael mimed putting a gun to his head and firing.

'OK, no lemons. Let's see. I do want to visit my grandfather's grave in the old cemetery at some point.' He might even spot the rectangle with the circle and two dashes, if it was a tomb.

'More dead people? Not today,' Michael pleaded.

Noah supposed the Nice war museum would come under the same heading. 'What about a gallery, then? The South of France has always been full of artists.'

'We did that already in Manhattan. The drainpipe pic.'

Noah licked his finger to collect a flake of

croissant. 'Are you going to say no to everything?'

The boy jerked his head toward the ceiling. 'Just leave me in the room, chillin'.'

'I can't do that.' Tempting, though. As a Person in Parental Relationship, surely Noah had the right to leave an eleven-year-old on his own once in a while? 'What about . . . there's a sort of zoo, with otters and iguanas and, ah, lemurs, I believe.'

'I'm not some little kid.'

Noah got to his feet. 'True. But you've used up all your vetoes.'

'My what, now?'

'Your no votes. Let's go.'

'Not the freaking lemons!'

'I promise, no lemons.'

They went up to the room for Noah to brush his teeth and collect his satchel. Michael insisted on taking the elevator back down; Noah, hurrying down the stairs with a childlike ambition to get there ahead of his great-nephew, almost tripped on the last flight. *Watch it*, he scolded himself.

As they walked away from the front desk, Michael asked, 'How come you gave back the key?'

'They hold it for you while you're out.'

'But they could go in and steal your shit.'

'They have duplicates anyway. How do you think the chambermaids get in to tidy up?'

Michael's face was horrified.

It struck Noah that the boy had never stayed in a hotel before.

214

'I don't want them going in.'

Did he fear they'd steal some treasure of his — his grandma's glasses? 'They're not going to take anything of yours.'

'They'll see.'

'What?'

Michael's face was suffused with red.

Noah put a hand on the boy's narrow shoulder.

Michael threw it off.

'What's up?' Softly. 'What'll they see?'

'The freaking bed.'

'What about it?'

A word barely mouthed. 'Wet.'

'Oh.' Like the other night in Noah's apartment, the sheets Michael had washed by hand. 'Oh,' Noah said again, mildly, in case he'd sounded stern the first time, 'is that all?'

The boy scowled, as if Noah was making fun of him.

He'd read something about this, hadn't he — bedwetting as a sign of extreme stress. He couldn't remember whether it was because the exhausted child was so tired he slept too deeply to wake, or so agitated he slept restlessly, which upped metabolic production of urine. 'Don't worry about it, is all I meant. It can happen when you have a lot on your plate. They'll change the sheets.'

Michael, through his teeth: 'They'll be mad.'

'Not a bit, it's routine.' Noah jerked his head toward the doors and led the way out of the lobby.

In the sunny street, he mentioned, 'Joan and I

215

were once staying in a five-star swanky hotel in Chicago, and she woke up in a gigantic puddle of blood. It looked as if there'd been a murder.'

The boy's eyes bulged.

'Just from her period,' Noah told him.

'That's revolting, dude!'

Noah thought of telling the boy that their bodies were just as messy as women's, but that discussion could be postponed. 'We'll tip the chambermaids when we leave, OK?'

Warily. ''Kay.' Michael crossed the road.

'Careful!' Noah hurried after him.

They worked their way through the streets.

'Where are we going?' Michael asked, at his side.

'Nowhere in particular. I'm waiting for inspiration to strike.'

Outside the Lycée Masséna, the boy eyed the white ornamented walls, the decorative frieze under the roofline. 'Pretty fancy for a school.'

Noah was reading a plaque. 'Students from here joined one of the first Resistance groups in Nice.'

'What happened to them?'

'Well . . . ' He read on, and sort of regretted bringing this up. 'They fought very bravely till the end of the war.'

'They won?'

'These particular boys died,' Noah had to admit, 'but their side won.'

He eyed the modern teenagers variously smoking and vaping against the wall, and tried to imagine how their forebears had managed to rise to the occasion, back in 1940. If the US were

216

invaded, Noah found himself wondering, where would he find himself on that spectrum from fighter to nervous bystander to *collabo*? He couldn't know for sure, but he'd lay money that heroism was not in his nature.

Michael had found another sign below a small tree. '*Oliver*. Is one of the Resistor guys buried under here?'

'No, it's *olivier*, an olive tree.' Noah patted the gray bark. 'A symbol of peace.' Because of the dove carrying the sprig to announce the end of the Flood? Noah had never liked bearing the name of that cranky patriarch. 'Olive trees grow so slowly, it's said you don't plant one for yourself or even for your kids, but for your grandkids.'

'What if you don't have any?'

'It's a metaphor. It just means future generations.'

What had Noah planted? He'd contributed to some minor discoveries in polymer science, he supposed. As a professor, he'd helped shape the minds of wave after wave of students; that probably counted for more.

Across the street was a long park stretching over several blocks, with huge trees and a bronze copy of Michelangelo's *David*. Michael sniggered. Because of the inevitable splatter of greenish guano on the statue's head, Noah wondered? Or the —

'Micro dick!'

'In the sixteenth century, they thought it looked better like that.'

'No way!' Michael zoomed in and snapped.

217

'Well, at least for sculptures: more discreet and elegant.' Presumably Renaissance Italians had valued big dicks in real life?

Noah went over to a sign about the native-plant garden. The scrawny carnations reminded him of watching flower-pickers toil in the hills above Nice — unless that was another false memory?

On the next block stood a bizarre playground of sea creatures. The silver tongue of a huge, wooden-ribbed whale was a slide; the rope-covered saucers that hung under the giant octopi were swings. The place was deserted except for a drunk asleep on a bench, and a couple of men in neon-orange uniforms armed with trash grabbers and plastic bags, as well as portable tanks. The grass turned out to be fake, when Noah looked more closely; they were spraying something, presumably to dust it. 'You need some exercise,' he told Michael.

'I'm eleven.' Scathing.

Noah went over to read the sign. 3–12 ACCOMPAGNÉ D'UN ADULTE. 'It's for up to twelve-year-olds. Think of it as a gym.'

'Only jocks go to the gym.'

'No need to classify yourself, this young. We've all got muscles.'

'Barely,' Michael muttered, tugging down his sleeves.

A security guard of some sort glided by on a Segway. Noah wondered if in a couple of generations the human race would live in wheelchairs. 'Go on, show me how high you can climb.'

An extravagant sigh. Spotting a vaguely pyramidal spider's web thirty feet high, the boy made a beeline for the top, then reclined there, dangling in the ropes.

Noah smoked a cigarette on a bench, thinking ruefully of the fostering leaflet: 'guidance, discipline, and a good example.'

He brooded over the rearview shot of the couple on the bench in his mother's photo: like a botched version of one of Robert Doisneau's iconic pictures of lovers.

After five minutes, Michael slithered down.

'Got a rope burn?'

'No,' Michael said unconvincingly, hiding his hands in his pockets.

He went over to stuff his legs into the ride-on fish that said it was for ages three to six, and made it plunge so far backward and forward that it almost hit the ersatz turf. Then he hopped in reverse along the rail of the wooden ship, hands in his pockets, refusing to look at his feet.

Noah shut his eyes and imagined the paperwork involved on both sides of the Atlantic if the kid were to smash his head, on Noah's watch. (In fact, by his order: 'The old dude made me go up there!') Social services and French people were two groups notorious for red tape. How would Noah ever get permission to bring the small coma patient — or corpse — back to New York?

The scarlet-faced man sleeping on the bench opposite sat up and rubbed his beard. Then folded up the long piece of cardboard he'd been lying on, with an odd fastidiousness, tucked it into the huge plastic bag that held his other possessions, and went off about his day.

Michael hung underneath the saucer, somehow clinging on. Then stood on the exposed springs of the manta ray, jumping up and down as if trying to break them. He came down the slide headfirst, gazing at the sky; Noah had to avert his eyes again for fear of some neck-cracking landing.

'Look, Great-Uncle Noah,' Michael squealed in what Noah supposed was meant to be an English accent, 'I'm having so much fun!' Riding on the head of the sad-looking wooden turtle, grinding his pelvis into its neck, taking a lewd close-up. Then he jumped down and said, in his own voice, 'I need a bathroom.'

Noah felt an irrational surge of exasperation. He scanned the park in all directions. 'There — over that door, it says *Public Toilets*.'

He savored the solitude for a minute.

Then Michael was back, glowering. 'Some woman in heels tried to hit me up.'

A mugging, did he mean? A beggar? Then Noah remembered that French bathrooms always had an attendant. 'How much, did her sign say?'

'Fifty cents.'

'That's how she gets her wages. Here's a euro — she'll break it for you.'

When he came back the boy said, 'Look at that big-ass Ferris wheel,' pointing toward the far end of the park where a vast circle stretched into the sky. 'Can we go on it?'

'Another day, maybe.' Distracted by a man

rolling on the grass in apparent agony, Noah didn't see the leaf of a low-hanging palm tree until it spiked him in the scalp, which Michael found hilarious. Actually there were three men, all belly down on the ground, all clutching their ankles, so Noah deduced that it must be in the service of fitness. 'I need a coffee.'

'You're a fiend for that stuff.'

'Well, you're just as bad with your soda, and that's worse for you.'

'You freaking smoke, dude. Touché!'

'See, you *do* know some French,' Noah said.

In the café, Michael played his Twenty Questions ball. He stretched in the chair, making the wicker creak.

Reading the chalkboard menu, Noah smiled. ''*Un café*,' one coffee — '*sept euro*,' seven euros.'

The boy didn't look up but he asked, 'For one cup, seriously?'

'Listen to the next item. '*Un café, s'il vous plaît*' — that means 'A coffee, please' — five euros.'

'Huh?'

Noah translated the third line. 'And '*Good morning, Madam, a coffee, please*' is only two euros.'

Michael got it. 'Like a fine for disrespect.'

'More like a discount for good manners.'

The woman finally came over, and Noah requested his coffee, and baguette and butter for Michael, as graciously as he could.

'*Merci*,' Michael muttered, surrendering his menu. After she walked away, he whispered,

221

'What's she looking so sour for?'

'That's a neutral expression here. The French save their smiles for people they like. They call us hypocrites for grinning at strangers.'

Michael nodded. 'I get that. Every damn morning, our first-grade teacher was like, 'Now who's got a big smile for me?''

Noah's mouth twitched. 'Still, could be worse. When I first came to New York, my nanny — if I didn't use my fork in what she considered the proper way, she'd bang my knuckles with it.'

'Bitch! Did she expect you to smile too?'

'No, Miss Sprule would probably have smacked me if I'd smiled. Different rules.'

'Did you tell on her?'

'Complain to my father, you mean? It never occurred to me. Kids generally didn't.'

'Then how come you're pro-snitching now?' Michael asked.

Noah stared. 'Am I?'

'You said I should have snitched on the dickheads that took my board.'

Noah barely remembered how that conversation had concluded. This boy had a Velcro mind; details stuck to it. 'Well, that was an actual crime.'

'So's whacking a kid with a fork.'

'I see that now. But back then . . . kids were meant to be grateful. Maybe especially because it was wartime, and we were lucky enough to be in the States, with plenty of food, instead of Europe.'

'Where other kids were getting gassed in ovens.'

Noah blinked; nodded. He supposed it was

good they still taught that much in school.

His *café crème* arrived, with a tiny rectangular speculaas. He dipped the cookie in the coffee to awaken the spices. No Proustian moment, but it was tasty.

Michael wriggled in the wicker chair, slathering his long cuts of baguette with butter.

'Drink your water,' Noah reminded him.

The boy sipped it like medicine.

Now Noah couldn't shake the thought of the gas chambers.

He'd slept reasonably well last night. How could he have slept well in that room?

Succumbing to a morbid impulse, he looked up 'Nazis Excelsior Nice.'

He couldn't stop himself from clicking on one link after another. *Adolf Eichmann's top aide, SS Captain Alois Brunner, watched night after night from one of the hotel's elegant second-story balconies as his men's black Citröens and trucks pulled up, loaded with Jews. By September 1943 the cafés and hotels of Nice were full of refugees who'd fled to that cosmopolitan haven from all over Europe. The first harvest was easy, but to hunt down the rest, the Nazis relied more and more on informers.*

Margot. No, no, no. This was pure speculation, and tacky, frankly. Just because she'd had to — chose to — no, felt she'd *had to* — stay away from her little boy for two years, had he any right to accuse her of being an informer?

Head reeling, Noah rested his eyes on Michael, who was spinning a euro coin on the polished table. Shouldn't the kid have only fifty

223

cents left? 'So the bathroom lady didn't charge you after all? Nice of her.'

Michael snorted. 'I didn't go back, that's wasting good money. Took a whiz behind a tree instead.'

Well, Noah could hardly tell him, 'Never pee outdoors,' when Frenchmen were so known for it that their cities always had a urinous waft. 'I don't think fifty euro cents is enough to buy you anything except a pee.' He pulled out his billfold. 'You really should have an allowance for this week.' He slid ten euros across the table. 'That's about twelve US dollars. Not to be spent on extra Cokes, OK?'

''Kay.' Michael pocketed the note. 'Thanks.'

Noah got to his feet, leaving coins on the saucer for the waitress.

Out in the sunshine, he led the way past cheap luggage stores. The Vieille Ville — Old Nice — had to be south of here, but he was all turned around. Ah, there was a tunnel roofed with gold, steps leading down: could it be through there? He ducked into the tunnel and descended into a warren of lanes, the boy behind him.

Noah stood staring around.

'Are we lost?'

'No, it's just that this part of town — it used to stink. Garbage, rats.' The old slum still had its picturesque proportions, barely changed since the seventeenth century — shadowed alleyways with terraced houses almost touching four or five stories overhead. But now every gutter was clean enough to eat out of, low doors leading to leather or jewelry workshops, bikini boutiques.

'They've polished it up so much, it's more like a film set.'

'This bit still stinks,' Michael said as they went around a corner.

'Only because of that fancy cheese shop over there.' Grinning plaster cows of various sizes stood below the gracious capitals of FROMAG-ERIE, and weird-looking rounds of cheese filled the window: blackish, and red, and green. 'France has more cheeses than days in the year. What's your favorite cheese?'

A shrug. 'American.'

'Shall we go in?' Noah suggested.

'*Pew.*'

'All right.' As they walked, he told the boy, 'The French say '*beurk*' when they're disgusted. And '*pan-pan*' for *bang-bang*, and '*aïe-aïe-aïe*' for *ouch*.'

'Freaky.'

Noah tried to think of a few others. 'Roosters go '*cocorico*' . . . ' Something just out of reach, over the rim of his memory. A song? *Chaque matinée, chaque matinée, cocorico, cocorico.* Had that been her name, the cleaner's child? How could a girl in the 1930s have been named Cocorico?

No, Coco, that was it. Coco, the daughter of Madame Dupont — she must have been named for Chanel. But Noah remembered that he used to call her Cocorico for a joke. Would she by any chance still be alive, he wondered, and living in or near Nice?

The tourists who were wandering in aimless appreciation through the Vieille Ville were clearly distinguishable from the inhabitants who had things to do: skinny kids, workmen, bowed old ladies filling their string bags with the day's provisions. Michael blew five euros on a selfie stick from a gaunt young North African selling them out of a basket on his back.

Noah didn't mention his view that the selfie stick represented early twenty-first-century culture at its shoddy, narcissistic nadir.

Michael struck a pose with another giant turd, then photographed himself mugging beside a theater poster that said *Le Sexe pour les nuls* — 'Sex for Idiots' — over a picture of a half-peeled banana encased in black leather.

'Why don't you take a picture of something old and beautiful, for once?' Noah pointed at a decorated facade (Adam and Eve?) high over their heads.

'Nah, my friends prefer funny.'

'Let's see what you've got so far?'

After a moment, Michael held out his phone.

Noah flicked through three blurred images in a row. 'Why don't you make sure they're in focus, at least?'

Michael shook his head at Noah's stupidity.

'So it's uncool to be in focus?'

'To look like you're trying,' Michael corrected him.

Noah reached a grotesque selfie the boy had clearly distorted afterward in a house-of-mirrors way. 'You really want that image of you to be online forever?'

Michael yanked the phone away. 'It'll disappear from their feeds as soon as they've seen it.'

'Really?'

'I guess they could do a screen grab, but nobody bothers except for sex pics.'

'Great,' Noah said, sardonic. 'These friends, I hope you actually know them? Do they go to your school?'

'Jason used to, till his mom took him to Atlanta. The rest I know from hanging out in chat rooms. Eyes on the prize!'

'What prize?'

'We're going to be streamers and make a million bucks.'

'Streamers?'

Michael broke it down into contemptuous syllables: 'Peo-ple will pay to watch us gam-ing.'

Noah postponed the question of whether that was a realistic career plan. 'But are you friends in the real world?'

With scorn: 'It's all real, dude.'

Spotting a small sign that said OPÉRA, Noah said, 'Oh, I grew up near here.'

'In the slum?' Michael asked.

'Well, no,' he admitted. 'On a nice street, just outside the Old Town, near the sea.'

Right after the ornate Opera House, Noah turned a corner; he'd remembered the name but he'd had to look up the street number in Max Harstad's index. 'When my grandmother died, Père Sonne and Margot moved down from the hills, into town, and rented the whole third floor of this building.' He pointed up at the faded pink walls, and scanned the top windows as if his mother might smile down from one.

Had she never considered starting wedded life

with Marc on their own, rather than cheek by jowl with Père Sonne? Both his parents probably could have been artists themselves, it struck Noah now. But they'd strayed off that path for different reasons (her father, his lost hand) and never found their way back. What had Margot's regrets been, Noah wondered now, and what had she done with them?

Not that. Not a *mouche*. He refused to believe it. That would mean Margot's life from her forties to her nineties had been one long cover-up.

He read the tiny plaques by the doorbells. 3IÈME KHOURY AISHAH MASSO-KINÉSITHÉRAPIE.

'Who lives there now?' Michael wanted to know.

'The third floor's the office of some kind of massage person.'

'Really?' The boy craned up.

Noah guessed his misunderstanding. '*Medical* massage, like physiotherapy.'

'Oh. Are we going in?'

Noah hadn't thought to try. 'They're probably on a long French lunch break.' But he pressed the bell once, for the heck of it.

Michael pecked at the wall with his selfie stick till a bit of plaster crumbled off.

'Stop that.' Noah turned away, mounting shallow marble steps in the deep shadow between two ancient tenements.

Rounding a corner, he and Michael almost trod on the heels of three soldiers with machine guns patrolling the empty alley. 'What are these motherfuckers doing here?' Michael asked, in a

228

voice that wasn't low enough.

Noah grabbed him by the elbow and hustled him back down the steps. He thought of trigger-happy police shooting kids.

'That's so fake.'

'What is?' Bewildered.

With his selfie stick, Michael pointed to shuttered windows painted on a blank cement wall.

'*Trompe l'oeil*, remember that phrase?'

'Hasn't tricked *my* eye,' the boy boasted. Again, a second later, 'Fake!'

Noah squinted against the hard light. 'Actually, I think those windows are real.'

'The bits underneath, though.'

Yes, the elaborate moldings were painted — and recently, by the looks of it. 'You're right, but they're not necessarily trying to fool us.'

'Then why bother?'

'It's an homage. A sort of shout-out to the ancestors. Architects around here have been using *trompe l'oeil* for centuries, so when house painters do it today, it's a little wink at the past.'

'Hey look, more Segways.'

A tour was rolling out of a doorway. Noah read the sign: 'Twenty euros for thirty minutes.'

'What a rip-off.'

'You think?' The boy wasn't used to Upper West Side prices. 'You're paying for the guide's time and expertise, as well as the use of the machine,' Noah pointed out.

'For that money, I'd want eight hot babes *carrying* me around town.'

Noah grinned at that image.

Next door was a *papeterie*, a purveyor of fine stationery, which claimed to be *By Appointment to Her Majesty Queen Victoria*. Hadn't Père Sonne captured Victoria on one of her holidays here, in her donkey carriage? It seemed as if everybody-who-was-anybody had come through Nice sooner or later; no wonder the photographer hadn't needed to leave. The city was a playground, a stage set, a still point in a turning world.

Oh, oh, that aroma — how it took Noah back three-quarters of a century. Socca! There it was, squares of thin gold that a woman was digging out of her dish, the diameter of a truck wheel. But it was nearly noon, and Noah needed to have his lunch sitting down, and he was determined not to miss the right slot for a meal as he had yesterday. So he turned away from the socca cart. Through an alley that was barely wider than his arm span, he found his way onto a shopping street and went along sniffing out appetizing scents.

'Gross!' Michael was eye to eye with a whole spitted pig.

'Well, where do you think your bacon comes from? Want a slice?'

'It's got a *face*, dude.'

That made Noah think of Alice in Wonderland; didn't she find it impossible to eat anything she'd been introduced to? The pig was indeed dazzlingly gross, a spectrum of shades from pink to orange. A blackened string like a prisoner's chain bound it, sunken and burned right in.

Michael took a close-up through the greasy glass.

Noah picked a little bistro simply because its chalk menu offered *testicules de mouton panés.* 'Crispy fried sheep's balls.'

'Order them,' Michael begged.

'Sorry, not in the mood. And not for *tête de veau avec langue* either — that's calf's head with tongue.'

Michael gagged.

At their table, Noah dithered over the menu: tripe, a terrine of foie gras, rabbit in its sauce (he loved that French idiom, as if each dish rightly had one and only one proper sauce). 'You know rabbits can have several hundred great-grandchildren in one year?'

'Nightmare,' Michael said.

Did they feel a glow of dynastic pride, Noah wondered, or had they no idea that these younger bunnies were anything to them — just more competitors for the limited grazing?

Michael rejected everything Noah suggested he might like, and there was no kids' menu here. (Nor credit-card payment nor even phone bookings, he noticed from the chalkboard; it was the bistro that time forgot.) 'Aha,' Noah said as he turned the card over, 'Pizza Margherita.'

'I don't want any margherita.'

'That's just the name for a cheese pizza here.'

''Kay.' Michael wanted Noah to order the *escargots à l'ail*, 'just so's I can watch.'

But Noah wasn't in the mood for snails. 'They're intersexed, you know.'

'What, now?'

'Snails. They each have a tiny penis and vagina right by the head.'

Michael's eyes narrowed. 'You know a lot of stuff, but most of it's sick.'

'Fair comment.' Noah finally picked *loup entier cuit à la plancha*, monkfish cooked on a plank. Though after the proprietor had gone into the kitchen, he realized he'd confused the words — *lotte* was monkfish, *loup* was sea bass.

Since you can't taste the difference, Joan asked, *what does it matter?*

'Why does everyone touch that thing on their way out?'

Noah looked where Michael was pointing. It was a little hunched man in bas-relief. 'He's called Gobbo,' he said, the word floating up from his childhood. 'You rub his hump for good luck.'

'Huh.'

The pizza arrived startlingly fast, seared with black from the woodfired oven. It smelled so good, Noah somewhat regretted ordering the fish.

Michael glowered. 'I knew there'd be god-damn margherita.'

'Those are just basil leaves, for a garnish.' Noah lifted one off with his fork.

'I don't eat fucking garnish.' Michael gouged them out and flicked them onto Noah's plate.

Noah wished Joan was alive. (Well, what else was new?) Not that she'd necessarily have known what to do with Michael, but at least the challenge would have been shared, even halved. What merciless fate had decreed that Noah turn eighty in this brat's company?

He ate the basil. *So the boy's moody this week*, he told himself. *Hasn't he good reasons?* 'Is your pizza acceptable, otherwise?'

'Too flat, and they kind of burned it,' Michael said, mouth full.

⋆ ⋆ ⋆

On their way out, Michael doubled back to rub the hunchback. 'Now you.'

'I thought we agreed I've had enough luck in my lifetime.'

'Do it!'

So Noah did.

Out in the sunshine, they got ice cream from Fenocchio, the gelateria that claimed to have more than a hundred flavors. After a brief reprise of their argument about waffle cones, Michael settled for a regular cone of Oreo (a suspiciously American-sounding flavor), whereas Noah chose olive, simply because he'd never find it anywhere else. Several licks in, he decided that there was a good reason ice cream was rarely flavored with olives, but he couldn't face getting in line again.

'Like your mom's photo.' Smeared brown and white around the mouth, Michael nodded at something behind Noah.

Noah tried to swivel around, and his chair's silver feet squealed on the stone slab. 'What? Where?'

Michael used his selfie stick as a pointer. 'Same shape, except it's portrait not landscape.'

Noah's eyes searched the square, the tourists, the lone violinist, the capoeira performers

233

vaulting over each other as they did in Central Park. Only when he finally tilted his face high enough did he spot the neoclassical bell tower in warm pastels rearing up against the sky and recognize the pattern from Margot's photo: dash, circle, dash. It wasn't a box or a tomb at all; he'd been looking at the image the wrong way, horizontally, when it was actually a vertical tower. The dashes were narrow-cut windows, and the circle was a decoration between them. 'Why on earth would my mother have taken a close-up of that?'

Michael put on a pirate voice: 'X marks the spot!'

When the boy had finished his ice cream — Noah had already tossed his — they walked over to investigate. The bell tower turned out to belong to the older church beside it, the little Cathedral of Sainte Réparate. 'I think Margot may have brought me to Mass here,' Noah murmured as they stepped into the glittering gloom.

The church reduced Michael to silence: an excess of gold, marble, glass, multiple pipe organs, statues of angels and saints flying out of every wall.

'I seem to remember being rather afraid of that bird.' Noah pointed at a gilt eagle holding up the lectern.

Michael telescoped out his selfie stick to take a picture of himself with the eagle. 'This is some seriously frilly shit.'

'It's called Baroque style.'

'I call it fugly.'

234

He couldn't disagree. But the crass splendor of this interior offered no explanation of why his mother had taken such a ham-fisted snapshot of the tower. If Margot had been one of the ladies who did the flowers, that would have been here in her local parish church, wouldn't it? How was the tower connected with the other photos — the dandy and the couple and the little boy, the empty street, the tree?

Noah went up close to a stand of lilies, and breathed in: a sickly tang of death. His eye was caught by a tapestry that showed a man with a little boy on his shoulders, stumbling across a river. What was the name of that saint? All Noah could remember was the twist in the story; when the man griped about how heavy the load had been, the kid — who turned out to be Jesus — told him, 'You were only carrying me, but I was carrying the whole world.' Noah had been a disbeliever for almost his entire life, but his head was still cluttered with this nonsense.

He leaned on a column — Corinthian, was it? — and read a leaflet he'd picked up. 'In the seventeenth century the nave, this central bit, fell down and crushed the bishop.'

'Like, creamed?' Michael asked. 'Game over?'

'Game over.'

Dozens of marble plaques concisely expressed gratitude: *Remerciement juillet 63 LB*, or *Merci à N.D. de Lourdes mars 1953 CMP HB*. Mostly from the 1920s and '30s, but Noah spotted one as recent as 1996. St. Anthony seemed far more popular than Jesus, but less than the Virgin. 'These are paid for by people who want to thank a saint for healing them, or doing them favors,' he whispered. '*Mille mercis*, see — that's 'a thousand thank-yous,' like 'thanks a million.''

'You think it's all bullshit,' Michael said, too loud.

'Well, the placebo effect . . . If you believe God's mom is zapping away your tumor, maybe it gives your immune system the power to do it.'

'You're probably going straight to hell.'

Noah shrugged, eyes on the plaques. 'Either way, it can't hurt to say thanks.'

In one of the tiny chapels he found an undistinguished nineteenth-century painting of the parish's patron, Sainte Réparate. When Michael came up behind him, Noah murmured, 'Roman soldiers arrested this Palestinian girl for being a Christian. It says she was only a teenager — maybe as young as you.'

'Did they throw her to the lions?'

'No, first they, ah . . . ' Noah was having qualms. 'It's a bit gory.'

'I'm not shockable,' Michael told him. 'I can see from the painting, soldier boy's about to whop her head off.'

'All right.' Noah translated the panel. 'First they tried burning Réparate in a furnace, but rain put the fire out. Then they made her drink . . . boiling tar.'

'Shit, man.' Michael stared at the little cauldron in the painting.

'But she wouldn't stop praying, so in the end they cut her head off.'

A frown. 'That's it?'

'Oh, you were expecting some Hollywood

ending? No. Réparate's body — and head — were put on a raft. The angels blew it all the way across the sea to Nice, and they wouldn't let the birds peck her, so she did arrive in perfect condition.'

'Still dead, though?'

'Afraid so.' The Mediterranean was full of drowned migrants, these days; Noah was unsettled by an image of that tiny Kurdish boy who'd washed up on the beach in Turkey. 'Those are supposed to be Réparate's bones up there,' he added, pointing at a gold-and-glass case, 'but I doubt that very much.'

'The angels couldn't have pulled their thumbs out of their asses and stopped her from dying in the first place?'

'That's superheroes you're thinking of.'

Michael gave Noah a sideways look as they stepped outside into the sparkling afternoon. 'If your mom was churchy, how'd she like you ending up a atheist?'

Noah knew he was being baited, so he didn't say *an atheist*. 'Well, she wasn't thrilled, but she knew I had the same basic values, that's what mattered.' (Though what did he know for sure about his mother's values, anymore?) 'When I stopped going to Mass, it was nothing personal.' He reached for an analogy. 'You know how salt is formed? Have you covered inorganic compounds yet, at school?'

Blank.

Don't get technical about anions and cations, Joan advised, *or even positive and negative charges.*

'For instance, sodium and chlorine are two

237

elements that . . . long to be together.' Noah was anthropomorphizing, but never mind. 'OK?'

'If you say so.'

'Every molecule of chlorine is desperate for an electron to fill up its shell' — he held up one fist — 'whereas every molecule of sodium has an extra electron it's dying to get rid of.' The other fist. 'So when they meet' — he brought his index fingertips together — 'they click into place like puzzle pieces and make a new thing, salt.'

'Like, their baby?'

'Well put. What I'm trying to say is, I just never had that' — *deficit? need?* too derogatory — 'attraction for religion that let it stick to me like it did to my mom and my sister.'

Michael nodded. 'My grandma wouldn't be asking did you want some salt, she just shook it on.' He bent to pick up discarded paper cones from a *glacerie*.

'Leave them, they're dirty.'

Which of course made the kid persist, fitting them over his fingers and collecting more till he had the full complement of ten.

Outside a tiny shop window, tin trays with reproductions of old posters caught Noah's eye. One bore a girl in not much more than a feathered hat, beckoning to a top-hatted gentleman. The caption said *Very Nice;* clearly that Anglo-French pun was centuries old. 'How does this look on me?' Noah asked, holding up an apron that imposed a bikini-clad woman's torso on his own.

'Horrible.' Michael shielded his eyes with his spiked talons.

238

There was a puff-skirted doll in bright Provençal cotton, meant to be hung up in a kitchen to hold plastic grocery bags. A mug featuring Van Gogh's face, with a tag promising the ear would disappear when you poured in a hot drink.

The boy was spinning the postcard rack, scanning obscene holographic images of huge-breasted sunbathers.

'Take off your paper cones if you're coming inside,' Noah told him, opening the door. 'You can't touch anything with them.'

'I won't.'

'You won't touch anything?'

'Won't go in.'

So Noah stepped into the store, where ceramic crickets chirped as if by magic. Maybe he should get Vivienne a stack of little slabs of handmade soap — rosemary, lemon, olive oil? But he couldn't settle to browsing through miniature sacks of lavender and *herbes de Provence*, sets of jars of flavored salts. He wished he could check on Michael through the window, but it was overfilled with oilcloth tablecloths in gaudy blue and yellow patterns. What if when he went out, the kid had wandered off? With only half his attention, Noah considered a bottle of pastis, remembering the sharply aniseed bite of the liquor. According to the label it was made by steeping twenty-four different plants and spices in alcohol for three months. No, if he bought it, he'd need to check in his suitcase.

Probably not worth it for a bottle you'll never finish, Joan pointed out.

Occasionally Noah got the feeling that his wife was waiting for him — briefcase over her arm, hovering by the door — which was patently ridiculous, because neither of them believed in souls, much less anywhere for them to go, so where exactly was she planning to lead him?

The ding of the door; Michael, hands still spike-blossomed with paper cones.

Noah glared. The store owner adjusted her glasses to scrutinize the boy.

'I need a bathroom.'

'I'll be out in a minute,' Noah told him, grabbing a ten-bar collection of soaps for Vivienne.

'*Allez, allez!*' The owner flapped at Michael as if hurrying a chicken into its coop.

The kid's eyes flared with panic and he backed up. An entire rack of monogrammed hand towels teetered, then crashed onto a table of pastel salts.

The owner screeched a diatribe Noah could barely follow, but he caught the phrase *sale garçon* — 'filthy boy.'

Noah saw red. In his crispest French he denounced the woman and her overstuffed, overpriced shop, even as he was hustling Michael out the door. In the alley, he slammed it with a clang of the bell.

Michael's face was ashen. 'I'm such a fuckup, I didn't mean to.'

Imagine being eleven and having to placate some old man you'd only just met, because you had no one else in the world to look after you. 'Don't worry, nothing's broken.' In case that

240

wasn't true, Noah hurried the two of them around the corner.

'Fucking fancy stores,' the boy said between his teeth.

Noah eyed him. 'True, there was barely room to turn around in there.'

'It's how they stare. When they come up going, 'Can I help you?' — it just makes me *want* to grab something.'

Noah wondered if the boy was half-confessing to a bit of shoplifting in his time. 'Let's find you a bathroom.'

'Oh yeah, I forgot.'

Noah asked in an Indian restaurant, then waved Michael in.

The kid cast an eye at the mirror-decorated hangings, the silver samovar taller than himself.

'It's fine, the waiter doesn't mind,' Noah assured him. 'Here, give me that thing.' Confiscating the selfie stick.

When Michael came back out with wet hands, Noah was looking up what bus they needed to get to the *Musée de la résistance azuréenne*. 'This is the Blue Coast, remember, so the name means 'the Museum of the Blue Resistance.' Sounds cool, doesn't it?'

'Have they got guns?'

'Ah, very possibly,' Noah said, doubting it.

It was a long ride on two buses, out to near the airport.

Finally, opposite one of several car dealerships, Noah found the right door and they trudged up a spiral staircase.

One room had flour sacks stamped with eagles

241

and swastikas. Noah pointed out ration cards for bread, butter, oil, coffee, even clothes. 'See, during the war I'd have been entitled to a J1 ration, for a child aged three to six.'

'Why coffee?' Michael objected. 'Nobody needs it, not like actual food.'

'I suppose adults feel they need it, to keep their spirits up.'

There was a hideous substitute drink called Cossac, Noah read, and dextrine from the pharmacy to replace sugar. 'Like your grandma's SNAP card. Rations always ran out early, then you just had to do without.' If there was nothing at all in the stores, one panel explained, you might resort to the brown market (buying directly from farmers), the gray (from Germans), or the black (from profiteers). During the war, the average Frenchwoman spent four hours a day standing in line for food.

Noah wondered with an awful flippancy: if Margot had to rustle up dinner for herself and her father every day, how could she have found the time to betray anybody?

She didn't, because it's nonsense, the whole theory. Not even a theory — just morbid speculations.

Noah followed Michael to a display about local sabotage. In one photo a train line had been blown up, lifted high into the air as you might undo the ribbon on a gift. He translated the posters in bold graphics: '*Résister pour exister.* That means, 'Resist in order to exist.' The next one says, 'Down with collaboration.''

He pushed away the thought of his mother.

242

"'Our sons and daughters are hungry, we demand five hundred grams of bread a day.''

'How much is that?' Michael asked.

'Hm, maybe two-thirds of a loaf.'

'That's a lot of bread.'

'But no hot dogs with it, no burgers, no cheese. Maybe turnip jam.'

'Ew!' Michael drifted ahead, then ran back to report, 'There *are* guns.'

Noah went to examine the tarnished Mauser MG 42s. Then the neat calligraphy on the label affixed to a small suitcase. 'A woman from a communist group used this to smuggle weapons.'

'Aren't communists bad, though?'

Noah sighed. 'It's complicated, but I'd say she was on the right side.'

Some forty percent of Jewish Resistance members in France were female, he read — which seemed a remarkable figure, considering Frenchwomen were so excluded from political life at that point, they couldn't even vote.

Michael liked the green silk parachutes, and a German helmet that the label said had washed up on the Promenade.

'See how somebody drew a French flag over this swastika?' Noah pointed. 'And this cross with two horizontal bars, that was a symbol of the Resistance.'

Michael curled his lip. 'We've got better graffiti in Brooklyn.'

'Well, these folks were working in a hurry so they wouldn't get shot.'

'Same with taggers. This one guy, they found him dead a couple blocks from my school.'

Noah had no response at all to that.

A man nearby threw a dirty look — not at Noah, he realized, but at Michael, who was resting his elbow on a case as he studied the toy tanks and other military miniatures inside.

'Don't lean on the glass,' Noah told him.

Michael went and slumped against a wall, pantomiming fatigue.

Noah shuffled on through the rooms, trying to soak up the information from the crowded boards while he was gathering his nerve to ask for this Monsieur Benoit whom Vivienne had mentioned. He didn't know enough to know what he was looking for, and he wasn't going to find it in the exhibits about the Holocaust, but he couldn't bear to skip them. A tiny clog carved from an olive pit by a detainee; graceful sketches drawn on thin toilet paper. Strange, the human impulse to create, even in a prison camp. *Ni haine, ni oubli*, said one caption: 'Never hate, but never forget.'

'Are these gang tats?' Michael had gotten ahead of Noah.

'Where?' Noah walked over to see what the boy was looking at: a color photo of several elderly people showing five- or six-digit numbers on their outer forearms. 'Ah, no, those are their prisoner numbers, from the camps. More like slave brands.' How to make it real? 'My friend Vivienne . . . she has cousins in Florida and Israel with camp numbers on their arms.'

'No way!'

'When she was only three, Vivienne got smuggled out of Czechoslovakia.' A country that didn't exist anymore, it struck Noah now. 'It was called the *Kindertransport* — the transporting of child refugees,' he added, translating awkwardly. She'd been sent to an uncle in Hampstead, then an aunt in Staten Island. (He thought of Amber's sister, Grace: when was she going to show up?) Vivienne's mother had survived the camp somehow and joined the girl in New York a few months afterward, but it took years for confirmation of how her husband had died. She'd held it together for two decades — by Vivienne's unembittered account, the best of mothers — then she'd swallowed a bottle of pills the year after Vivienne and Frank's wedding, as if her job was done.

Where had Michael gone?

Noah found him two rooms back, smirking at the mannequins of prisoners standing at ungainly angles in their uniforms striped black and white. They wore triangles — red, pink, black — but also less familiar badges; a bizarrely detailed taxonomy. A purple triangle inverted over a yellow one meant (Noah read) a Jehovah's Witness of Jewish descent.

He tried to remember whether Amber's uniform had been exactly like those of the other inmates. He'd heard about a new initiative in some US prisons: color-coding of uniforms according to offenses committed, gang membership, vulnerability. The sheriff quoted claimed it was 'for the inmates' own protection.' Noah stared at an outlined black triangle over yellow now, which meant — he checked the chart — a Jew guilty of *métissage*, mixing Christian blood with their own.

That's me, quipped Joan.

Old love, like a kick in his solar plexus.

'Noah?'

He followed the child's call into the next room.

'Is that your mom's guy?' Michael asked.

'Where?' Horrified, Noah stared over the boy's shoulder at a group of Nazi officers giving the Sieg Heil salute in Place Garibaldi. 'Shh, I don't know for sure that she even — '

Michael cut in. 'No, down here. With the stick.'

Yes, the suave man leaning on a cane had a familiar air to him. This could very well be the dandy shown in profile in Margot's photograph.

Maurice Brener (alias 'Zazou') was known for sartorial grace, according to the note below the photo, and never seen without jacket and tie, although in constant pain from childhood polio. An old friend of Abadi's (who was that, Noah wondered?), Brener supplied false identity papers to the Marcel Network; he also secured funds from French and American Jewry to support its work.

Hang on, who were these people? Noah stared up at the large letters: GROUPES DE LA RÉSISTANCE. He must have walked by this whole section the first time. So his mother had taken a photo of a natty Jewish hero? 'It says Zazou was his *nom de guerre* — his code name in the war,' he murmured as he read.

'Z, like *MZ* on the back of the hair picture!'

Could there possibly be a connection? Brener had a wife back in Paris, Noah discovered from the next paragraph. But could the *MZ* woman in the photo have been a comrade of his, passing as Madame Zazou in Nice?

Head whirling, Noah pulled out his envelope of small snaps. The *MZ* picture was clearly taken indoors, but from behind — and maybe without its subject's knowledge? Whereas this Zazou guy had been standing in the street. Outdoor photography had been *verboten*, so had Margot crept up behind the man, doing her best to record his face, but managing no more than a side perspective?

Noah was feeling sick. 'I have to go talk to someone for a minute, Michael. Don't get in any trouble.'

In a conference room, a small cluster of people were chatting over some open folders. They had the air of a study group rather than an organizational meeting, and after all the door was open, shifting slightly in the draft. So Noah steeled himself and tapped on it to apologize for disturbing them. He was visiting from America and he had these photographs . . .

They were very kind, and one of them found Monsieur Benoit in the archive for him.

He wasn't the old Niçois Noah had been expecting but a middle-aged man wearing a yarmulke over short cornrows; an Ethiopian Jew, Noah guessed from his accent. Monsieur Benoit switched from French to English, in which he was even more fluent. Yes, he confirmed that the

247

dandy picture could very well be Brener, aka Zazou. But the *MZ* photograph rang no bells for him. 'And this I would say with a degree of certainty is Odette and Moussa themselves,' he added, plucking out Noah's shot of the couple on the bench.

'Sorry, who?'

'Moussa Abadi and Odette Rosenstock, I should say. They founded, they effectively were, the Marcel Network. To hide the children?'

'Sorry, I never heard of any of this till today. My mother . . . all I know is that she was in Nice during the war.' Noah stared at the back of the bench in the photo. 'You can't even see the people's faces in this shot.'

'True, but if you look at other images of Odette and Moussa . . . ' Benoit led him back to the room where Michael had spotted the photo of Brener with his cane.

Noah stared dully at Rosenstock and Abadi in close-up, then walking arm in arm down the Prom, as the archivist explained that this extraordinary pair and the little knot of allies they'd enlisted had managed to save many hundreds of Jewish children. Yes, Noah could see the resemblance now; something about how they sat together, as well as their individual outlines. Such an ordinary-looking pair; angels in disguise.

'Perhaps your mother knew them?' Monsieur Benoit suggested.

'Perhaps.' Noah writhed inside. He wished he'd never brought Margot's strange pictures into this building. Was Monsieur Benoit too

248

polite to wonder aloud why the photographer and her subjects weren't looking one another in the eye? If she'd been anything to these Marcel people, Margot had been their Judas.

'That one was probably her boyfriend.' Michael, popping up at Noah's elbow and pointing at Zazou like some glib ghost.

'Don't be silly.' Underneath his coat, Noah's armpits were dripping. 'I think my young great-nephew's got the wrong end of the stick.'

Monsieur Benoit shook the boy's hand and said he was delighted to meet him.

Scowling, Michael pulled away and headed for the door.

Noah knew he'd better follow him.

'Oh, and one more thing, about your photograph of the young child?'

'Yes?' Noah hung back, holding that one out.

Monsieur Benoit read the scrawled leters, *RJ*. 'All I can speculate is that it was taken for an identity document.'

'But . . . isn't the format wrong? And he's smiling.'

'There was no rule against smiling.' Its dimensions were rather unusual for an identity photograph, Monsieur Benoit agreed, but there was no compulsory shape or size, and after all, the same negative could have been printed for different purposes.

Noah's nose was dripping; he had to go into the bathroom to wipe it with toilet paper.

Behind a stall door, a familiar beeping.

'Michael?' he asked.

A pause. 'What?'

'Come out of there.'

The boy emerged. 'I was just playing my game and a woman told me off for making noise.'

'It's OK.' Noah's head was still whirling. 'Let's go. Wash your hands.'

'I don't need to.'

'Just wash them.'

But Michael was pushing out through the door already.

Noah thought he'd better use the toilet himself before the long bus ride back to the hotel.

Outside, the February breeze cut sharply and he couldn't see the boy at all. Panic flared. 'Michael!'

He found him around the corner, slashing at a flowerbed with a stick.

'Stop that this instant.'

Michael beheaded another.

'Those are for everyone to enjoy,' Noah told him. 'I let you out of my sight for two minutes and you disgrace me — '

Michael's eyes narrowed. 'I *disgrace* you?'

Noah was already regretting the word. 'Well, you're my relation, and you're behaving like — '

The kid cut him off with a contemptuous sound in his throat. 'Just a few goddamn flowers, dude.' He dropped his flail and fell into line behind Noah, pushing his earbuds in. Music thumped from his hood.

After they'd walked for a few minutes, Noah turned and made a gesture that meant 'Take them out.'

'I can hear you fine,' Michael said, too loud.

250

'That's not the point.' Noah spoke deliberately softly.

Michael poked his screen to pause the music. 'What?'

'I don't want to have to guess whether you can make me out over your music, so please be civil enough not to wear your earbuds when you're talking to me.'

'I *wasn't* talking to you.'

'Listen, I'm sorry I called you 'silly.'' Noah heaved a breath. 'I was embarrassed. Ashamed, actually.'

'Because she *was* running around on your dad?'

He shook his head. 'It's me who got hold of the wrong end of the stick. The people in the photos — they were in the Resistance, rescuing kids from the Nazis, and my mom . . . I don't think she was their friend at all.'

The pause was awful.

'What was she, then?'

Noah's voice dropped to a whisper, even though there was nobody else on the street. 'My best guess is that she was surveilling them. Recruited, because she could take covert photos and print them.'

Michael frowned. 'Recruited, like the army?'

'Recruited by . . . the enemy.'

★   ★   ★

They caught the wrong bus — Noah's fault, his eyes confusing a 5 with a 6 — so they had to double back. By the time they got out at Place

Masséna, he was dog-tired.

The plaza was vast, paved in a black-and-white checkered pattern with an oddly 3D effect: Michael called it 'kind of *Minecraft*.' There were red neoclassical arcades but the square was dominated by seven immense poles on which sat cross-legged figures (Buddhas?) that lit up with different pastels, fading and changing hue as Noah watched. The stands for watching the Carnival Corso stood empty, a little ominous.

To board the crowded tram he and the boy had to squeeze chest to chest between strangers. Noah couldn't help thinking of cattle cars; of trains on their way to the camps. Whether Margot had been unfaithful to Marc, or even had a child, didn't matter a damn compared with this. What had she done, who had she been in the darkest of the *années noires*?

For their dinner, Noah stopped at a hole-in-the-wall around the corner from the Excelsior, because he couldn't face a proper meal.

Standing in line, he tried to remember: who was that Egyptian god who weighed hearts?

When he carried the steaming bag into their room, the beds were made, as crisp as ever. Michael stiffened and went to check under his covers. Impeccable sheets.

They ate chicken skewers and rice, all of it startlingly yellow. Noah eyed the threadbare Pick-Pick Bird on his bedside table. He thought of children watching its motion, rapt, laughing.

The little boy. That photograph didn't fit with the others; he was smiling right into the lens, with curiosity, with trust. If R.J. wasn't one of Margot's targets, then, could he have been her child? Noah's head hurt. Two and a half years. Spying, and an affair, and the birth of a baby? (*Not* Brener's — a German's, then, maybe a German who'd won her over politically as well as personally?) All in two and a half years, and all in utter secrecy?

On his tablet, he thought to check the phone listings for a Madame Coco Dupont. If the cleaner had by any chance talked to her daughter about Margot's movements during the war . . . and if the daughter was still alive, and still in Nice . . . He found Duponts, no Cocos. But that was Coco's maiden name, of course, and odds were she'd have married.

A quick email to Vivienne: 'How might I go about tracking down a woman born Coco Dupont, in Nice, around 1938 or 1937?' Then — since the little girl could have been a bit older than Noé but certainly hadn't been any younger or less verbal — he added, 'Possibly 1936?'

Rosa sounded busy: her reply from this afternoon said only, 'Good, keep me posted.'

Noah googled the Ancient Egyptians. It was Anubis who set your heart on the scales against the Feather of Truth, and if your crimes weighed it down at all, it was thrown to the crocodile-faced demoness Ammit like any other scrap of meat. Only the clean-hearted got to walk forever in the Field of Reeds.

When he thought to check the Correctional Communications app, there was a message from Amber for Michael, headed *Hey yourself.*

Scrupulous, he didn't open it.

'From your mom,' he told the boy, holding out the tablet.

Michael dropped the plastic fork with a piece of chicken still on it.

From under his eyebrows, Noah watched him as he read the screen; tried to interpret that closed face. The boy's knuckles went up to his temple briefly; could that have been a tear? 'You can answer her,' Noah said.

''Kay.'

'Go ahead.'

The boy started pecking at the screen.

Lying on his bed to give Michael some privacy, Noah traced a faint watermark on the paint with his eyes. He found the food had settled like lead in his stomach; he struggled up on the bolster and pillow. Had this room had the same ceiling when the Nazis had taken over the hotel and turned it into their own private hell?

Turning toward the wall, leaning on one elbow, Noah looked up the Marcel Network on his phone. Starting in 1942, a Syrian Jewish graduate student in theater, Moussa Abadi (aka Monsieur Marcel), and a doctor, Odette Rosenstock (alias Sylvie Delattre), had cycled around Nice and its hinterland persuading the managers of Catholic schools and convents, as well as Protestant families, to take in Jewish children under assumed names. Children too religious to touch non-kosher food, or foreign refugees who couldn't pass for French, Abadi and Rosenstock sent off to Spain or Switzerland

254

instead, in the care of *passeurs* (people smugglers).

He glanced over his shoulder. 'You must be done emailing her, are you?'

'Have you got like zero games on this thing?' Michael asked.

'Just two: chess and checkers come built in.' Noah held out his hand for the tablet. He couldn't stop himself from asking: 'How's Amber?'

A shrug.

To push it or leave it? Noah wished he had more experience at this.

But Michael went on after a minute. 'As soon as she gets moved to a facility that has Family Reunion, we're going to have a trailer visit.'

Surely if there were any immediate prospect of Amber being moved, Rosa would have said. 'What's that?'

'Forty-four hours, dude! Just us two in a trailer. Mom's promised to make a cake for my last birthday and we're going to watch TV and sleep all curled up all night, *two* nights.'

Noah's eyes pricked with sorrow. Who'd decided on forty-four hours as the limit? 'Sounds fantastic.' He waited, in case any more was forthcoming. 'Maybe you could update your journal?'

Michael groaned, but got out his ballpoint.

Noah googled on. Bishop Paul Rémond, head of the Catholic church in Nice, had provided a room in his episcopal palace and the services of his staff to help the Marcel Network forge baptismal certificates and ration cards. A Baptist minister, Edmond Evrard, and Pierre Gagnier of the Reformed Church had been in on the conspiracy too. One particular image struck Noah as surreal: Moussa Abadi had sent children off to their places of refuge all over this lovely countryside in horse-drawn carriages, with Jewish Boy Scouts for escorts.

And Margot: when had she started tracking the Marcels? And had she managed to capture these heroes' likenesses well enough for them to be identified and seized?

Noah asked the question with a fingertip so clumsy that he had to go back and respell it twice.

Rémond's status as Bishop of Nice seemed to have protected him; likewise the ministers and their families. Abadi had somehow evaded capture too. The Gestapo had hurried up the stairs of Brener's office one day, brushing right past him — but he had gone into hiding and managed to survive the war. He wasn't the only one who owed his life to a fluke: Georges Isserlis, a schoolboy messenger for the network, had been scooped up and avoided Drancy only by climbing out the window of the train.

As for Rosenstock, she'd kept out of the Nazis' reach for a full seven months, but in April 1944 she'd been interrogated in the Excelsior. Noah swallowed hard. He put one palm against the wall and thought of what the word *interrogated* might cover. He looked at his mother's photo of Moussa Abadi and Odette Rosenstock again; Monsieur Benoit had identified the couple at a glance because he was familiar with other images of them, but surely on its own this rear view of them on a bench wouldn't have been enough to expose them?

From the Excelsior, Rosenstock had been moved to the Hotel Hermitage up in Cimiez, Noah read, and then to Auschwitz-Birkenau, and then to Bergen-Belsen, where typhus had put her into a coma. Inexplicably, she'd lived through the war and — as if further proof of her goodness were needed — stayed on at Bergen-Belsen for some time after, to help other former inmates. In 1959 she and Abadi had married at last (he in his fifties, she in her forties), maintaining their silence about the Marcel Network pretty much unbroken for the rest of their lives.

So the network's agents had all survived? Then Margot couldn't have had any blood on her hands.

Relief, like sugar in Noah's mouth.

But he read on, and learned about two young Jewish social workers who'd joined the Marcels in the autumn of 1943: Nicole Weil (alias Nicole Salon) and Huguette Wahl (Odile Varlet). Weil had been denounced by an anonymous informer after just three weeks, he read, Wahl after a matter of days. They'd both been killed at Auschwitz.

Noah squeezed his eyes shut. Of course his mother could have taken other photographs, better ones. Maybe the handful in her envelope were just the rejects, the ones she didn't bother handing over to her masters at the Excelsior.

Michael tossed the notebook across the gap

between their beds, making Noah jump.

'You didn't spend long on that.'

The boy tapped his cropped head. 'Work smarter, not harder.'

At the top of the page was what Noah realized was a diagrammatic representation of the Promenade des Anglais, *Famous Street of Death* scrawled over it. *Jihadi psycho killer*, Michael had added, with an arrow to the truck and a dotted line showing its zigzag progress, stick figures littering the pavement behind. At the other end of the street, by a sketched-in car, a figure labeled *Air-head Dancer Managed to Strangle Her Self With Her Scarf*. Then, a little inland, several crime-scene body outlines: *Nazis Shot Teen Resistors HERE*. Floating well offshore, on a raft, with sketched cupids overhead, was Sainte Réparate's young skull separated from her dripping limbs, labeled *Medeeval Martyr With Angels to Keep Off the Vultures*.

Noah's first instinct was to tear out the pages and make the boy start again. What on earth would his teacher say to this?

Joan weighed in: *Well, at least he's been paying attention.*

'Very vivid,' he commented, handing the journal back, and went to brush his teeth.

Getting into bed, he noticed Michael's phone tucked under his pillow. 'Never leave that there!'

Too stern: the boy's eyes narrowed.

'I just mean — a man was burned to death in his sleep one time, when his phone burst into flames.'

'Got it.' Michael moved his phone to the bedside table.

'And by the way' — Noah looked away, buttoning up his pajamas — 'if you happen to have an accident tonight, just throw a towel over it.'

Raging: 'I won't.'

'It's only a stress symptom.'

'Just stop.'

'OK.' The room felt oppressive; too small for two. Noah risked a grain of humor. 'All I'm saying is, even if you wet the bed every night, it's not a problem.'

'*You* wet the fucking bed.'

'I might well. Oldies are known for losing control of their functions.'

'Shit in it too for all I care,' Michael growled.

'Now there I draw the line. It would be too sticky.'

That got a very small laugh.

★　★　★

After midnight, Noah lay listening to a cacophony outside the window that reminded him of some sci-fi movie about the rise of the machines. He got up to finger the curtain aside and see what was going on. Just garbage trucks.

He was tired, doubtful, not one thing or the other, *neither here nor there*. He'd returned to his homeland, but he wasn't at home there; on the other hand, where in the world was Noah really at home at this point? The apartment in New York was his *place of residence*, as bureaucrats would put it, but it still echoed with Joan's absence almost a decade on. Perhaps Noah should make the break; throw away Mendeleev's heated pad and chew toy; move out.

As for his mother, she eluded him. Noah was working blind, fumbling in the dark to form a new, clear, awful image of Margot.

'Can't sleep.' Michael spoke huskily, out of the dark.

'Me neither. Our clocks are still wonky. But you don't really expect to sleep, at my age.'

'You don't sleep anymore?' the boy echoed, aghast.

'I just mean you can't make it happen when you want it to. So you get used to lying awake sometimes.' Attempting — though Noah didn't say this — to be at least slightly grateful not to be dead yet.

6

The Law of Closure

In the dazzling sunshine, over a late breakfast, watching a fat pigeon pecking at a pizza crust in the gutter, Noah found the whole spy theory almost comically implausible. Really, who kept documentation of her own war crimes in an envelope with random snapshots of trees and streets, and passed it on to her daughter?

'How long are you going to live?'

He blinked at the boy. Did Michael expect every adult in whose care he was placed to keel over, or was he just curious about the aging process? 'Quite a while yet, I hope. My father died at seventy-nine, so from Monday morning I could be considered to be in overtime. But my mother lasted till ninety-two. If I've inherited more of her DNA than his, I still have plenty of time to start a business or something.' *Repair the world*, Noah thought ruefully.

'Don't we get half of each?'

'Mother and father? It's more like shuffling two packs of cards together and dealing enough for a new pack. Also, some cards get dropped, duplicated, turned the wrong way or a corner folded down . . . '

Michael looked a little unnerved by this.

'The unpredictability's half the fun.' Noah finished his croissant and drained his coffee.

Such luxury, forbidden in New York, to light a cigarette at the table. Today was remarkably warm, for February; sunshine was burning through his left sleeve. 'Actually, I'm a lucky man to have lived this long already. I think life expectancy when I was born in the '30s was under sixty.'

A grin. 'So you should be dead?'

'Statistically speaking, I've already beaten the roulette wheel, just by being on this side of the grass.'

Michael objected: 'Grass doesn't have two sides.'

'It means above the grass' — Noah sketched a gesture — 'rather than under it.'

The boy's eyes lit. 'Like, 'Your ass is grass.''

'That's what you say for death?'

'It's a threat: 'Your ass is grass and I'm going to mow it.''

That made Noah chuckle. He tapped ash off his cigarette and drew on it.

'Dying a bit faster now,' Michael commented.

'Yeah, yeah.'

'So what about me, what's my life expecta-thingy?'

Noah tried to remember the current estimate for American males: about eighty? 'I'd have to look that up.'

'Do it.'

'But your odds are better than some kids', remember, because you've already made it to eleven.' Noah logged into the café's Wi-Fi and tapped in 'New York life expectancy borough.'

There was Brooklyn on the chart. Noah

clicked on a link to break it down by neighborhood. Then looked incredulously at the figures for Michael's notorious area. Seventy-four years, as compared with the city average of eighty-one. He read silently: 'Contributing factors are thought to include: environmental lead/mercury/organophosphates, nutritional deficits, violence, tobacco, alcohol, substance abuse, mental illness, substandard healthcare, chronic stress.' What a cornucopia of unnatural causes. It was like some horrifying tale in which you bargained with a goblin and lost seven years of your life. Noah couldn't bring himself to tell the boy. 'Ah, can't seem to find an exact figure,' he murmured. 'And remember, you have some of my mother's long-lived DNA, through Victor.' As soon as it was out of his mouth, Noah heard the stupidity of that remark.

Michael spoke low and hard: 'Didn't do shit for him, did it?'

Noah struggled for words. 'I believe drugs are very hard to shake, once they get hold of you.'

Seconds went by. Then the boy said, 'Vic did get clean in the end, though.'

Noah didn't want to say that wasn't true at all.

As if he had heard, Michael added, 'He gave me his maroon chip.'

Noah reran the phrase in his head. 'What's a maroon chip?'

Michael dug deep into his pants pocket and held out a small purplish disk on his palm. 'The last time I saw my dad, he asked me to keep it safe for him.'

Noah picked it up. Plastic, marked NA.

263

'Narcotics Anonymous,' Michael translated.

'I see.' On the back, *Ninety Days*. But anyone could get hold of a plastic token: buy them by the dozen online, pick one up off the sidewalk. It proved nothing, except to a gullible child. 'And Victor seemed . . . all right, did he, the last time?'

Michael nodded.

Noah handed the precious disk back. Well, he supposed it could just possibly have been true: if ever his nephew had made a real effort to sober up, surely it would have been when he'd just sent the woman he loved to prison for five years, leaving his son motherless. An even bigger pity, if Victor had made it to the three-month mark before his final lapse.

'About my longevity,' Noah said, to change the subject, 'I should have factored in something else: chemists have unusually high rates of death. A long tradition of blinding and scarring and poisoning ourselves.'

Michael perked up. 'On purpose?'

'Sometimes suicide, but generally by accident. Lab practices were terribly casual till the '70s. Not bothering to turn on the fume hood, sloshing mercury around, pipetting by mouth . . . '

'Huh?'

Noah mimed it with the boy's straw. 'We sucked up chemicals to transfer them between beakers.'

'That's crazy.'

He shrugged his shoulders. 'We were macho about it.'

'Show me something,' Michael demanded.

'What?'

'Anything cool. An experiment.'

'Hmm. Not sure I can think of anything to whip up in a hotel room . . . '

Go on, Joan incited him, *impress the child.*

But Noah had no supplies; couldn't even turn a penny gold or do the burning-money trick. Making a Mentos-and-diet-soda fountain was guaranteed to be messy, and growing salt or sugar crystals seemed too slow to appeal to this particular kid.

★   ★   ★

Later, on the Promenade, Noah wrenched off his jacket. There were steps down to the sea, with a civilized blue railing, but Michael had vaulted that already and was running down the wall of slanted, mortared rocks. His ankles so skinny above his big, precious Jordans.

By the time Noah reached him, the boy was sitting down, smashing one stone on another, *whack* after satisfying *whack*. Shards were jumping everywhere. Like some busy young Cro-Magnon, devising the most useful flint by endless trial and error.

Beside him, Noah piled stones up, making a little cavern. Then a tall cairn, tottering on its base. Finally he covered his own bare feet with astonishingly hot pebbles. His favorites were the pale grays with rings of white. He thought of that time-management parable about how everything could fit in the jar if you made sure to start with the rocks, and only then add the gravel, and finally the sand. If it were granted to Noah to

265

know how many years were left to him, he could estimate how many more pebbles he might be able to fit into the jar. Which reminded him of the announcement on the airplane: 'It is easier to pack coats around bags than bags around coats.'

A family nearby with three little girls; Noah thought of Grace and the small cousins. The problem was that the woman had moved, he supposed; or maybe had her phone cut off if she hadn't been able to pay the bill. But surely the tireless Rosa would be able to track her down one way or another?

These girls' T-shirts said U DO U, OMG GOSH WOW, and LOVE LIGHT SPARKLE FOREVER respectively. Noah wouldn't mind the French taste for English slogans on their clothes if the ones they chose weren't so platitudinous.

Michael was watching teenagers on a parasail being tugged into the air by a speedboat. When the boat turned back on its track, the billowing balloon sank and dipped the youths briefly into the water before they soared again. 'Is it getting higher?'

'Is the tide coming in, you mean? Maybe a bit, but the Med only goes up and down by a few feet, because it's really more like a lake.'

Michael shook his head, impatient. 'Is it true about the sea rising, everywhere? The ice melting.'

'Oh, the climate crisis? Afraid so.'

The boy's eyes narrowed. 'Are we all going to drown?'

'It doesn't happen quite that fast, but it is a disaster. The big disaster of our time.'

'It was fast in Japan.'

'You're thinking of a tsunami. Rising sea levels, that's over decades . . . New York will lose ground, for instance. Coney Island's toast.'

'Me and Cody have a plan, we're going to hide out in that new skyscraper on Flatbush Avenue that's seventy-three stories high.'

'Michael. Use that excellent brain of yours. What does it matter how high the building is, if the lobby's underwater?'

The kid's face contorted. 'By then there'll be . . . ziplines between the tops of the towers.'

Noah sighed, lacking the energy to go step-by-step through the probabilities of apocalypse. His eyes rested on something blowing along the beach. 'Is that a diaper?'

'Ew!'

'No, it looks like a clean one — still folded. Want to grab that for me?'

'Are you about to piss your pants?'

'You wanted a chemistry demonstration. I can do something with a diaper.'

'I didn't ask for an experiment with *diapers*.'

'Your call.' Noah pulled out his satchel, as well as that microfiber towel he'd bought for going to the gym and so rarely used.

Out of the corner of his eye he saw Michael crunching along the pebbles to retrieve the folded diaper.

'I believe I'm going to brave a dip,' he said when the boy came back and dropped it on the pebbles.

'No *way*.'

'*Way*.' Noah unbuttoned his pants; he already

had his swim trunks on. Odds were, this would be his last chance to immerse himself in the sea of his childhood; to go back to the source. Wasn't there a poem, something about growing old and wearing your pants rolled? He lifted his shirt. 'You coming? You can swim in your underwear, no one will give you a second glance.'

'Hell no.'

He can't swim, Joan guessed.

Never had lessons? An alarming percentage of low-income kids didn't. 'Why don't you come in just for a minute?' Noah suggested. 'Maybe I could teach you how to float on your back.'

Michael gave him the finger.

'Water's the most common molecule in the universe. And in us: it makes up two-thirds of your body. What a beautiful spring morning,' he added to convince himself, because the sun had slunk behind a cloud now. It struck him that the sea would have gradually lost heat over the course of the winter, so the water would be almost at its coldest point now. Noah pressed on regardless, shoes off, losing his balance on the knobbly stones as he unbuttoned his shirt. No sunscreen; he never bothered with that. There was a funny mole on his arm that Fernande used to nag him to have biopsied, but at this stage what was the point? 'Want to paddle, even? Come in up to your knees? I'll hold your hand so you won't fall over.'

'You can hold your dick.'

'No need to be nasty.' These stones hurt so much to walk on; however had Noah managed it as a child? Something to do with the ratio of body weight to sole surface area. Or were kids just more distracted by the excitement of running into the waves? Or braver? Noah should have bought himself a pair of those water shoes the locals wore. Still, no turning back. In fact the beach sloped so steeply that he was beginning to lose control; he wasn't sure he could reverse his tracks now even if he chose.

Joan's siren call. *Come on, Professor — if not now, when?*

Oh, don't you quote Primo Levi at me.

He thought of the chemist-turned-novelist, and the eleven months Levi had somehow survived at Auschwitz, and all who'd ended up in the camps. A great swirling vortex of hate that had sucked down the ordinary and the geniuses, the frail and the strong, the old and the young. The Marcel agents. Could it really have been Margot who'd had four of them sent to the camps, two of them to their deaths? If this was true, what was Noah meant to do with the information now?

His first step into the water, it was like piranhas nibbling his shin. But he couldn't let himself cry out or squirm or shrink back, because Michael was watching. He set his teeth and made himself plunge farther into the numbing water. His feet felt damaged. *The sea of my childhood*, he told himself; *the sea of my goddamn childhood*. Another step. The incoming wave had a heft to it, and a bite. Noah couldn't remember why he'd committed himself to this merciless immersion.

Boom! There went the noon cannon, making Noah jerk. A greasy stone slithered under his right foot, caved in, tipped him sideways . . .

Panting in the flood as it rushed up to his chin and locked his chest in an icy embrace, Noah wondered for a moment if he'd managed to fracture a hip.

Behind him, he heard Michael whooping.

Noah lurched to his knees, salt on his lips. No, nothing was broken, it was just the shock. Since he couldn't stand up, better pretend he'd meant to do this. He lay sideways awkwardly, something between a clown and a cadaver; let the next wave take him as far as his cheekbone. A sound like a frightened hoot came out of his mouth.

It doesn't count as a swim unless you go all the way in, Joan reminded him.

Noah grimaced, locked his eyes and mouth, and put his head under the next wave.

Afterward he clawed his way up the slope on hands and knees, the icy sea alternately yanking his shanks back in and bashing his ribs on the stones. Like the self-punishment of a pilgrim. When he got to his feet, he almost fell over again; he had to paw at the sliding pebbles with desperate hands.

He finally limped back to the little towel spread out above the water line.

Michael seemed content as he held up his cracked phone. 'Caught the whole thing. Want to see yourself?'

'No need,' Noah gasped.

'How was it? Like, cold at all?'

Noah lied, shaking his head, licking his lips.

270

'Saltier than the Atlantic,' was all he could get out.

★   ★   ★

For lunch he took Michael to one of the clubs on the beach itself, under the blue parasols, even though it cost double for the privilege. He was feeling shattered by his swim, but also buoyed up.

Michael looked askance at every item on the menu. Finally Noah begged the waiter for some pasta with just butter and cheese.

While the boy tried to fake out his Twenty Questions ball by lying to it, Noah buried himself in *Père Sonne: A Life's Work*. He propped the book open between the pepper shaker and the salt, but its pages flapped loose to show a photo of Josephine Baker floating on her back with her face lifted in ecstasy.

'Who's that?' Michael asked.

'Josephine Baker. Dancer, singer, film star, had this famous costume made of bananas?'

The boy's face was blank.

'Well, that's her swimming right here.' Noah gestured out the window. His grandfather — in his sixties by then — must have waded waist-deep into the water to get the extreme close-up. Water dripping from one of Baker's perfect lobes made a pendant earring. Was it an echo of Vermeer's *Girl with a Pearl Earring*?

'Oh, a visual pun,' Noah said, reading Harstad's paragraph below. 'See the drop of water, like a pearl? Well, Baker was known as the Black Pearl.'

'Pretty hot, for back in the day,' Michael conceded. 'When's my spaghetti coming?'

'As soon as it's cooked. This set of photos is called '*En Fête*' — partying, basically,' Noah translated, 'celebs goofing around on or near the Prom. Here's the first female tennis star, Suzanne Lenglen.' Ermine coat, bob in a jeweled bandeau, champagne flute in hand as she strode out of a casino at dawn. 'See that homeless guy asleep on the bench behind her?'

'What about him?'

'It strikes me that Père Sonne would have had to set up the shot carefully in advance,' Noah said.

'Unless he paid the guy to lie there.'

'True.' The camera did often bullshit, and not just since digital. 'Do you know, the first faked photo dates from 1840?'

'Huh. They even had cameras back then?'

Noah nodded. 'It was a selfie, too — the guy posed himself as a drowned man.'

'I do that!' The boy flicked through the camera roll on his phone and held it out. 'There's one.' Michael as a corpse on the grass, eyes shut, tongue lolling, head sideways.

'Very dramatic.' Noah fingered the small screen, fissures showing through its tattered-edge tape.

'Give it.'

'I'm just looking at your photos.'

'Yesterday all you did was bitch about them being out of focus.'

There was a freshness of approach in the composition of one or two; more than a touch of wit. 'This one taken out of our hotel window — was it? — of the little guy with the big dog, that's not a bad photo at all.'

Michael grunted and reached for his phone.

Noah went back to the biography and paged through the playfully framed faces. The Thurbers, the Stravinskys, the Hemingways, James Joyce and Nora Barnacle.

'Nice car.' The boy was assessing it upside down.

Noah turned the book to show him the shot taken inches from the grille. 'That's a writer called Aldous Huxley in his Bugatti.' Diaghilev on the next page. Pavlova, Valentino . . .

'They all look high.'

'On life, or fame. But very possibly the other kind of high as well, or drunk at least,' Noah told him. 'You've heard of Pablo Picasso?' In bathing trunks and a Stetson, the painter was captured graffitiing a wall.

Michael studied the picture. 'Definitely high.'

Père Sonne made family life look a blast, Noah thought. Matisse and his daughter in their canoe. Scott and Zelda Fitzgerald on the Prom, swinging their little girl between them. *Un, deux, trois, soleil!* (One, two, three, sunshine!) That's what Margot and Marc used to chant, Noah remembered, each gripping one of his sticky paws through Central Park, and heaving him high on *soleil*. She'd been a good mother. But didn't the children of monsters often believe that?

Michael grinned at an image on the next page: a man in a tiny alley in the Old Town, clown legs

273

braced horizontally between two buildings. At the top of the image, a housewife looked down on him from a high window as if to ask, what nonsense is this?

'That's one of the Marx Brothers — Harpo, maybe,' Noah told him.

'Oh yeah, seen them on YouTube.'

Noah checked the date: 1929. 'A year later, my grandpa suddenly stopped photographing celebrities.'

'How come? Had enough of their ego-tripping?'

'Well, maybe, after fifty years . . . and he'd just been widowed, but that doesn't explain it.' Max Harstad discussed the theory that the photographer's mood had been darkened by the crash of the US stock market, but pointed out that France hadn't really started feeling the effects till 1931. Noah put his finger on the woman at the window above Harpo. 'Père Sonne got interested in the nobodies instead. *Les riz.* My mother had an old saying about *les poivres et les riz* — the rich were pepper because it used to be expensive, whereas the poor were plain old rice.'

'Who's she?' Michael tapped the next page: a lipsticked face looming in a mirror at a market stall in the Cours Saleya.

'A cross-dresser.' Noah said, reading Max Harstad's caption. 'It's in a 1930s series called '*La Nuit*,' 'The Night'.' Taken after dark, mostly during Carnival. Workingmen in false noses and head scarves, crammed together behind a fence like animals at the zoo. 'Lots of street performers — look at this one-legged organ-grinder.'

Rouged girls resting on benches, maybe an allusion to a Toulouse-Lautrec painting? It was hard not to take a voyeuristic pleasure in their limp curves, Noah found. A woman had her face down on a bar table while a baby sat up wide-eyed in the pram beside her.

That one made Michael nod. 'Good one. He's not even crying yet but you're like, 'Uh-oh, any second now . . . ' '

Did Père Sonne ask permission of the subjects of these apparently candid shots? This wiry family in worn leotards, for instance, packing up their painted wagon.

'That could be the same circus we're going to,' Michael said.

Noah had forgotten that half-promise. He touched his finger to the arc of bright canvas in the upper left corner of the picture. 'See this bit of the big top?'

'Uh-huh.'

'Your eye — well, your brain — imagines the rest, the whole huge circle of the tent.' Noah traced the circumference past the edge of the page, across the snowy tablecloth. 'That's called the law of closure. Like *closing* a gap. The viewer fills in what they don't see, what's missing.' Noah was having trouble explaining this. He used to be a good lecturer, but his students had never been eleven. 'Do you by any chance know the FedEx logo?'

'The arrow. I never *didn't* see the arrow,' Michael crowed. 'But Cody couldn't tell what I was talking about till I drew it for him.'

Noah's fish soup arrived just then with all its

275

little accoutrements: a puddle of *rouille*, garlic croutons, grated Gruyere. Michael complained about how small his plate of pasta was, but tucked in.

★ ★ ★

At the bus shelter, Noah squinted at the schedule.

'So, the circus this afternoon, maybe? I saw the trucks, it's really near our hotel.'

'Well, I don't know. There's a bus we could take to a Roman arena,' Noah said as enticingly as he could.

'An arena like for basketball?'

'Ah . . . similar. Gladiator fights, that sort of thing.' What he really wanted to see up at Cimiez was the episcopal palace, but he'd have trouble selling that.

'The arena, *then* the circus,' Michael decided.

Their bus lurched in zigzags through the hills, slowly rising above Nice. It hung behind a knot of bicycles for a while, then overtook them. Now there was a very French sight, Noah thought: skinny men (and one woman) in lurid spandex bib shorts.

Nudging Michael, he held *A Life's Work* open and showed him an action shot of newsboys in shirtsleeves dashing by with bundles of papers. 'There's a sort of rule in photography that moving subjects should go left to right, the direction we read in, but you notice my grandpa broke it here?'

'By mistake?'

Noah shook his head. 'I think he wanted to shock the eye — like, 'Whoa, those boys are going to knock me over!'' Another picture, of dockworkers dwarfed by the gigantic barrels they were rolling off a ship. A scrawny woman with a thickened right arm working an olive mill. These overworked subjects had paused in their trades to pose with gravitas for Père Sonne, and in return he'd done them the courtesy of framing them like saints or scholars in a fresco: with respect, but no sentimentality.

Here was an enigmatic fisherman regarding the viewer through his net. 'That's genius,' Michael said. 'Like, is he the fish, is it him that's trapped?'

'Ooh, you're getting deep now,' Noah told him, only a little mockingly. 'Do you notice how there's often an odd man out in the group? Like this one brick-carrier who's stopped to sneak a cigarette.' Which made Noah itch for one.

'This little girl's bored out of her skull.' Michael pointed to a shot of a family in procession behind a coffin.

'Exactly.' The collective, and its discontents. The children in the series titled 'Les Gens' were a force of anarchy erupting from the shadows of their slum: squeezed into huge pipes, peeking down from balconies, splashing in foul puddles.

'He called this series 'Les Gens,' another pun — it means 'The People,'' Noah explained, 'but it sounds a little bit like légendes, legends — as if ordinary working people were superheroes.'

'With secret powers?'

'Well . . . the power to keep going at hard jobs

for not enough pay.' Noah couldn't shake the image of Amber welding for twenty cents an hour. Did she focus all her rage into that small flame? Was it her sentence she was burning away, a moment at a time?

Now the bus passed a sign about a colloquium on Nice in 1918. With uniquely French grandiloquence, it said LE SOUVENIR EST UN HONNEUR. OUBLIER SERAIT UNE HONTE. 'It's an honor to remember, and it would be shameful to forget,' he translated for Michael's benefit.

'An honor to remember what?'

'The dead. It's a conference to mark a hundred years since the end of World War One.'

Michael frowned, thinking that through. 'Not much honor for you, though.'

Noah gave the boy a look.

'Remembering your mom, I mean. If it turns out she was snitching to the Nazis.'

A woman sitting nearby stared.

Noah asked, 'Keep your voice down, would you?'

''Kay.'

Noah leaned his mouth on his knuckles.

After a few seconds, the boy whispered: 'No offense, dude.'

'None taken. I don't know if *snitch* is quite the right word for it,' Noah murmured, troubled by the parallel. 'See, your no-snitching code . . . it's really important to tell the police if you have information about a crime in your neighborhood.'

The boy's mouth twisted.

'That's different from the terrible thing

Margot may have done, sneaking off to betray her own people to the invaders. If she really did that . . . that's unforgivable,' Noah said heavily. 'But cops are not the same as Nazis.'

One eyebrow went up. 'Tell that to the black kids at my school.'

'I take that point, but — '

'What about Michael Brown Junior? Or Tamir Rice, he was fucking *twelve* when they gunned him down.'

'OK, OK.' Noah noticed on the electronic sign that they'd just missed their bus stop, so he lurched to his feet.

★   ★   ★

The suburb of Cimiez was all quiet green and shade. 'See, the Romans had no interest in lying around on the beach,' he told the boy, 'so they settled up here in the hills where it was cooler.'

A vast, dark red house across the park turned out to be the Musée Matisse, but Michael said he wasn't looking at any art today.

'All right, the Archaeological Museum, then.'

'The arena, with the gladiators.'

'The arena's part of the museum, and I meant there *were* gladiators, a couple of thousand years ago.'

In a wounded voice: 'You said gladiators.'

'Michael! You could not have believed there'd be actual live gladiators.'

The kid smirked, dropping the act.

The woman at the ticket counter seemed

irritated to have her espresso and magazine-reading disturbed. She asked where they were from, for statistical purposes.

To spite her assumptions, Noah said France.

He could tell she didn't believe him. Whether she was suspicious of Americans, or children, or both, she kept a beady eye on the pair of them.

In the museum's barnlike and almost entirely empty first room, Noah showed the boy coins, ivory-handled knives, even hands-on replicas — the puzzle pieces of an ancient amphora you could try to fit together. Michael slapped a reproduction helmet on his head (dull gold, with cheek flaps and a little point on top) and roamed around touching everything, spinning a marble head of Antonia on its stand, taking selfies with a mask of Silenus. 'Shit, I forgot my selfie stick in the hotel.'

'Bad luck.' Noah had slid it under the bed before the boy woke up.

The woman from the desk clearly knew enough English to catch the word *shit*. She click-clacked on her stilettos through the cavernous space, scowling at Michael, and reminded Noah that children were to be supervised at all times by their . . . responsible adults.

Noah told her he quite understood.

'*Ce n'est pas un jouet*,' she barked at Michael, tapping her head.

'She says the helmet's not a toy.'

The boy was at the pretend-you're-an-archaeologist table, scooping and brushing red sand too vigorously, so it puffed into the air.

The woman hovered in the entrance. Perhaps

the young man should take the helmet off now, she suggested, and put it back on the stand for the next visitor?

Noah's temper flared. He pointed out that there were currently no other visitors.

'*Attention!*' she shot at Michael, who was getting some sand on the floor.

'Watch it,' Noah told him.

'My bad,' Michael said glibly.

Noah got him to put back the helmet before they went into the next room, where they sat through a video about life in ancient Cemenelum, full of creepily identical CGI soldiers.

It was a relief to step out into the ruins of the town. Founded in the first century, Cemenelum had been the same size as Pompeii, Noah read, with a temple to Mars, a market square, and a vast bath complex. He walked to the center of the ruined white amphitheater and raised his voice. 'Five thousand Romans would sit on these tiers and watch Christians get torn apart by lions.'

The boy called back: 'Nothing much going on here today, though.'

'Oh come on, Michael, even you have to admit this is pretty cool.'

The kid clambered onto an arch that was a single stone thick and snapped a picture of himself in a heroic pose.

As they wandered around the vast diggings, Noah found a row of Roman toilet holes in a bench. 'See, you'd sit there beside total strangers, and take turns wiping with the same sponge-on-a-stick.'

'Ew!' Michael climbed over the warning string for a closer look.

'Get back here.'

'Just one pic, sitting on the Roman crapper.'

'No! You'll dislodge something.'

'It survived a few million centuries, I don't think my skinny ass is going to break it.'

'Get back here *this minute*.'

Indoors again, in the little gift shop, Michael flipped through a volume with translucent pages showing how Nice had looked at hundred-year intervals since the Greeks. Noah wondered whether the kid's interest would dissipate if Noah actually bought it for him.

The woman came scuttling out from behind her counter again to say that the books were not to be read before purchase.

Noah's teeth clamped together so hard, his jaw ached. 'Come on, let's pee before we go, if her ladyship doesn't object to that.'

He came out of the stall afterward to find Michael gone, and for a moment he panicked.

But there was the boy outside the museum with his backpack, studying a sticker someone had put slightly askew on a lamppost. 'What's this about kebabs?'

Burqas, kebabs, mosquées — assez! 'It's an anti-Muslim thing: no more burqas, kebabs, or mosques.'

'Kebabs? Who doesn't like kebabs?'

'Idiots,' Noah sighed.

'Are we going back down to the sea now?'

'Yeah,' hedging, 'but by a different bus so I can have a look at a garden near here.'

'A garden?' Disgustedly. 'Can we get it over with real fast?'

'Really fast,' Noah told him. 'It's an adverb.'

'It's a pain in the ass is what it is.'

★　★　★

This bus took only five minutes. As Noah followed his satellite map down one flowery avenue and along another, he told Michael what he'd looked up this morning. 'The Marcel Network — '

'The couple on the bench, and the dude who wasn't your mom's boyfriend?'

He nodded. 'They had to change all these Jewish kids' names to Christian-sounding ones so the Nazis wouldn't arrest them, right?' Noah had come across a partial list of the Marcel children in a database. Born from 1927 to 1942, hundreds of -steins, -manns, -blums, -baums, -ovitches. No R.J.s, though; no *J*s at all, not among the real surnames or the false. He'd skimmed the stories; nothing heartwarming about them. Moussa Abadi had felt guilty for the rest of his life about drilling his fellow Jews in the ersatz identities that were their only hope of survival, after they'd been entrusted to him by weeping parents who in many cases they would never see again. 'But imagine if you forgot your real name and date of birth, and when the war was over you couldn't remember who you really were, or find . . . any of your family who were left?'

'I'd remember.' Michael's voice was stern.

'Well, some of them were just toddlers. So

Abadi and Rosenstock, what they did was, they wrote down all the kids' true facts, made three identical cards for each, with photographs, fingerprints, addresses, relations, the whole works.'

'Why three?'

'Safer, I suppose, because if there was just one it might get lost.'

'But riskier because more cards the Nazis might find.'

'You're a smart cookie, Michael.'

The boy shrugged off the compliment.

The paradox was that these cards had endangered the entire Marcel Network, hiders and hidden alike. But then, it wasn't fair to save a child's life at the cost of stripping him of who he was. 'Rosenstock and Abadi kept their own set tucked between books in their friend the bishop's library, that's just over there.' He nodded at the stately building coming up on the left. 'They buried a second copy in his garden, and sent a third off to the International Red Cross.' How much they'd gambled, these imperfect heroes. What could have possessed Margot to wish, no, to do them harm?

Noah's hip was throbbing as they got off the bus and walked along the wall topped with decorative fencing. Here were the gates, but they wouldn't open, even when he shook them. He checked the entrance hours listed for the diocesan office — yes, Friday 2:30 to 4:30 — then noticed a slip of paper taped at the bottom: *Fermé exceptionellement.* 'Damn it. Shut today, doesn't say why.'

284

'What did you want to see, anyway?' Michael asked.

'Just where they did their secret work, these Marcel people.' Noah pressed his forehead to the bars. A lush garden, with lofty trees. No sign of light in the building. 'I had a notion that just maybe this picture was taken here.' He pulled out his mother's envelope and found the image of the tangled roots.

'Your mom was spying on *trees*?'

Noah managed a smile; that did sound ridiculous. 'I don't know, possibly marking the spot where the third set of cards was buried?'

'Like pirate treasure.' Michael seized the photo. Then shrugged off his backpack. 'Give me a boost.'

'What? Why? There's nothing to see now.'

'Come on,' the boy ordered.

So Noah laced his fingers and let Michael step into them. Pressing down on Noah's shoulders, even his head, the boy clambered up and then leaped onto the wall.

'Hang on, I just meant for you to get a better view. Get down before you fall.'

'I'm not going to fall.' Michael held onto the short spikes and swung his butt from side to side like a triumphant chimp.

'It's too high.'

'This isn't high.'

'Remember how you broke your collarbone?'

'It wasn't from *falling*. Those eighth-grade dickwads threw me into a dumpster.'

Noah stared up at him.

The boy lifted one leg over the fence.

'Michael! What are you *doing*?'

'Going to look for your tree.'

'Come back down right now.'

But the boy had already dropped onto the grass below, with a thump.

'There'll be security cameras, a burglar alarm!' Noah couldn't hear anything from the episcopal palace itself, but sensors might have triggered a call to the emergency services. Up on his toes, he craned through the bars.

Michael walked away, throwing over his shoulder: 'It's not like I'm breaking in.'

'You already have!'

'It's only a freaking garden.'

'The police could be on their way already. And what if you can't climb back up?'

But Michael was preoccupied with comparing the picture in his hand to the nearest palm tree. The next looked like a yew to Noah. Then a knobbly plane tree.

'Come back,' he wailed. 'It's pointless, I'm sorry we came.' He was preparing an explanation for when the *gendarmes* roared up. A misunderstanding; a confused child. Did French municipal police carry guns? *Ne tirez pas!* Don't shoot the kid!

'It's *kind* of like this one.' Examining, what was it, some kind of oak now, Michael held up the picture beside it. He pulled out his phone and photographed the base of the tree.

'It's been seventy-five years,' Noah called. 'Think how much the roots would have grown in that time, or the tree could have fallen down long ago.'

Michael's face fell. 'Then why are we here?'

Because I need to weigh my mother's soul. 'Please!'

A faint siren in the distance; an ambulance?

Michael cantered over to the gates. Tucking the toe of his sneaker into a scroll of ironwork —

'Don't spear yourself,' Noah groaned.

The boy was up and over in two seconds, and thudded down onto the sidewalk.

Noah didn't waste any breath rebuking him; he picked up the backpack, seized the sleeve of Michael's jacket, and turned to go.

The boy tugged his arm out of Noah's grasp, but did follow him around the corner.

* * *

Sitting on the bus coming back into the center of Nice, Noah compared his mother's small print to the image on Michael's phone. They were not dissimilar, these tangle-rooted trees, if you allowed for the passage of three-quarters of a century.

'Could be, right?'

'Could be.' Noah didn't want to sound ungracious. The kid was doing everything he could to help this old man with a quest that wasn't his own.

'Hey, I nearly forgot. Shut your eyes.'

Noah did. When he opened them again, he recoiled from the granite-eyed gaze of a soldier. The kid was wearing the replica Roman helmet. 'Michael Young!'

A giggle from behind the nosepiece. 'Bitch was asking for it.'

Noah couldn't deny that, but — 'She was suspicious, and you just confirmed her worst suspicions. You stole from a *museum*.' He was trying to remember whether there'd been CCTV cameras there.

'It's just plastic.' Michael drum-rolled his fingertips on the helmet.

'What about all the other kids who won't get to try it on now?'

'Like they could give a shit.'

'Listen to me. Trespass, theft, all in one day. You'll end up' — Noah stopped himself from saying *in prison* — 'in deep trouble if you carry on like this.'

The boy's face was set, behind the brassy cheek flaps; the lower lip jutted.

'We're taking back the helmet this minute. Well, first thing tomorrow, because I'm tired,' Noah corrected himself, unable to face the return trip right now, as the afternoon shadowed into evening.

★ ★ ★

At the stop by the Galeries Lafayette with their displays of masked, pirouetting mannequins, Michael said he was starving. Noah found the nearest café with a takeout counter. Their shtick turned out to be that they formed your ice cream, petal by petal, into the shape of a rose.

'More frilly shit.' Michael was already daubed with strawberry pink around the nose.

Remembering the chemistry demonstration he'd promised the boy, Noah discreetly helped

288

himself to a packet of salt, a plastic spoon, and three plastic cups from the side of the counter.

The electronic sign said the next tram was due in four minutes. Noah leaned against a vaulted pillar and knuckled his hip to ease the muscle. He shut his eyes to rest them. When he opened them next, they focused on a marble plaque: PENDU ICI. 'Hanged here,' he murmured, pointing at the plaque. 'A farmer called Séraphin Torrin.' The name of an angel. 'The Seventh of July: that was nearly the end of the war. The Nazis left him strung up here as a warning to his comrades.'

'Did it work?'

'Nope,' Noah said with a sorrowful satisfaction. 'Before the end of August, the Resistance got tired of waiting for the Yankees and liberated the city themselves.'

And what about Margot, had she found herself on the losing side of history? Could she possibly have regretted the ousting of the Germans?

Don't indict the woman without evidence, Joan reminded him.

But if Margot had been loyal to France, why had she fled its shores the minute the war was over?

Words chiseled in a little wreath below the marble plaque: 'PASSANT, INCLINE-TOI, SOUVIENS-TOI. That means, 'You who pass by, bow down, remember.''

'Yeah yeah yeah, we've been remembering all week,' Michael said through a huge yawn. 'Streetcar's coming.'

Have some respect. But Noah managed not to say it; pressed his lips against his teeth.

As they walked from the tram stop, Michael got only the occasional glance from a passerby. They probably assumed his helmet was a Carnival costume.

'Here we are.'

'No, we're still a few blocks from the hotel,' Noah told him.

Michael gestured down a street to where a slice of big top was lit up in the dusk.

Noah nearly dropped down on the sidewalk at the prospect. 'Really, the circus, now?'

'We had a deal.'

'All right. If you let me have a nap first.'

'Big baby!'

'That's how it is.' Noah checked the complicated website on his phone; almost two hours before the evening show. Yes, he'd have time to stretch out on starched sheets in his room . . .

In *their* room. Being alone, his normal condition for the past decade, was forbidden to Noah this week.

★   ★   ★

When he forced himself back to consciousness after just forty-five minutes in bed — the alarm on his phone like a barbed sliver of sound in his brain — Noah sat up and massaged his haggard face to get some muscle tone back.

The camp bed was empty. He gulped — then registered the sound of the pipework. Michael was taking a shower without even being asked.

There was a brief email from Vivienne. 'Colette Estelle Lamarche née Dupont born Nice December 4, 1937, don't suppose she could be your Coco? Here's her number in case.'

That was it, *Colette*, the cleaner's little girl. Coco had just been her nickname.

'Bless your cotton socks,' Noah wrote back to Vivienne.

He dialed this Colette's number and it went to voicemail, so he left an awkward *don't-know-if-you'll-remember-me* message, making sure to use the polite *vous* form.

Michael came back out, dressed in the same pants and hoodie, and threw himself down. He turned the pages of what looked like a tiny scrapbook.

'Are those photos?'

A few seconds passed. Then he held it up. 'Mom made it for me, for Christmas.'

A four-by-six photo album, carefully covered in old denim. (Noah thought of that clog carved with infinite patience from an olive pit in a concentration camp.) Snaps of Michael as a baby, in the arms of a younger, more sparkling Amber; one in which he sat high on the shoulders of Victor, holding on to his father's perfectly shaped ears.

That maroon chip: could Victor really have been clean when he'd seen his son last? All the more of a tragic waste, then, when he'd injected heroin and fentanyl into the back of his knee.

Averting his face now, Noah put a hand up to wipe his leaking eyes. None of it made any sense to him, neither his nephew's lucky breaks nor his unlucky ones. Arrested with Amber, let go the next day; dead on a motel carpet three months later.

'That's Grandma.' Michael showed one of her clutching him tight.

'This would be Cody?' Noah put his finger to a grinning face.

Michael nodded. 'Used to give me rides in his wheelchair.'

There were recent-looking ones of Amber in her uniform, posed with her son on a stretch of almost convincing sand, or against a forest thick with trees. Unsmiling, Michael rode on a toy truck with his knees sticking up. 'Where was this?'

'Children's room at the prison. Shit's always broken.'

'And here?' Noah pointed to another photo in which Michael held his mother around the waist in what seemed like full-spectrum sunlight, against a brick wall.

'That was last Family Day. Races and Sno-Kones,' Michael added appreciatively. 'The click click let us out into the yard for that pic.'

'The click click?'

Michael put his right hand up by his eye and mimed pressing a button. 'The guard that takes the photos. And the photos, too, they're called click clicks, or flicks.'

Noah couldn't bear it: this little plasticated book of love.

'Look at this one.' Michael flicked the pages till he reached a slightly blurred image of an *M* in the crook of a pale elbow. 'Mom did that.'

'Tattooed herself?' Noah was appalled.

'With a needle and a ballpoint. *M* for *Michael*, see?'

'That must have been painful.'

A shrug. 'It's not all that.' The boy hesitated, then pushed up one sleeve and showed Noah his own inner arm.

FOE, Noah read, inside a lopsided heart. 'Who did this?' Trying not to let Michael hear his outrage.

'My friend Jason, last year, before he went to Atlanta. I had to make sure Grandma never saw it, she hates tats.'

Noah was more concerned about infection than tastefulness. But the skin looked healthy enough now; no point in panicking retrospectively. 'Is *FOE* supposed to declare, what, that you're enemies with the whole world?'

Michael considered him, head tilted. 'You're so ignorant, you *disgrace* me.'

Every word Noah let out of his mouth came back to bite him on this so-called vacation. Michael would grow up to be an autodidact, or a holder of lifelong grudges, or both.

'F dot O dot E dot,' the boy spelled out. 'Family. Over. Everything.'

'Ah.'

'So when are we going to do this experiment?'

Noah was lost. What was this whole week but an experiment, with the most uncertain of outcomes?

'With the diaper.'

'Oh. Yes.' He dragged himself up.

Over the bathroom sink, with Michael watching, he ripped open the diaper's dry-weave skin and reached for the plastic spoon. Then he handed it to Michael. 'Dig out a spoonful of that powder.'

Excited: 'It's going to blow up?'

'Don't you think if diapers were explosive we'd have heard about a few cases of vaporized babies by now?'

Michael laughed. 'Like tiny suicide bombers.'

'Go ahead, scoop the stuff into one of the cups.'

'Which one?'

'They're all the same.' When the boy had done that, Noah dropped the gored diaper into the trash and carried the three plastic cups into the bedroom. 'Now. Ever played Cups and Balls?'

'You know you sound like a chomo?'

Noah kept forgetting to google the word. 'What *does* that mean?'

'Cho-mo, child molester.'

'Ah.' Relieved to get it at last. 'Anyway, maybe you know it as the Shell Game?'

'Yeah, yeah. We play that one with bottle caps. Hide a bread clip under one . . . '

'Right. So you sit over there.' Noah fetched the glass of water from his nightstand and poured it into the cup of powder. 'Watch closely now.'

'I see what you're doing,' Michael warned him. 'Can't trick *my* eye.'

'Keep watching, wise guy.' Noah made some cursory movements, swapping the cups around. 'Where's the water?'

Michael pointed at the middle cup.

'You sure?'

'Hundred percent. Want to make this interesting?' The boy rubbed thumb and fingers together.

'Financially? No. Scientifically, it's interesting already.' Noah switched the cups on the left and right.

'You suck at this. My friend Jason, you should see him play the shells.'

Noah swapped the middle with the left. 'Would you care for one more try?'

'Nah, because boo-ya, I win.' Michael pointed at the cup on the left.

'Your funeral.' Noah turned the cup upside down. Nothing spilled.

The boy stared.

'I thought you were a hundred percent sure the water was in this one?'

'What the *fuck*?' Michael dived for it.

Noah held it high, out of his reach.

The kid snatched at the other two cups: dry. 'Where'd the water go?'

Noah put down the first cup so Michael could look into it. 'It's still there, just not liquid anymore. The stuff from the diaper is called sodium polyacrylate.'

Michael probed the plumped-up gel with his finger. 'Ew.'

'Its molecules are shaped like telephone cords.' A dated example. 'Spirals. When it bonds with water, all the little coils straighten out and form sandwiches — two chains of polymer on either side of each chain of water. So diapers can absorb up to three hundred times their weight.

Try and squeeze a drop out?'

Michael scooped the fat cylinder out of the cup, mashed the gel, crushed it.

'Force won't do it. You need salt to break the bond.' Noah offered him the tiny sachet.

The boy sprinkled the salt on. They watched it puddle and release water across the table.

★ ★ ★

Night, now. Just inside the alley beside the hotel, the beggar in the military cap was sorting through his things as Noah and Michael passed — swapping them according to some mysterious rationale among a dozen or so plastic bags. Perhaps their possessions gave street people the only sense they had of a *place of residence*, Noah thought.

For a quick bite before the circus, he stopped at a crêperie counter and chose a buckwheat galette with ham and an egg.

'Nutella,' Michael ordered.

'Oh come on, this is your dinner. What about ham and cheese? Spinach? Chicken?'

The kid shook his head, immovable.

Noah thought of buying Michael a savory one, and seeing if the boy would eat it if he had no other options. But why match wills with an opponent so stubborn, unless the issue was life-or-death? '*Alors, Nutella, s'il vous plaît,*' he said to the man behind the counter.

At the circus ticket booth, Noah was startled by the prices: wasn't this traditionally a shabby kind of entertainment? He rejected the premium charms of the *tribunes de privilège* and the *tribunes d'honneur*. When he asked for two seats in the *tribunes populaires*, the man made a sour face and offered his opinion that, being at the very back, Monsieur and the boy wouldn't see much . . .

Noah agreed to the *tribunes d'honneur;* he knew he was being upsold, but there wasn't much point in going at all if the view was going to be that bad.

A young nincompoop in a bright red uniform led them to their seats, for a tip.

Tinny, distorted, hectic tunes. 'I think the music might have been live, in my day. Or maybe from a gramophone?'

'What's that smell?'

'Big-cat urine.'

That made Michael hoot.

As soon as the show began, Noah realized it was going to be god-awful. Had old-style animal circuses always been like this, and had he simply been easier to impress at three or four? Or maybe he was remembering a circus in New York when he was older. He had a sense of bouncing in Margot's lap. Had Fernande been with them, or not born yet? He'd gotten *barbe-à-papa* in Margot's hair, Noah remembered now, and she hadn't even lost her temper. A good mother, by any measure. But even if that was true, how to set that against what she'd done in the war?

Might have done, he told himself. There was no hard evidence.

These horses seemed cowed; the dogs, creepily eager. The tigers, when they finally emerged in

297

their wheeled cage, were limp and mangy. How humiliating for kings of the jungle to be forced to stand over each other, bridge-style, or roll on their backs like kittens.

But Michael fizzed with elation at each entrance.

The human acts were easier for Noah to bear. One juggler spun five huge metal bowls at once; another danced in a spinning maze of hula hoops. An acrobat played at being caught inside a sort of spider's web. A man and woman climbed and wound themselves up a rope to the top of the tent, then suddenly let go and hurtled almost to the floor, making Noah's pulse thump. Beside him, Michael let out a wild yip.

At least half the performers were black, which Noah hadn't expected of a French circus, and there were dancers from Eastern Europe who somehow caught and threw laser beams. An old-school clown drove into the ring in a miniature car, then came back in on a deconstructed bike that had its back wheel connected to its front only by a loose chain. Michael seemed particularly fascinated by a skinny contortionist who bent backward and walked his legs around in a circle, past his own face, and finished by somehow feeding his whole body (belly first) through a metal tube; Noah had to look away.

At the intermission the kid begged for a glow stick, a rattle, a souvenir top hat.

'Pick one, or a snack if you'd rather.'

'OK, cotton candy. At least my helmet was free.' Michael knuckle-drummed on it.

Noah enjoyed watching the girl in spangles and tights tease up the sugar fluff from the whirling cauldron onto her stick. 'The French call it *barbe-à-papa*, dad's beard. Hey, don't make your helmet sticky.'

Michael lifted it off before taking a huge bite of the pink stuff. 'Vic had a beard for a while. Mom showed me a pic on her phone.'

Noah's vision suddenly blurred with tears. Victor's perfect face, in all its disguises.

The music was rising; the speakers screeched with feedback, and a deep voice in Italian-accented French asked patrons to be so good as to take their seats.

The second half began with a complicated act involving motorcyclists (two brothers and a sister, the master of ceremonies claimed) in a ball-shaped cage. Lots of revving and suspense-ful bass before they began to spin terrifyingly . . . but Noah soon saw how reliably each rider stayed on their particular track. It was a matter of trusting geometry.

The next performance was a quick-change act, as old as vaudeville. It began as a conventional fox-trot, then the woman's outfit changed, and then the man's, and then both of theirs again. Michael let out a groan of delighted protest. Mostly the pair changed behind hastily whisked tablecloths, or in elasticized tubes they pulled up around each other, but for the last change the man threw a fistful of confetti over the woman, and her skimpy lingerie somehow transformed into a full-length white evening gown.

Noah cringed when a whole so-called family

of elephants came in, with men somersaulting on their backs and a woman dangling from one soft gray mouth. The beasts seemed both strong and frail, desperate to please. Three of them were made to get up on tiny stools and dance to 'Gangnam Style,' shaking their sagging bottoms. They seemed so old, and so appalled that it had come to this.

The father figure of the troupe ordered the smallest boy to lie down on the sawdust for an elephant to step over. Noah couldn't avoid thinking of Abraham preparing Isaac on the altar. The child quailed stagily and ran off; the man chased and caught him.

'Shithead!' Michael pressed his small fists together.

Noah thought of reassuring him, but there was no need because the crowd, incited by the ringmaster, began to chant 'Le Papa, le Papa!'

'They're saying the dad should do it himself,' he told Michael.

The boy nodded, rigid.

With a show of bowing to the crowd's will, the man threw himself down, supine. The elephant approached, and stroked the man's sternum tenderly with one giant foot. (Noah had to remind himself that this wasn't a sign of affection, just the result of hundreds of weary hours of training.) Groans of pleasurable terror went up all across the stands.

'Jesus Christ!' Michael breathed the words.

The man patted the elephant's wrinkled leg . . . then she stepped forward, over him, and he was somehow up on top of her, waving in

300

triumph, as the crowd applauded wildly.

'Maybe they're the ancestors of the crew in your grandpa's picture,' Michael shouted in Noah's ear.

'You mean the *descendants*. Could be. Circus does run in families.' Like a disease.

'Hey, I've got a joke,' Michael said on their way out.

He was really just a little boy, Noah registered; eleven years old, cotton candy on his chin. 'Oh yeah?'

'What did the elephant say to the naked man?'

'This is going to be smutty, isn't it?'

'You know the answer or not, dude?'

Noah could just imagine, but he didn't know exactly how it would be worded. 'So what did the elephant say to the naked man?'

Michael put on a shaky old lady voice: 'It's cute, but can you pick up peanuts with it?'

Which made Noah laugh more than he had in some time.

7

Nom de Guerre

Noah lay in the dark, a patient, crazed prosecutor building a case against his own mother. *Petit à petit, l'oiseau fait son nid;* 'little by little, the bird makes its nest.'

The photos: at her death last year his sister Fernande had in her possession prints from war-time Nice that seemed unlikely to have come from anyone but Margot, including images of three Marcel Network members: Maurice Brener (Zazou), Odette Rosenstock (Sylvie), and Moussa Abadi (Marcel), none of them taken face-on. Also a close-up of the door of the hotel the Nazis had commandeered. Also — though this didn't make the story any clearer — images of a small boy, a bell tower, a tree, children's feet, a woman (*MZ* on the back), an empty street.

The facts: Margot had sent her husband to New York in 1940, then two years later, her son; she'd stayed away a further two and a half years. She'd gone missing for three days in August 1944, and as soon as she'd buried her father, she'd left France and never gone back.

It didn't seem to add up to as much as Noah thought it would. He should be relieved; he'd rather not have to think these dreadful things of his mother. But every day he spent in Nice, he found himself more desperate to know for sure.

He touched his fingers to the painted wall. Over three thousand Jewish detainees had passed through this hotel from September to July, which was an average of — he reckoned it in his head — about ten newcomers a night. Vacationers shivering in shorts, snatched off the beach; wet runaways fished out of the Var. The waiting, the wailing, the yanking of children away from mothers and fathers. The interrogations.

Noah let himself look up 'Nice Excelsior 1943–1944.' Some of those held here had poisoned themselves and their children, he learned, or jumped from the pretty windows. He found himself on a World War Two forum in which an American reminisced about a night concierge in 1983 who'd taken him into the basement to see the cells and the special room with the drain.

Noah found himself picturing young Sainte Réparate as she swallowed the burning pitch. He couldn't stop himself from tapping in, 'Nazi torture.'

Oh for God's sake, Joan snapped, *are you planning to keep yourself up till dawn?*

Ignoring the links to porn sites, he found some useful articles. The word *torture* turned out to mean *twisting;* a literal torsion, but also a wringing-out of the self. Torture was an unreliable way of getting information, apparently; it tended to elicit the false or irrelevant. The French Resistance had a code of trying not to spill until the third day, to give comrades time to escape, but in fact it seemed that few had

303

spilled anything at all. Some found the pain inflamed their resolve. Some admitted they would probably have revealed names and addresses except that their captors, interested only in hurting them, had never asked. In those rare cases where a Resistance member had cracked, it was generally unclear if they'd done much harm, since what they'd said was out of date or known to their captors already.

Noah puzzled over that. Should your betrayal be measured by the secrets you'd thought you were revealing, or by what the consequences had been? The same went for drunk drivers, he supposed; some wound up in prison for manslaughter and some happened not to hit anyone. It made his head spin, the randomness of it. Would Anubis accept that argument when weighing hearts against the Feather of Truth, he wondered — that morality had an element of what could only be described as luck?

The dark seemed stifling now, the bedroom walls closing in.

Techniques varied under the Occupation, he read, but two were particularly common. The Paris method, or *baignoire*, was usually inflicted on women, who were stripped naked, with their legs tied to a bar across a bathtub filled with icy water, and pushed in backward. Next the interrogators might add electric current. This was known as the *gégène*, slang for *génératrice*, a portable generator that had been used initially for mobile telephones on the battlefield. The French had pioneered this technique in Indochina in the '30s, to interrogate Vietnamese

304

nationalists. Alligator clips might be attached to hands, feet, ears, genitals. Often victims lashed out and dislocated their own tied limbs.

'What's up?'

Noah blinked at Michael's faint silhouette on the other bed.

'You went like — ' The kid hissed dramatically through his teeth.

'Did I? Sorry. I'm looking up . . . upsetting things.'

'Which things?'

'Just stuff that happened in this hotel, in the war.'

'Pulling fingernails out and shit?'

Noah was meant to be making this boy feel safe. 'It's nothing you need to worry about, and it was all over a long time ago.'

'I've seen, like, beheadings,' Michael assured him.

He reeled. 'But why?'

'Isis, Boko Haram, they upload them.'

What could the boy's grandma have been thinking — no, that wasn't fair. She'd been chronically ill, for one thing. And Noah was a hypocrite, because it wasn't as if he had any idea which murky passages of the internet this boy moved through, or how to go about monitoring, let alone controlling it. He asked instead, 'Why put such images in your head, though?'

Silence crackled in the stuffy room.

'Michael?'

'If the world's like that,' the boy muttered, 'I'd rather be ready.'

Noah had no answer.

'But I have to admit, I need some eye bleach after.'

'You rinse your eyes with *bleach*?'

Michael let out a snort. 'Eye bleach, dude. It's pics of kitties and stuff, to wipe your mind after grossing yourself out.'

What a curiously prim notion; like a napkin to dab the lips. 'That's not how memory works. There's nothing that can wipe horrifying information away.'

'Cute kitties, though.'

'Go back to sleep now,' Noah pleaded.

'Nah, I'm up.'

And so was the sun, Noah realized, a narrow beam knifing under the blind.

★ ★ ★

Saturday morning. They were leaving in two days. Michael's T-shirt said WINTER IS COMING, which seemed belated, in February.

For breakfast they happened on a café where all the crockery was artistically askew: cups, juice glasses, bowls made to tilt sideways. Noah kept thinking he was going to spill something, but Michael found it funny.

'Shit, I left my helmet at the hotel.' Michael licked his buttery fingers.

'You mean the property of the people of France, temporarily stolen by an American, which will be returned later today.'

Michael grinned. 'That makes it sound even cooler. Can we go back to the hotel and get it?'

Noah couldn't face the kid wearing the helmet

around town all day; what if they ran into the museum's custodian, out doing her shopping? 'Too far.'

'At least I found my selfie stick.' The boy telescoped it in and out. 'Want to try?'

'Sure,' Noah made himself say.

Michael showed him how to slot his phone into the holder at the end of the rod. 'Hey, do one with the cup, it'll look freaky.'

Gamely, Noah held the diagonal cup to his lips and extended the selfie stick.

'Bend your head the other way,' Michael ordered. 'One eyebrow up.'

Noah tried.

'The other eyebrow, dude.'

'I don't think I can move them separately.'

'Bet your mom could, if she could lick her own nose.'

Noah nodded. 'She was an excellent winker, too.'

When the two of them examined the shot, Noah said, 'I look like something out of a ghost train.'

Michael nodded in approval.

The flower market in the Cours Saleya had been transformed into a *marché aux puces* today. 'It's called a flea market, because they sell old things that might have fleas living in them.'

'Gross!'

'Though everything here seems pretty clean.' The prices suggested there was little chance of anyone snapping up an overlooked bargain, either. Not that Noah cared; he was so bemused by the variety that it didn't occur to him to try to buy anything. He could make no judgment on this jumble of linen napkins, carpets, wicker handbags, ceramic owls, fur hats, theatrical necklaces in rubber or aluminum, decorative gourds pierced to make lampshades, holy cards (a mawkish one of a little girl offering her teddy bear to the crucified Christ) . . . Noah enjoyed picking through a basket of those blotchily painted figurines you baked into cakes for the *Fête des Rois* in January — *fèves*, that was the word — but he didn't want to own any. He handled a bronze nineteenth-century letter opener that had a stylized feather on one end and a chicken claw on the other. When he saw the tiny price tag (€195) he flinched and returned the thing to its spot.

Michael hung back. Did this count as a *fancy store*, Noah wondered? He beckoned the kid closer, showing him tiny collectible cars and a mug of Tintin on his motorcycle with his terrier Milou riding in a basket on the back. Michael was more entertained by vintage tech, Noah found: a rotary phone with a separate earpiece labeled *c. 1900*, a Speed Graphic camera with its bulky bellows . . . 'Père Sonne used one of these until the '30s,' he told the boy. 'My mother would have had to change the cut-film holder for him after every shot, with her hands inside a bag to keep the light out.' He thought of Margot's stamina; her patience. If she'd had some engrossing career of her own, instead of serving her father's, would she have been less likely to succumb to whoever had recruited her, if it was true that she'd been recruited?

'*Touchez pas, Monsieur!*' The stall owner snapped at Noah to take his hands off the camera's brittle leather.

Noah had inherited a few of his *pépère's* smaller cameras, and he'd passed them on to Victor one by one because the adolescent had claimed to be fascinated by shooting on film. Only years later had Noah come to the conclusion that Victor had scammed him, selling each camera the moment he'd gotten his hands on it. But now, eyes on his plausible nephew's son, his ribs seemed to creak with the hurt of it all. If Noah could dial the years back, he'd surrender anything Victor asked for. We spend most of our lives holding on to objects, he thought, and finally they fall from our cold dead hands and those who tidy up after us have the worry of what to do with all this stuff.

Michael was leaning so far over a knife stall that Noah thought he might fall into it. Noah stood beside him, admiring a huge, ornate, nineteenth-century knife and fork for serving fish.

'Nice,' the boy murmured, stroking the filigree handle of a small dagger.

Noah gestured at a fanned-out display of antique pocket-knives. 'We all carried these in my day. I mean, the boys, and some of the tougher girls. Used to play something called Nerve.' He mimed stabbing between his spread fingers.

Michael's face lit up. 'Yeah, yeah, The Knife Game.'

'Is that what you call it?'

'Or Stabscotch, or Five-Finger Fillet.'

'I seem to remember the biggest risk was that the knife would fold up and slice the hand you were holding it with.'

'There's this YouTuber does it supersonically fast . . . ' Michael launched into a jingle about the knife going *chop chop chop*.

'Probably best to practice with a blunt pencil,' Noah suggested. 'We had a version where you threw your knife near your feet, or the other boy's feet. If you got it a few inches in, he — '

Michael interrupted. 'Into his *foot*?'

'Into the ground,' Noah said, scandalized. 'The loser had to pull it out of the ground with his teeth. Mumblety-peg, we called that.' He retrieved the word with satisfaction, like some dust-coated heirloom.

'That'd be *so* banned now,' Michael lamented. 'All the fun stuff is.'

'Snowballs! I got sent to the Mindfulness room for throwing one goddamn snowball.'

'What's the Mindfulness room?'

'New name for *detention*.'

Noah's eyes rolled back in his head. 'What next — will they ban walking in case you fall down?' Maybe it was because there was so little schools could do to shield kids from the real threats: drive-by crossfire, pedophiles, opioids . . .

He caught a whiff of socca and hurried across the market to the woman dishing it out. 'You must try this, Michael,' he called. 'It's, ah, a local thing, a salty pancake.' Probably best not to mention that it was made of ground chickpeas.

310

Noah asked the woman for two portions — one without pepper, for the kid. It amused him to notice *Sans gluten / No gluten* scrawled on her sign; for the Yanks, presumably, because since when did the French try to avoid gluten?

His Proustian moment at last, the hot, greasy taste in his throat. 'Good, am I right?'

'It tastes funny,' Michael mumbled, but kept eating. 'Do you think the massage woman's in today?'

Yes, they were right by the Opera House. The French insisted on their time off, more than other nationalities, but then Saturday might be the most popular day for people needing physiotherapy. 'Why, would you like to see inside my old apartment?'

'*I* don't care,' Michael said crushingly.

Noah decided it was worth a try, and led the way down the narrow street. This time when he rang the bell beside KHOURY AISHAH, there was a buzz and he heard the front door unlock.

They climbed the stairs, Noah's hip speaking to him. Tourism was such an odd mixture of the tiring and the hedonistic.

In an elegant head scarf, Madame Khoury welcomed them in accented but impeccable French and said they must indeed look around since they'd come all the way from New York. She was only updating files and didn't mind being interrupted. She knew his grandfather's work, of course, and what a shame this place hadn't been preserved as a memorial.

Noah peered around in hopes of finding the drainpipe from the photo. Of course the floor plan was quite altered. He remembered their living room, how the piano had stood by the sea-facing windows — that had been cut into two treatment rooms — but as for the rest, he couldn't even decide where the bedroom he'd shared with his parents had been. Linoleum on the floor, that was the only detail he recalled.

Dr. Khoury's practice in Damascus — she'd been an orthopedic surgeon there, but was having trouble getting her qualifications accepted in France — had been obliterated by a bomb. But she could still shut her eyes and walk through it.

Well, Dr. Khoury was so much younger than Noah, he pointed out. And he'd left when he was only four.

'What kind of stuff did you play with back then?' Michael asked him.

'Oh, lead soldiers, a catapult, Meccano trains . . . Monopoly.'

'I freaking hate Monopoly. Goes on forever and the bank always screws you.'

Noah nodded, opening a door to what turned out to be a supply closet. 'I think the darkroom may have been here. *La chambre noire*,' he told Dr. Khoury.

She clapped her hands with pleasure.

Trays, shelves, stains on the walls: all gone now, but Noah could picture them. 'No windows, because developing has to be done in a total blackout,' he explained to Michael. 'Margot would open the cassette in the dark, pull out the film' — he mimed it — 'tear off the end, roll it onto the reel — that was the trickiest part. Then

312

she'd put it in the tank, fit the cover on, and shake it gently, for the right number of minutes, before she pegged the photos up on a washing line to dry.' *Maman, who were you?*

'How'd you know what she did? If it was dark.'

'I suppose . . . I must have learned about it when I was older, or maybe she told me. At least for the printing, she could turn on a safelight, red or amber.' Which wall had that hung on? Or overhead, with a pull cord? 'The crucial thing was to avoid dust, because it makes white spots on the prints.' Noah seemed to recall Père Sonne giving Madame Dupont hell for that. 'The whole room stank of fumes.' He sniffed at the sterile air now and tried to conjure them up: sulfurous, vinegary, metallic, ammoniac?

'Like, poisonous?'

'Not if you just caught a whiff, but once I smashed a bottle with my soccer ball and my grandpa *roared*. Oh, and it had to be kept warm in here all year, warmer than the rest of the apartment,' Noah remembered. 'One winter, we burned the chairs.'

'Cool.' Michael wandered off.

Noah thought he could see the flames rise, hear the crackle, but perhaps that was just a family story come to life in his imagination.

★　★　★

Down in the Old Town he paused at a window holding marzipan diamonds in white and pale brown . . . *calissons*, that was the word, sudden on his tongue. Beside them, *guimauves à la rose*.

313

'Rose-flavored marshmallows,' he said aloud.

Michael made a retching sound. 'Why would you put *roses* in them?'

'Flavor. The French are always trying to make life taste stronger.'

'In fifth grade, the teacher made us play this dumb game. If you had enough self-control to hold on to a marshmallow for fifteen minutes, you'd get two.'

Noah was amused. 'She was doing a classic psychology experiment on you.' Was that even legal?

'I told her she could stick them up her ass.'

'Michael!'

'Actually I went, ''No thanks, I don't like marshmallows,'' the boy said in a saccharine singsong.

'So you got none?'

'I got the satisfaction.'

Noah wondered whether, in the long run, this kind of defiance might come in just as handy as self-control. He pointed into the shop window. 'Those marzipan pebbles ... ' Amazingly realistic in variegated, veined greens and grays. 'I think I ate a real rock once. Another kid had told me it was one of those candies.'

'You swallowed it? Sucker!'

'Not quite, but I cracked a tooth.' His tongue moved around his mouth, but of course these were his adult teeth; he couldn't have had any of these at four.

'That kid, he *schooled* you.'

'It was a girl.' Noah added, 'Coco. Her mother came in twice a week to clean our apartment.'

Michael's brow contracted. 'I did that a couple times, with my mom.'

'Cleaned your apartment?'

'Other people's.'

Noah couldn't tell if this was a nostalgic memory of a time when Amber had still been right there, on top of everything . . . or one of the recollected humiliations of poverty. Had she let him keep the TV on while they were working? Had the cleaning products reeked and stung? 'How was it?'

A shrug.

Thinking of Madame Dupont's daughter, Coco, he checked his phone.

Yes, she'd left him a message, in a voice he didn't recognize. She'd be delighted to meet him on Sunday after Mass. Noah was surprised; he thought of French Catholics as pretty much nonpracticing these days, though he supposed they couldn't all be or the churches would be shuttered by now. 'We're actually going to meet her for coffee tomorrow,' he told Michael, 'the pebble girl.'

'Bring her a bag of these,' the boy suggested, nodding at the shop window, 'and throw in a couple real ones from the beach.'

Noah grinned at that.

His eyes rested on a stream of figures rolling into a doorway: that must be where the Segway tour began. 'Would you like to go on one of those?'

'Right now?'

'Why not?'

A hesitation. 'Not on my own.'

It was only apprehension that was making the boy ask for Noah to do it with him, but still, it warmed Noah.

The guide looked about seventeen and spoke fast and casually, with such a Provençal accent that he had trouble following him. Of course, Noah probably wouldn't have understood the technical terms for the parts of the wheeled transporter even in English. He signed the waivers without reading them, then struggled to tighten his helmet's strap.

Selfie stick slotted through a loop in his jeans like a sword, Michael got the hang of the thing as soon as he stepped onto the little platform and seized the handlebars. 'It's all in the hips,' he told Noah. 'Like flossing.'

Noah was thrown by that. 'I floss with my fingers.'

'The floss *dance*, dude.' Michael jumped down and swung his body and his arms different ways, blindingly fast.

On the Segway, Noah tried some pelvic action, like Elvis in slow motion, and found that it did help to steer the device.

But as the little group set off through the cobbled streets, Noah bringing up the rear, it occurred to him: *so this is how I'll break my hip.* (The good one, probably, just as a falling slice of bread always landed butter-down.) French hospitals were renowned, but how would Noah manage with Michael if he were trapped in traction? Could he have him shipped back to Rosa like some valuable parcel?

The guide pointed out a tiny shrine, high up

on a corner building; one of those relief carvings in which a gigantic Virgin sheltered dozens of tiny people under her cloak. The next alley was redolent of freshly cut leather; wallets and handbags hung on stone walls in a rainbow of shades. Noah thought he remembered this *confiserie* they were passing, which sold fruits — pears, apricots, whole clementines — steeped in syrup for days on end.

Michael pointed as they rolled past a giant gold thumb outside the Hotel de Ville. Noah supposed it counted as art, but he couldn't work out the symbolism. A thumbs-up for encouragement? Or a more sinister hint that everyone lived under the thumb of the municipal bureaucracy? He thought of *mouches* lining up to tattle at the Excelsior. Margot, with an envelope in her handbag that put, if not clear faces, then profiles and shapes to the aliases that masked the Marcels. But if she'd handed over her best photos, he wondered, why hadn't the Resistance agents all been arrested at once? None of it made sense.

The boy lagged behind, ogling the contents of a window: swords, guns. 'Keep up or we'll lose you,' Noah called over his shoulder.

This time the *Boom!* from behind took Noah unawares, and he almost toppled off his Segway.

'Just that twelve o'clock thing.'

Breathless, Noah tried for nonchalance. 'Right, the cannon.'

Their guide led them past a flower stall. Noah breathed in the overwhelming sweetness and concentrated on not knocking anyone down. The

317

next stall held bizarre fruits; a kind of citrus with crooked, devilish fingers.

Out onto the Promenade, where — once they'd survived crossing the six lanes — it was easier on the broad, smooth pavement. Michael was at the front of the pack, working up alarming speed and — could he be? — videoing himself with his selfie stick held high. But if Noah shouted *Slow down*, Michael would only pretend not to hear. Besides, Noah hadn't the heart, because at last, on the sixth day of knowing him, he'd hit on something that thrilled the boy.

They had to turn back at the point where the Prom had been blocked off for something called — rather Franglais, Noah thought — *La Nice Carnaval Run 10km*. Revelers in outrageous costumes and rainbow clown wigs jogged along to the strains of thumping American pop. Noah would have expected anyone capable of running more than six miles to look lithe and limber, but many of these had the baggy, knock-kneed, or stooped bodies of ordinary mortals.

His phone went off, startling him. He couldn't stop the Segway or he'd lose his party, and he doubted he'd be able to find his way back to the rental shop on his own. He thought of ignoring the ringtone, but what if it was Coco Lamarche? Or Rosa, from New York, with urgent news about Grace Drew? He fumbled the phone out of his pocket. 'Hello,' keeping his right forearm pressed on the handlebars and leaning into the phone . . . which made the Segway speed up. Noah straightened up, came

318

to a sharp halt, and almost fell.

'Monsieur Selvaggio?'

It was Monsieur Benoit from the Resistance museum, Noah worked out after a confused exchange. 'Sorry, it's really noisy here and I'm on a . . . a rolling thing.' Eyes searching for Michael.

'One of my colleagues has dug up some information that might be of interest to you, but perhaps this is a bad time?'

Noah managed to get a better grip on the handlebars and glide forward. 'No, carry on, please.'

'Well, this might not be the same person as in your mother's photograph, but there is an individual with the initials M.Z.'

Coincidence, Noah told himself.

'A woman,' Monsieur Benoit went on, 'Marie Zabel. Though that was almost undoubtedly a *nom de guerre*.'

'Marie Zabel?' Noah almost shouted into the phone.

'Yes, a very obscure figure. She's not mentioned in any publications about the Marcel Network, but it's thought she did some forgery work for them.'

Another of Margot's targets, then; Noah's stomach knotted. He hardly dared ask. 'Did she . . . survive the war?'

'Since she seems to have dropped out of view after the summer of 1944, we assume not.'

Noah found he'd come to a halt again. Captured, then; sent to the camps.

'I'm sorry I can't tell you anything more.'

'No, no, you've been more than helpful, Monsieur.' His voice guttural.

'I wish you well with your researches.'

Noah wished he'd never begun his mother-fucking *researches*; wished he'd thrown out Fernande's last box without looking inside.

'Noah!' A shriek, very young. Michael zoomed up to him. 'Where were you, dude?'

'Right here.'

'I couldn't see you.'

'Sorry.' Still discombobulated. 'I had a phone call.'

When they were on the final stretch, approaching the rental shop down a steep cobbled alley, Michael took a corner too fast and fell off his Segway.

Jesus Christ! Noah parked his own machine and hurtled down to the boy. 'Are you hurt?'

'I'm good,' Michael insisted, clutching his elbow.

All the guide did was remark that this happened, sometimes; probably the wheel had caught on the curb.

'You're bleeding, Michael.'

'Not much.' The boy hopped up, proud of himself, and remounted his machine.

'Did you hit your head?'

'You're as bad as my grandma.'

Noah, fumbling in his satchel for an antibacterial wipe and a Band-Aid, decided to take that as a compliment.

At the rental counter, he was inclined not to put a tip in the guide's basket because of the fellow's laxity about safety standards, but

Michael kept nudging him with his unbandaged elbow until he did.

★ ★ ★

The boy munched chicken and fries. Noah toyed with a salade Niçoise. 'So the man from the museum identified our M.Z.' Holding her up. 'You guessed right: it was an alias of another of the Marcel people — someone who made fake documents for the kids.'

'Shit, your mom was spying on them *all*?'

'Looks like it,' Noah admitted, leaden.

Michael pulled the picture out of his hand. 'This one doesn't go with the others, though, because they're outdoors.'

True, it looked like a studio shot, carefully posed. Could Margot have known this M.Z. socially? On what pretext could she have gotten her to pose: had she asked for a memento, but hadn't been able to persuade M.Z. to risk revealing her face? Was it perhaps through this friend that Margot had come across the Marcels in the first place? And at what point had his mother decided to shop them to the Nazis, and (the question he might never be able to answer) why?

'That's a weird last name.'

'Zabel? Jewish, probably.' Noah got out his phone and looked it up. 'German, meaning *board game*,' he reported. 'Sometimes Jewish, but not necessarily.'

'Marcel Network Marie Zabel,' he tried. No hits.

321

'Marie Zabel,' Michael chanted, 'Marie Zabel, Marie Zabel.'

Noah looked at him crazily.

'What?'

His throat was dry. 'It sounds like . . . Mar-Isabelle.' He sipped his wine. 'Isabelle was my grandmother's name, as well as my mother's middle name. Margot Isabelle Personnet.'

'Margot, Mar — plus Isabelle,' the boy yelped. 'It's her, dude. Your mom.'

Could it possibly be true: had Margot been Marie Zabel? A helpful forger, rather than a traitor?

'Mar-Isabelle, Marie Zabel, we fucking nailed it!'

'Hang on, now, we can't be sure.' But Noah's pulse was scudding along. Yes, it could be, it almost had to be. He should have guessed as soon as Monsieur Benoit had supplied him with the *nom de guerre*. Daughter of a someone whose *nom d'artiste* insisted he was *personne*, no one. Had Margot not been able to resist playing games even in the most serious of times? The photos were clues his mother had left behind, for her future self or for her children. 'Zazou with the cane and Odette, Moussa — I think my mother wanted a record of her comrades,' he told the boy, 'but she couldn't show their faces without endangering them, so that's why she photographed them from behind.'

'And herself too.' Michael flapped the coiled-hair picture. 'Bet it *was* a selfie, she must have took it with a string or something.'

Noah managed not to kill the moment by

322

saying *must have taken*. 'And the cathedral! The picture with the circle and dashes.' Another private joke. 'She did the flowers at Sainte Réparate, so that's where she'd have met the bishop, and he was a Marcel too.' Of course Bishop Rémond would have heard about the great photographer's daughter and assistant, a parishioner with unusual skills and access to a private darkroom; it must have been Rémond who'd brought her in, Noah saw now. He'd appealed to Margot's conscience, but her stifled ambition too; even her craving for adventure. That would have been, what, 1942? The summer she'd put Noah on the ship at Marseilles. 'That's why she sent me away.' His voice caught, jerked. 'She had to, because her work was so dangerous.' ID cards, passports, visas, baptismal certificates, ration cards. Identity photos for the cards that would spend the rest of the war tucked in the bishop's books, or buried under one of his trees. Margot had been one thin link in the chain: an archivist of human beings, a filer of children.

'So my great-great-grandma was some heroine,' Michael said sternly, 'and you said she was a snitch?'

'I was only guessing. I still am,' Noah warned him.

'Nah, we got her. Marie Zabel!'

Relief, so vivid it made Noah dizzy. But also he was imagining his mother's constant dread. During all the pedestrian tasks of her days, her heart must have been in her mouth. Each document she worked on like a land mine underfoot.

★ ★ ★

The buildings of the old port rang a faint bell for Noah: two long flame-peach and pink neoclassical blocks. 'Isn't that rather lovely?' he asked, still shaky from the good news.

Michael wrinkled his nose. 'Kind of Baskin-Robbins.'

The white nineteenth-century church was topped with the Virgin, the inevitable gull on her head. On the steps outside, sunburned drunks with bottles in paper bags lay dead to the world in an encampment of sleeping bags and boxes.

In the little harbor at the bottom of the granite steps, Michael ran up to the first of the motor yachts, huge and sleek. They looked more like floating hotels to Noah. 'Owned by Russian mobsters, most of them,' he told the boy.

'Cool.'

'*Not* cool. Probably funded by, ah, exploiting a lot of North African teenagers.' Noah had read something about how the Russians had the French Riviera sex trade sewn up.

'This is a sweet ride, though.' Michael's hand traced a shining prow in the air. He turned his back on the yacht and posed with it, grandiose, holding up his phone on its stick.

As the two of them strolled westerly around the port, the motorboats became reasonably sized, even shabby, with faded canopies. Michael was fascinated by the giant metal rings set into the pavement; he lifted one and let it drop with a clang.

'Don't smash your foot.' So many ways Noah

324

couldn't protect this boy; it was like traveling with a bag of bananas he had little chance of delivering unbruised.

A smaller ring, bolted into the wall: the kid put his head right through it and posed for a dying-prisoner-in-dungeon shot.

Noah was up ahead, at a line of tiny sailboats with upright masts and angled cross masts, bright paint flaking, names scrawled on: *Ninou*, *La Galinette*, *Lou Calanque*, *M'en Bati*. It didn't look as if any of them were used for fishing anymore, just for nostalgic pleasure boating.

Michael thumped down one of the little boardwalks, then sat down, sneakers dangling over the water.

'That's private property, and be careful not to fall in.'

'There's *fish* down there,' the boy remarked.

'Where do you expect them to live?'

'Smart-ass.' Michael stared into the water. 'We had fish.'

Puzzled, Noah asked, 'Where?'

'At my grandma's.'

'For dinner?'

'Pets, dude!'

'Ah, sorry.'

'But they didn't last long.'

'Often the way, with fish.'

'Mom says when she comes home we'll get a dog, if the landlord's cool with that.'

Two years and nine months; thirty-three months from now, so long as Amber managed to pick her way through the contingencies of prison life. If she put a foot wrong at any point, it would be longer than that. Michael would be what, at least fourteen? And what hypothetical *home* was Amber imagining?

As they walked on past the harbor, every bench seemed to hold someone who looked older and more content than Noah. What a strange city of transients this was: sun worshippers, invalids, mobsters, retirees, cruise-ship tourists, refugees with bleeding feet . . .

The sea came in and out with a rush and suck of sound that satisfied Noah's ear. Laid out on a little pebbly triangle of beach were locals with orange leather skin, and more of them basked like seals on the great boulders farther on. He saw an INTERDIT DE FUMER sign, but nobody seemed to be paying it any attention, so he lit a cigarette. Michael threw stones in the sea, not skimming them with any skill, just heaving them far and hard.

'Careful,' Noah called at one point; 'you're too close to that swimmer.'

Out of the glittering waves an ancient-looking woman emerged, head enclosed in the hood of her black wetsuit, weird rubber webbings over her hands. She'd probably live to be a hundred, Noah thought, stubbing out his cigarette. 'Let's walk on a bit farther.'

He ignored the boy's groan.

They took a little coastal path, meandering west away from the city. Bright blooms grew in crevices in the salt-splashed rocks. A nude man lay like a sacrifice, flat on his back.

'If a flasher showed off his junk like that back

326

home, cops would slam his ass in jail.'

'Well, context is everything,' Noah said. 'He's not showing off, he's napping. Americans are such prudes, freaking out at a glimpse of the human body.'

'No, you're the freak, making me look at that. I could tell Ms. Figueroa on you.'

'Fire away.' Noah could just imagine the message: HELP, MR. SELL-VAG SHOWED ME A NAKED DICK. But he didn't care, not this afternoon. *Margot Isabelle was Marie Zabel*, he told himself again. A boulder, lifted off his chest. *She was better than I'll ever be.*

Out to sea, a kite string of white triangles. 'Look,' Noah said as they clambered back up onto the coast road again, 'kids learning to sail in tiny dinghies.'

'They're going to get swamped by that big ship.'

'The ferry?' A huge liner with a bandit's head on the side was moving toward the port. 'No, the sailing instructors must know what they're doing.' A massive horn shook the air, and foam heaved high on the rocks. 'There was a ferry that sank — this must be thirty years ago.'

'How come?'

'Somebody forgot to shut the doors, so the sea poured in and the ship tipped on its side. Hundreds drowned in the first minute. Passengers tried to scramble up, away from the sea, but there was a hole they couldn't get across, with the water pouring through . . . and this one guy, a tall guy,' Noah remembered, 'he lay down.'

'Collapsed, like?'

'No, he lay across the gap on purpose, so twenty other people could climb over him.'

Michael frowned. 'Like a rug?'

'Like a bridge.'

'You can't lie on a gap, you'd fall through. That's gravity.'

'Well, I guess he was gripping on with his arms and feet.'

'Face up or down?'

'I don't know.'

'Face up, you could see what was happening, tell people what to do, but they might step on your junk.'

Noah nodded. 'Face down, it might hurt a bit less to be walked on, but you'd have to watch the water rising toward you.'

'Wasn't the guy afraid they'd be too heavy for him, and he'd get pushed through?'

'I bet he was, if he had any sense.' Had the hero thought of himself as anything special before that day, Noah wondered?

He and the boy squeezed onto the first orange bus jolting back to town, swerving around the coastal bends. No seats, so they hung on to a pole.

★ ★ ★

In Place Masséna, young reenactors in medieval tunics and floppy caps were fighting laboriously with wooden swords. A stall of plastic kitsch was staffed by a man in a bizarre costume that made him look like he was riding a two-legged horse.

Michael blew his last five euros on something

called a sound machine: a rectangular orange device with buttons on it that produced various horrible effects.

'You know that leaves you with nothing for the rest of the week?'

'Yeah, yeah.' A burst of plasticky applause from the box. 'What about next week?'

Noah forced himself to consider the prospect. Back in New York, could he put the kid on the subway to school every morning, or should he go with him? The pair of them would be jet-lagged, too. No, actually, that would work; they'd be waking up early. 'More allowance, you mean? TBD.'

'What's that mean?'

'To Be Determined. Negotiated.'

Michael's machine let out a ghostly laugh, then the *ka-ching* of a cash register.

After the boy had put the thing through its paces, over and over, Noah said, 'Maybe give it a rest now.'

The only response was the losing horn from a game show: *wah wah*.

'Oh, very funny.'

The drum that marked a joke, what was that called? *Ba dum tsssss!* Then the applause.

'Don't you think we've heard enough silly sounds for the moment?'

Here came a belch, so deep and open it was halfway to a retch.

'Michael, frankly, I don't know how much more of this I can stand.'

A tinny falsetto — Mickey Mouse's — assured him, 'You can do it!' Then glass smashed, and a rifle was cocked and fired.

'Not that one in public places,' Noah said seriously. 'You could start a panic.' He walked on.

Michael cantered to keep up. 'Listen, man, these are the best.' The scream and the laugh. A loud raspberry — or was it a fart?

Put that thing in the nearest trash can, Joan advised.

It's his money, Noah argued. *He likes what he likes, and who am I to* —

Fart. Fart. Fart.

Noah spun around. 'Enough!'

Michael nodded, deadpan. From his pocket came the demonic laugh. 'Hey,' he said, gesturing at the marble figure in the fountain, 'another giant showing his junk.'

The marble figure had a curious crown made of . . . four horses, could it be? Noah couldn't imagine which naked Roman deity this was.

He looked it up on his phone. Greek, in fact: Apollo, with a weird crown of small horses. In the spouting water around him, full-size bronze ones cavorted with their riders. 'The sculptor finished the big horses first, but then the war broke out, so they were buried in a garden for safekeeping till it was over.' He thought of Michael's keepsakes: his grandma's drugstore glasses, that maroon chip that proved to the boy's satisfaction at least that his dad had won his second-to-last battle against drugs. A pity people couldn't tuck away their sons and daughters in the ground for safekeeping, in bad times. Noah thought of the carefully filled-in cards under the bishop's tree: had they been dug up in 1944?

He looked that up too, sitting on the cold ledge of the fountain. No complete set of the records had survived, he learned. The batch buried in the episcopal garden, in their paper wrapping, had rotted to mush, and it didn't seem as if the *passeurs* had ever delivered their cards to the International Red Cross in Geneva. Rosenstock and Abadi's own set, from the bishop's library, had gaps; the couple had burned many cards out of fear of raids. But fortunately they'd kept one last failsafe — a complete list of the real and false names — so it seemed as if none of the children had lost their identities. Lost everything else, of course, so many of them: homes, parents, siblings, uncles, aunts, community. They got to hold on to their lives, and their names, but in many cases that was about it.

'What's up with you?'

Noah met Michael's gaze. 'Oh, just the war. Those children.'

'It's a long time ago.'

'True.'

'And we know your mom was on the right side, now.'

Noah nodded. The right side of a sad story.

He found they'd strayed into a viewing area for what turned out to be the Bataille des Fleurs. Why hadn't Noah remembered to buy tickets? Floats were going by encrusted with flowers. A girl whose dress seemed to be made of clementines tossed gladioli at the crowds seated in the stands. A man with ten-foot legs — he had stilts under his striped trousers — was roaring incomprehensible encouragement through a megaphone. 'French people stand too close,' Michael complained in Noah's ear.

It was just too noisy for Noah to attempt to parse this cultural difference. A police officer in a short-sleeved uniform was letting passersby pat her horse. 'Like horses?' he mouthed at Michael.

'What's like horses?'

'Do you *like* them?'

Michael shrugged.

He'd probably never been to summer camp. 'Want to pet this one?'

'What for?'

Noah walked up to the horse and waited his turn. Michael's eyes were nervous, but he moved closer.

The policewoman smiled down and beckoned him. Michael stepped up to the horse and ran his fingers down the glossy coat.

'You can be firm,' Noah told him, lightly slapping the chestnut flank with the flat of his hand.

Michael did the same.

'Stroke down the nose, too.'

'This a he or a she?'

Noah was reminded of some novel in which a boy from an orphanage saw a camel and thought it was a diseased or mutant horse. 'Take a look.'

Michael ducked and craned sideways. 'Oh yeah, he's all dude.'

Just then a carnation came winging its way through the air; a leaf struck Noah's temple, an inch from his eye.

Michael laughed, and lunged for the next bunch, but an old lady got them first, snatching them out of the air. The boy let out a gasp of annoyance.

'She's probably had seventy years of practice,' Noah told him.

Blooms had fallen down the sides of the stands; gladioli and that yellow stuff (mimosa?), mashed underfoot.

'How come you gave me shit for whacking a few flowers,' Michael wanted to know, 'but today everybody's allowed to trample them?'

'Ah . . . those ones were still growing.' Noah was aware his logic was weak. 'These have been cut and paid for, specially for the battle. Besides, it's a tradition. History.'

''Kay, if it's *history*,' Michael said, sardonic.

Noah peeled the sepals off a crushed carnation to see how they fit together. 'Well, that's Carnival. It's supposed to be nonsense. Once a year, everything should get turned upside down.'

'I'm starving.'

'What about something healthy, for once?' Noah kept thinking of the kid's life expectancy; those seven years Michael might be robbed of by growing up in his particular neighborhood. He wondered where Grace Drew was living. 'Some fresh vegetables?'

Michael put the sound machine to his head and made the noise of a gun cocking and firing.

'*Not* in public,' Noah hissed.

The boy stuffed it back in his pocket and held his hands up in surrender as he walked backward.

They lined up for panini the length of the kid's arm, then ate them crossing the raucous plaza. Michael's hand strayed into his pocket once to make an electronic belch.

Revelers went by with armfuls of broken flowers. Noah was picking a piece of lettuce from his lapel when — *whap!* — a sensation like that of a heavy cloth slammed over him, blinded him; a blow to the skull.

His first thought was that Michael had ripped off his hoodie and tackled Noah with it. He spun around, bewildered; where had his panini gone?

Behind him Michael was gasping with laughter. Applause burst from his pocket, over and over. 'A gull, man! You got jacked by a goddamn seagull!'

Noah followed Michael's finger. Yes, there on the edge of the fountain, a muscular, triumphant bird held Noah's panini with one orange foot, ripping and rending the bread. 'Oh come *on.*'

'I wish I'd had time to snap it,' Michael told him. 'Best thing I've seen in Europe.'

'Delighted to have entertained you,' Noah said sourly. Tourism always corrupted the locals — even the gulls.

'You going to get yourself another?'

'I'm not quite hungry enough to bother.'

★   ★   ★

In the Excelsior, Noah collapsed on his bed. The hotel still spooked him, but he wasn't weighed down by guilt now.

Michael came out of the bathroom.

334

Noah roused himself to say, 'Hey, you should update your journal.'

'Tomorrow.'

'OK. Brushed your teeth?'

'Uh-huh.'

'I didn't hear you.'

'I did it quiet. Quiet*ly*,' Michael corrected himself.

Person in Parental Relationship, Noah reminded himself. He heaved himself off the bed, went into the bathroom, and touched the toothbrush. 'Your brush is dry.'

'It dries quick*ly*.'

'Now you're being childish.'

'Nah, I'm behaving childish*ly*.'

'Michael — '

Barely moving, the small hand in the pocket made the sound of gunfire over and over.

Noah covered his ears.

'What the fuck do you care if my teeth fall out ten years from now?'

The accusation winded him. 'Of course I care.'

'You're only in this for a couple weeks, max. You've got no skin in the game.'

'Listen, Michael, I — '

'You're pepper, and I'm fucking rice,' the boy roared. 'So I guess I'm going to be all toothless and mumbling while you're laying in your coffin with a full set.' He bared his teeth like a wolf.

Noah could think of no response except, 'Would you just brush them already?'

Michael shoved his way past him into the bathroom, slammed the door and locked it.

As so often, Noah was left with the sense that he'd picked the wrong battle — and lost it. This was Victor's son, he reminded himself. Michael was never going to be easy. He had his father's perversity as well as his wit.

What kind of cleverness or charm had gotten Victor out of custody the day after he and Amber had been arrested with her car full of drugs? Noah's mind picked at the problem like a knot: what did Victor have that his girlfriend lacked? Only a record; dirty hands. He'd already served time as a boy and as a man. But it made no sense that innocence could have sent Amber to prison while experience set Victor free.

Noah pulled out his tablet and typed in 'drug arrest charges dropped.'

Nothing helpful; mostly lawyers offering tips to the nervous that ended with 'Nothing on this website is to be understood to constitute legal advice.'

He tried rephrasing it: 'Drug arrest release let go no charges filed.'

Just a jumble.

What was it Rosa had said about *factors* that might have gotten Victor off? That word she'd used: *arrangements*.

Noah tried 'drug charge drop arrangement deal.'

This time he blinked at the screen and tried to make sense of the flood. Article after article about state and national drug task forces, desperate to boost the conviction rate to which their funding was pegged, relying on CIs (an

336

abbreviation that could stand for *Confidential Informant* or *Criminal Informant*). When someone was convicted on drug charges these days, he learned, they might well be offered what was called a 'substantial assistance deal': the prosecutor offered to recommend a lower sentence if the offender helped convict an agreed number of others.

But hang on. Victor hadn't been convicted of anything that night; not even charged.

Noah read on. The American Civil Liberties Union condemned the widespread practice of using CIs (often college students, generally lower-income or minorities, some as young as fourteen) wearing wires in undercover stings to buy drugs or even guns. It might sound heroic if you pictured toppling the linchpin of an evil cartel, but often it was a matter of the CI being told to entrap an acquaintance or workmate into selling them a few pills. 'Up to 80% of all drug cases in the US may be based on information provided by informants.' All in the pointless cause of inflating conviction rates. According to one article, the no-snitching ethos so widespread in impoverished communities was a reaction to the fact that these communities were riddled with snitches.

That threw Noah. Spies around every corner . . . it sounded like France during the war. Though it wasn't the same thing at all, he argued with himself. These CIs weren't choosing to turn on their neighbors; they were forced into it by the hope of going home to their families a few years sooner, or staying out of prison altogether.

337

But Victor. Noah's fingers fumbled over the keys. 'CI charges dropped,' he tried.

He struggled with the jargon. Occasionally the filing of charges might be postponed; if an arrestee had just enough familiarity with the drug scene to be useful to the police, he might win his freedom 'on the promise of reeling in bigger fish within a set period.'

That was it! What had happened to Victor. It had to be. Amber was collateral damage; she'd been bullied into accepting a plea of five years. Vic had been full of regret, Michael had reported. *He'd trade places with her in a second* ... Was it a choice between both of Michael's parents being locked away for years and only one of them? Had Amber been party to this deal, or at least not spoken up about it? Maybe that was part of the 'arrangement': that Amber promised not to scream the precinct down about how the stash was Victor's, and in return he got to walk away a free man? Well, Noah corrected himself, as a CI; an owned man; tethered. *He had to travel for work*, that's what he'd told Michael.

And the couple's gamble had gone horribly wrong. Victor had been clean, if the boy's plastic amulet was to be believed, when he'd walked into the motel that night. The strain of all those months of deception had proved too much for him, and he'd given in to his old consolation; in fact, gone farther out from shore than ever before.

It all sounded more than possible to Noah. People held such secrets, lived with such

338

complications. He tapped the Correctional Communications app. 'Dear Amber,' he typed, 'Michael and I are having a good trip. There's something I need to ask you about — '

Then he stared at the screen and backspaced till the words were gone. How naïve of him: of course every word in or out would be vetted. If the guards learned from Noah's message that Amber had been a CI's girlfriend, and if they let that slip to any prisoners . . . Noah wondered, with a shudder, what happened to 'snitches' bitches.'

He tried to think how to ask it in a coded or casual way, such that Amber would read between the lines. But no, this was ridiculous; Noah would only botch it. Maybe he could whisper his question, in person, when next he visited.

Not with Michael; Noah would go on his own. This wasn't like Bond movies or *Mission: Impossible*; there was no glamour to spying on your own peers. Given Michael's belief in the no-snitching code, how could Amber ever tell him, bring him to understand the deal (never to be spoken of) that his dad had had to make? A deal that had backfired, too. Her great generosity punished; her child left alone.

Just then the boy came out of the bathroom. 'Night.' Getting into bed.

'Night.' Noah put on his pajamas, brushed his teeth, and snapped off the light.

He shouldn't get ahead of himself and jump to conclusions, as he had about his mother. (All those bad habits built into the human brain because they were useful shortcuts: confirmation, framing, hindsight bias.)

Surely there'd be evidence sitting in some prosecutor's filing cabinet in Brooklyn. Rosa had her friend in the police. Could she — and would she, if he asked — get Noah proof that Victor had been a CI? He reached for his tablet in the dark and wrote the social worker an email, spelling out his theory. 'Surely Victor's family has a right to know,' he finished, a little self-importantly. Then added, 'I'd be very grateful for your help.'

A terrible volley of farts.

Noah thought it was the machine at first. Then, 'Michael!'

The kid's voice was only a little sheepish: 'Got to let it out.'

'You could have gone into the bathroom.'

'I was too sleepy to move.'

Noah switched his tablet off and set it on the nightstand. 'Did you hear about the man who died of inhaling his own gas?'

'This one of your unfunny jokes?'

'Not a bit. Back in the '90s, I think it was. He'd eaten a lot of beans and cabbage, he was sleeping in a tiny bedroom, and he inhaled so much of the methane he released in his sleep that he never woke up.'

'You're shitting me.'

'The paramedics got poisoned too when they came in, but they recovered.'

'Why would you tell me that?' Michael demanded. 'Now I can't get back to sleep from thinking about dying of the fumes.'

'Believe me, I'll put you out in the corridor if it builds up to dangerous levels. Good night,' Noah added.

'Night.'

8

Schooled

Noah woke late to a weirdly warm Sunday, like summer in February.

'I've been awake for hours,' Michael told him.

'OK. Give me a minute.'

'You mean like half an hour to get your socks on.'

'You're learning.'

The boy's journal was splayed on the floor between their beds, which Noah took as an invitation to look at the latest double spread. The teacher would have a field day with this — possibly the principal and the psychologist too, if the school had one. In a nightmarish comic strip, a stick figure in a fedora and glasses was being attacked by a seagull the size of a pterodactyl. Next, the cartoon Noah was sprawling in a pair of obscenely small swim trunks on a stony beach. Then attacked by a hailstorm of thorny flowers. In the next panel, Noah was trodden — literally 'creamed,' as Michael would say — by an elephant; and finally (as far as he could make out from the smeared ink) devoured by a lion in a surprisingly accurate Roman arena. The caption beneath said, with unusual brevity, *My 'Great' Uncle*.

Noah put the notebook back on the carpet.

'I was looking at your mom's pics,' Michael said. 'Is that OK?'

'Sure.' Noah straightened up and rubbed his face.

'This one of the feet going by, I reckon these are the kids she saved.'

'Why's that?'

'Duh, because of the suitcase,' Michael said.

'What suitcase?'

'There.' Michael put his finger to a black shape in the upper right corner.

Now the boy said it, yes, it could be a valise one of them was carrying. Somehow Noah's eye had skipped over the shape because nowadays roller bags moved at ground level. 'Huh. Well done.' He imagined the weight of the case in the child's tired hand. 'But Michael . . . ' Should Noah be honest? 'This photo, now that you've pointed out the luggage, it looks to me like lots of children all walking along together.' Burdened by whatever they'd been allowed to take with them. 'But the hidden kids — the Marcel people tucked them away all over the countryside, in ones and twos. They wouldn't have risked drawing attention to them by walking along in a big group in the street.'

'So who would these kids be?'

'Well, maybe . . . ' He hated to say it. 'The others.'

Michael frowned in puzzlement.

Noah went to the window and looked down: tourists with backpacks, locals with shopping bags, a girl in a feathered and spangled mask. 'The ones who weren't hidden in time. The

Nazis would have marched them from here to the train station, just five minutes up the street.' (Then on to Drancy, then to Auschwitz.) Had Margot stood in the street and watched them go by, these small ones who'd slipped through the Marcels' hands? Discreetly (through a gap in her coat) positioned her father's Leica? She'd done what all war photographers managed to do, no matter how they shook or wept, so that each abomination would be recorded, at least: pressed the shutter.

'But what about RJ?' Michael pulled out the photo of the small smiling boy.

Noah studied the soft lines of the boy's face. 'He could certainly be one of the hidden ones, if she was making him an identity card.' A random representative? Perhaps there'd been something about RJ that had particularly moved her, lodging him in her memory. Please let him not have been a lost one, whose picture Margot had saved because she hadn't been able to save the boy.

Michael went back to his game, and Noah took a shower.

Once he was dressed, he checked his email.

'I suspect you're right about Victor,' Rosa wrote, 'and the same thought had actually occurred to me, but it didn't seem the time (or my place) to speculate. I'm afraid there's unlikely to be anything about a deal in police files. Generally no record gets kept, for the CI's own safety.'

But Victor hadn't been safe, in fact, had he? It must have been his puppetmasters who'd told him to go to Long Island that night, Noah saw; the encounter made no sense unless it was a sting. He did trust the maroon chip, now; believed that Victor had been three months clean and sober when they — law enforcement and dealers, two jaws of a pincers — had forced him back in. And under such perilous conditions, too: a wire taped under the young man's shirt, flop sweat pooling. Was that why Victor had agreed to take heavy-duty narcotics with whoever he was meeting in that motel — had that been the only way to convince them he was the real thing?

Surely the autopsy would have mentioned the wire, though. No? Noah fired off a quick follow-up to Rosa about that, apologizing for bothering her again on the weekend. Funny, he didn't even know if she had a family of her own, but he could imagine how wiped out she'd be after checking in with her twenty-four cases.

* * *

In the café around the corner from the pealing bells of the church, Michael polished off a chocolate chip-studded roll. Today his T-shirt said LEVEL UP, and he had the Roman helmet on his lap because Noah had made him take it off.

The door tinkled as another customer came in, but it was a middle-aged man, not the woman Noah was waiting for. He dipped his napkin in his water and handed it to Michael.

'What's that for?'

'Your mouth.'

Michael swiped at his face, eyes still on his screen.

'You're making it worse.' Noah took back the napkin and finished the wiping himself, holding Michael by the chin. 'Listen, would you please be polite to her when she comes?'

'Does this lady speak English?'

'I don't think so.'

'Then she won't understand even if I say, *Sup, bitch?*'

Noah fixed him with a look.

'OK, OK, I'll be nice.'

A woman of Noah's vintage coming in: he leaped to his feet. Could it be Madame Lamarche? 'Colette? Coco?' he asked, faltering. He yanked at Michael's sleeve to get him to stand.

She had pink lipstick, overplucked eyebrows filled in with pencil, and a shining silver bob. Smiling broadly, she kissed Noah on both cheeks. Some classic perfume. Yes, she told him with a strong Niçois accent, it had always been Coco, but the priest hadn't been willing to baptize a baby with such a name, so officially she was Colette.

Neither recognized the other's face, they admitted once their coffees were ordered, but she did think Noah had something of his *pépère* about the eyebrows. And so did his young relation, she added, nodding at Michael. She liked his helmet.

The boy produced a choirboy smile before going back to his game.

346

Noah realized that he and this woman had slipped right back into addressing each other as *tu*, as when they were small.

They'd buried a swallow together, Coco mentioned.

He drew a blank. '*Oui, oui,*' he said, pretending to remember.

It had flown into the window and broken its neck.

Where was it they'd made the grave, could she remind him?

On the beach, under the stones.

Noah didn't mention her getting him to chew the pebble. He cast around for some more small talk before he broached what was really on his mind. He remembered her mother warmly, all of Madame Dupont's kindness to his family. He didn't believe he'd ever met Coco's father, had he?

He wouldn't have, no; Papa was sent away to a German factory during the war.

The *Service du Travail Obligatoire*, a forced-labor program for Frenchmen and -women: Noah had almost forgotten about that.

When a compensation scheme was set up about fifteen years ago, Coco said, she and her siblings had applied — not for the measly seven thousand euros, which wouldn't have gone far among the three of them, but for the principle of it. Anyway, they were informed that what their father had gone through didn't count as slavery, because he'd received some wages.

Noah shook his head in sympathetic outrage. This seemed as good a moment as any to bring up Margot. Back in the 1960s, he mentioned, Madame Dupont had told a journalist a strange story of his grandfather being worried sick when Noah's mother was absent from the apartment for two nights in August 1944. He had the article here. (Reaching for his tablet.) He didn't suppose Coco happened to know anything more about that?

'*Mais bien sûr*.' She waved the tablet away. Then seemed to hesitate. She didn't want to speak ill of the dead . . .

Of her mother or mine? Noah wondered privately.

But Madame Dupont had, well, harbored suspicions of the photographer's daughter. Staying on when Marc went to New York, then sending their child after him — some saw that as daughterly devotion, but Coco's mother had her own thoughts on the subject.

Noah pushed it: she'd believed his mother had a lover?

Coco pursed her lips. He should forgive her mother for wondering; those were judgmental times. And of course Madame Selvaggio had been more than punished, if by any chance it was true.

'*Punie?*' Noah repeated. How had Margot been punished?

Coco blinked at him. Hadn't he been asking about the three days his mother had stayed out, at the end of the war? Well, she'd come back black and blue, with a dislocated knee.

Noah nodded, his hand trembling on the warm rim of his coffee bowl.

348

Frankly, Madame Dupont had assumed Madame Selvaggio had been beaten for fraternizing with a German. Those last weeks of the war, such rage had been unleashed; the streets were chaos. But Coco's mother had asked no questions and had managed to find a doctor, who'd done his best to patch up Madame Selvaggio as well as treat poor Monsieur Personnet's pneumonia.

Noah's head was spinning. Margot's bad leg, yes; bad for the rest of her life. But if it hadn't in fact been a punishment beating . . .

Coco put her hand lightly over his. Please, he wasn't to think badly of his mother. Many women did what they had to, for the sake of better rations for their families.

In a husky voice he told her that Margot hadn't had a lover that he knew of, German or French. She'd been forging documents to help save children from the Holocaust.

Coco sat back, her eyes compassionate.

Noah thought she was moved by that — Margot's nobility — but then he realized she didn't believe a word of it. It was true, he insisted, he had a picture. He fumbled for the envelope in his satchel.

Well, she said awkwardly, it was just that so many did claim they'd been in the Resistance, afterward, didn't they? Lined up for praise and thanks, medals, even money from de Gaulle's new government. And maybe they even half-believed it. Memory was deceptive, *n'est-ce pas?*

'*Non, mais* — ' Hang on, there was the photo of the tree, the children's feet, where was the one of Margot? Noah plucked it out and slapped it down on the tiny table, almost upsetting the sugar bowl. That was his mother, he said, with — look, on the back — *MZ* for Marie Zabel: *Margot Isabelle*, Marie Zabel, see?

A nickname? Coco asked gently.

No, no, her *nom de guerre*. This M.Z. was a known forger for the Marcel Network, according to the archivist at the *Musée de la résistance azuréenne*.

Coco's drawn-on eyebrows went up.

Noah felt a childish satisfaction that he was convincing her at last.

But why had Madame Selvaggio not said?

Well, Noah imagined Margot didn't want to endanger her father. (He didn't say: *And how could she have been sure of the sympathies of anyone else — Madame Dupont included?*) The fewer who'd known, the better.

Ah yes. But Noah had grown up hearing the stories?

Not a word, he admitted. Just this week, he'd found some old photos in a box and put two and two together. With the help of his clever great-nephew.

'Huh?' Feeling eyes on him, Michael looked up.

'I'm telling her how I couldn't have figured it out without you — my mother's story.'

Michael nodded and went back to his screen.

Many of the best of them had kept quiet about it, Coco was saying. *Un sentiment de culpabilité.*

A sense of guilt. That they'd survived, Noah asked?

She nodded. And that they hadn't managed to do more. Save more. *Les femmes*, women in particular, Coco had the impression that many had plunged back into private life after the war, making babies, wanting to bury the whole horror in silence.

Noah thought of his little sister's pudgy cheeks.

Coco discreetly checked her watch for the second time, so Noah said he was sure she had things to do. A granddaughter's birthday party? How nice. If she could help him understand one last thing, though . . . in 1968, why had her mother not told the journalist about Margot coming home injured?

Oh, she wouldn't have done that, Coco said, tutting. Maman was loyal to Monsieur Personnet and would never have brought shame on his memory. Whereas Coco didn't mind answering Noah's questions, since he was one of the family. Besides, it seemed now that her mother had misjudged his mother; Coco was very sorry about that.

That was all right, Noah assured her, getting to his feet. He'd done plenty of misjudging himself.

Coco was tugging her coat on with difficulty; Noah helped it over her shoulder. Better to forgive them all, at this point, she supposed. '*Il vaudrait mieux passer l'éponge.*'

He hadn't heard that idiom in decades, probably not since Margot's death: *best to pass the sponge.* (Incongruously, it made him think of the Roman toilets at Cemenelum.) *Wipe the*

351

slate clean, he supposed you'd say in English; *let bygones be bygones*.

★ ★ ★

'I need a rest,' Noah told Michael, turning back in the direction of the hotel.

'Already?' The boy's voice echoed inside the helmet. 'All we've done today is sit in a café.'

'Afraid so. Especially if we'll be out late at the Carnival tonight.' Noah stopped just outside the Excelsior, so Michael walked right into him. 'Oh Christ.'

'What?'

The black doors, how they swung closed, like teeth. 'Of course.'

'*What?*' Michael demanded.

'I think my mother was arrested.' Noah turned wild eyes on the boy. 'Held here for three days.'

'Is that what your Coco lady said?' Michael asked, heading into the lobby.

He shook his head, letting Michael go into the elevator ahead of him. 'Her mother, our house cleaner, she didn't know where Margot had been except that when she got home she was in bad shape, with a smashed knee.'

'You figure the Nazis smashed it?'

Noah covered his mouth.

Her eye as well, though Coco hadn't mentioned that. He supposed that sort of injury didn't show. Was it in this hotel that Margot had lost half her vision, which afterward she'd blamed on an infection?

Michael didn't break the uneasy silence.

I'm really in no state to be in charge of anything, Noah thought. *Not a child. Particularly not this child.*

Once through their door, he went straight into the bathroom to collect himself. Sitting on the toilet lid, his eyes fell on the shallow bathtub, the unyielding rectangle of ceramic. Margot had had their tub in New York ripped out.

Michael thumped on the door. 'What's going on? You made a terrible noise.'

Had he?

'You having a heart attack in there?'

Noah stood up and opened the door in the boy's face. The helmet was off, and clutched to Michael's chest. 'No,' he managed to say.

'I thought you were dying on the toilet like fucking Elvis.'

'Sorry to scare you.'

'I wasn't *scared*.'

Noah tried for a hint of levity. 'Mildly concerned? Or just curious?'

Michael puffed out his breath.

Weak at the knees, Noah sat back down on the toilet lid. There was no hiding from this boy. 'They'd have tortured my mother,' he said, very low. 'Not just her knee, but . . . I think that's why her left eye could only see shadows.'

'Shit,' Michael murmured.

Noah wouldn't describe the half-drownings, the electrocutions; that was too much. And he didn't want to make the child phobic about bathtubs.

'Did Nodaddy Ding know?'

'Good question.' Still shielding the Marcel

353

Network, Margot had kept her mouth shut rather than defend herself against Madame Dupont's suspicions, but surely Père Sonne would have coaxed the truth out of his battered daughter? Maybe it was that shock that had brought on his final illness. The agony of not having been able to protect his child.

Not that Margot would have let him protect her. Père Sonne had been so careful to keep out of the world's mucky struggles, but after more than four decades of being his quiet helpmeet, his daughter had had no such qualms: she'd done what had to be done.

'I don't know who she told, if anyone. And here's something that's really odd, Michael: when the Nazis let her go, Margot doesn't seem to have gotten in touch with any of her friends in the network. They didn't even hear that their 'Marie Zabel' had been arrested; she just went silent. So they had to assume she'd been sent to the camps.'

'Like, dead?'

'Exactly.'

'Huh.' Michael cracked his knuckles.

'It was all pretty crazy in the last days of the war, but still. Margot got over the worst of her injuries, her dad died, and then the first chance she got, she sailed to New York.' Surely she must have told Marc, at least, what she'd been through — if not when it happened, then months later, when she'd disembarked?

Those who survived torture said the worst scars were in the mind. Margot had been a loving wife and mother in New York, but how

354

much effort had that required of her? All her lies of omission. 'The photo of the hotel entrance.' Noah stepped past the boy to get it out of the envelope. 'Maybe she went back to take this shot, once the Germans had left.'

'Like a souvenir?'

'I suppose.' To mark what had been done to her in one of these rooms, for three days and two nights. Such a nondescript image. A door from one reality into another. The gates of the underworld.

Had Margot told Fernande, at some point, when she'd entrusted her with the box of photos? Noah felt ridiculously hurt that neither of them had shared the painful history with him. Then again, maybe their mother hadn't told a soul; left the photos in the bottom of a drawer, and the truth on the other side of the ocean.

'Hey. No offense, but . . . '

'What?'

Michael shifted from one foot to another. 'You think maybe she squealed?'

Noah heard the verb literally: his mother, legs lashed to a bar, screaming and choking as the freezing bathwater filled her mouth. Then he got it. 'Broke under torture, you mean?'

A reluctant shrug. 'If she dropped out of sight, after . . . It doesn't look good, dude.'

Noah swallowed bile. His mother's silver story was tarnishing, corroding, as he tugged it into the light. Could that have been why Margot had kept her wartime work a lifelong secret, to hide a more terrible one — that she'd helplessly betrayed her comrades and the hidden children?

355

'But that can't be true. Almost all the kids survived, more than five hundred of them.' His voice came out angrily. 'And the Marcel people too, wouldn't they all have been rounded up if she'd given their names?' Most of them — Abadi and Brener and the various clerics — had never been arrested. Noah answered his own question: 'Except of course this was in the last weeks of the war, so maybe the Nazis ran out of time.'

Noah sat on the edge of his bed and dropped his face into his hands. For Margot to have done so much, more than she'd ever have imagined was in her . . . and then to crack apart. After the war, had she been forced to live with the fact that only an accident of timing had saved her comrades from the destruction she'd unleashed? Had shame dogged Margot for half a century, till her death at the age of ninety-two?

Enough! Noah wished, irrationally, that he believed his mother was still out there, up there in the sky, looking down, listening; that he could tell her to stop blaming herself. He tried to picture the two of them meeting again, in Margot's Catholic notion of heaven in the clouds, or what the Ancient Egyptians called the Field of Reeds. 'Lord knows I would have broken,' he said now, 'long before the second night.' Who was Noah to cast the first stone, or even a pebble?

★ ★ ★

Michael was hungry, so they went out for lunch. Noah had half a dozen oysters. He tried to

356

savor each slowly; one with minced shallot, one with vinegar, one with lemon . . . 'They don't taste as tangy as they used to in my day.' Pollution, maybe? The warming of the oceans? And why did they have to be served with such arid rye bread?

'It must be your mouth that's different.' Michael inserted bits of chicken nuggets through his helmet. 'I guess most of your taste buds have retired by now.'

Noah considered the last oyster without appetite. It was a waste to leave it, but then the money was already spent. To force down an oyster, on the last day of his eightieth year, seemed absurd.

Michael got a free ice cream in a plastic penguin. He gouged at it with his spoon.

Noah failed to catch the waiter's eye. He noticed a poster for an exhibition of photos by Cartier-Bresson — that famous shot of the man leaping over the puddle. 'My grandpa knew that photographer.' Pointing. 'The guy had this notion of the decisive moment — watch and wait until the split second when all the elements in the shot are in perfect balance, then press the shutter.'

'Why not just take a burst?'

'Film cost so much, remember? You had to want every shot.'

'That must have sucked.'

'Well, but pre-digital, maybe they paid more attention,' Noah argued. 'Saw better.'

The kid shook his head. 'Pre-Netflix, you all must have been bored out of your minds.' He switched to a different game on his phone; engine revs, brake screeches.

'Can you turn down the sound on that thing?' Noah turned around to see if other customers were looking irked.

'Nah.'

'Are you sure? Let me see.'

Michael gave him a withering glance. The game rampaged on.

'It's very loud,' Noah said.

'Not as loud as that.' He jerked a thumb toward a speaker overhead.

True, the restaurant was blasting some particularly grating pop music in English. Noah went to find the waiter to ask for the bill.

As he and the boy were walking out of the café into the sunshine, three teenage girls passed on a single bicycle: one riding, one sitting on the back carrier, and one perched on the handlebars. Maybe that was what distracted Michael. 'Shit!'

Noah looked back to find the boy with one sole turned up and an expression of wrath recognizable even through the helmet's visor. 'Stepped in something?'

Michael pawed at the ground with his foot like a stallion. He ran over to the curb to scrape his sneaker on it.

'Let's find you some grass to rub it on.'

'This is an Air *Jordan* I got dogshit all over.'

The shoes his grandmother had paid for month after month, Noah remembered. 'Bad luck. Want to go dip it in that fountain back there?'

'Are you kidding? They're suede.'

'Well, then, just let it dry and the poop will flake off.'

Michael was shaking his head as he picked at the treads with — what was it? — a plastic straw from the gutter.

'Let's find a bathroom and try warm, soapy water.'

'No water, dude, they're suede!'

'We'll fix this,' Noah assured him. He had a travel nailbrush he could sacrifice to the cause. 'We'll buy a special cleaning fluid.'

'My sneaker reeks, the dog must have been diseased.'

Noah let out his breath. 'OK, do you want to go back to the hotel and change your shoes?'

'I don't have any others,' Michael admitted.

How could Noah not have noticed that? 'Then let's pick you up something basic right away. What about . . . ' There was a narrow store nearby festooned with beach umbrellas and lurid towels (lions, hot dogs, Johnny Depp for some reason). 'Espadrilles?' Noah suggested, finding a rack of the canvas slip-ons. 'What's your size?'

Michael looked as if Noah had to be pulling his leg. 'Are those made of straw?'

'The base is rope, actually. Classic French summer shoes.' Forty-five euros, Noah noted with shock.

'Not me, not in this lifetime.'

He pressed his lips together hard. 'I'm sorry this store doesn't meet your style needs, Michael. Would you rather go barefoot?'

'Hell yeah.'

Noah had walked into that one. 'But then they won't let you into any building.'

'Fine by me.'

He was backed into a corner. 'You're worshipping a brand. I bet Michael Jordan doesn't design your Nikes, he just puts his name on the box.'

'What the fuck do you know about sneakers?'

They were just tired of each other, Noah told himself; of being together morning, noon, and night. Vacationing together was a strain even on the best of relationships, and he and this kid had spent almost a week at close quarters. 'Look, try these on' — he flapped a pair of espadrilles in their crinkly plastic wrapper — 'and I'll do my best to clean your stinky Jordans later.'

Michael gave him the finger and stomped away.

★   ★   ★

By five forty-five the dusk was darkening, and the warmth of the day had thickened. Noah and Michael were stuck in the security line for the Corso outside Place Masséna. Michael wiped sweat off his cheeks under the metallic flaps of his helmet. 'Just looking in bags, what does that do?' he demanded. 'They need to pat us all down and walk us through a metal detector for guns and clips and knives.'

'Voice *down*, or talk about something harmless.'

'Bunnies, kitties, sweetie pie!' Dropping the falsetto: 'No, but seriously, dude, anything can

360

be a weapon. A really sharp pencil, if you drive it in behind someone's eyebrow . . . '

'Zip it.'

Michael did.

'Now,' Noah said, 'what's our plan if we bump into the lady from the museum and she takes one look at you in the helmet and shouts, *Stop, thief?*'

'Run.'

At last their section of the line was allowed through, and Noah — peering at the fine print on their tickets — found their places high in the hard-seat *tribunes*. Because of the bass thump of the music, the announcer's over-amped declamations, and occasional shrieks from the audience, his head was pounding already. Every now and then a boom made him jump, as a confetti cannon sprayed multicolored paper over the crowd.

'*Bienvenu au Corso Illuminé,*' caroled the man with the loudspeaker, welcoming everyone to the Corso. The hired dancers — one in every aisle — were trying to work the crowd up into a frenzy. The announcer kept repeating that the eyes of the world's media were on Nice tonight, so if they didn't want to bring shame on the glorious, historic tradition of Carnival, they should *make some noise!*

It seemed a curiously self-conscious form of festivity, to Noah: to dance and scream just because the TV cameras might be turned your way. But some excitable members of the audience were roused to start squirting cans of foam into the air.

'Can I get some of that Silly String?'

'I don't know. Do you have any of your allowance left?'

'You're cold, dude.'

Now that he'd made his point, Noah felt a little bad. The Silly String was environmentally unfriendly, but a genuinely cheap thrill; all the pleasures of polymers in a can. He produced a ten-euro note. 'And say *s'il vous plaît* and *merci*, remember?' he called after the boy vanishing into the crowd.

Michael came back with three cans of Silly String. 'Five euros for one, ten for three — that's seriously good value.'

'I meant *one*.'

'You never said.' Michael shot a test streak into the air; it rose in an arc and fell in what Noah had to admit was a most satisfying way.

'You'll have noticed that it's a liquid that turns into a solid as the solvent evaporates in — '

Michael pressed his finger hard against Noah's lips. 'Nope, you're not educating me tonight.'

Noah subsided.

'*Il ne reste que cinq minutes*,' the announcer warned: only five minutes to wait. The dancers in the aisles were coordinating the crowds in doing the wave, now; even Noah heaved to his feet when it was their section's turn. *Bang!* Confetti showered the multitude, and the response was a mass screech. Noah took off his fedora and brushed paper dots off it. Would it be safer in his lap? Or under the seat? Could he rest it on the back of his heels so it didn't touch the dirty boards? But then he might forget and tread on it,

362

or it could fall down under the bleachers. Noah wished he had something to cover it with; a plastic bag or a newspaper, even.

'Historians can tell what people used to throw at Carnival by what the city laws have banned over the centuries,' he said to the side of Michael's helmet.

'Like what?'

'Oh, do you want to know, now, or would that be too educational?'

'Get on with it,' Michael told him.

'Plaster, flour, beans, eggs, oranges . . . '

'That shit must have hurt.'

'Blinded a few paraders, I'd imagine. The richer ones rented metal-mesh face guards. If you came without some kind of mask — that was seen as killing the buzz, see? — you'd get flogged with a stocking filled with flour.'

'Ow!' Michael laughed. 'Sounds like they wasted tons of food.'

'That was part of the fun. Like eating way too much at Thanksgiving.'

When the floats finally began to file one by one into the floodlit plaza, the crowd went berserk, filling the air with strings of foam from their cans. Michael was on his second can already, nodding along to the tinny pop music. Would Silly String stain clothing, Noah wondered? Already he'd found a tangled line strewn across his fedora, and hurried to lift it off. Like spider web, the stuff could be scrunched up to almost nothing.

The effigies were huger than Noah had imagined from photos; spectacular. There were dozens of people pushing them along, dancing inside them, operating mysterious mechanisms to create weird or lewd movements on a gigantic scale. Noah recognized Macron, Trump, Kim Jong Un. 'They're made of papier-mache,' he roared at Michael. 'Can you imagine all the layers you'd have to paste on?' This year's theme was space, which meant a lot of shiny surfaces, and ranks of dancers in rocket costumes moving in zombie-like synchronicity. Despite the futuristic references, this bacchanal felt ancient to Noah.

A wet glop fell on the shoulder of his jacket.

Michael turned his head to the man behind them, who was wearing bobbing antennae. 'Shake it, or it doesn't spray right.'

'He may not speak English,' Noah reminded him, swabbing at his jacket with a handkerchief.

'Shake it, dude!' Michael repeated, demonstrating with his own can for the man's benefit; he shot a dry squiggle into the air.

The insect man gave him a thumbs-up and sprayed his can, but he hadn't shaken it. The stuff spat all around him, and an awful ejaculation landed on Noah's fedora.

Noah let out a groan. Twisting around, he brandished the hat at the insect man, who only giggled, his antennae wobbling. 'Idiot!' Noah swabbed at the fedora. But the pale blue slime was spreading across the felt, soaking into it.

'You're making it worse,' Michael told him.

Noah inflated with rage. 'Two world wars this hat has survived, and it has to get trashed on my watch.'

'Hey, I have an idea.' Deadpan. 'Wash it in the fountain!'

Noah wanted to slap the kid.

'Or maybe buy yourself some shitty rope one?'

Noah didn't trust himself to answer that.

Another wave, then; all around them the crowd leaped up and sank down. More extraordinary effigies wheeled into view, followed by hundreds of performers in purple, gold, red. But Noah couldn't get back into the Carnival spirit; he found he'd fallen through a lightless chink somewhere. Everything looked soiled to him, ersatz, pointless.

When the parade was over and the crowd was dispersing from the stands, Michael clicked his fingers at Noah. 'Gimme another ten.'

'I beg your pardon?'

'Euros. I want three more cans before the guy goes,' nodding at a Silly String seller packing up.

'You've got to be kidding.' Noah walked over to an almost-full garbage can and pushed the wrecked fedora down into it.

Deep in Michael's pocket, the machine honked its faux-sympathetic horn: *wah wah!*

Noah whipped around and stared.

All trace of humor had left the face of the small, helmeted centurion. 'You're mean.'

'And you're a savage.'

Michael's machine released a contemptuous belch.

'Give me that thing.' Noah strode over, hand outstretched.

'Like hell I will.'

'This instant.'

The imaginary gun was cocked and fired, cocked and fired, cocked and fired.

'Michael!' Out of the corner of his eye Noah could see a few tourists twitch. '*Not* that sound.' This was how mass panics started and people ended up trampled.

Again: *cock, fire.*

Noah was on Michael, trying to dig the hateful device out of his pocket.

Michael fought hard. 'Get your hands off me!' He bent Noah's finger back.

But Noah got hold of the sound machine and threw it to the ground so hard that it emitted a mad laugh. He stamped on it; applied his full weight until the orange plastic corners popped and the thing was in pieces on the ground.

He turned to face the boy, already regretting it, as his frenzy ebbed.

Nowhere to be seen in the thinning crowd.

'Michael?'

Fear had Noah in its mouth and was chewing him up. A blur, a running figure that could be the boy. As if in belated response to some half-heard starter's pistol, Noah was off.

Strangely enough he found he had time — as he ran, walked, lurched, stumbled through the sticky, nighttime streets of Nice — to regret everything he'd done this week, and everything he'd failed to do. 'Michael,' he shouted every now and then, in a random direction. A petty quarrel, running away, this was probably how children ended up caught by traffickers, smuggled over borders, sold to pedophile rings.

Two or three times Noah spotted a boy who

could have been Michael, but never was. Checking his watch: almost half an hour now. It felt like a whole night. His lungs were burning and his armpits were dripping. He couldn't think of anywhere else to try but the hotel. Why would Michael go back to their room, though, if all he wanted was to get away from the evil great-uncle who'd smashed his toy? It was time to go to the police; Noah should have done it half an hour ago.

But Michael thinks of cops as Nazis, he argued with himself.

Still. Any adult who found a foreign child distressed and alone would surely take him to the police. So Noah stopped the next person in uniform — a street cleaner — and asked, voice uneven, for the nearest *gendarmerie.*

He'd have hailed a cab if he'd spotted one. He stumbled as fast as he could through sultry streets still crowded with revelers. He had a half-remembered statistic stuck in his head like a seed between his teeth, something about the percentage of missing children who got murdered within three hours.

You're distorting the statistics, Joan told him. *It must be that of children who are subsequently found murdered, a certain percentage turn out to have been killed in the first three hours. Whereas most missing children probably find their way home.*

You're no help, he raged. *Michael has no home.*

★　★　★

367

257. In the police station, Noah sat and held the number between trembling fingers.

Two police on wheeled chairs were shooting the breeze with a third who leaned on their counter, as if this was their night off — no prospect of any public disorder to quell during Carnival. Could Noah jump the line for a situation as grave as this, he wondered? Was his mislaying of Michael reason enough for a red alert, or amber, or whatever the color was?

OPERATION TRANQUILLITÉ VACANCES, said a poster; Operation Holiday Tranquility. (Which had a sinister ring to it, but it was nothing more than advice about not leaving valuables in parked cars.) A sign over the row of conjoined seats prohibited anyone from moving them to improvise a bed. One cracked windowpane was mended with opaque tape. These did not seem like good signs.

Noah leaned back in his hard plastic seat and closed his eyes.

When one of the officers called out 'Deux cent cinquantesept,' Noah heard his number belatedly and leaped up.

The handsome uniformed man placidly dug out a form.

Noah could only give Michael's name, not his date of birth; the nearest he could offer was 2006, and June, maybe? As for where the child's parents were . . . These were circonstances spéciales, Noah explained. The father was dead and the mother was in the US; Noah was only a gardien temporaire.

The officer tapped on his computer, but Noah

368

got no sense of an Interpol alert being sent out.

Height and weight?

Too embarrassed to say he didn't know, Noah guessed wildly.

No medical conditions? Birthmarks, scars?

None that he knew of. Oh, one tattoo, on the inside of the arm: *F.O.E.* (*Family Over Everything*, he thought, cringing. How had he found this child and lost him again, all in a week?)

Any recent pictures?

Not that Noah had on him, no. Michael's passport was back at the hotel.

On Monsieur's phone, even?

He had to admit that he never took any photos.

What was Michael wearing?

Noah drew a complete blank, at first. Then described the Roman helmet. He could tell the man thought this sounded like a weird setup, what with the headgear and the tattoo and the old man's ignorance about this child he was claiming to have brought to France. Perhaps the officer thought Noah had dementia, and the boy was a figment of memory or imagination.

How much money had Michael had on him?

None, Noah admitted.

Places to which the boy was attached, where he might be likely to go?

But they were visiting for only a week, and Michael didn't know Nice. '*Nous sommes des touristes ici, Monsieur.*' Or should it be *Officer*?

Michael's telephone number, email, social-media accounts?

Noah shook his head, pathetic. He really should have bought a French SIM card for the wretched cracked phone, to be able to reach Michael if they got separated; he saw that now. What was he was going to say to Rosa, when he'd finally have to call her?

'*Demain.*'

Dazed, he realized the officer was telling him to come back tomorrow.

★　★　★

At the desk of the Excelsior, wiping his forehead, Noah asked for their key. The clerk handed it down, and only then mentioned that Noah's young relation was in the lounge.

Michael was watching TV with his feet up on an antique-trunk coffee table, helmet still on.

Noah let himself down heavily and put up his own feet beside the kid's sullied sneaker. Michael didn't turn his head.

'What are we watching?' Noah asked after a minute.

A long pause. 'Victoria's Secret fashion show. On a loop.'

It struck Noah as a cross between soft porn and wildlife; all those masks and plumes.

'You took your sweet time,' Michael muttered.

'I was at the police station, reporting that you'd been kidnapped.'

'For real?'

Was the boy amused? Touched? Or just scornful of Noah's misjudgments? 'How did you find the hotel?'

370

Michael shrugged. 'I kept saying, 'Train station'? People pointed.'

'Excellent life skills.' A great yawn split Noah's face. 'Shall we?' Nodding toward the elevator.

'We never had any dinner.'

In all the hullabaloo, Noah hadn't thought to feel hungry. The Excelsior's kitchen was clearly shut. He summoned his last reserves. 'OK, let's see what's still open . . . '

On the street he lit a cigarette. But he was too tired to savor it, somehow. He spotted a Greek place. A Moroccan beside it.

Michael kept shaking his head. 'I want churros.'

'They're not dinner, they're just fried dough. Look, there's souvlaki, falafel . . . Kebabs, you said you like kebabs.'

Michael shook his helmet, immovable. 'I passed churros down on the Prom, and they smelled so good.'

'All right, churros it is.' Because Noah couldn't handle another argument tonight. It was the repetition that appalled him; the stop-and-start, petty, Whac-A-Mole wrangling that died down and flared up over and over. 'But surely we can find some a bit closer?'

No, it turned out that churros were sold only from vans on the seafront. So Noah and Michael trailed all the way back down to the Prom, through confettied streets with a wrecked and dissolute look to them. Better not to talk; to let the exhausting evening wind down like a clockwork train.

Instead Noah found himself reflecting out

371

loud about everybody having electrical charges in the brain, prompting chemical signals that had been useful to our hunter-gatherer ancestors but were obsolescent in a modern urban society.

'*You're* obsolescent.' Michael spoke through his teeth.

'I'm only pointing out, as someone with a great deal of life experience, that following those fight-or-flight impulses can get you into trouble in various ways, medically, legally . . . '

'Shut the fuck up, old man.'

'I don't think you should speak to me that way, especially considering I'm one of the few relations you have left.'

'No you aren't,' the kid snarled. 'It'd take more than a couple spirals of DNA to make us blood.'

'Michael — '

But the kid was gone again, racing off through the crowd, fleet with fury.

Argh!

Noah just didn't have it in him to chase the boy this time; after a few steps he slowed, coughing. The most he could do was weave through the late-night promenaders, keeping the Roman helmet in view. 'Michael!' he yelled hoarsely, just once. All it did was make strangers stare. Noah almost collided with three giggling girls on those blue rental bikes, and had to lunge out of the path of a pair of twins in a stroller.

Michael was almost at the giant sundial now. Should Noah give up, walk back to the Excelsior and wait for him to show up again? No. The

372

truth was, Noah had provoked this latest quarrel by preaching and pontificating, so —

Jesus Christ, what was the kid doing?

Michael was climbing around the fence at the point where they'd seen teenagers dive from the high rocks the other day. Was he meaning to sulk on a ledge, out of sight?

Adrenaline-fueled now, Noah broke into a trot, almost crashing into a Rollerblader. But by the time he got to the fence and stepped up to peer around it, the boy had disappeared among the rocks, outside the lamp's circle of light. 'Michael!' Noah panted. 'Come back, you might slip.'

And if Michael did fall in . . . He couldn't swim. The lunatic, didn't he register the danger? Now Noah was scared to climb after him, not just because he mistrusted his own balance but because it might provoke the boy.

If this was a standoff, was it best to wait it out? Or would Michael interpret Noah's silence as indifference? 'Michael,' he pleaded.

No answer.

If Noah descended to the stony beach below, it struck him, he'd be able to see the high rocks better.

He hurried down the pavement, down the steps, gripping the flaking rail so he wouldn't trip. His shoes wallowed among the slippery, grinding pebbles. He staggered, almost fell. Head tilted back, he searched the line of rocks. Yes, there was the small figure of Michael, alone on the divers' ledge, hunched with chin on fist like Rodin's *Thinker*. 'Careful,' Noah wailed. No dignity, now; no authority; no idea what else he could do.

Was the kid . . . yes, he was setting down his helmet. Slipping his sneakers off. Was he going to make some dramatic gesture by tossing them in the sea?

No, it was the other way around. Michael meant to jump.

'I apologize!' It came out of Noah as a shriek. 'I'm sorry for everything. I'm an asshole. Come down!'

Michael showed no sign of hearing, eyes fixed on the foaming waves.

From day one, Noah had failed to grasp the reality of what this kid had been through. Behind the braggadocio, such grief. After all, what did Michael have left to keep him anchored to the world?

'No!'

Young people smoking dope on the stones nearby turned to stare.

'Don't!' Noah howled.

Cleanly, no flailing, arms by his sides, Michael dropped like a knife, and the dark sea swallowed him.

Noah didn't make a sound, not even a call for help. He was on his knees, watching the water. He couldn't speak, couldn't take a breath. When, if, when he spotted Michael's head, he told himself, he'd be able to fix his eyes on it — point both hands — roar to those potheads to help him get the kid out of the water.

A shape, a figure in the sea halfway between the foam line and where Michael had fallen. Was it? Backstroking smoothly, face tilted up to catch the lamplight. No. Could it —

'Michael!' Noah waited, in his painful crouch.

There was the boy, walking out of the waves like some miracle. Clothes flattened into sodden armor, face bejeweled by salt drops.

Noah pounded, then slithered his way toward the boy. Up to his knees in the icy wash, he flung his arms around Michael, almost knocking them both into the surf. Pressed the small frame to him, very hard. 'I didn't know you could swim.'

Michael was panting a little, but his voice was oddly calm. 'Why wouldn't I be able to swim?'

'You never said!'

'You never asked. My mom's been taking me to the Y since I was three.'

Up on the wide sidewalk of the Prom, the two of them making pools of water like mermen, Noah noticed something: 'Your foot's bleeding.'

'I bashed it on a rock,' Michael said with pride, 'but it's OK.'

'It doesn't look OK.'

'I don't feel anything.'

'That's because you're numb from the water.'

Going back to the base of the fence, Michael clambered around it to retrieve his helmet and Jordans. Then he jumped back down. 'Can we get churros now?'

Noah weighed the risk of Michael getting hypothermia against the certainty of his whining all night about being hungry, and went to line up for a white paper sack of churros.

Michael spared him half a stick: stiff, warm,

greasy under the powdered sugar.

Noah checked his watch. Past midnight; it was technically Monday. 'I just turned eighty.'

'Cheers, dude.' Michael toasted him with the little sack.

★   ★   ★

Back in their room at the Excelsior, Noah got out his hydrogen peroxide.

'Hell no.'

'It's just to clean your foot and keep it from getting gangrenous.' Exaggerating a little, for effect. 'Its formula is H_2O_2. Like water, H_2O, but with an extra atom of oxygen per molecule that gives it amazing antiseptic powers.' Over the bathroom sink, he dabbed at the boy's gashed toe.

Michael winced.

'Oh, I thought of a chemistry joke — a classic. Two guys walk into a bar,' Noah began, to distract him. 'One of them says, 'I'd like a glass of H_2O.' The bartender asks the other guy what he'd like. He says, 'Well, I guess I'll have H_2O too.''

It took only a second before Michael snickered. 'What happened to him — the second guy?'

'Burns, respiratory distress, stroke, death.' Noah dried the cut with a tissue, then applied an adhesive bandage. 'There you go. Only a Band-Aid solution, as they say.'

★   ★   ★

In the night he lay awake, still wired; horrified by what could have happened if the kid had hit his head rather than his foot on that rock. Noah never had put him on his travel insurance.

A grunt from Michael. 'You got any more chemistry jokes?'

'Hm, let's see.'

He practiced a couple silently in his head: *What do you do with sick chemists?* Joan had tried this one on Noah a few days after her diagnosis. *Helium and curium.* Michael would know about helium from balloons, but what were the chances he'd heard of curium? The same went for *What do you do with dead chemists? Barium.*

'Oh, I do have another joke,' he said aloud, 'but it's not about chemistry.'

''Kay.'

'Will you remember me in a second?' Noah asked.

'Huh?'

'This is how the joke starts. Will you remember me in a second?'

'Sure. I'm not a goldfish.'

An honor to remember . . . shameful to forget. 'Will you remember me in a minute?'

'Of course,' Michael said.

'In an hour?'

'Uh-huh.'

'In a day?'

'This joke's taking forever.'

'In a week?'

'Just get it over with,' Michael pleaded.

'In a month?'

'Are you trying to bore me to sleep?'

'Answer the question. Will you remember me in a year?'

'Yeah, yeah, I swear.'

'In a century?'

'OK, whatever.'

'Knock-knock.' Noah came to the punchline at last.

'Who's there?'

He put on a hurt tone. 'I thought you said you'd remember me?'

A long pause. 'That's the unfunniest joke ever.'

Noah smiled in the dark.

9

Decisive Moments

Noah woke late and sat up in bed slowly, like an invalid. 'You awake yet, Michael?'

'Nope.'

'I'm maxed out this morning.'

'Me too,' the boy said into the mattress.

'We're not flying to New York till late this afternoon.'

'Good.'

Noah called down to the front desk and agreed to pay their extortionate fee for late checkout. Then he reached down for his tablet, in the slim hope that Rosa might have answered late last night.

'I got a look at the report on Victor's death,' her email began. 'No mention of his wearing a wire, but I did notice there was no gear (drug paraphernalia) in the motel room, which suggests that whoever was with him took it away.'

Bastards! They'd left without checking to see that Victor was all right. Or worse, they'd panicked when he'd lost consciousness and run off without even calling 911.

'Also, the pathologist noted that there were no track marks, just the fresh injection site behind Victor's left knee.'

Noah rubbed between his eyebrows. What did that mean — that the very first time his nephew had tried injecting, it had gone wrong? 'That shit was never his poison,' Amber had insisted. Did she mean the method as much as the substance? Had Victor been obliged to shoot up for the first time in his life to win the trust of the strangers he was aiming to entrap?

He must have been so torn, as well as terrified. 'Snitches get stitches. Snitches end up in ditches.' And he'd had good reason to be afraid, hadn't he? Dead by morning.

Noah stared at the liver-spotted backs of his fingers. Who would pick behind their knee for a first try if the veins in their arms and hands were unscarred?

It hadn't been an accidental overdose; he found he didn't believe that story anymore.

He tapped in 'confidential criminal informant CI sting wire death,' and the cases filled his screen like some wave of filth:

'Bullet-ridden body found in a ditch . . . Beaten with a bat, run over by a car . . . Pulled from the river with a gunshot wound in the head and a backpack full of rocks . . . Torso found ablaze beneath an old mattress . . . Behind her knee.'

One case caught Noah's eye. A woman of twenty-four, pressured into working as a CI, found dead in a trailer. 'The medical examiner concluded that heroin and alprazolam (Xanax) had been injected behind her knee.' Afterward her grandparents 'heard rumors the people she was with may have known she was an informant.'

That motel on Long Island. Had the dealers found Victor's wire, then held him facedown on the carpet and stuck that syringe in the back of his knee?

Possible. Likely even. But unproven. Unprovable, now?

I'm so sorry, Victor. Sorry that wrong had been done to him and none of his family had understood. Sorry for what had come before, and after.

Michael was playing a game on the cracked screen resting on his ribs. 'What?' he asked without shifting his gaze.

'What?' Noah said back.

'You were looking at me.'

Instead of explaining, Noah changed the subject. 'What are you playing now?'

'Just spectating, I died already.'

'So you can keep watching after you die? That's better than the real world, all right.'

'No contest,' Michael muttered. 'And in most games you can respawn.'

'What's that?'

'Come back to life.'

'Handy.'

'I like save states, too. You freeze the moment you're in, so if you fuck up you can go back to it.'

Noah thought of Victor lying on that carpet. Because he was a fuckup, they'd all assumed he'd fucked himself up, but sometimes even fuckups got fucked up by forces beyond their control. By life itself.

If Victor had been murdered because he'd been a snitch, how was Noah ever going to find a way to break it to Michael? How to begin to

381

explain the strain the young man had been under, the moral gray areas, the awful ambiguities of the so-called war on drugs?

It occurred to Noah with a pang of relief that he had no right to (like the ghost in *Hamlet*) blurt out a wild theory about a father's murder. It would be for Amber to make that judgment call. Noah would talk to her about Victor's death; she might have her suspicions already, but he doubted anyone would have shown her the autopsy report. Maybe he and she could figure out together whether it was worth trying to prove Victor had been a CI, or that he'd been killed.

Noah could also hire a good attorney to see what could be done for Amber, if she let him. Might she appeal her sentence on the grounds that her public defender hadn't represented her adequately?

The future was more urgent than the past, he decided, even if the two were entangled. Like the line he'd read in the Resistance museum: never hate, but never forget.

★   ★   ★

Waiters came out of restaurants to hose the sidewalks; Monday morning smelled of pine cleaning fluid. A single window caught the sun, like a covert signal. The peaks in the distance were acute. 'That sharpness,' Noah said, 'that's how you know the Alps are still young mountains.'

Michael scanned the horizon like Julius Caesar contemplating an invasion.

'Mature mountains are curvy. They get lower as they get older.'

The boy grinned. 'So I'm super sharp, and you're practically flat?'

'True. How's your foot this morning? Any redness or swelling?'

'Nah.'

They had bananas from a convenience store. Noah rested his back against a wall while Michael went off to watch a gold-painted living statue stand frozen until enough children gathered around him. Finally the statue winked and made them scream.

Putting the peels in a garbage can, Noah caught sight of an angel silhouetted high on the hill. 'Oh, I nearly forgot, I need to visit my grandfather's grave.'

A token groan from the boy.

'The cemetery's just up there, at the back of the Colline du Château.'

'The hill with nothing on it ever since the King of France blew it up?' Michael asked.

'A-plus for attention.'

At the base of the higgledy-piggledy staircase, Michael shook his head, which made his helmet shimmy. 'Go ahead and climb if you want, I'll be here.'

'Come on, you're a lot fitter than I am.'

The boy shrugged. 'You do you.'

Which Noah realized must be a modern way of saying no.

Then Michael pointed at the letters over a red brick archway through which a little knot of people seemed to be disappearing right into the hill, Pied Piper-style. 'What's *ask-an-sewer*?'

'*Ascenseur* . . . elevator,' Noah read. Could it really be an elevator in a hill?

'Cool! Can I get a ticket?'

'It says it's free,' he admitted.

'Score!' Michael cantered off that way.

As a matter of pride, now, Noah had to toil up the zigzag staircase on his own. His feet thumped the flat paving stones, and he counted, to keep his mind off his lungs. This was more of a hill than he'd realized. Seventy-seven, seventy-eight, seventy-nine, eighty (just like him, today), eighty-one . . . He paused at a turn to catch his breath, pretending to take in the flowering slope. Then climbed again. One-twenty-seven, one-twenty-eight.

Maybe you should have ridden up with the boy, Joan suggested.

Noah pressed on to show her she was wrong. One-ninety-three, one-ninety-four, one-ninety-five. Christ, how much farther? He looked down at the steeples, terra-cotta roofs, little domes tiled in multicolored Genoese style, the greenery, the cyan sea, but he couldn't enjoy it. Was Michael cutting in line, deep in the bowels of the hill? Messing with the elevator controls? To soothe himself he glanced to the right, toward Cannes in the gauzy distance. Climbed again. Paused to gasp, and examine a huge pink disk-shaped flower. Clinging inside it was a green grasshopper of some sort.

After another turn, Noah thought he was done — but the path curved and flourished into more steps. Breathless, he'd lost count.

Michael was lounging against a wall at the very top, arms crossed, helmet pushed back on his head like some disdainful warrior. 'You took forever.'

Noah didn't have enough breath to answer. He led the way past a flattened-earth court where ceremonious old men were taking turns throwing metal balls. '*Pétanque*,' he said after a minute, enjoying the recollected word. 'You have to get your ball near a smaller ball.' Had his *pépère* played it? He thought of Père Sonne and Margot, fox-trotting to keep warm. 'In New York there's a different version, *bocce*. Ever try it?'

Michael shook his head. 'We play basketball, handball, skelly . . . '

'We called that skully. Shooting metal bottle caps into chalk squares?'

'Milk-jug caps, we use.'

'I was rather good at skully in my day,' Noah said.

'Why do you keep saying that? In your day.'

'Do I? It just means *when I was young*.'

'But isn't this still one of your days? Just about.'

'Well, I suppose.' At the overlook, Noah stared down at the gorgeous jumble of yachts in the old port, the hills rising on the other side of the harbor. Soft saxophone notes drifted up from below, and the faint cries of children. (Always hard to tell, at a distance, if they were happy or screaming.)

Michael had his phone up and was taking a burst of photos, which Noah decided was a compliment to the view.

Crossing the hilltop, they came across archaeological remains, and modern mosaics in the Roman style; one was a sailboat, with the classic verse *Heureux qui, comme Ulysse, a fait un beau voyage.* 'Like Odysseus, you're happy if you've . . . had a good trip,' Noah translated. No, that made it sound like a tourist-board slogan. The original was about travel in the older, more active sense. And not bland happiness, either. He tried again: 'Lucky the man who's gone voyaging.'

Michael scoffed: 'Lucky if you can afford the tickets.'

'Good point.'

The first cemetery they found was the Jewish one. The Holocaust memorial just inside the gate held an urn containing ashes from the gas chambers, and another of soap made with rendered human fat. Speechless, Noah couldn't bear to translate any of that for Michael. The kid had to know the truth, but not all of it quite yet.

He swiveled away and pointed out the prewar tomb of a little boy, topped by a stylish stone car.

Michael nodded. 'Nice. I wouldn't mind one like that.'

The Catholic graveyard was next: a vast city of the dead arranged in orderly gravel paths. Noah found the protector angel who could be seen from so many points in the streets below; it turned out to be a monument to a nineteenth-century couple, the Grossos, who'd left all their worldly goods to the city. (They'd lost their two children, whose marble portraits were shown in disconcerting bas-relief.) 'See the broken

386

anchor? That means death.'

'How come?' Michael asked.

'I suppose your anchor snaps and your boat drifts free.'

'Look, a head's sticking right out of this one!' The boy trotted over to a figure with deep-cut features, shadowed with black; a long drip from one eye, as if the marble mourner was crying ink.

'Those stains are algae, or maybe fungus,' Noah told him. 'And see where this other one's fingers have almost melted away? Acid rain, due to sulfur in the air.'

'You're a downer, and so is this place.'

'Death's very useful, though, to the species if not to the individual.'

The boy put his head to one side. 'Because otherwise the earth would be so full of us we'd be tripping over each other?'

'True, but also because it stops our accumulated cellular mutations from being passed on.'

Michael puzzled that out. 'You mean, like, you shouldn't make any babies at eighty because they might have three eyes?'

Noah nodded. A clearing of accounts, biologically speaking; an editing of errors. From a truly scientific point of view, who could be afraid of that?

Mind you, from an evolutionary perspective, having three eyes might be an advantage.

Michael marveled at an elegant pair of stone feet protruding from a tomb; then a beautiful, limp youth held up in a giant three-taloned bird foot; and the most gothic, a black slab with a golden braid (clutched by two little hands) bursting out of it. 'Like some psycho walled-up Rapunzel!' He sprawled back on the tomb for a selfie.

When Noah finally located the right grave, it was rather an anticlimax: a plain slab.

Isabelle Personnet née Gaspard
1865–1930
Pierre Jean Personnet, dit Père Sonne
1860–1944

'What's *dit*?'

'Called,' Noah told him.

'It doesn't say much.'

'I suppose he didn't feel the need to blow his own trumpet.' Or perhaps Margot had made that last decision for her father. 'The photographs are his real memorial.' Genius had rung through Père Sonne like a bell. It occurred to Noah that Joan had been the same way: no dithering, no grousing. Perhaps geniuses had to be a little ruthless; always aware of their task and of the fact that there'd never be quite enough time to get it done.

Graves really didn't matter. Still, Noah wished he'd thought to bring a few flowers for his grandparents. (Something less miserable than those chilly daffodils for Victor, in Central Park; something Mediterranean, scented.) He felt in his pockets and in his satchel for something to leave. Nothing but lint.

'Do you want a pic with Nodaddy Ding?' Michael waved his phone. 'Since you brought his old hat all the way back for a visit.'

388

Noah stood by the headstone, then managed to crouch beside it.

Michael pressed the shutter.

Noah was straightening up with difficulty when he thought to say, 'One of you too, I mean one with you? Their great-great-grandson.' A postscript, one more *PS*. DNA chiming down through four generations; some kind of inheritance.

The two of them stood on either side of the headstone, a little awkward. 'Where's your selfie stick when we need it?'

'Don't remember. I think maybe I lost it,' Michael said gloomily.

Noah was secretly delighted. 'OK, lean in and take off your helmet. Give me your phone — my arm's longer.' He fumbled and almost dropped it. But managed to take the picture in the end.

They considered the image together. 'Well, aren't we the odd couple,' Noah said. Sixty-nine years between them, for starters; a smooth beech sapling beside a gnarled oak.

'It's not a bad ussie,' Michael said.

'A what?'

'Like a selfie for more than one. I'll send you a copy.'

'Thanks.' Was that a sort of goodbye in advance, Noah wondered?

He flicked back through more of Michael's photos: odd angles on buildings, people cavorting in Carnival masks, fish in the water between two boats. Noah liked one of himself taken from directly overhead, defamiliarized: his hairless head like some unevenly colored planet. When and where had Michael taken that one? The boy had an artist's eye as well as a scientific mind. 'That's a great shot.'

A shrug. 'It's not all that.'

'Yes it *is* all that, actually. Learn to take a compliment.'

A roll of the eyes.

Noah risked it: 'I think you're all that.'

Michael turned away. 'You don't count. You're family.'

A strange hiss behind them, then an explosion so loud that Noah staggered. He reeled around and spotted a plume of smoke going up behind a cypress. The whole hill still seemed to be shaking. Was someone blowing up the whole city?

Michael was laughing. 'Your face!'

Noah swallowed hard. 'That was just the cannon? It's so much louder up here.'

★   ★   ★

'Can I get a hot dog?' Michael asked as they emerged from the cemetery.

'This is a historic site,' Noah reminded him. 'I really don't think there'll be — '

The boy pointed his finger like a gun at a parked van that said *Le Giant Hot Dog New-Yorkais*. The same one as the other day, or was there a whole fleet?

'Water,' Noah called as Michael ran ahead.

'Nah, I haven't had my Coke of the day.'

Noah was still full from breakfast, so he

checked his phone while Michael ate his lunch, the helmet on the wall between them.

He was surprised to see an email from Monsieur Benoit at the museum. *Possibly of interest?* the header said, with a link to an article in a Nice paper from August 2014.

Once it loaded, Noah glanced through: celebrations for the seventieth anniversary of the Liberation, nothing very interesting there . . . In the last paragraph, the journalist quoted a local named Lucien Demetz.

'Listen to this.' Noah's voice wavering as he translated for Michael. 'In 1943, when I had — when I was only three years old, it was necessary for my parents to give me into the, ah, safekeeping of Monsieur Abadi. He gave me a new name, René Jacques, and hid me at a boarding school run by monks. When he came to collect me at the end of the year, I asked for my parents, and he wept.'

Michael nodded. 'Poor kid.'

'No, but . . . René Jacques, that was this Lucien Demetz's *nom de guerre*, the war name the Marcel Network gave him. René Jacques — R.J.'

'The smiley boy in your mom's photo!'

'It must be. And what's more, it says he lives in a *maison de retraite* — an old folks' home — in Cimiez, where we were the other day. Or he *was* living there three and a half years ago, anyway,' Noah added, suddenly doubtful. This Lucien would be only seventy-seven now, but still that was getting on, for a man. 'Let's go see if we can talk to him.'

First they went back to the Excelsior for Noah to collect his photos and the Pick-Pick Bird.

When they stepped off the bus in Cimiez, Michael recognized the ruined silhouette of the Roman arena. 'This place? You're going to make me give the helmet back.'

'Of course.' Though it hadn't actually occurred to Noah, in his state of preoccupation with Lucien Demetz. 'You know it's the right thing to do.'

'I'm not apologizing to that bitch. She wouldn't understand my English anyway.'

'Oh, I think she'd know the word sorry.' Noah weighed the matter. 'But she was so nasty, I'm not sure she deserves an apology.'

Michael brightened.

Noah beckoned for him to hand over the helmet.

The boy took it off slowly, as if it was made of lead, and planted a kiss on the crest.

Noah would have to find the kid another one like it for his birthday.

He had an idea for how to avoid a mortifying conversation with the museum attendant. He crossed the grass to intercept a tour party gathering around its leader (identified by the tiny Chinese flag she held above her head) outside the doors. He handed the helmet to a random man and gestured toward the interior of the building.

Honored, the man put the helmet on and bowed to Noah.

Hidden behind a tree, Michael was watching in disbelief.

'Done and dusted.'

'What if she calls the cops on *that* poor sucker?'

'She won't — she knows it was you.'

Michael sniffed, watching the tour party disappear into the museum. 'I've got to say, I wore it better.'

Noah was only half-listening as he checked his phone for the correct turn to the *maison de retraite*.

It was behind a high wall (because some of the residents had to be prevented from wandering, he supposed). He pointed out the heavy branches of the fruit trees: 'Clementines.'

'What?'

'Like satsumas. Mandarins? Little oranges.'

Michael studied the gate's elegant metalwork and official signage. 'Will they let in a couple of strange Americans?'

Noah hadn't tried calling ahead, because he figured his chances were better in person. 'I'm going to say my mother knew him.'

'That is total bull.'

'Partial bull,' Noah corrected him. He held down the button on the little box and in his crispest French announced himself as a family friend, *un ami de la famille de Monsieur Demetz*. Fingers crossed that the man wasn't dead yet. Who'd raised him after he'd been orphaned in the Holocaust, Noah wondered? If he'd stayed around Nice, that might be an indication that he did have some family here.

393

The gate swung open with only a tiny creak.

Noah lingered on the path, pretending to smell the trees; he dreaded going into the building, even though this was what he'd come here to do. He wondered if Michael sometimes felt this way about his visits to Amber in prison.

After he rang the buzzer on the front door, it took a few minutes for a tiny woman in uniform to come and unlock it.

It was the smell that made Noah stiffen, as much as the locks on all the doors. Nothing rancid, only institutional; disinfectant? (Please, please let Noah drop down dead crossing Broadway before it came to this.) He signed them in and asked — casually, as if they were frequent visitors — where Madame thought they might find Monsieur Demetz?

They could try his room. The care worker pointed upward.

Noah took the carpeted stairs. When he turned on the landing Michael was still at the bottom, sitting on the stairlift.

'Where's the On button?'

'Get off,' Noah hissed, beckoning.

Michael loped up the stairs three at a time, one hand on the rail.

They read the names on the doors until they finally got to DEMETZ LUCIEN. It struck Noah that the French habit of putting the surname first could give situations an almost military tinge. *Davis*, he remembered the guard calling Amber. *Inmate Davis!* But really he supposed it was a matter of whether you saw yourself primarily as a member of a clan or as an

394

individual. *Family Over Everything*, as Michael's tattoo said?

Noah tapped softly on the thin wood. 'Monsieur Demetz?'

Nothing.

The man could be napping, or reading, or anything. Noah had no right to barge in. But he'd come all this way . . .

He opened the door an inch, then another. A small bedroom, nobody in it. Some kind of safety rail around the bed. How a life could shrink to a handful of square feet, toward the end.

Noah led Michael downstairs again. Through a square of glass he spotted dozens of people sitting around the edge of a big room as if having a silent meeting; a TV on in a corner. Old people: definitely *decrepitus* rather than *senectus*. He steeled himself to go in, but it was locked.

'This place creeps me out,' Michael whispered.

'Me too.'

'Can we go?'

'It's worse for me,' Noah told him. 'One fall and I'll end up here, in diapers.'

That made the boy giggle.

Noah waited for the next nursing assistant to come through and appealed to him.

Ah yes, Monsieur Demetz was in the sunroom, at the other end of the building, and he'd be glad to see some old friends.

Noah was feeling bad about his cover story. What if the Frenchman took one look at these Americans and said he'd never seen them in his life?

In the conservatory there were perhaps a dozen figures, two of them men — as far as Noah could tell from a quick scan, because age made everyone more androgynous. One man in a hat at the piano, hands motionless on the keys; another between some potted plants, staring out the window. Noah hesitated, then touched the aide's sleeve as the young man turned to go. 'I can't — *Pardonnez-moi*,' but it had been some time and he couldn't quite recall . . .

The aide led him over to the plants. 'Lucien,' he said gently, rousing the starer.

Lucien Demetz had a full head of hair, much of it still black. Physically he looked younger than Noah. Something about the gaze, though; not vacant, but misty. Damn it: Noah could tell they'd come several years too late.

But he did his best, introducing himself and Michael as *visiteurs des États-Unis* and hurrying on to say that he thought Monsieur Demetz had known — had once met — Noah's mother? Noah had reason to believe that she'd taken Monsieur Demetz's picture when he was a little boy. 'Pour Monsieur Abadi — Moussa Abadi?' he added in a low voice, awkward about raising painful history in a public space. (But none of the other residents paid any attention. *Do they all have dementia*, he wondered?)

Not a spark in those brown eyes.

If this was indeed Monsieur Demetz in this photo? Noah produced it from his envelope.

The man's face lit up at the sight of the small boy.

But that proved nothing; he might think it was

a grandson of his. Noah would bet the residents were constantly being shown old photos. And who didn't like the sight of a smiling child? '*C'est bien vous, Monsieur?*'

'*Oui, oui, bien sûr.*'

'Does he say it's him?' Michael asked.

'Mm, but I think he's, you know, gone in the head.' Noah turned the photo over and pointed to the initials on the back: '*R.J., c'était bien votre faux nom pendant la guerre, René Jacques?*' Was it true that had been Monsieur's false name in the war?

Lucien Demetz kept nodding.

Noah's mother, Madame Selvaggio, had taken that photograph, a friend of Moussa Abadi's.

The face was uncertain now.

Did the name *Margot Selvaggio* mean anything to Monsieur? Or — Noah corrected himself — *Marie Zabel*? He should have thought to bring a picture of his mother from New York. All he could do was flick to a marked page in the biography and point to a photo captioned *Margot on her wedding day*. This was her, Marie Zabel.

Lucien Demetz's eyes wandered across the page.

Noah tapped just below Margot's glowing face. Marie Zabel, a lady with a camera?

'*Et un oiseau.*'

'And a bird.' Had Noah heard the man right?

'*Le petit oiseau va sortir.*' Eyes veering to the window again, Lucien Demetz barely breathed it.

'The little bird's coming out,' Noah translated under his breath.

Michael nodded excitedly. 'Watch the birdie.'

But it wasn't just Margot who'd said that; anyone photographing a child would have used the phrase. 'Probably just because I mentioned a camera,' Noah whispered. Word association, the last game of a failing mind; language falling from prose to bare, enigmatic poetry.

'Show him the actual bird,' Michael suggested.

A little sheepish, Noah took the Pick-Pick Bird out of his pocket and unwrapped it from its sheet of bubbles. He stood it on his palm.

Lucien Demetz beamed. '*C'est l'oiseau!*'

'It's the bird!' But perhaps he just meant it was *a* bird; any colorful toy might have elicited the same response. Even if this was the very model of plush bird the woman had shown Lucien Demetz when she'd been taking his picture — there were millions of Pick-Pick Birds out there. It must have been a nightmarish day when the Demetzes told little Lucien he had to go away and pretend to be a Christian boy; why would he have paid any attention to the photographer?

Lucien Demetz reached out and Noah let him take the bird. The man touched the velvet, especially the bald patches, as if soothing the creature.

How could Noah possibly extract from Lucien Demetz's soupy brain the information he needed? But he tried again. So did Monsieur remember her, the lady with the bird who'd taken this photo of him when he was three years old?

Lucien Demetz nodded again, but this struck

398

Noah as just a tic, a way to keep the conversational ball in the air. The man's eyes stayed on the bird. His mouth was doing something curious. His tongue was out, not in a lax or dribbling way.

'Trying to touch his freaking nose!' Michael squealed it.

'Hang on.' Noah watched Lucien Demetz, wary. His mottled gray-pink tongue was reaching upward, urgent, as if to catch the last drip of something delicious.

'Ask him! Ask him if she did that.'

Noah put his own tongue out and curled it, aiming vainly upward. By any chance, could the lady touch her own tongue to her nose?

'*Oui! Oui! Elle l'a léchée!*' Lucien Demetz burst out laughing.

'She licked it,' Noah told the boy.

'That's got to be your mom, then.'

'Ten percent of the population have Gorlin sign.'

'Yeah, but come on, dude! You said she did it like a party trick.'

Though maybe every mother who could do a thing like that, did. Wouldn't you use all the tricks in your bag to distract children, especially in bleak situations? Still, Noah reckoned the odds. Drew a Venn diagram of overlapping traits. A woman taking identity shots of kids in Nice for the Marcel Network, in 1943; a woman who wound up a velvety orange, black, and gold Pick-Pick Bird, and licked her nose to make her subjects smile.

'It's her,' Michael crowed.

Lucien Demetz's tongue was back in his mouth now, his lips still, his hands stroking the bird.

Watching him, Noah thought of the emperor whose gorgeous clockwork bird had seized up in the end; on his deathbed he'd called for the dark-feathered nightingale, knowing he never should have chosen a shiny substitute, because nothing but her real song could save him now. Was there any music that would bring back memories once they were lost in the fog? What were we, once our stories had drifted off like smoke?

He thanked Lucien Demetz.

Who paid no attention, but caressed the Pick-Pick Bird as if it had flown back to him after a lifetime.

Had the man made a new family, as Vivienne had, in place of all he'd lost? Did his descendants come to see him every Sunday afternoon? Noah could have asked one of the staff, but he realized he couldn't bear it if the answer was no. Besides, it wasn't as if there was anything Noah could do about it; he was just passing through.

He jerked his head at Michael to mean they should go now.

'The bird.'

'I'm going to leave it with him.'

'But it's yours.'

Noah waved that off. *How much longer do you think I'll get to hold on to my things before I have to give them all away anyway?*

But he did put the photo of little R.J. back in the envelope, to keep the whole set together.

Getting off the bus, Noah said there was something he wanted to do at Place Masséna, where they'd watched the Carnival Corso last night.

'Can we ride the Ferris wheel?'

'All right, but my thing first.'

'Let's take the tram.'

'Oh, Michael, it's just two stops down the street.'

'Faster, though, and we have to use up our ten-ride card, don't we?'

'Your logic is irresistible.'

The carriage was crammed, and just as the high-pitched *ping* announced that the tram was about to move off, a man hauled the doors back open and a horde of schoolkids came squirreling in. Young ones — seven or eight years old, maybe. The teacher held the doors and asked everyone to move up because more children were still on the platform waiting to get in.

Could the teacher not have broken up the group, Noah wondered, or waited for the next tram? This one seemed dangerously over-crowded. Children pushing, shoving, leaning against poles and one another . . . A cluster fell over as the tram braked to let a car cross the intersection. Noah was afraid an adult would trip over them. They were snorting with glee, and one girl wiped her nose on her sleeve as she hopped up, then scratched her calf with the other shoe. When the tram stopped suddenly at Jean Medecin she toppled again, right through the wave of bodies. Noah leaped up, pointing. '*Attention!*'

People stared at him.

Michael looked away, shaking his head in embarrassment.

But the little girl had sprung up already, her bobble head wobbling on its spindly neck. She sang out: '*Quelqu'un a pété!*'

And it was true, someone *had* farted: that warm agricultural smell. Gales of laughter went up; even their teacher's hard face cracked.

As the tram moved off and gained velocity, Noah's irritation surged. This pack of brats was lurching back and forward again, *trying* to cause an accident . . .

Then he found his eyes jellied with tears. The sheer merriment of these children; maybe this was the funniest moment they'd ever know in their lives. (Noah remembered bursting out laughing in Mass, one time; his mother's urgent eyes on him, the hoots and snorts exploding out of his body.) It was well and good, all in all, that these particular kids had no reason to be afraid, today; they still had time to be childish. If one of them leaned too far and slipped, well, people would pull back, make space, and pick up the fallen. No need to fight for scraps or air. This was enough for Margot and all of them to have fought for, Noah saw now: the freedom of these kids to mock and fart, to break and remake; even to forget.

For a moment he saw his mother in that bath at the Excelsior, like some martyr of old, singing through her pain.

At Place Masséna, workers in oddly smart, futuristic uniforms were dismantling the stands and trucking the pieces away. It all looked so different in the light of day. Noah couldn't be sure which garbage can he was looking for, so he peered squeamishly into three or four.

'You're wishing you hadn't thrown away Nodaddy Ding's old hat.'

'Well, if I can spot it . . . '

'It's not in any of those cans,' Michael told him.

'Where is it, then?'

The boy loped in a different direction over the black-and-white paving squares, right across the square.

'Are you sure? Careful!' Because the kid was dipping into a trash can. 'Watch for broken glass — or needles — '

Michael emerged with a gigantic cone dripping with melted ice cream.

'Don't eat that!'

'What do you think I am, a raccoon?' He tossed it aside and dug in farther.

'Just leave it.' If Rosa could see them now . . . 'It's not worth it. It's just a hat.'

'It's my great-great-grandpa's fucking hat.' With a final grunt, Michael hauled it out. The once-beautiful — so-long beautiful — fedora.

Noah hurried up to examine it. Crushed, gluey with Silly String and other disgusting substances. 'Well done.' Doing his best to sound appreciative. He held it stiffly by his side, away from his pants, as he led the way toward the gigantic Ferris wheel.

★ ★ ★

The views of Nice were magnificent, but Michael — although excited to be up so high — soon tired of them. It was Noah who noted each slate spire and brightly tiled dome, each little terra-cotta roof; he who watched (probably for the last time) the ancient city spread its arms to embrace the sea.

It took a while to unload the cars one by one. Michael's head dipped to his phone. 'What are you playing?' Noah asked as their car dangled and wobbled.

'Just the dinosaur game. There's no Wi-Fi.'

'What's the dinosaur game?'

'You don't know it?' Michael showed Noah his screen — *There is no internet connection*, with a roughly pixelated T. rex.

'How is that a game?'

'Hit the space bar, he starts running, has to jump over cactuses . . . '

'Cacti.'

Michael squinted at him. 'Are you correcting me again?'

'Live with it.'

The boy held out the cracked phone. 'Try it if you want.'

Noah did his best, tapping the bar to make the dinosaur leap. 'You know in reality T. rex and cacti never shared the earth?' A whisker too slow, he crashed at the fifth cactus: GAME OVER.

'Pathetic, dude.' Michael pointing to Noah's score of 68. 'One time I got past four thousand. Sometimes there's birds . . . The colors invert, too, when it's night for the dinosaur.' He got to work again, utterly focused. 'I guess this is what we're all going to be playing, in the end.'

Noah didn't follow. 'What end?'

'After the crash.'

Noah's eyes stayed on the racing, jumping T. rex; it was oddly mesmerizing. 'After you crash into the cactus?'

'*The* crash, dumb-ass. When the sea rises and the internet's down and all. This is going to be the only game left.'

Noah looked out for each cactus on the boy's behalf, stomach tight in sympathetic tension, cringing in case the dinosaur wasn't quick enough to leap, or too quick . . .

GAME OVER.

He and this boy were quite alien to each other, he decided. Yet, in an odd way, akin.

Michael put away his phone. 'We're up.' Their car finally dipped to the platform, and he shoved at the restraining bar.

★ ★ ★

Back at the hotel, while the boy was taking a long shower, Noah thought to check that their plane was on time.

At the bottom of his phone's screen, he noticed the +1 on the voicemail icon.

'Mr. Selvaggio, Noah, it's Rosa, on Monday, 8 a.m. New York time.'

405

She'd left the message while they were on the Ferris wheel, he realized; he hadn't heard the ringtone through the noise. Her voice was oddly muted.

'I wanted to speak with you in person. I have to tell you, I managed to contact Amber's sister, Grace Drew, in Cincinnati — '

A sinking feeling; a disappointment that this story was coming to an end already. But how irrational for Noah to feel flattened.

Really, Joan asked, *what else could you have been hoping for?*

'Unfortunately, her current circumstances don't allow . . . She and her daughters have just moved in with a new partner, and the situation's not the most stable. She says to give Michael her love, but she's in no position to take him on, to take him in, at the moment.'

Noah let out a long, ragged breath. So that's why Rosa sounded regretful — not because she was taking Michael away from him, but because she couldn't.

Behind the wall, he heard the boy flush the toilet.

'We can meet up again on your return to New York, talk it through. Maybe another visit with Amber. But as of now, if you aren't able or willing to keep Michael for the foreseeable . . . I don't see any alternative but to take him into our agency's custody.'

Noah gritted his teeth. *Hell no, motherfucker!*

'So let me know. Talk to you soon, I hope.'

He took a breath.

Joan spoke sharply in his head. *Call back and*

say you're not equipped for this.

Zip it, he told her. *You're just a verbal algorithm.*

Joan wasn't abashed. *What are any of us but chemical algorithms, when we're alive?* Oxygen and hydrogen, stiffened by carbon. Some nitrogen, calcium, phosphorus, potassium, sulfur, sodium, chlorine, magnesium . . . molecules forming their lovely equations, temporarily following the rules for how to make a human.

Noah was packing socks into shoes when Michael came out of the bathroom.

'The chambermaids,' the boy reminded him.

'Thanks for remembering.' He tucked a twenty-euro note under the clock radio. 'I'd better give you a regular allowance once we're back in New York.'

Seconds passed.

Noah kept packing. *I can do this, Joan. At least, maybe I can. Very possibly. Worth a try. Isn't an experiment always worth making?*

'Regular like how?' Michael asked.

He still didn't turn his head; this seemed easier without eye contact. 'Well, it looks as if you might be staying with me for a while longer. Your aunt — Rosa left me a message — it turns out your aunt Grace can't look after you right now.'

No answer.

Panic, Noah wondered? *Grief? The final death of hope?*

'She and her girls have moved in with a new boyfriend, and I'm afraid there just isn't room, for the time being.'

407

''Kay.'

Was Michael unsurprised because his aunt was generally not to be counted on? Or because he expected all plans to fall through?

'So I'll be staying in your apartment?'

'That's right,' Noah told him.

'How'll I get to school?'

'By subway.' He thought of the hour and seven minutes Google estimated it would take. Would Michael be allowed to stay in that school if he was living in Manhattan? 'Or maybe you could switch to a different one.' He'd ask Vivienne's advice. What better woman to instruct him on how a child could endure the impossible?

'Who says I want a different school?'

'Suit yourself. It's mostly a distance issue.' Noah folded a shirt. 'I suppose I could — we could think about moving, if you prefer.' The words squeezed out of his tight throat. 'Closer to where your grandma's was.'

Michael said nothing.

It struck Noah for the first time that he could sell the Manhattan apartment. It wasn't as if he really cared about it anymore. And — a further shock, when he formulated this question — who but Michael would he be leaving it to, anyway?

'We'd visit your mother every week or two,' he added. 'Your Uncle Cody, as well. I could, ah, take you to your choir on Sundays.'

Michael screwed up his nose.

Was he doubting Noah's promises?

'Do I have to?'

'Fine, no choir.'

'How much allowance?'

'As I said, TBD.'

'And 'a while longer,' how long are we talking about?'

'I really can't say.' That came out too stiff.

The boy's mouth tightened. 'So if it all goes south, like if I break your fancy-pants lounger, are you going to call Rosa and send my ass back?'

'Why, are you planning to break my lounger?'

A shrug. 'Shit happens.'

'Indeed it does. But all I meant by 'a while longer' was that your aunt's circumstances might change.' Or a new lawyer might get Amber out early, though Noah mustn't tantalize the boy with that slim possibility. 'Also, let's be realistic: old men shouldn't make promises.'

'Because you should be twenty years dead already.'

Noah smiled.

Michael corrected himself: 'Twenty-*one* years, as of today.'

'Better pack up now.'

Noah quarantined his soiled, salvaged fedora in a plastic bag at the bottom of his carry-on; he'd have to see what a specialty dry cleaner could make of it. Whether he wore the hat again or not, he would hold on to it. Someday he'd pass it on to Michael along with Marc's bionic hand. Such random objects, freighted with meanings; the stuff of dream analysis. The boy might fail or refuse to treasure them; sell them, mislay them, throw them away. All right. The matter — all matters — would be out of Noah's hands. Which made him feel rather less sad than relieved.

409

They still had a little time to kill. Browsing on Noah's tablet, Michael beckoned him over. 'Here, it's *your day*.'

Old black-and-white footage; it turned out to be an experimental silent short about Nice from 1930. Rich people were shown in a paradise of restaurants and balls while workers pruned their palm trees and scrubbed dogshit off the pavements. Carnation-pickers labored in the hills, and tourists tossed the same blooms in the Bataille des Fleurs . . . But the director couldn't help relishing the beauty even as he denounced it, Noah noticed: a tiny plane landed on the glittering sea, and the elegant sails of a ship glided through the frame.

He caught himself looking for his mother as the camera pushed through the crowds on the Prom; searching for a thirty-year-old Margot Personnet in every cloche-hatted chatterer or paper-reader. Crossed legs in ladylike stockings, bobbing to the unheard tune of a busker's violin; could that possibly be her? 1930, so two more years before she'd marry Marc Selvaggio; eight more before she'd have a baby boy; more than a decade before she'd remake herself into Marie Zabel, to do the most important job of her life. Yes, even more important than being his mother.

And who would Noah have been if he'd been a father, he found himself wondering? Softer than he was now, harder? Whatever he might manage to be to Michael Young, it was too late for faux-fatherhood; Noah wouldn't even constitute a formative influence. But any port in a storm. Actually, no, Noah was more like a *passeur*

410

hurrying a child to the border, to entrust him to stronger arms. *Just don't break anything.*

Now the camera was moving though the murky slum of the Vieille Ville, the odd sheet flapping from a washing line like a flag of surrender, and boys were playing something rapid and warlike with their hands. Memory stirred. '*La Mourre*,' Noah said, the phrase suddenly striking him as sounding like *l'amour*, love. 'That's what we called it. You had to guess what everyone's fingers would add up to.'

'Oh yeah — Odds and Evens.'

'You play it?' He was charmed by the notion of the game's survival.

'Nah, it's for kids,' Michael said with contempt. 'These days, at school, we're all about Ballgazing.'

'All about what?'

'You make a circle' — Michael put his thumb and index finger together in the OK sign — 'and hold it low, like below your waist. If you catch anyone looking at the circle, you say 'Ballgazer!' and whack him on the arm.'

'That's the most ridiculous excuse for hitting someone I ever heard.'

Michael shrugged. 'He shouldn't be looking at your junk.'

'But you're trying to get him to do exactly that!' Noah didn't point out how homoerotic the whole thing sounded, too.

'That's the game, dude.'

The footage had run out without Noah's noticing. He googled the director. Jean Vigo, who turned out to have shot *À Propos de Nice* on

411

scraps of film filched from his employer, before he'd died of TB at twenty-nine. Here was his work, still flickering away online, eighty years after his death.

What would be left of Noah in eighty years? Not even that much. Only any individual's short, incalculable tally.

★ ★ ★

Waiting for the taxi outside the Excelsior, he wouldn't turn his head to give the hotel's doors one last look.

He was only two puffs into his cigarette when it hit him that he'd have to give up the goddamn things. The facts were clear: if he was taking on this temporary guardianship for the foreseeable future, the least he could do was stay upright and functional. He had *skin in the game* now. (Which reminded him of the raggedy mole on his forearm; all right, he'd have the thing cut out, just in case.) If in the next year or two Noah happened to be felled by natural causes, he wouldn't blame himself. But if it was by one of the innumerable problems that could be blamed on *lifestyle factors* such as smoking up to seven cigarettes a day? Then he'd feel like a criminal fool for having accepted this challenge, but loused it up for want of a little self-discipline. Like ballsing up an experiment by knocking over a beaker, or bleaching a whole roll of shots by leaning against the light switch.

'Why are you looking so sour?' Michael wanted to know.

412

'That was my last cigarette.' Rash to boast before Noah had achieved even a single day off nicotine, but saying it aloud committed him; he'd be too ashamed to go back on his word now.

'I'll believe that when I see it.'

'Oh, you'll see it,' Noah answered in an equally menacing voice.

This taxi had to be theirs.

'*Par le tunnel ou la Prom, Monsieur?*' the driver asked as they climbed in.

By the Prom, please. Taxis here cost so much, Noah decided to think of the ride as a tour with a private chauffeur, and pretended this was Grace Kelly beside him rather than a kid picking wax out of his ear.

'An unaffected smile is permitted.' At seventy-nine it was imperative to be a realist, but at eighty it was time to be an optimist. The cab rolled along the Promenade des Anglais, where generation after generation of the frail had strolled, faces up to the sun in hope of lasting just a little longer. One more sip of this improbable phenomenon: life.

While they were stalled in traffic, Noah began to fret about what awaited him — them — in New York. Decisions, disruptions. *You're going to have to help me with the boy.*

Joan laughed a little. Hadn't she helped him with everything else life had thrown at them? Even her cancer, her old adversary, their only home-wrecker. *We had almost forty years.* Put another way, not quite forty. Not enough, never enough. But still.

413

'Fake,' Michael muttered. 'Total fake.'

Noah craned to see out the window. In a city with many murals of palm trees, this one was smarter: it showed a man up a ladder, painting three palm trees. 'No, that did trick your eye, actually. One of those trees is real.'

'No way!'

'The palm on the left, it's growing in front of the wall.'

Michael looked out the back of the taxi in chagrin.

They drove on, past the children's hospital. This was the stretch driven by the terrorist in the white truck, Noah remembered. Strange, how all killing fields eventually took on a benign look, especially on a sunny morning when teenagers were walking along licking ice cream.

Beside him, Michael was playing Twenty Questions now. ''Can you lie on it?'' he muttered. 'No. 'Do you use it at work?' Maybe.'

Nothing in the seat back for Noah to read except that glossy magazine, *Plaisirs d'Azur*. One article claimed the Bay of Angels was named for the *requin-ange* once so populous there, a small member of the shark family with rear fins that looked slightly like wings. But Noah preferred the story of the angels blowing Sainte Réparate's raft across the Mediterranean. Not able to perform anything as impressive as resurrection, only to keep the gulls from pecking out the girl's dead eyes, because angels were no more powerful in their sorrow than mortal mourners.

''Can it fit in an envelope?' No,' Michael told the ball. ''Could you balance it on one finger?'

414

Yes. 'Could it exist in outer space?' How the fuck should I know?'

Noah would probably need a policy on Michael's language now; a program of bribery, maybe. Also screen time, and diet. These questions were waiting for them, the minute they got off the plane.

But really all Noah was attempting to do was fill a gap; throw his ungainly self down so the kid could cross over this abyss. Weren't all of us bridges for each other, one way or another? Just a few years, fingers crossed, till Amber got out of prison. It wasn't a matter of Noah planting any olive trees, at this point, just watering one sapling, attempting to shield it from hard winds.

And then it struck him that it was really the other way around. This boy was saving Noah. Rescuing him from the trap of habit, the bleak tedium of counting down the years of his retirement. Michael was the little ark, crazily bobbing, in which one lucky old man could go voyaging.

' 'Did it exist a hundred years ago?' Maybe,' the boy said, pressing buttons.

Noah got out his mother's envelope of pictures, a history in fragments. Margot had averted her face from her own lens, but jotted *MZ* on the back of the print to record who she'd been. Likewise, her comrades. The bell tower to mark the spot where she'd been charged with her task. The doomed children carrying their cases, and one smiling one. The tree whose roots had held secrets. The hotel where perhaps she'd broken and spilled them. (Would Noah ever know for sure?)

The only picture that still baffled him was the street scene with the bicycle, the parked car, the seagull. What had Noah missed? An empty street. Nothing was going on here. A moment in between; a gap in time.

Unless that was the whole point? Perhaps before or even during those chaotic years of occupation, Margot had caught a split second when nothing had been happening. How unbearably sweet she must have found this ordinariness, afterward. Cars drove, people promenaded, leaves blew. One of those moments that didn't usually make it into the record; a respite from history. No tanks rumbling by, no soldiers marching, no feet fleeing, no truck accelerating, no pavement exploding, no blood. Undisturbed brick, stone, air. A chance to catch your breath.

''Could you break it?' Hell yes,' Michael told his machine.

Noah was unlikely to find any more hard evidence about his mother's war. He supposed it was always that way with the dead; they slid away before we knew enough to ask them the right questions. All we could do was remember them, as much as we could remember of them, whether it was accurate or not. Walk the same streets that they'd walked; take our turn.

Michael let out a yawn and let his head roll on the back of their seat till it almost rested — no, did rest, tentatively — on Noah's shoulder.

Noah tipped his own head that way till it

416

leaned lightly on Michael's warm one. He shut his eyes and said, *Merci, merci, mille mercis.*

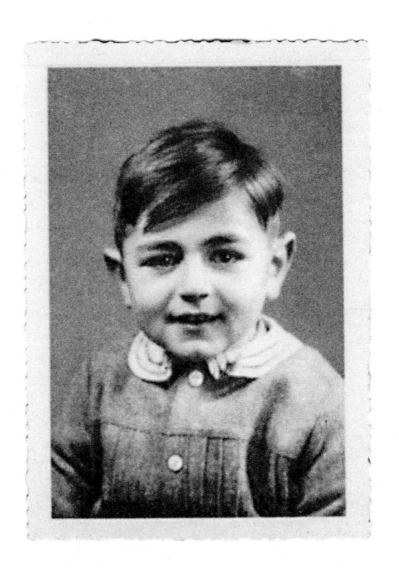

One of the unnamed children hidden around Nice by Yvonne Dandoy Rocques (1912–2002) working with Bishop Paul Rémond, donated by her to the Yad Vashem Archive Collection, M 31.2/6954

Acknowledgments

Père Sonne and his family are my invention, though I've drawn on the careers and work of many European photographers. Margot is in small part my homage to Marguerite Matisse Duthuit, daughter, model, and right-hand woman to the painter; the story of her extraordinary war was first pieced together by Hilary Spurling in *Matisse the Master*.

The real Marcel Network managed to save 527 children from the camps by hiding them in and around Nice from 1943 to 1945; just two were captured and sent to their deaths in Auschwitz. For the rest of their lives, the surviving members of the network preferred not to speak publicly about what they'd done.

I've been lucky enough to spend two separate years in Nice (2011–12 and 2015–16) and I'm grateful to everyone who has enriched my understanding of this lovely city. Thanks to my mother-in-law, Claude Gillard, for stories of your France, and for reading the novel in draft (as did my friend Zoë Sinel). To my father, Denis Donoghue, a professor for six decades, who combines a tireless mind with a soft heart. And to my beloved Roulstons — Finn, Una, and Chris — for all the inspiration you've given me on both sides of the Atlantic. Finally thanks to my dear friend for thirty years, image maker Margaret Lonergan, who created Margot's photographs.

We do hope that you have enjoyed reading this large print book.

Did you know that all of our titles are available for purchase?

We publish a wide range of high quality large print books including:
Romances, Mysteries, Classics
General Fiction
Non Fiction and Westerns

Special interest titles available in large print are:
The Little Oxford Dictionary
Music Book
Song Book
Hymn Book
Service Book

Also available from us courtesy of Oxford University Press:
Young Readers' Dictionary
(large print edition)
Young Readers' Thesaurus
(large print edition)

For further information or a free brochure, please contact us at:
Ulverscroft Large Print Books Ltd.,
The Green, Bradgate Road, Anstey,
Leicester, LE7 7FU, England.
Tel: (00 44) 0116 236 4325
Fax: (00 44) 0116 234 0205

THE WONDER

Emma Donoghue

Lib Wright, a young English nurse, arrives in an impoverished Irish village on a strange mission. Eleven-year-old Anna O'Donnell is said to have eaten nothing for months, but appears to be thriving miraculously. With tourists thronging to see this child, and the press sowing doubt, the baffled community looks to an outsider to bring the facts to light. An educated sceptic, trained by the legendary Florence Nightingale and repelled by what she sees as ignorance and superstition, Lib expects to expose the fast as a hoax right away. But as she gets to know the girl, she becomes more and more unsure. Is Anna a fraud, or a 'living wonder'? Or is something more sinister unfolding right before Lib's eyes — a tragedy in which she herself is playing a part?

ROOM

Emma Donoghue

Jack is five and excited about his birthday. He lives with his Ma in Room, which has a locked door and a skylight, and measures eleven feet by eleven feet. He loves watching TV, and the cartoon characters he calls friends, but he knows that nothing he sees on screen is truly real — only him, Ma and the things in Room. Until the day Ma admits that there's a world outside . . . Told in Jack's voice, *Room* is the unsentimental and sometimes funny story of a mother and son whose love lets them survive the impossible.

SWALLOWTAIL SUMMER

Erica James

For many years, Alastair and his best friends Danny and Simon have spent summers together with their families at his gorgeous holiday home, Linston End, against the idyllic backdrop of the Norfolk Broads. The memories are ingrained in their hearts: picnics on the river, gin and tonics in the pavilion at dusk, hours spent seeking out the local swallowtail butterflies. There's no reason to believe the good times won't continue down the generations, though there are surprises in store for them all? After Alastair's wife Orla passes away in a tragic accident, he goes travelling — and when he returns, it's not just adventures and memories he brings back, but Valentina, his new love interest. Is this just a holiday romance? What will Alastair's decisions mean for the long-time friends?

SAVING MISSY

Beth Morrey

It was bitterly cold, the day of the fish-stunning. So bitter that I nearly didn't go to watch . . . Missy Carmichael's life has become small. Grieving for a family she has lost or lost touch with, she's haunted by the echoes of her footsteps in her empty home; the sound of the radio in the dark; the tick-tick-tick of the watching clock; a fish-stunning. Spiky and defensive, Missy knows that her loneliness is all her own fault. She deserves no more than this; not after what she's done. But a chance encounter in the park with two very different women opens the door to something new. Another life beckons for Missy, if only she can be brave enough to grasp the opportunity. But seventy-nine is too late for a second chance . . . isn't it?